ED McBAIN

WIDOWS

"RICH...ROUSING...
Hot enough to spontaneously combust"
Boston Sunday Herald

"GRIPPING...FASCINATING...
Filled with tension, action and human drama...
McBain has stood the test of time.
He remains one of the very best."
San Antonio Express-News

"FORMIDABLE...
Grabs one's total attention...
A brilliant job"
The New York Times Book Review

"LITERARY GENIUS!"
Denver Rocky Mountain News

"THIS ONE HAS IT ALL—
multiple murders; a city awash with crime;
tight and unerring characterizations—
and a stunning denouement...
McBain remains a literary boss
on his chosen turf."
Tulsa World

WIDOWS

AN 87TH PRECINCT NOVEL

ED McBAIN

AVON BOOKS  NEW YORK

This is for
JANE POWELL AND DICK MOORE

AVON BOOKS
A division of
The Hearst Corporation
1350 Avenue of the Americas
New York, New York 10019

Published in hardcover by William Morrow and Company, Inc.; for information address Permissions Department, William Morrow and Company, Inc., 1350 Avenue of the Americas, New York, New York 10019.

First Avon Books International Printing: December 1991
First Avon Books Printing: January 1992

AVON TRADEMARK REG. U.S. PAT. OFF. AND IN OTHER COUNTRIES, MARCA REGISTRADA, HECHO EN CANADA

Printed in Canada

UNV 10 9 8 7 6 5 4 3

The city in these pages is imaginary.
The people, the places are all fictitious.
Only the police routine is based on
established investigatory technique.

1

She'd been brutally stabbed and
slashed more times than Carella chose to imagine. The knife
seemed to have been a weapon of convenience, a small paring
knife that evidently had been taken from the bartop where a bottle
opener with a matching wooden handle sat beside a half-full
pitcher of martinis, an ice bucket, and a whole lemon from which
a narrow sliver of skin was missing.

Someone had been drinking a martini. With a twist. Presumably the paring knife had been used to peel back the skin of the
lemon before the knife was used on its victim. The martini was
still on the coffee table alongside which she was lying. The lemon
twist lay curled on the bottom of the glass. The paring knife was
on the floor beside her. The blade was covered with blood. She
was bleeding from what appeared to be a hundred cuts and gashes.

"Natural blonde," Monoghan said.

She was wearing a black silk kimono patterned with oversized red poppies. The kimono was belted at the waist, but it had
been torn open to reveal her long, slender legs and the blonde
pubic patch upon which Monoghan had based his clever deduc-
tion. Her blue eyes were open. Her throat had been slit. Her face

had been repeatedly slashed, but you could still see she'd been a beauty. Nineteen, twenty years old, long blonde hair and startling blue eyes, wide open, staring at the ceiling of the penthouse apartment. Young beautiful body under the slashed black kimono with poppies the color of blood.

The men in suits and jackets stood around her, looking down at her, plastic-encased ID cards clipped to their coat collars. Monoghan and Monroe from Homicide North; Detective/Second Grade Steve Carella from the Eight-Seven; Detective/Third Grade Arthur Brown, same precinct. Nice little gathering here at a little past eight o'clock on a hot, muggy night late in July. Monoghan and Monroe kept staring down at the body as if pondering the mystery of it all. There were slash and stab marks on her breast and her belly. Her wounds shrieked silently to the night. The insides of her thighs had been slashed. There was blood everywhere you looked. Torn white flesh and bright red blood. Shrieking. The men were waiting for the medical examiner to arrive. This weather, cars and people all over the streets, it took time to get anywhere. There was a pained look on Carella's face. Brown looked angry, the way he normally did, even when he was deliriously happy.

"Girls like this, they can get in trouble, this city," Monroe said.

Carella wondered Girls like *what*?

"You get a young, pretty girl like this one," Monoghan said, "they don't know what this city is like."

"What this city can do to you," Monroe said.

"This city can do terrible things to young girls," Monoghan said.

They stood there with their hands in the pockets of their suit jackets, thumbs showing, identical navy-blue suits and white shirts and blue ties, looking down at the dead woman. Girl, they had called her. Nineteen, twenty years old at most. Carella wondered if she'd thought of herself as a woman. On all the subsequent reports, she would be labeled merely FEMALE. Generic labeling.

No fine distinction for feminists to pursue, no quarrel over whether it should be girl or woman, no such bullshit once you became a victim. The minute you were dead, you became *female,* period.

The pained look was still in his eyes.

Dark brown eyes, slanting downward to give his face a some-what Oriental look. Brown hair. Tall and slender. His nose was running, a summer cold. He took out his handkerchief, blew his nose, and looked toward the front door. Where the hell was the M.E.? The apartment felt sticky and damp, was there a window open someplace, diluting the air-conditioning? No window units here, everything hidden and enclosed, this was an expensive apart-ment. High-rise, high-rent condo here on what passed for the precinct's Gold Coast, such as it was, overlooking the River Harb and the next state. Two blocks south you had your tenements and your hot-bed hotels. Here, on the floor of the building's only penthouse apartment, a young woman in an expensive silk kimono lay torn and bleeding on a thick pile carpet, a martini in a stemmed glass on the coffee table behind her. Liquid silver in the glass. Yellow twist of lemon curling. Lipstick stain on the glass's rim. Enough still left in the pitcher on the bar to pour half a dozen more glasses like this one. Had she been expecting company? Had she voluntarily admitted her own murderer to the apartment? Or *was* there a window open?

"They say it's gonna be even hotter tomorrow than it was today," Monoghan said idly, and turned away from the victim as though bored with her lifeless pose.

"Who's *they*?" Monroe asked.

"The weather guys."

"Then why didn't you say so? Why do people always say *they* this, *they* that, instead of who the hell *they* is supposed to be?"

"What's the matter with you tonight?" Monoghan asked, surprised.

"I just don't like people saying *they* this, *they* that all the time."

"I'm not people," Monoghan said, looking offended and hurt. "I'm your partner."

"So stop saying *they* this, *they* that all the time."

"I certainly will," Monoghan said, and walked over to where a second black leather sofa rested under the windows on the far side of the room. He glanced angrily at the sofa, and then heavily plunked himself down onto it.

Brown couldn't believe that the M&Ms were arguing. Monoghan and Monroe? Joined at the hip since birth? Exchanging heated words? Impossible. But there was Monoghan, sitting on the sofa in a sulk, and here was Monroe, unwilling to let go of it. Brown kept his distance.

"People are always doing that," Monroe said. "It drives me crazy. Don't it drive you crazy?" he asked Brown.

"I don't pay much attention to it," Brown said, trying to stay neutral.

"It's the *heat's* driving you crazy," Monoghan said from across the room.

"It ain't the goddamn heat," Monroe said, "it's people always saying *they* this, *they* that."

Brown tried to look aloof.

At six feet four inches tall and weighing two hundred and twenty pounds, he was bigger and in better condition than either of the two Homicide dicks. But he sensed that the argument between them was something that could easily turn against him if he wasn't careful. Nowadays in this city, a black man had to be careful, except with people he trusted completely. He trusted Carella that way, but he knew nothing at all about the religion or politics of the M&Ms, so he figured it was best not to get himself involved in what was essentially a family dispute One thing he didn't want was a hassle on a hot summer night.

Brown's skin was the color of rich Colombian coffee, and he had brown eyes and kinky black hair, and wide nostrils and thick lips, and this made him as black as anyone could get. Over the years, he had got used to thinking of himself as black—though that wasn't his actual color—but he was damned if he would now start calling himself African-American, which he felt was a phony label invented by insecure people who kept inventing labels in order to reinvent themselves. Inventing labels wasn't the way you found out who you were. The way you did that was you looked in the mirror every morning, the way Brown did, and you saw the same handsome black dude looking back at you. That was what made you grin, man.

"You get people saying things like 'They say there's gonna be another tax hike,' " Monroe said, gathering steam, "and when you ask them who they mean by *they,* they'll tell you the investment brokers or the financial insti . . ."

"You just done it yourself," Monoghan said.

"What'd I do?"

"You said you ask them who they mean by *they,* they'll tell you the investment . . ."

"I don't know what you're talking about," Monroe said.

"I'm talking about you complaining about people saying *they* this and *they* that, and you just said *they* this yourself."

"I said nothing of the sort," Monroe said. "Did I say that?" he asked Brown, trying to drag him into it again.

"Hello, hello, hello," the M.E. said cheerily from the door to the apartment, sparing Brown an answer. Putting down his satchel, wiping his brow with an already damp handkerchief, he said, "It's the Sahara out there, I'm sorry I'm late." He picked up the satchel again, walked over to where the victim lay on the carpet, said, "Oh my," and knelt immediately beside her. Monoghan got off the sofa and came over to where the other men stood.

They all watched silently as the M.E. began his examination.

In this city, you did not touch the body until someone from the Medical Examiner's Office pronounced the victim dead. By extension, investigating detectives usually interpreted this regulation to mean you didn't touch *anything* until the M.E. had delivered his verdict. You could come into an apartment and find a naked old lady who'd been dead for months and had turned to jelly in her bathtub, you waited till the M.E. said she was dead. They waited now. He examined the dead woman as if she was still alive and paying her annual visit to his office, putting his stethoscope to her chest, feeling for a pulse, counting the number of slash and stab wounds—there were thirty-two in all, including those in the small of her back—keeping the detectives in suspense as to whether or not she was truly deceased.

"Tough one to call, huh, Doc?" Monoghan asked, and winked at Monroe, surprising Brown.

"Cause of death, he means," Monroe said, and winked back.

Brown guessed they'd already forgotten their little tiff.

The M.E. glanced up at them sourly, and then returned to his task.

At last he rose and said, "She's all yours."

The detectives went to work.

The clock on the wall of the office read eight-thirty P.M. There was nothing else on any of the walls. Not even a window. There was a plain wooden desk probably salvaged from one of the older precincts when the new metal furniture started coming in. There was a wooden chair with arms in front of the desk, and a straight-backed wooden chair behind it. Michael Goodman sat behind the desk. *Dr.* Michael Goodman. Who rated only a cubby hole office here in the Headquarters Building downtown. Eileen Burke was singularly unimpressed.

"That's Detective/Second, is it?" he asked.

"Yes," she said.

"How long have you been a detective?"

She almost said Too long.

"It's all there in the record," she said.

She was beginning to think this was a terrible mistake. Coming to see a shrink recommended by another shrink. But she trusted Karin. She guessed.

Goodman looked at the papers on his desk. He was a tall man

with curly black hair and blue eyes. Nose a bit too long for his face, mustache under it, perhaps to cradle it, soften its length. Thick spectacles with rims the color of his hair. He studied the papers.

"Put in a lot of time with Special Forces, I see," he said.

"Yes."

"Decoy work."

"Yes."

"Mostly Rape Squad," he said.

"Yes," she said.

He'd get to the rape next. He'd get to the part that said she'd been raped in the line of duty. It's all there in the record, she thought.

"So," he said, and looked up, and smiled. "What makes you think you'd like to work with the hostage team?"

"I'm not sure I would. But Karin . . . Dr. Karin Lefkowitz . . ."

"Yes."

"I've been seeing her for a little while now . . ."

"Yes."

"At Pizzaz. Upstairs."

Psychological Services Assistance Section. P.S.A.S. Pizzaz for short. Cop talk that took the curse off psychological help, made it sound jazzier, Pizzaz. Right upstairs on the fifth floor of the building. Annie Rawles's Rape Squad office was on the sixth floor. You start with a Rape Squad assignment on the sixth floor and you end up in Pizzaz on the fifth, Eileen thought. What goes up must come down.

"She suggested that I might find hostage work interesting."

Less *threatening* was what she'd actually said.

"How did she mean? Interesting?"

Zeroing right in. Smarter than she thought.

"I've been under a considerable amount of strain lately," Eileen said.

"Because of the shooting?" Goodman asked.

Here it comes, she thought.

"The shooting, yes, and complications arising from . . ."

"You killed this man when?"

Flat out. You killed this man. Which, of course, was what she'd done. Killed this man. Killed this man who'd murdered three prostitutes and was coming at her with a knife. Blew him to perdition. Her first bullet took him in the chest, knocking him backward toward the bed. She fired again almost at once, hitting him in the shoulder this time, spinning him around, and then she fired a third time, shooting him in the back, knocking him over onto the bed. At the time, she couldn't understand why she kept shooting into his lifeless body, watching the eruptions of blood along his spine, saying over and over again, "I gave you a chance, I gave you a chance," until the gun was empty. Karin Lefkowitz was helping her to understand why.

"I killed him a year ago October," she said.

"Not this past October . . ."

"No the one before it. Halloween night," she said.

Trick or treat, she thought.

I gave you a chance.

But had she?

"Why are you seeing Dr. Lefkowitz?"

She wondered if he knew her. Did every shrink in this city know every other shrink? If so, had he talked to her about what they'd been discussing these past several months?

"I'm seeing her because I'm gun-shy," she said.

"Uh-huh," he said.

"I don't want to have to kill anyone else," she said.

"Okay," he said.

"And I don't want to do any more decoy work. Which is a bad failing for a Special Forces cop."

"I can imagine."

"By the way," she said, "I don't particularly like psychiatrists."

"Lucky I'm only a psychologist," he said, and smiled.

"Those, too."

"But you *do* like Karin."

"Yes," she said, and paused. "She's been helpful."

Big admission to make.

"In what way?"

"I have other problems besides the job."

"First tell me what your problems with the job are."

"I just told you. I don't want to be placed in another situation where I may have to shoot someone."

"Kill someone."

"Shoot, kill, yes."

"You don't see any difference?"

"When someone's coming at you and you've got three seconds to make a decision, there's no difference, right."

"Must have been pretty frightening."

"It was."

"Are you still frightened?"

"Yes."

"Just how frightened are you, Miss Burke?"

"Very frightened."

She could admit this now. Karin had freed her to do this.

"Because you killed this man?"

"No. Because I was raped. I don't want to get raped again, I'd *kill* anyone who tried to rape me again. So I don't want to be . . . to be constantly put in situations where someone may *try* to rape me, which frightens the hell out of me, and where I'll . . . I'll have to kill him, which . . . which also frightens me, I guess. Having to kill someone again."

"Sort of a vicious circle, isn't it?"

"If I stay with Special Forces, yes."

"So you're thinking of the hostage team."

"Well, Karin thought I should come up here and talk to you about it. See what it was all about."

"It's not about killing people, that's for sure," Goodman said, and smiled again. "Tell me about these other problems. The ones that *aren't* related to the job."

"Well, they're personal."

"Yes, well, hostage work is personal, too."

"I understand that. But I don't see what *my* personal problems have to do with . . ."

"I just interviewed a detective who's been with Narcotics for the past ten years," Goodman said. "I've been interviewing people all day long. There's a high burnout rate on the team, lots of stress. If the inspector and I can keep a good negotiator for eight months, that's a long time. Anyway, this detective hates drug dealers, would like to see all of them dead. I asked him what he'd do if we were negotiating with a hostage-taker who was a known drug dealer. He said he'd try to save the lives of the hostages. I asked him who he thought was more important, the hostages or the drug dealer. He said he thought the hostages were more important. I asked him if he'd kill the drug dealer to save the hostages. He said yes, he would. I told him I didn't think he'd be right for the team."

Eileen looked at him.

"So what about these personal problems you're working on?" he asked.

She hesitated.

"If you'd rather . . ."

"The night I shot Bobby . . . that was his name," she said, "Bobby Wilson. The night I shot him, I had two backups following me. But my boyfriend . . . "

"Is he the personal problem? Your boyfriend?"

"Yes."

"What about him?"

"He figured he'd lend a hand on the job, and as a result . . ."

"Lend a hand?"

"He's a cop, I'm sorry, I should have mentioned that. He's a detective at the Eight-Seven."

"What's his name?"

"Why do you need to know that?"

"I don't."

"Anyway, he walked into what was going down, and there was a mix-up, and I lost both my backups. Which is how I ended up alone with Bobby. And his knife."

"So you killed him."

"Yes. He was coming at me."

"Do you blame your boyfriend for that?"

"That's what we're working on."

"You and Dr. Lefkowitz."

"Yes."

"How about you and your boyfriend? Are *you* working on it, too?"

"I haven't seen him since I started therapy."

"How does he feel about that?"

"I don't give a damn *how* he feels."

"I see."

"I'm the one who's drowning," Eileen said.

"I see."

They sat in silence for several moments.

"End of interview, right?" she asked.

They found the letters in a jewelry box on the dead woman's dresser.

They had ascertained by then—from the driver's license in her handbag on a table just inside the entrance door that her name was Susan Brauer and that her age was twenty-two. The picture on the license showed a fresh-faced blonde grinning at the camera. The blue cloth backing behind her told the detectives that the license was limited to driving with corrective lenses. Before the M.E. left, they asked him if the dead woman was wearing contacts. He said she was not.

The box containing the letters was one of those tooled red-leather things that attract burglars the way jam pots attract bees. A burglar would have been disappointed with this one, though, because the only thing in it was a stack of letters still in their envelopes and bound together with a pale blue satin ribbon. There were twenty-two letters in all, organized in chronological order, the first of them dated the eleventh of June this year, the last dated the twelfth of July. All of the letters were handwritten, all of them began with the salutation *My darling Susan.* None of them was signed. All of them were erotic.

The writer was obviously a man.

In letter after letter—they calculated that he'd averaged a letter every other day or so—the writer described in explicit language all the things he intended to do to Susan . . .

. . . *standing behind you in a crowded elevator, your skirt raised in the back and tucked up under your belt, you naked under the skirt, my hands freely roaming your* . . .

. . . and all the things he expected Susan to do to him . . .

. . . *with you straddling me and facing the mirror. Then I want you to ease yourself down on my* . . .

As the detectives read the letters in order, it seemed possible that Susan had been writing to him in return, and that her letters were of the same nature, his references to her requests . . .

. . . *when you say you want to tie me to the bed and have me beg you to touch me, do you mean* . . .

. . . indicating an erotic imagination as lively as his own. Moreover, it became clear that these were no mere unfulfilled fantasies. The couple were actually *doing* the things they promised they'd do, and doing it with startling frequency.

. . . *on Wednesday when you opened your kimono and stood there in the black lingerie I'd bought you, your legs slightly parted, the garters tight on your* . . .

. . . *but then last Friday, as you bent over to accept me, I wondered whether you really enjoyed* . . .

. . . *quite often myself. And when you told me that on Monday you thought of me while you were doing it, the bubble bath*

*foaming around you, your hand busy under the suds, finding that
sweet tight . . .*

*. . . known you only since New Year's Day, and yet I think
of you all the time. I saw you yesterday, I'll see you again tomorrow, but I walk around eternally embarrassed because I'm
sure everyone can see the bulge of my . . .*

The letters went on and on.

Twenty-two of them in all.

The last one was perhaps the most revealing of the lot. In
part, before it sailed off into the usual erotic stratosphere, it dealt
with business of a sort:

My darling Susan,

I know you're becoming impatient with what seems an
interminable delay in getting you into the new apartment. I
myself feel uneasy searching for a taxi when I leave there
late at night, knowing the streets to the south of the Oval
are neither well-lighted nor well-patrolled. I'll be so much
happier when you're settled downtown, closer to my office,
in a safer neighborhood, in the luxurious surroundings I
promised you.

But please don't take the delay as a sign of
indifference or changing attitude on my part. And please
don't become impatient or forgetful. I would hate to lose
this apartment before the other one comes free—which I've
been assured will be any day now. I'll make sure you have
the cash to cover any checks you write, but please pay all
of the apartment bills promptly. You can't risk losing the
lease on default.

I've been going to my post office box every day, but
nothing from Susan. Is little Susan afraid to write? Is little Susan losing interest? I would hate to think so. Or
does sweet Susan need reminding that she's mine? I
think you may have to be punished the next time I see
you. I think I'll have to turn you over my knee, and pull
down your panties, and spank you till your cheeks turn
pink, watch your ass writhing under my hand, hear you
moaning . . .

This letter, too, was unsigned.

It was a shame.

It made their job more difficult.

The clock on the squadroom wall read twelve minutes to midnight. The Graveyard Shift had just relieved, and Hawes was arguing with Bob O'Brien, who didn't want to be the one who broke the news to Carella. He told Hawes he should stick around, do it himself, even though he'd been officially relieved.

"You're the one the sister talked to," O'Brien said. "You're the one should tell Steve."

Hawes said he had an urgent engagement, what did O'Brien want him to do, leave a note on Carella's desk? The urgent engagement was with a Detective/First Grade named Annie Rawles who had bought him the red socks he was wearing. The socks matched Hawes's hair and the tie he was wearing. He was also wearing a white shirt that echoed the white streak of hair over his left temple. Hawes was dressed for the summer heat. Lightweight blue blazer over gray tropical slacks, red silk tie and the red socks Annie had given him.

This was the seventeenth day of July, a Tuesday night, and the temperature outside the squadroom was eighty-six degrees Fahrenheit. By Hawes's reckoning that came to thirty degrees Celsius, which was damn hot in any language. He hated the summer. He particularly hated *this* summer, because it seemed to have started in May and it was still here, day after day of torrid temperatures and heavy humidity that combined to turn a person to mush.

"Can't you just do me this one simple favor?" he said.

"It's not such a simple favor," O'Brien said. "This is the most traumatic thing that can happen in a man's life, don't you know that?"

"No, I didn't know that," Hawes said.

"Also," O'Brien said, "I have a reputation around here as a hard-luck cop . . ."

"Where'd you get *that* idea?" Hawes said.

"I got that idea because I have a habit of getting into shoot-outs, and I know nobody likes being partnered with me."

"That's ridiculous," Hawes said, lying.

"Now you're asking me to tell Steve this terrible thing, he'll confuse the messenger with the message and he'll think Here's this hard-luck cop bringing hard luck to *me.*"

"Steve won't think that at all," Hawes said.

"I won't think what?" Carella said from the gate in the slatted-rail divider, taking off his jacket as he came into the room. Brown was right behind him. Both men looked wilted.

"What won't I think?" Carella asked again.

O'Brien and Hawes looked at him.

"What is it?" Carella said.

Neither of them said anything.

"Cotton?" he said. "Bob? What is it?"

"Steve . . ."

"What?"

"I hate to have to tell you this, but . . ."

"*What*, Bob?"

"Your sister called a little while ago," O'Brien said.

"Your father is dead," Hawes said.

Carella looked at them blankly.

Then he nodded.

Then he said, "Where is she?"

"Your mother's house."

He went directly to the phone and dialed the number from memory. His sister picked up on the third ring.

"Angela," he said, "it's Steve."

She'd been crying, her voice revealed that.

"We just got back from the hospital," she said.

"What happened?" he asked. "Was it his heart again?"

"No, Steve. Not his heart."

"Then what?"

"We went there to make positive identification."

For a moment he didn't quite understand. Or didn't choose to understand.

"What do you mean?" he said.

"We had to identify the body."

"Why? Angela, what happened?"

"He was killed."

"Killed? What . . . ?"

"In the bakery shop."

"No."

"Steve . . ."

"Jesus, what . . . ?"

"Two men came in. Papa was alone. They cleaned out the cash register . . ."

"Angela, don't tell me this, please."

"I'm sorry," she said.

And suddenly he was crying.

"Who's . . . who's . . . is it the . . . the . . . it's the Four-Five, isn't it? Up there? Who's working the . . . do you know who's working the . . . the . . . Angela," he said, "honey? Did they . . . did they hurt him? I mean, did they . . . they didn't *hurt* him, did they? Oh God, Angela," he said, "oh God oh God oh God . . ."

He pulled the phone from his mouth and clutched it to his chest, tears streaming down his face, great racking sobs choking him. "Steve?" his sister said. "Are you all right?" Her voice muffled against his shirt where the receiver was pressed fiercely to his chest. "Steve? Are you all right? Steve?" Over and over again. Until at last he moved the phone to his mouth again, and still crying, said, "Honey?"

"Yes, Steve."

"Tell Mama I'll be there as soon as I can."

"Drive carefully."

"Did you call Teddy?"

"She's on the way."

"Is Tommy there with you?"

"No, we're alone here. Mama and me."

"What do you . . . ? Where's Tommy?"

"I don't know," she said. "Please hurry."

And hung up.

2

The two detectives from the 45th Squad in Riverhead felt uncomfortable talking to the detective whose father had been killed. Neither of the men knew Carella; the Eight-Seven was a long way from home. Moreover, both detectives were black, and from all accounts the two men who'd robbed Tony Carella's bakery shop and then killed the old man were black themselves.

Neither of the detectives knew how Carella felt about blacks in general. But the murderers were blacks in particular, and the way the black/white thing was shaping up in this city, the two Riverhead cops felt they might be treading dangerous ground here. Carella was a professional, though, and they knew they could safely cut through a lot of the bullshit. He *knew* what they'd be doing to apprehend the men who'd killed his father. They didn't have to spell out routine step by step, the way you had to do with civilians.

The bigger of the two cops was named Charlie Bent, a Detective/Second. He was wearing a sports jacket over blue jeans and an open-collared shirt. Carella could see the bulge of his shoulder holster on the right-hand side of his body. Left-handed, he figured. Bent spoke very quietly, either because he was naturally soft-spoken or else because he was in a funeral home.

The other cop was a Detective/Third, just got his promotion last month, he mentioned to Carella in passing. He was big, too, but not as wide across the shoulders and chest as Bent was. His name was Randy Wade, the Randy being short for Randall, not Randolph. His face was badly pockmarked, and there was an old knife scar over his left eye. He looked as mean as Saturday night, but this was ten o'clock on Wednesday morning, and they were inside the Loretti Brothers Funeral Home on Vandermeer Hill, and so he was speaking softly, too.

Everyone was speaking softly, tiptoeing around Carella, who for all they knew might be as bigoted as most white men in this city, but whose father had certainly been killed by two black men like themselves, bigot or not. The three detectives were standing in the large entrance foyer that separated the east and west wings. Carella's father was in a coffin in Chapel A in the east wing.

There was a hush in the funeral home.

Carella could remember when he was a kid and his father's sister got run over by an automobile. His Aunt Katie. Killed instantly. Carella had loved her to death. They'd laid her out in this very same funeral home, in one of the chapels over in the west wing.

Back when Aunt Katie died, the family still had older people in it who'd come from the Other Side, as they'd called Europe in general. Some of them could barely speak English. Carella's mother, and sometimes his father—but not too often because his own English showed traces of having been raised in an immigrant home—laughed at the fractured English some of their older relatives spoke. Nobody was laughing when Aunt Katie was here in this place. Aunt Katie was twenty-seven years old when the car knocked her down and killed her.

Carella could still remember the women keening.

The women keening were more frightening than the fact that

his dear Aunt Katie lay young and dead in a coffin in the west wing.

Today, there was no keening. The old ways had become American, and Americans did not keen. Today, there was only the hush of death in this silent place where two black cops tiptoed around a white cop because his father had been killed by two black men like themselves.

"The witness seems reliable," Bent said softly. "We've been showing him . . ."

"When did he see these two men?" Carella asked.

"Coming out," Wade said.

"He was in the liquor store next door. He thought he heard shots, and when he turned around to look, he saw these guys . . ."

"What time was this?"

"Around nine-thirty. Your sister told us your father sometimes worked late."

"Yes," Carella said.

"Alone," Bent said.

"Yes," Carella said. "Baking."

"Anyway," Wade said, "he saw them plain as day under the street lamp . . ."

"Getting into a car, or what?"

"No, they were on foot."

"They'd been cruising, we figure, looking for a mark."

"They had to pick my father, huh?"

"Yeah, well," Bent said sympathetically, and shook his head. "We've got the witness looking through mug shots, and we've got an artist working up a drawing, so maybe we'll come up with some kind of positive ID. We're also checking the M.O. file, but there's nothing special about the style of this one, we figure it was maybe two crack addicts cruising for an easy score."

Nothing special about it, Carella thought.

Except that it was his father.

"They're both black," Bent said. "I guess your sister told you that."

"She told me," Carella said.

"We want you to know that our being black . . ."

"You don't have to say it," Carella said.

Both men looked at him.

"No need," he said.

"We'll be doing our best," Wade said.

"I know that."

"We'll keep you informed every step of the way," Bent said.

"I'd appreciate that."

"Meanwhile, anything we can do to help your family, look in on your mother, whatever you need, just let us know."

"Thanks," Carella said. "Whenever you have anything . . ."

"We'll let you know."

"Even if it seems unimportant . . ."

"The minute we get anything."

"Thanks," Carella said.

"My father was killed in a mugging," Wade said out of the blue.

"I'm sorry," Carella said.

"Reason I became a cop," Wade said, and looked suddenly embarrassed.

"This city . . ." Bent started, and let the sentence trail.

Brown had been in the apartment for an hour before Kling arrived to lend a hand. Kling apologized for getting there so late but he didn't get the call from the lieutenant till half an hour ago, while he was still in bed. This was supposed to be his day off, but with Carella's father getting shot and all—

"Are they any good up there?" he asked Brown. "The Four-Five?"

"I don't know anything about them," Brown said.

"That's like the boonies up there, isn't it?"

"Well, I think they have crime up there," Brown said dryly.

"Sure, but what *kind* of crime? Do they ever have murders up there?"

"I think they have murders up there," Brown said.

Kling had taken off his jacket and was looking for a place to hang it. He knew the techs were finished in here and it was okay to touch anything he liked. But he would feel funny putting his jacket in a closet with the dead woman's clothes. He settled for tossing it over the back of the living-room sofa.

He was wearing brown tropical-weight slacks and a tan sports shirt that complemented his hazel eyes and blond hair. Loafers, too, Brown noticed. Mr. College Boy. They made a good pair, these two. Most thieves figured Kling for an innocent young rookie who'd just got the gold shield last week. With all that blond hair and that shit-kicking, apple-cheeked style, it was hard to guess he was a seasoned cop who'd seen more than his share of it. Your average thief mistook him for somebody he could jerk around, play on his sympathies, get him to talk Big Bad Leroy here into looking the other way. Kling and Brown played the Good Cop/Bad Cop routine for all it was worth, Kling restraining Brown from committing murder with his bare hands, Brown acting like an animal just let out of his cage. It worked each and every time.

Well, once it hadn't.

"How's Steve taking it?" Kling asked.

"I haven't seen him this morning," Brown said. "He was pretty shook up last night."

"Yeah, I can imagine," Kling said. "Is your father alive?"

"Yes. Is yours?"

"No."

"So I guess you know."

"Yeah."

"Did the lieutenant say how long you'd be on this?"

"Just till Steve's done with the funeral and everything. He pulled me off a stakeout me and Genero are working on Culver. These grocery-store holdups."

"Yeah," Brown said.

"What are we looking for?" Kling asked.

"Anything that'll give us a line on the guy who wrote these letters," Brown said, and tossed the packet to Kling. Kling sat on the sofa and undid the blue ribbon around the envelopes. He unfolded the first letter and began reading it.

"Don't get too involved there," Brown said.

"Pretty steamy stuff here, Artie."

"I think you may be too young for that kind of stuff."

"Yeah, I agree," Kling said, and fell silent, reading. "*Very* good stuff here," he said.

"It gets better."

"You go on and do whatever you have to do, I'll see you next week sometime."

"Just read the last letter."

"I thought I might read all of them."

"Last one's got everything you need to know."

Kling read the last letter.

"Paying for the apartment here, huh?" he said.

"Looks that way."

"He sounds old, don't you think?"

"What's old to you?"

"In his fifties, maybe. Doesn't he sound that way to you?"

"Maybe."

"Just the words he uses. And the tone. How old was this girl?"

"Twenty-two."

"That sounds very young for this guy."

"You might want to look through some of that stuff in her desk, see if you find anything about anyone named Arthur. I think his name might be Arthur."

"That's *your* name," Kling said.

"No kidding?"

"You sure *you* didn't write these letters? Listen to this,"

Kling said, and began quoting. "*And afterward, I'll pour oil onto your flaming cheeks, and should any of this oil accidentally flow into your . . .*"

"Yeah," Brown said.

"Some imagination, this guy."

"Check out the desk, will you?"

Kling folded the letter, put it back into its envelope, retied the bundle, and tossed it onto the coffee table. The desk was on the wall opposite the sofa. The drawer over the kneehole was unlocked. He reached into it for a checkbook in a green plastic cover.

"What makes you think his name is Arthur?" he asked.

"I've been going through her appointment calendar. Lots of stuff about Arthur in it. Arthur this, Arthur that. Arthur here at nine, Arthur at Sookie's, call Arthur . . ."

"That's a restaurant on The Stem," Kling said. "Sookie's. He probably figured the turf up here was safe."

"What do you mean *safe*?"

"I don't know," Kling said, and shrugged. "He says his office is downtown, so I figure he knows people down there. So up here would be safe. He may even *live* downtown, for all we know. So up here would be safe from his wife, too. I figure he's married, don't you?"

"Where do you see anything about that?"

"I don't. But if he's single and he lives *downtown* . . ."

"There's nothing there that says he lives downtown."

"How about him taking a cab when he leaves late at night?"

"That doesn't mean he's going downtown."

"All right, forget downtown. But if he isn't married, then why's he keeping a girl *any*place? Why don't they just live together?"

"Well . . . that's a point, yeah."

"So he's this old married guy keeping this young girl in a fancy apartment till he can get her an even *fancier* one."

"Is 'Phil' another restaurant?"

"Phil? I don't know any restaurant named Phil."

"It says here 'Arthur at Phil, eight P.M.' "

"When was that?"

"Last Wednesday night."

"Maybe he's a friend of theirs. Phil."

"Maybe."

"You know how much the rent on this joint comes to each month?" Kling said, looking up from the checkbook.

"How much?"

"Twenty-four hundred bucks."

"Come on, Bert."

"I'm serious. Here are the stubs. The checks are made out to somebody named Phyllis Brackett, for twenty-four hundred a shot, and they're marked Rental. Rental March, Rental April, Rental May, and so on. Twenty-four hundred smackers, Artie."

"And he's trying to find her a *better* place, huh?"

"Must be a *rich* old geezer."

"Here he is again," Brown said, tapping the calendar with his finger. " 'Arthur here, nine P.M.' "

"When?"

"Monday."

"Day before she caught it."

"I wonder if he spent the night."

"No, what he does is take a taxi home to his beloved wife."

"We don't know for sure that he's married," Brown said.

"Got to be," Kling said. "*And* rich. I'm clocking five-thousand-dollar deposits every month on the first of the month. Here, take a look," he said, and handed Brown the checkbook. Brown began leafing through it. Sure enough, there were deposits listed for the first of every month, each for an even five thousand dollars.

"Probably won't help us," Brown said. "His letter . . ."

"Cash, I know," Kling said.

"Even if those deposits were checks, we'd need a court order to get copies of them."

"Might be worth it."

"I'll ask the loot. What was that woman's name again?"

"Brackett. Phyllis Brackett. With a double *T* on the end."

"Take a look at this," Brown said, and handed Kling the calendar.

In the square for Monday, the ninth of July, Susan had scrawled the name *Tommy!!!!*

"Four exclamation points," Kling said. "Must've been urgent."

"Let's see what we've got," Brown said, and picked up a spiral book bound in mottled black plastic, Susan Brauer's personal directory.

The only possible listing they found for anyone named Tommy was one under the letter *M: Thomas Mott Antiques*. Brown copied down the address and phone number and then leafed back to the pages following the letter *B*. There was a listing for a Phyllis Brackett at 274 Sounder Avenue. A telephone number was written in below the address. He copied both down, and then they read through the calendar and the directory and the checkbook yet another time, making notes, jotting down names, dates, and possible places Susan Brauer might have visited with the elusive Arthur Somebody during the weeks and days before her murder.

They went through every drawer in the desk and then they turned over the trash basket under the desk and sorted through all the scraps of paper and assorted debris that tumbled out onto the carpet. They spread newspapers on the kitchen floor and went through all the garbage in the pail under the sink. They could find nothing that gave them a last name for the man who was paying the rent on this apartment.

In Susan's bedroom closet, they found a full-length mink coat and a fox jacket . . .

"He's getting richer and richer by the minute," Kling said.

. . . three dozen pairs of shoes . . .

"Imelda Marcos here," Brown said.

. . . eighteen dresses with labels like Adolfo, Chanel, Calvin Klein, Christian Dior . . .

"I wonder what his *wife* wears," Kling said.

. . . three Louis Vuitton suitcases . . .

"Planning a trip?" Brown said.

. . . and a steel lockbox.

Brown picked the lock in thirty seconds flat.

Inside the box, there was twelve thousand dollars in hundred-dollar bills.

The doorman was a dust-colored man with a thin mustache under his nose. He was wearing a gray uniform with red trim and a peaked gray hat with red piping, and he spoke with an almost indecipherable accent they guessed was Middle Eastern. It took them ten minutes to learn that he had been on duty from four P.M. to midnight last night. Now what they wanted to know was whether or not he'd sent anyone up to Miss Brauer's apartment.

"Dunn remembah," he said.

"The penthouse apartment," Kling said. "There's only one penthouse apartment, did you send anybody up there last night?"

"Dunn remembah," he said again.

"Anybody at all go up there?" Brown asked. "A whiskey delivery, anything like that?"

He was thinking about the martinis.

The doorman shook his head.

"Peckage all the time," he said.

"*Package,* is that what you're saying?"

"Peckage, yes."

"People delivering packages?"

"Yes, all the time."

"But this didn't have to be a delivery," Kling said. "It could've been *anyone* going up there to the penthouse. Do you remember *anyone* going up there? Did you buzz Miss Brauer to tell her anyone wanted to come up?"

"Dunn remembah," he said. "Peckage all the time."

Brown wanted to smack him in the mouth.

"Look," he said, "a girl was killed upstairs, and you were on duty during the *time* she was killed. So did you let anyone in? Did you send anyone upstairs?"

"Dunn remembah."

"Did you see anyone suspicious hanging around the building?"

The doorman looked puzzled.

"Suspicious," Kling said.

"Someone who didn't look as if he belonged here," Brown explained.

"Nobody," the doorman said.

When finally they quit, it felt as if they'd been talking to him for a day and a half. But it was only a little after three o'clock.

274 Sounder was a brownstone on a street bordered by trees in full summer leaf. It had taken them close to an hour in heavy traffic to drive from the penthouse apartment on Silvermine Oval all the way down here to the lower end of Isola, and they did not ring Phyllis Brackett's doorbell until almost four o'clock that afternoon.

Mrs. Brackett was a woman in her early fifties, they guessed, allowing her hair to go gray, wearing no makeup, and looking tall and slender and attractive in a wide blue skirt, thong sandals, a sleeveless white blouse, and a string of bright red beads. They had called before coming, and not only was she expecting them, she had also made a pitcher of cold lemonade in anticipation of their arrival. Brown and Kling almost kissed her sandaled feet; both men were hot and sticky and utterly exhausted.

They sat in a kitchen shaded by a backyard maple. Two children were playing in a rubber wading pool under the tree. Mrs. Brackett explained that they were her grandchildren. Her daughter and her son-in-law were on vacation, and she was baby-sitting the two little blonde girls who were splashing merrily away outside the picture window.

Brown told her why they were there.

"Yes," she said at once.

"You were renting the apartment to Susan Brauer."

"Yes, that's right," Mrs. Brackett said.

"Then the apartment is yours . . ."

"Yes. I used to live in it until recently," she said.

They looked at her.

"I was recently divorced," she said. "I'm what is known as a grass widow."

Kling had never heard that expression before. Neither had Brown. They both gathered it meant a divorced woman. Live and learn.

"I didn't want alimony," she said. "I got the apartment and a very large cash settlement. I bought this brownstone with the settlement money, and I get twenty-four hundred a month renting the apartment. I think that's a pretty good deal," she said, and smiled.

They agreed it was a pretty good deal.

"Was anyone handling this for you?" Brown asked. "Renting the apartment uptown? A real estate agent, a rental agent?"

"No. I put an ad in the paper."

"Was Susan Brauer the one who answered the newspaper ad?"

"Yes."

"I mean *personally*," Brown said. "Was she the one who wrote . . . or called . . . ?"

"She called me, yes."

"She herself? Not anyone calling for her? It wasn't a man who called, was it?"

"No, it was Miss Brauer."

"What happened then?" Brown asked.

"We arranged to meet at the apartment. I showed it to her, and she liked it, and we agreed on the rent, and that was it."

"Did she sign a lease?"

"Yes."

"For how long?"

"A year."

"And when was this?" Kling asked.

"In February."

Fast worker, Kling thought. He meets her on New Year's Day, and he's got her set up in an apartment a month later. Brown was thinking the same thing.

"I don't know what to do now that she . . . well, it's just a terrible tragedy, isn't it?" Mrs. Brackett said. "I suppose I'll have to contact my lawyer. The man who drew the lease. I guess that's the thing to do."

"Yes," Kling said.

"Yes," Brown said. "Mrs. Brackett, I want to make sure we've got this absolutely right. You were renting the apartment *directly* to Miss Brauer, is that right?"

"Yes. She sent me a check each month. To this address."

"No middleman," Brown said.

"No middleman. That's the best way, isn't it?" she said, and smiled again.

"Do you know anyone named Arthur?" Kling asked.

"No, I'm sorry, I don't."

"Did Miss Brauer ever introduce you to anyone named Arthur?"

"No. I only saw her once, in fact, the day we met at the apartment. Everything since then has been through the mail. Well, several times we spoke on the telephone, when she . . ."

"Oh? Why was that?"

"She needed to know how to work the disposal . . . there's a switch on the wall . . . and she wanted the combination to the wall safe, but I wouldn't give her that."

"Did she say why she wanted the combination?"

"No. I assume to put something *in* the safe, wouldn't you guess?"

I would guess, Kling thought.

Like twelve grand, Brown thought.

"Thank you very much for your time," Kling said. "We appreciate it."

"Some more lemonade?" she asked.

Outside, the little girls kept splashing in the pool.

Thomas Mott was a man in his late forties, early fifties, with stark white hair, deep brown eyes, and a face that seemed carved from alabaster. Brown guessed his height at five-eight, his weight at a hundred and forty. Slender and slight, wearing skintight black jeans, a red cotton sweater, and black loafers without socks, he flitted among the treasures in his Drittel Avenue shop like a dancer in a Russian ballet. Brown wondered if he was gay. There was something almost too delicate about the way he moved. But he was wearing a narrow gold wedding band.

Kling could not have named or dated any of the antiques here if he were being stretched on a rack or roasted on a spit, but he knew he was in the presence of objects of extreme beauty. Burnished brass and wood rubbed to a gleaming patina, tiny clocks that ticked like chickadees, stately clocks that tocked in counterpoint, beautiful bottles in ruby reds and emerald greens, silver-filigreed boxes and bronze lamps with stained-glass shades that glowed with vibrant color. There was a hush in the place. He felt as if he were in an ancient cathedral.

"Yes, of course I know her," Mott said. "A terrible shame, what happened to her. A lovely person."

"Why'd she come in here on the ninth?" Brown asked.

"Well, she was a customer, she stopped by every now and then, you know."

"But was there something special about the ninth?" Kling asked. He was thinking of those exclamation points.

"No, not that I can remember."

"Because her appointment calendar made it look like something important," Kling said.

"Well, let me see," Mott said.

"How well did you know her?" Brown asked, biting the bullet.

"As well as I knew any of my customers."

"And how well was that?"

"As I said, she came in every now and . . ."

"Well enough to call you Tommy?"

"All my customers call me Tommy."

"When was the last time she came in?"

"Last week sometime, I suppose."

"Would it have been last Monday?"

"Well, I . . ."

"The ninth?"

"I suppose it could have been."

"Mr. Mott," Kling said, "we've got this idea that Miss Brauer felt it was important for her to come in here last Monday. Would you happen to know why?"

"Oh," he said.

Comes the dawn, Brown thought.

"Yes, now I remember," Mott said. "The table."

"What table?"

"I'd told her I was expecting a butler's table from England . . ."

"When did you tell her that, Mr. Mott?"

"Well . . . last month sometime. She came in sometime last month. As I told you, she stopped by every . . ."

"Every now and then, right," Brown said. "So when she was in last month, you mentioned a butler's table to her . . ."

"Yes, that was coming from England on or about the ninth, was what I told her."

"What kind of table is that?" Kling asked. "A butler's table?"

"Well, it's a . . . I'd show it to you, but I'm afraid it's already gone. This was solid cherry, quite a good buy at seventeen hundred dollars. I thought she might be able to find a place for it in her apartment. She jotted down the date I was expecting it, and said she'd give me a call.''

"But instead she came to the shop."

"Yes."

"On Monday the ninth," Kling said.

"Yes."

"So that's what was so urgent," Brown said. "A cherry-wood butler's table."

"A quite beautiful piece," Mott said. "She couldn't use it . . . from what I was able to gather, she was renting a furnished apartment . . . but it went in a minute. Well, only seventeen hundred dollars," he said, and raised his eyebrows and moved his hands in an accompanying extravagant gesture.

"What time did she come in here?" Kling asked. "Last Monday."

"It was toward noon. Shortly before noon. Sometime between eleven-thirty and twelve o'clock."

"You remember, huh?" Brown said.

"Yes. It was about that time." As if on cue, somewhere in the shop a clock began chiming the hour. "A Joseph Knibb," Mott said, almost idly. "Quite rare, quite valuable, such lovely chimes."

The clock chimed six times.

Mott looked at his watch.

"Well, I guess that's it," Brown said. "Thanks a lot, Mr. Mott."

"Thanks," Kling said.

The moment they were out on the street again, Brown said, "You think he's gay?"

"He was wearing a wedding band."

"I caught it. That doesn't mean anything."

"What's a butler's table?" Kling asked.

"I don't know," Brown said, and looked up at the sky. "I hope Carella gets good weather tomorrow," he said.

*   *   *

Deputy Inspector William Cullen Brady was telling the trainees that he took no credit for organizing the hostage negotiating team. Listening to him, Eileen felt uncomfortable because she thought she was overdressed.

This was the first meeting of the training class.

Thursday morning, the nineteenth day of July. Nine o'clock.

For work she'd normally have worn either slacks or a wide skirt, comfortable shoes, big tote bag—unless they were dolling her up for the street. But she hadn't decked herself out as a decoy since the night she'd killed Robert Wilson. Bobby. She supposed that was known as shirking the work. Not precisely doing the job for which she was getting paid. Which was why she was here today, she guessed. So she could go back to doing an honest job someplace in the department.

She was wearing a simple suit, brown to complement her red hair and green eyes, tan blouse with a stock tie, sand-colored pantyhose, low-heeled pumps, fake alligator-skin bag. Service revolver in the bag, alongside the lipstick. Overdressed for sure. The only other woman in the room, a tiny brunette with a hard, mean look, was wearing jeans and a white cotton T-shirt. Most of the men were dressed casually, too. Slacks, sports shirts, jeans, only one of them wearing a jacket.

There were five trainees altogether. Three men, two women. Brady was telling them that the unit had been organized by former chief of patrol Ralph McCleary when he was still a captain some twenty years back. ". . . never would have *been* a team," he was saying. "We'd still be breaking down doors and going in with shotguns. His ideas worked then, and they still work. I take credit for only one new concept. I put women on the team. We've already got two women in the field, and I hope to have another two out there . . ."

A nod and a smile to Eileen and the brunette.

". . . by the time we finish this training program."

Brady was in his early fifties, Eileen supposed, a tall, trim man with bright blue eyes and a fringe of white hair circling his otherwise bald head. Nose a bit too prominent for his otherwise small features. Gave his face a cleaving look. He was the only man in the room wearing a tie. Even Dr. Goodman, who sat beside him at the desk in front of the classroom, was casually dressed in a plaid sports shirt and dark blue slacks.

"Before we get started," Brady said, "I'd like to take a minute to introduce all of you. I'll begin here on the left . . . *my* left, that is . . . with Detective/First Grade Anthony . . . am I pronouncing this correctly . . . Anthony Pellegrino?"

"Yes, sir, that's it, Pellegrino, like the mineral water."

Short and wiry, with dark curly hair and brown eyes. Badly pockmarked face. Olive complexion. Eileen wondered why Brady had questioned the pronunciation of a simple name like Pellegrino. Especially when it *was* the brand name of a widely known mineral water. Hadn't Brady ever been to an Italian restaurant? But there were people in this city who got thrown by any name ending in an *o*, and *a*, or an *i*. Maybe Brady was one of them. She hoped not.

"Detective/First Grade Martha Halsted . . ."

The petite brunette with the Go-to-Hell look. Cupcake breasts, the narrow hips of a boy.

"Martha's with the Robbery Squad," Brady said.

Figures, Eileen thought.

"I forgot to mention, by the way, that Tony's with Safe, Loft and Truck."

He kept going down the line, Detective/Third Grade Daniel Riley of the Nine-Four, Detective/Second Grade Henry Materasso —had no trouble pronouncing *that* one—of the Two-Seven, and last but not least Detective/Second Grade Eileen Burke . . .

"Eileen is with Special Forces."

Martha Halsted looked her over.

"I'm not sure whether Dr. Goodman . . ."

"Mike'll do," Goodman said, and smiled.

"I'm not sure whether *Mike*"—a smile, a nod—"explained

43

during the interviews that while you're attached to the hostage unit, you'll continue in your regular police duties . . ."

Oh, terrific, Eileen thought.

". . . but you'll be on call here twenty-four hours a day. As I'm sure you know, hostage situations come up when we least expect them. Our first task is to get there fast before anyone gets hurt. And once we're on the scene, our job is to make sure that nobody *gets* hurt. That means *nobody*. Not the hostages and not the hostage-takers, either."

"How about *us*, Inspector?"

This from Henry Materasso of the Two-Seven. Big guy with wide shoulders, a barrel chest, and fiery red hair. Not red like Eileen's, which had a burnished-bronze look, but red as in carrot top. The butt of a high-caliber service revolver was showing in a shoulder holster under his sports jacket. Eileen always felt a shoulder holster spelled macho. She was willing to bet Materasso had been called "Red" from the day he first went outside to play with the other kids. Red Materasso. The Red Mattress. *And* the class clown.

Everyone laughed.

Including Brady, who said, "It goes without saying that *we* don't want to get hurt, either."

The laughter subsided. Materasso looked pleased. Martha Halsted looked as if *nothing* pleased her. Poker up her ass, no doubt. Eileen wondered how many armed cowboys she'd blown away in her career at Robbery. She wondered, too, what Detective/First Grade Martha Halsted was doing here, where the job was to make sure nobody got hurt. And she also wondered what she *herself* was doing here. If this wasn't going to be a full-time job, if they could still put her on the street to be stalked and—

"How often do these hostage situations come up, Inspector?"

Halsted. Reading her mind. How often do these situations come up? How often will we be pulled off our regular jobs? Which in Eileen's case was strutting the streets waiting for a rapist or a murderer to attack her. Wonderful job, even if the pay wasn't so hot. So how often, Inspector? Will this be like delivering groceries part time for the local supermarket? Or do I get to work more regularly at something that doesn't involve rape or murder as a consequence of the line of duty?

I don't want to kill anyone else, she thought.

I don't want anybody to get hurt ever again.

Especially me.

So how often do I get a reprieve, Inspector?

"We're not talking now about *headline* hostage situations," Brady said, "where a group of terrorists takes over an embassy or an airplane or a ship or whatever. We're lucky we haven't had any of those in the United States—at least not *yet*. I'm talking about a situation that can occur once a week or once a month or once every six months, it's hard to give you an average. We seem to get more of them in the summer months, but all crime statistics go up during the summertime . . ."

"*And* when there's a full moon," Riley said.

A wiry Irishman from the Nine-Four, as straight and as narrow and as hard-looking as a creosoted telephone pole. Thin-lipped mouth, straight black hair, deep blue eyes. Matching blue shirt. Tight blue jeans. Holster clipped to his belt on the left hand side for a quick cross-body draw. Plant him and the dame from Robbery in the same dark alley and no thief in the world would dare venture into it. Eileen wondered how the people in this room had been chosen. Was compassion one of the deciding factors? If so, why Halsted and Riley—who looked mean enough to pass for the Bonnie and Clyde of law enforcement?

"That's statistically true, you know," Goodman said. "There *are* more crimes committed when the moon is full."

"Tell us about it," Materasso said, grinning, and looked around for approval.

Everyone laughed again.

It occurred to Eileen that the only person in the room who

hadn't said a word so far was Detective/Second Grade Eileen Burke. Of Special Forces.

Well, Pellegrino hadn't said much, either.

"This might be a good time to turn things over to Mike," Brady said.

Goodman rose from where he was sitting, nodded, said, "Thanks, Inspector," and walked to the blackboard.

Actually, it was a greenboard. Made of some kind of plastic material that definitely wasn't slate. Eileen wondered if the movie she'd seen on late-night television last week would have made it as *Greenboard Jungle.* She also wondered why everyone in the room was on a first-name basis except Deputy Inspector William Cullen Brady, who so far wasn't either William or Cullen or Bill or Cully but was simply and respectfully Inspector, which *all* deputy inspectors in the police department were called informally.

Goodman picked up a piece of chalk.

"I'd like to start with the various types of hostage-takers we can expect to encounter," he said.

His eyes met Eileen's.

"Inspector Brady has already mentioned . . ."

Or was she mistaken?

". . . terrorists, the political zealots who are the most commonly known of all takers," Goodman said, and chalked the word onto the board:

TERRORIST

"But there are two other types of takers we'll . . . let's get used to that shorthand, shall we?" he said, and chalked another word onto the board:

TAKER

"The takers we'll most frequently encounter . . ."

No, she wasn't mistaken.

". . . can be separated into three categories. First, as we've seen, we have the terrorist. Next, we have the criminal caught in the . . ."

He rode in the limo with the three women dressed in black. Sat between his mother and his wife, his sister on the jump seat in front of them, everyone silent as the big car nosed its way through the Thursday morning heat and humidity, moving slowly in convoy toward the cemetery where Aunt Katie was buried. His father was in the hearse ahead. He had talked to his father on the telephone only last week. It occurred to him that he would never talk to his father again.

Teddy took his hand.

He nodded.

Beside him, his mother was weeping into a small handkerchief edged with lace. His sister, Angela, stared woodenly through the window, gazing blankly at the sunlit landscape moving past outside the car.

It was too hot to be wearing black.

They stood in the hot sun while the priest said the words of farewell to a man who had taught Carella the precepts of truth and honor he had followed all his life. The coffin was shiny and black, it reflected the sun, threw back the sun in dazzling bursts of light.

It was over too soon.

They were lowering the coffin into the ground. He almost reached out to touch it. And then his father was gone. Gone from sight. Into the ground. And they moved away from the grave. His arm around his mother. A widow now. Louise Carella. A widow. Behind them, the gravediggers were already shoveling earth onto the coffin. He could hear the earth thudding onto the hot, shiny metal. He hoped his mother would not hear the earth hitting the coffin, covering his father.

He left his mother for a moment, and walked up the grassy

47

knoll to where the priest was standing with Angela and Teddy. Angela was telling the priest how beautiful the eulogy had been. Teddy was watching her lips, reading them, eyes intent. They stood side by side in black in the sun, both of them dark-haired and dark-eyed—he wondered suddenly if that was why he'd chosen Teddy Franklin as his wife all those years ago.

Angela was in her early thirties now, enormously pregnant and imminently parturient with her second child. She still wore her brown hair long, cascading straight down on either side of eyes surprisingly Oriental in a high-cheekboned face. The face was a refinement of Carella's, pretty with an exotic tint that spoke of Arabian visits to the island of Sicily in the far-distant past.

Teddy was a far more beautiful woman, taller than her sister-in-law, her midnight-black hair worn in a wedge, intelligence flashing in her dark eyes as she turned now to study the priest's mouth, translating the articulation of his lips into words that filled the silence of her world: Teddy Carella was deaf; nor had she ever spoken a word in her life.

Carella joined them, thanked the priest for a lovely service, although secretly—and he would never tell this to a soul, not even Teddy—he'd felt that the priest's words could have applied to *anyone,* and not to the unique and wonderful man who'd been Antonio Giovanni Carella, so-named by an immigrant grandfather who'd never once realized that such names would never be in fashion in the good old U.S. of A. Nevertheless, Carella invited the priest to join the family at the house, where there'd be something to eat and drink—

"Well, thank you, no, Mr. Carella," the priest said, "I must get back to the church, thank you anyway. And, once again, be cheered by the knowledge that your father is now at peace in God's hands," he said, which caused Carella to wonder whether the priest had even the faintest inkling of how *much* at peace his father had been while he was still alive. To make this point clear, the priest took Carella's hand between both his own and pressed it, from God's hands to Father Gianelli's hands, so to speak, in direct lineage. Carella remained unimpressed.

Teddy had noticed that her mother-in-law was now standing alone some ten yards or so down the knoll. She touched Carella on the arm, signed to him that she was going to join his mother, and left him there with the priest still sandwiching Carella's hand between his own, Angela looking on helplessly. Standing in black, her hands resting on her big belly, her back hurting like hell, she knew damn well that the priest's eulogy had been boilerplate. Fill in the blanks and the dead man could have been anyone. Except that it had been her father.

"I must be on my way," the priest said, sounding like a vicar in an English novel. He made the sign of the cross on the air, blessing God only knew whom or what, picked up his black skirts, and went off toward where his sexton was standing beside the parish car.

"He didn't know Papa at all," Angela said.

Carella nodded.

"You okay?" he asked.

"Yes, fine," she said

The sexton gunned the priest's car into life. Down the knoll, Teddy was gently hugging Carella's mother, who was still crying into her handkerchief. The car moved off. On the lawn below, the two figures in black were etched in silhouette against the brilliant sky. On the knoll above, Carella stood with his sister.

"I loved him a lot," she said.

"Yes."

He felt inadequate.

"We'd better get to the house," she said. "There'll be people."

"Have you heard from Tommy?" he asked.

"No," she said, and turned suddenly away.

He realized all at once that she was crying. Mistaking her tears as grief for his father, he started to say, "Honey, please, he wouldn't have wanted . . ." and then saw that she was shaking her head, telling him wordlessly that he did not understand the tears, did not know why she was crying, stood there in black in pregnancy in utter misery, shaking her head helplessly in the unrelenting sunlight.

"What is it?" he asked.

"Nothing."

"You told me you thought he was still in California . . ."

Shaking her head.

"You said he was trying to get back in time for the funeral . . ."

Still shaking her head, tears streaming down her face.

"Angela, what is it?"

"Nothing."

"*Is* Tommy in California?"

"I don't know."

"What do you mean, you don't know? He's your husband, where is he?"

"Steve, please . . . I don't know."

"Angela . . ."

"He's gone."

"Gone? Gone where?"

"Gone. He left me, Steve. He walked out."

"What are you saying?"

"I'm saying my husband walked out on me."

"No."

"For Christ's sake, do you think I'm making this *up*?" she said fiercely, and burst into fresh tears.

He took her in his arms. He held her close, his pregnant sister in black, who too many years ago had been afraid to come out of her bedroom to join her future husband at the altar. She'd been wearing white that day, and he'd told her she was going to be the prettiest bride the neighborhood had ever seen. And then he'd said . . .

Oh, Jesus, as if it were yesterday.

He'd said . . .

Angela, you have nothing to worry about. He loves you so much he's trembling. He loves you, honey. He's a good man. You chose well.

His sister was trembling in his arms now.

"Why?" he asked her.

"I think he has someone else," she said.

Carella held her at arm's length and looked into her face. She nodded. And nodded again. Her tears were gone now. She stood in bloated silhouette against the sky, her brother's hands clasping her shoulders.

"How do you know?" he asked.

"I just know."

"Angela . . ."

"We have to get back to the house," she said. "Please, it'll be a sin."

He had not heard that expression since he was a boy.

"I'll talk to him," he said.

"No, don't. Please."

"You're my sister," he said.

"Steve . . ."

"You're my sister," he said again. "And I love you."

Their eyes met. Chinese eyes meeting Chinese eyes, dark brown and slanting downward, the Carella heritage clearly evident, brother and sister reaffirming blood ties as powerful as life itself. Angela nodded.

"I'll talk to him," he whispered, and walked her pregnant down the grassy knoll to where Teddy and his mother stood waiting in black in the sunshine.

3

The gun had been a gift from him.

Everyone in this city should have a gun, he'd said, should know how to use a gun if and when the need arose. Said the police were worthless when it came to protecting the lives of ordinary citizens. The police were too busy tracking down prostitutes and drug addicts.

Where he'd bought the gun was anybody's guess.

He traveled a lot by car, he could have picked it up in any of the states that thought America was still the Wild West with hostile Indians massing to attack, better get those wagons in a circle and unholster the Mac 10s. *Bought you something*, he'd said. *I'll teach you to use it.*

That was the irony of it.

The gun was a .22-caliber Colt Cobra.

He'd explained that it was a part-aluminum version of the higher-caliber Detective Special, but people shouldn't let the caliber of a gun fool them, a .22 could do as much damage—even more damage sometimes—as a higher-caliber gun. The reason for this was that the lower-caliber slug would bounce around inside the body without the power to exit, and it could wreak havoc with all the organs in there. Wreak havoc. Those had been his exact words. Wreak havoc. Which was exactly what was planned for tonight. The wreaking of a little more havoc.

The gun was a revolver with a six-shot capacity. It weighed only fifteen ounces, and he had chosen the one with the two-inch barrel, which made it nice in that it wouldn't snag on your clothing. A nice gun. It had been easy learning how to use it, too, he'd kept his promise. That was the irony.

This time, it would be deliberate.

Malice aforethought, wasn't that what they called it?

Tuesday afternoon had been different.

Tonight would be simpler.

Tonight there was the gun.

The building was tree-shaded, and so the sidewalks had not been baking under a merciless sun for hours on end; the street at nine o'clock was refreshingly cool. Cool here in the shadows across the street from the building. Cool waiting here under a big old tree with thick leaves, right hand wrapped around the butt of the Cobra, index finger inside the trigger guard. He would walk his dog at nine o'clock sharp. A creature of habit. Walk a dog at nine, fuck a mistress any chance he got. In ten minutes, he would be dead.

Waiting.

Dressed entirely in black, a black cotton jumpsuit, black socks and jogging shoes, black woolen ski hat pulled down over the ears, sweltering in the woolen hat, but it covered the hair, concealed the color of the hair, no stray pedestrian or motorist would later be able to come up with a good description.

He came out of the building at two minutes to nine, eight fifty-eight on the digital watch, said something to the doorman who was out taking the air, and then started toward the corner, leading his dog. Eight fifty-nine now, and a dark empty street. No cars, no people. Even the doorman had gone back inside again. *Go!*

Cross the street diagonally . . .

Gun out and ready . . .

Step onto the sidewalk and into his path and level the gun at him . . .

"Are you crazy?" he said.

"Yes."

Calmly.

And shot him four times in the head.

And shot the whimpering dog, too, for good measure.

The neighborhood was still largely Italian, the bakery shop wedged between a grocery store and a sausage shop that had an Italian sign in the window, SALUMERIA. Two- or three-story buildings along the street here, clapboard and frame, stores on the ground-floor level, owners usually occupying the upper floor or floors. There were still trees along this street. No graffiti on the buildings. Still something Old World about it.

Carella could remember growing up in this neighborhood when many of the cadences were still Italian, when Italian-language radio stations still played songs like "*La Tarantella*" and "*O Sole Mio*" and "*Funiculì-Funiculà*," the music floating out on the summertime air through open windows all up and down the street. He could remember helping his father in the bakery shop on weekends, when the crowds were thickest, kneading the dough for the bread while his father handled the more delicate art of pastry-making. Carella's hands would be covered with flour. Kneading the dough. When he turned fourteen, fifteen—who could remember now, he'd been a late bloomer—he began to think the dough felt exactly like a girl's breasts. Kneading the dough. Well, exactly like Margie Gannon's breasts, in fact, because this was after he'd experienced his first heavy petting session with her. Or with anyone, for that matter.

Margie Gannon.

Freckled all over, including her breasts, which he'd released from her blouse and her bra one Saturday afternoon while the rain and her breasts came tumbling down, he and she feverish and intent in the living room of the two-story brick house two houses down from his own, her parents out doing the marketing or the shopping or wherever they were, the only thing that mattered was that they'd be gone all afternoon—*They won't be back till four or five,* she'd told him, *come in out of the rain, Steve.*

He had gone there to read comic books with her. Margie had the best comic-book collection in the neighborhood. Kids used to come from blocks away, boys and girls, all of them barely pubescent, to read Margie Gannon's comic books. Her parents encouraged it as a nice clean way of socializing. But they should not have left their lovely young daughter (hch-hch) in the clutches of the mad beast named Stephen the Horny, certainly not on a sultry afternoon in August, with lightning flashing and thunder booming outside, and with all his adolescent juices coming to a boil, not to mention hers.

Alone with Margie Gannon in the ground-floor living room of her house. Parents gone. Rain pelting the windows. Their heads bent over the comic book. Heads almost touching. His arm on the couch behind her. She was holding one side of the comic book in her right hand, he was holding the other side in his left. Heads together. There was the sudden feel of her hair against his cheek. Long reddish-blonde hair. Silken hair against his cheek. Green-eyed, freckle-faced, Irish Margie Gannon sitting beside him with her hair touching his cheek. He was suddenly erect in his pants.

He could not remember now which comic they were reading. Something to do with cops and archcriminals? He could not remember. He remembered what she was wearing, though, still remembered *that*. A short, faded blue-denim skirt and a white, short-sleeved blouse buttoned up the front. Freckled pretty Irish face, freckled slender arms, freckled everything, he was soon to discover, but for now there was only the tingling thrill of her silken hair touching his cheek. She reached up with her left hand, brushed the hair back from her face. Their cheeks touched.

It was as if an intensely sharp light suddenly spilled onto the open comic book. Not daring to look at her, he concentrated his vision on the brilliantly illuminated pages, alive now with pulsating primary colors, red and blue and yellow outlined in the blackest black, focused his white-hot gaze on the action-frozen figures and the shouted oversized words, POW and BAM and BANG and YIIIIKES leaping from the pages, repeating in print the triphammer of his heart, POW, BAM, BANG, echoing the fierce erection in his pants, YIIIIKES!

He turned his face toward hers, she turned her face toward his.

Their noses banged.

Their lips collided.

And oh, dear God, he kissed sweet Margie Gannon, and she moved into his suddenly encircling arms, the comic book POW-ing and BAM-ing and BANG-ing and sliding off her knees and falling to the floor with a whispered YIIIIKES as lightning flashed and thunder boomed and rain relentlessly drilled the sidewalk outside the street-level living room. They kissed for he could not remember how long. He would never again in his life kiss anyone this long or this hard, pressing her close, lips fusing, adolescent yearnings merging, steamy young passions crazing the sky with blue-white flashes, rending the sky with blue-black explosions.

His hand eventually discovered the buttons on her blouse. He fumbled awkwardly with the buttons, this was his goddamn *left* hand and he was *right*-handed, fumbling, fearful she would change her mind, terrified she would stop him before he managed to get even the *top* button open. They were both breathing audibly and hard now, their hearts pounding as he tried desperately to get the blouse open. She helped him with the top button, her own trembling hand guiding his, and then the next button seemed to pop open magically or possibly miraculously, and the one after that and oh my God her bra suddenly appeared in the wide V of the open blouse, a white bra, she was wearing a white bra.

Lightning flashed, thunder boomed.

He thought Thank you, God, and touched the bra, the cones of the bra, white, her breasts filling the white bra, his hand still trembling as he touched the bra awkwardly and tentatively, fumbling and unsure because whereas he'd *dreamt* of doing this with girls in general and Margie Gannon in particular, he never thought he would ever really *get* to do it.

But here he was, actually *doing* it—thank you God, oh Jesus *thank* you—or at least *trying* to do it, wondering whether he should slide his hand down inside the bra, or lower the straps off her shoulders, or get the damn thing *off* somehow, they fastened in the back, didn't they? Trying to dope all this out in what seemed like an hour and a half but was only less than a minute until Margie moved out of his arms, a faint flushed smile on her face, and reached behind her, arms bent, he could see the freckles on the sloping tops of her pretty breasts straining in the bra as she reached behind her to unclasp it, and all at once her breasts came tumbling free, the rain kept tumbling down in torrents, and oh dear God, her breasts were in his hands, he was touching Margie Gannon's sweet naked breasts.

He wondered what had ever become of her.

He could never walk the streets of this neighborhood without thinking of Margie Gannon on that rainy August afternoon.

Carella did not know what had led him back here tonight. Perhaps he wanted only to be near the place where his father had spent most of his waking hours. Be there to feel again the essence of the man he had been. Until it faded entirely. There was a light on in the back of his father's bakery shop. Nine-thirty on a Friday night, a light burning. Just as if his father were still alive, baking his pastries and bread for the big weekend rush. The guys from the Four-Five must have forgotten to—

A shadow suddenly appeared on the shade covering the upper glass panel of the rear door to the shop.

Carella tensed, threw back the flap of his jacket, unholstered his gun.

The shadow moved.

He walked stealthily to the side of the building.

A good policemen never entered a room or a house without

first listening at the door, ear pressed to the wood, trying to ascertain whether anyone was inside there. He knew someone was inside his father's shop, but he didn't know how many were in there or who it was. There was a window on the side of the shop, better than a door in that he could *see* who was in there without having to guess at sounds or voices filtered through a door. He skirted the window, approached it from the side, and ducked below the sill. Cautiously, he raised his head.

It was his mother inside there.

He sat alone in the living room, crying. The room was dark except for the soft glow of the imitation Tiffany lamp behind him. He sat in the big easy chair under the lamp, his shoulders quaking, tears streaming down his face.

Teddy could not hear his sobs.

She went to him, sat on the arm of the chair, gently pulled his head to her shoulder. He had never been a man who'd thought of crying as shameful or embarrassing. He cried because he was pained, and whereas the emotion was painful, the act itself was not; this was a distinction someone more macho might not have appreciated. He cried now. His head cradled on his wife's shoulder, he cried until there were no more tears left in him. And then he raised his head and dried his face with a handkerchief already soggy and looked at her and nodded, and sighed heavily and forlornly.

She signed *Tell me*.

He told her with his mouth and with his hands, words forming on his lips and his fingers, spilling into the silence of the living room where only the imitation Tiffany glowed. The grandfather clock standing against the far wall struck the hour, eleven o'clock, but Teddy could not hear the bonging, could not hear her husband's words except as she watched them on his lips and on his fingers.

He told her he'd watched his mother through the window at the side of the shop. Watched her touching things. Moving around the shop touching things his father had used. The rolling pins and baking pans, the spatulas and spoons, the pastry sheets—even the handles on the big oven doors. He'd watched her for a long time. Moving about the shop silently, touching each item lovingly.

He'd gone around back at last to where the Crime Scene signs were tacked to the back door of the shop, the police padlock gone, but the signs still there. The shade was drawn, his mother's shadow flitted on the shade as she moved silently about the shop. He rapped gently on the glass panel.

She said, "Who is it?"

"It's me," he said. "Steve."

"Ah," she said, and came to the door and unlocked it.

He went in and took her in his arms. She was a good head shorter than he was, wearing the mourning black she would wear for a long time to come, following the tradition of the old country even though she'd been born here in the United States. He held her gently and patted her back. Tiny little pats. I'm here, Mama, it's all right. I'm here.

She spoke against his shoulder.

She said, "I came here to see if I could find him, Steve."

Patting her. Comforting her.

"But he's gone," she said.

Carella looked up at his wife now, looked directly into her eyes intent on his face, and said, "I've been crying for her, Teddy. Not Papa, but her. Because she's the one who's alone now. She's the widow."

The doorman at 1137 Selby Place was telling the detectives that he'd talked to the victim not three minutes before he heard the shots.

"We exchanged a few words about the weather," he said. "That's all everybody talks about these days is the weather. 'Cause it's been so hot."

It had cooled off a bit, the forecasters said there'd be rain tonight.

The detectives were standing on the sidewalk where the technicians still worked within the rectangle defined by the yellow crime-scene tapes stretching from trees and police stanchions to the wall of the apartment building. Monoghan and Monroe had left half an hour ago. So had the medical examiner and the ambulance taking the body of the dead man to the morgue. Hawes and Willis had caught the squeal and they were the only ones left with the technicians, who were busily searching the sidewalk and gutter for whatever they could find.

The doorman was shorter than Hawes but taller than Willis—well, almost everybody was taller than Willis, who'd barely cleared the department's five-foot-eight-inch height requirement when he joined the force all those years ago. Things had changed since then. Now you had women cops who were a lot shorter than that, though Hawes still hadn't seen any midgets in uniform. He didn't like being partnered with Willis. The man was too damn sad these days. He could understand grieving for a loved one, but that didn't mean you had to inflict the pain on everyone around you.

Hawes had scarcely known the woman Willis was living with. Marilyn Hollis. Victim of a felony murder, pair of burglars broke in, put her away, something like that, Hawes never had got it straight. There'd been a lot of tiptoeing around this one, something about Willis being at the scene and blowing the two perps away, Carella and Byrnes both advising Hawes not to ask too many questions. This was two, three months ago, time moved like molasses in this precinct, especially in the summertime.

Willis was handling the questioning now.

Asking about the dead man in a dead man's voice.

"His name?"

"Arthur Schumacher."

"Apartment number?"

"Sixty-two."

Sad brown eyes intent on his pad. Curly black hair, the slight slender build of a matador. Detective Hal Willis. The sadness seeping out of him like sweat.

"Married, single, would you know?"

A dead toneless voice.

"Married," the doorman said.

"Any children?"

"Not living here. He's got grown daughters from a previous marriage. One of them comes to see him every now and then. *Came* to see him."

"Would you know his wife's name?" Hawes asked.

"Marjorie, I think. She's away just now, if you planned on talking to her."

"Away where?"

"They have a summer place out on the Iodines."

"How do you know she's there?"

"Saw her when she left."

"Which was when?"

"Wednesday morning."

"You saw her leaving?"

"Yes, said good morning to her and all."

"Do you know when she's coming back?"

"No, I don't. They usually split their time between here and there in the summer months."

The doorman seemed to be enjoying all this. Except for the killer, he was the last person to have seen the victim alive, and he was clearly relishing his role as star witness, looking ahead to when they caught the killer and the case came to trial. He would take the stand and tell the district attorney just what he was telling the detectives now, though it was hard to believe the tiny little guy here was actually a detective. The big one, yes, no question. But the little one? In the doorman's experience, most detectives in this city were big, that was a fact of life in this city. You hardly ever saw a small detective.

"What time would you say Mr. Schumacher came downstairs with the dog?" the little one asked.

"Little before nine." Practicing for what he'd tell the district attorney. "Same as every night. Unless him and his wife were going out someplace together, in which case he'd walk the dog earlier. But weeknights, it was usually nine o'clock when he took down the dog."

Hawes guessed the doorman considered Friday night a weeknight. Hawes himself considered it the start of the weekend. He would be spending this weekend with Annie Rawles. Lately, he had been spending *most* of his weekends with Annie Rawles. He wondered if this could be considered serious. To tell the truth, it was a little frightening.

"What happened then?" Willis asked.

"He started walking up the street," the doorman said. "With the dog."

"Where were you?"

"I went back inside."

"Did you see anyone before you went back in?"

"Nobody."

"Across the street? Or up the block?"

"Nobody."

"When did you hear the shots?"

"Almost the minute I went back in the building. Well, maybe a few seconds later, no more than that."

"You knew they were shots, huh?"

"I know shots when I hear them. I was in Nam."

"How many shots?"

"Sounded like a full clip to me. The dog got shot, too, you know. Nice gentle dog. Why would anyone want to kill a dog?"

Why would anyone want to kill a *human*? Willis wondered.

"You'll want these," one of the technicians said, walking over. He was wearing jeans, white sneakers, and a white T-shirt. He handed Willis a small manila envelope printed with the word EVIDENCE. "Four bullets," he said. "Must've went on through."

Overhead, there was a sudden flash of lightning.

"Gonna rain," the doorman observed.

"Thanks," Willis said to the technician, and took the envelope, and sealed it, and put it in the right-hand pocket of his jacket. Hawes looked at his watch. It was a quarter past eleven. He wondered how they could reach Mrs. Schumacher. He didn't want to hang around here all night.

"You have a number for them out on the Iodines?" he asked.

"No, I'm sorry, I don't. Maybe the super has. But he won't be in till tomorrow morning."

"What time tomorrow?"

"He's usually here by eight."

"Would you know which island?"

"I'm sorry, I don't know that, either."

"Was the dog barking or anything?" Willis asked.

"I didn't hear the dog barking."

"Did you hear Mr. Schumacher say anything?"

"Nothing. All I heard was the shots."

"What then?"

"I came running outside."

"And?"

"I looked up and down the street to see where the shots had come from . . ."

"Uh-huh."

". . . and saw Mr. Schumacher laying on the sidewalk there." He glanced toward where the technicians had chalked the outline of Schumacher's body on the pavement. "With the dog laying beside him," he said. The technicians had not chalked the dog's outline on the sidewalk. "Both of them laying there. So I ran over, and I knew right away they were both dead. Mr. Schumacher and the dog."

"What was the dog's name?" Willis asked.

Hawes looked at him.

"Amos," the doorman said.

Willis nodded. Hawes was wondering why he'd wanted to know the dog's name. He was also wondering where they'd taken the dog. They didn't take murdered dogs to the morgue for autopsy, did they?

"Did you see anyone at that time?" Willis asked.

"No one. The street was empty."

"Uh-huh."

The technicians were still working the scene. Hawes wondered how long they'd be here. Another lightning flash crazed the sky. There was a crash of thunder. When it rained, the blood would be washed away.

"Was she carrying a suitcase when she left?" he asked. "Mrs. Schumacher?"

"Yes, sir, a small suitcase."

"So you're pretty sure she went out to the Iodines, huh?"

"Well, I can't swear to it, but that's my guess, yes, sir."

Hawes sighed.

"What do you want to do?" he asked Willis.

"Finish up here, then start the canvass. If we can't get a phone listing for her, we'll just have to talk to the super in the morning."

"Tomorrow's my day off," Hawes said.

"Mine, too," Willis said.

Something in his voice made it sound as if he was wondering what he would do on his day off.

Hawes looked at him again.

"Well," Willis said to the doorman, "thanks a lot, we'll get in touch with you if we have any more questions."

"Okay, fine," the doorman said, and looked again at the chalked outline on the pavement.

Suddenly, it was raining.

On Saturday morning, the twenty-first day of July, Steve Carella went back to work. The first thing he found on his desk was a copy of a Detective Division report signed by Detective/Third Grade Harold O. Willis and written by him before he'd left the squadroom at one o'clock this morning. At that time, he had not yet been able to contact Arthur Schumacher's widow. There *was* a phone listed to an Arthur Schumacher in Elsinore County, but the number was an unpublished one and the late-night telephone-company supervisor refused to let Willis have it until someone from Police Assistance okayed it in the morning.

Lieutenant Byrnes's memo, paper-clipped to Willis's report, suggested that someone—he did not recommend who—should contact the telephone company again in the morning and get to Mrs. Schumacher as soon as possible. Neither Willis nor Hawes, who'd caught the squeal, would be back in the squadroom till Monday morning, and someone—again, Byrnes did not say who—should set the 24-24 in motion. Because the report had been left on his desk, Carella shrewdly detected that the someone the lieutenant had in mind was he himself.

Elsinore County consisted of some eight communities on the Eastern Seaboard, all of them buffered from erosion and occasional hurricane force winds by Sands Spit, which—and with all due understanding of the city's chauvinist attitudes—*did* possess some of the most beautiful beaches in the world. Sands Spit ran pristinely north and south. The Iodines were the smaller islands that clustered around it like pilot fish around a shark.

There were six Iodine islands in all, two of them privately owned, a third set aside as a state park open to the public, the remaining three rather larger than their sisters and scattered with small private houses and, more recently, high-rise condominiums and hotels, their fearless occupants apparently willing to brave the hurricanes that infrequently—but often enough—ravaged Sands Spit, the clustering Iodines, and sometimes the city itself.

The Schumachers had shared a house on Salt Spray, the Iodine closest to the mainland. It was there that Carella reached the dead man's widow at nine-fifteen that morning, after having finally pried the phone number loose from a telephone-company liaison officer in the Police Assistance section. It was his sorry task to tell her that her husband had been murdered.

They arrived at the Schumacher apartment on Selby Place at two o'clock that Saturday afternoon. Margaret Schumacher (and not *Marjorie,* as last night's doorman had surmised) had started into the city from Sands Spit shortly after talking to Carella, and was waiting to greet them now. She was in her late thirties, Carella guessed, an attractive woman with blue eyes and blonde hair rather too long for her narrow face. She was wearing a brown skirt cut some two inches above her knees, a tangerine-colored blouse, and low-heeled pumps. She told them that she'd just got home an hour or so ago. Her eyes, puffy and red, indicated that she'd been crying all morning. Carella knew exactly how she felt.

"This is a second marriage for both of us," Margaret said. "I was hoping it would last forever. Now this."

She told them she'd been divorced for almost three years when she met Arthur. He was married at the time . . .

"He's a good deal older than I am," she said, without seeming to realize she was still using the present tense. Her husband had been shot dead the night before, four gunshot wounds in his head according to the autopsy report, but she was still talking about him as if he were alive. They did this. It caught up with them all at once sometimes, or sometimes it never did. "I'm thirty-nine, he's sixty-two, that's a big age difference. He was married when I met him, with two daughters as old as I was—one of them, anyway. It was a difficult time for both of us, but it worked out eventually. We've been married for almost two years now. It'll be two years this September." Still the present tense.

"Could you tell us his former wife's name, please?" Carella asked.

He was thinking that divorced people sometimes did more terrible things to each other than any strangers could. He was thinking there were four bullet holes in the man's head. One would have done the job.

"Gloria Sanders," Margaret said. "She went back to using her maiden name."

Which perhaps indicated a bitter divorce.

"And his daughters?"

"One of them is still single, her name is Betsy Schumacher.

The other one is married, her name is Lois Stein. Mrs. Marc Stein. That's with a *c*, the Marc.''

"Do you have addresses and phone numbers for them? It would save us time if . . .''

"I'm sure Arthur has them someplace.''

Something there, Brown thought. The way she'd said those words.

"Did you get along with his daughters?'' he asked.

"No,'' Margaret said.

Flat out.

No.

"How about your husband? How was his relationship with them?''

"He loved Lois to death. He didn't get along with the other one.''

"Betsy, is that it?'' Carella asked, glancing at his notes.

"Betsy, yes. He called her an aging hippie. Which is what she is.''

"How old would that be?''

"My age exactly. Thirty-nine.''

"And the other daughter. Lois?''

"Thirty-seven.''

"How'd he get along with his former wife?'' Brown asked.

Circling around again to what he'd heard in her voice when she'd said her husband probably had the phone numbers someplace, whatever it was she'd said exactly. The peculiarly bitter note in her voice.

"I have no idea.''

"Ever see her, talk to her, anything like . . . ?''

"Him or me?''

"Well, either one.''

"There's no reason to talk to her. The daughters are grown. They were grown when we met, in fact.''

The daughters.

Generic.

"Any alimony going out to his former wife?" Brown asked.

"Yes."

The same bitter note.

"How much?"

"Three thousand a month."

"Mrs. Schumacher," Carella said, "can you think of anyone who might have done this thing?"

You asked this question of a surviving spouse not because you expected any brilliant insights. Actually, it was a trick question. Most murders, even in this day and age of anonymous violence, were incestuous affairs. Husband killing wife or vice versa. Wife killing lover. Boyfriend killing girlfriend. Boyfriend killing boyfriend. And so on down the line. A surviving husband or wife was always a prime suspect until you learned otherwise, and a good way of fishing for a motive was to ask if anyone *else* might have wanted him or her dead. But you had to be careful.

Margaret Schumacher didn't give the question a moment's thought.

"Everyone loved him," she said.

And began crying.

The detectives stood there feeling awkward.

She dried her tears with a Kleenex. Blew her nose. Kept crying. They waited. It seemed she would never stop crying. She stood there in the center of the living room of the sixth-floor apartment, sealed and silent except for the humming of the air conditioner and the wrenching sound of her sobs, a tall, good-looking woman with golden hair and a golden summer tan, seemingly or genuinely racked by grief. Everyone loved him, she had said. But in their experience, when *everyone* loved someone, then *no* one truly loved him. Nor had she said that *she* loved him. Which may have been an oversight.

"This is a terrible thing that's happened," Brown said at last, "we know how you must . . ."

"Yes," she said. "I loved him very much."

Perhaps correcting the oversight. And using the past tense now.

"And you can't think of any reason anyone might have . . ."

"No."

Still crying into the disintegrating Kleenex.

"No threatening letters or phone . . ."

"No."

". . . calls, no one who owed him money . . ."

"No."

". . . or who *he* may have borrowed from?"

"No."

"Any problems with his employer . . .?"

"It's his own business."

Present tense again. Swinging back and forth between past and present, adjusting to the reality of sudden death.

"What sort of business would that be?" Carella asked.

"He's a lawyer."

"Could we have the name of his firm, please?"

"Schumacher, Benson, and Loeb. He's a senior partner."

"Where is that located, ma'am?"

"Downtown on Jasper Street. Near the Old Seawall."

"Was he having trouble with any of his partners?"

"Not that I know of."

"Or with anyone working for the firm?"

"I don't know."

"Had he fired anyone recently?"

"I don't know."

"Mrs. Schumacher," Brown said, "we have to ask this. Was your husband involved with another woman?"

"No."

Flat out.

"We have to ask this," Carella said. "*You're* not involved with anyone, are you?"

"No."

Chin up, eyes defiant behind the tears.

"Then this was a happy marriage."

"Yes."

"We have to ask," Brown said.

"I understand."

But she didn't. Or maybe she did. Either way, the questions had rankled. Carella suddenly imagined the cops of the Four-Five asking his mother if *her* marriage had been a happy one. But this was different. Or was it? Were they so locked into police routine that they'd forgotten a *person* had been killed here? Forgotten, too, that this was the person's wife, a person in her own right? Had catching the bad guy become so important that you trampled over all the good guys in the process? Or, worse, did you no longer believe there *were* any good guys?

"I'm sorry," he said.

"Mrs. Schumacher," Brown said, "would it be all right if we looked through your husband's personal effects? His address book, his appointment calendar, his diary if he kept . . ."

"He didn't keep a diary."

"Anything he may have written on while he was making or receiving telephone calls, a notepad, a . . ."

"I'll show you where his desk is."

"We'd also like to look through his clothes, if you don't . . ."

"Why?"

"Sometimes we'll find a scrap of paper in a jacket pocket, or a matchbook from a restaurant, or . . ."

"Arthur didn't smoke."

Past tense exclusively now.

"We'll be careful, we promise you," Carella said.

Although he had not until now been too overly careful.

"Yes, fine," she said.

But he knew they'd been clumsy, he knew they had alienated her forever. He suddenly wanted to comfort her the way he'd comforted his mother, but the moment was too far gone, the cop had taken over from the man, and the man had lost.

"If we may," he said.

Margaret showed them where her husband's clothes were hanging in the master bedroom closet. They patted down jackets and trousers and found nothing. A smaller room across the hall was furnished as a study, with a desk and an easy chair and a lamp and rows of bookshelves bearing mostly legal volumes. They found the dead man's address book and appointment calendar at once, asked Margaret if they might take them for reference, and signed a receipt to make it all legal. In the desk drawer above the kneehole, in a narrow little box some three inches long and seven inches wide, they found a stack of blank wallet-sized refill checks and a small red snap-envelope containing the key to a safe-deposit box.

Which was how, on Monday morning, they located another bundle of erotic letters.

4

Hi!

I'm putting on my new sexy lingerie, a red
demi-bra (so-called because it pushes up my
breasts and leaves my nipples uncovered) a
garterbelt with red silk stockings, and the
tiniest red panties you ever saw in smooth soft
silk. On top of that I'll wear the new suit I
got yesterday. It cost an arm and a leg but it
was irresistible, a prim-looking blue thing
with a short, double-breasted jacket and—the
pièce de résistance—a skirt with an
interesting arrangement in front: a big split
artistically draped with intricate folds so
that it looks very decent when I stand up but
when I sit down and spread my legs a little I'm
practically inviting the man sitting next to me
to put his hand through that split and touch me
between the legs.

Is this the sort of letter you want me to
write? I think I may enjoy this.

In my fantasy, we'll check into a hotel and then
go down to the restaurant together and find a
booth in an out-of-the-way corner somewhere and
you would be that man sitting next to me and you
would put your hand through that split in the
skirt and you would touch my cunt, which would
be very hot, very wet, and very very hungry for
your attention. In no time at all, you would
bring me to climax, and then it would be my
turn. I would unzip your fly and find your cock,
which I'm sure would already be stone hard. It
would spring out into my hand, and I would play
with it under the table until it got harder and
harder, and then when nobody was looking, I
would pretend to pick up a napkin from the floor,
and I would lower my mouth onto your cock, and
suck you till you begged me to let you come but
I wouldn't let you no matter how hard you
begged. I'd just keep sucking your big cock until you were almost weeping, and then I'd say,
''Come on, let's go up to the room.''

We would compose ourselves, leave the
restaurant, and take the elevator back
upstairs. And inside the room, I'd take off the
blue suit, and you'd tear off that wisp of red
panty, and you'd say something about me driving
you crazy, and I'd unzip you once again, and
sink to my knees, and put your big cock in my
mouth again. You'd take off the rest of your
clothes, and slowly slip out of my mouth, and
then you'd lift me to you and start licking my
breasts. I would come again, you always make me
come so fast, even just sucking my nipples, but
I would know you weren't finished with me yet, I

would know you wanted more from me, you always
want more and more from me. You would pick me
up and carry me to the bed, and you would kneel
over me with my legs wide open and your cock in
your hand, and you would begin fucking me slow
and steady, and then harder and harder and
harder, give it to me, baby, fuck me now.

See you later.

Bye!

"Gives me a hard-on, this woman," Brown said, and shook his head, and said, "Whooosh," and slid the letter back under the rubber band that held the stack of letters together. He was sitting beside Carella in one of the squad's unmarked cars, a three-year-old Plymouth sedan with the air conditioner on the fritz, both men sweltering as they drove uptown again to the Schumacher apartment. It had taken them an hour and a half this morning to get a court order to open Schumacher's safe-deposit box, and another half hour to get to the bank, not far from his office on Jasper Street. The box had contained only the letters and a pair of first-class airline tickets to Milan, one in Schumacher's name, the other in Susan Brauer's.

There were seventeen letters in all, five fewer than Schumacher had written. The first one—the one Brown had been reading—was dated three days after Schumacher's first letter, and seemed to be in direct response to it. Like his letters, none of these were signed. Each of the letters was neatly typed. Each started with the same salutation and ended with the same complimentary close. *Hi!* and *Bye!* Like a vivacious little girl writing to someone she'd met in camp. *Some* little girl, Brown thought.

"You think he was losing interest?" he asked.

"I'm sorry, what?" Carella said.

His mind had been drifting again. He could not shake the

image of his mother in the bakery shop, wandering the shop, touching all the things that had belonged to his father.

"I mean, he meets her on New Year's Day, and this is only June when he gets her to write him these hot letters. Sounds as if he was maybe losing interest."

"Then why would he be taking her to Europe?"

"Maybe the letters got things going again," he said, and was silent for a moment. "You ever write any kind of letters like these?"

"No, did you?"

"No. Wish I knew how."

They were approaching the Selby Place apartment. Carella searched for a parking spot, found one in a No Parking zone, parked there anyway, and threw down the visor to display a placard with the Police Department logo on it. It seemed cooler outside the car than it had inside. Little breeze blowing here on the tree-shaded street. They walked up the street, announced themselves to the doorman, and then took the elevator up to the sixth floor.

What they had already concluded was that Arthur Schumacher and Susan Brauer had been exchanging intimate letters and that they'd been planning to fly to Italy together at the end of the month. What they did *not* know was whether Margaret Schumacher had known all this. They were here to question her further. Because if she *had* known . . .

"Come in," she said, "have you learned anything?"

Seemingly all concerned and anxious and looking drawn and weary; her husband had been buried yesterday morning. They had to play this very carefully. They didn't want to tell her everything they knew, but at the same time it was virtually impossible to conduct a fishing expedition without dangling a little bait in the water.

Carella told her they were now investigating the possibility that her husband's death may have been connected to a previous homicide they'd been investigating . . .

"Oh? What previous homicide?"

. . . and that whereas when they were here on Saturday they'd merely been doing a courtesy follow-up for the two detectives who'd initiated the investigation into her husband's death . . .

"A *courtesy* follow-up?" she said, annoyed by Carella's unfortunate choice of a word.

"Yes, ma'am," he said, "in order to keep the investigation ongoing . . ."

. . . but under the so-called First Man Up rule, the previous homicide demanded that *both* cases be investigated by the detectives who'd caught the first one. This meant that her husband's case was now *officially* theirs, and they'd be the ones . . .

"What previous homicide?" she asked again.

"The murder of a woman named Susan Brauer," Carella said, and watched her eyes.

Nothing showed in those eyes.

"Do you know anyone by that name?" Brown asked.

Watching her eyes.

"No, I don't."

Nothing there. Not a flicker of recognition.

"You didn't read anything about her murder in the papers . . ."

"No."

". . . or see anything about it on television?'"

"No."

"Because it's had a lot of coverage."

"I'm sorry," she said, and looked at them, seemingly or genuinely puzzled. "When you say my husband's death may have been connected . . ."

"Yes, ma'am."

". . . to this previous homicide . . ."

"Yes, ma'am, that's a possibility we're now considering."

Lying, of course. It was no longer a mere possibility but a definite probability. Well, yes, there *did* exist the remotest chance that Arthur Schumacher's death was totally unrelated to Susan Brauer's, but there wasn't a cop alive who'd have accepted a million-to-one odds on such a premise.

"Connected how?"

The detectives looked at each other.

"Connected how?" she said again.

"Mrs. Schumacher," Carella said, "when we were here on Saturday, when we found that key in your husband's desk, you said the only safe-deposit box you had was up here at First Federal Trust on Culver Avenue, that's what you told us on Saturday."

"That's right."

"You said you didn't know of any box at Union Savings, which was the name of the bank printed on that little red envelope. You said . . ."

"I *still* don't."

"Mrs. Schumacher, there *is* a box at that bank, and it's in your husband's name."

They were still watching her eyes. If she'd known what was in that box, if she now realized that *they*, too, knew what was in it, then something would have shown in her eyes, on her face, something would have flickered there. But nothing did.

"I'm surprised," she said.

"You didn't know that box existed."

"No. Why would Arthur have kept a box all the way downtown? We . . ."

"Union Savings on Wellington Street," Brown said. "Three blocks from his office."

"Yes, but we have the box up here, you see. So why would he have needed another one?"

"Have you got any ideas about that?" Carella asked.

"None at all. Arthur never kept anything from me, why wouldn't he have mentioned a safe-deposit box down there near his office? I mean . . . what was *in* the box, do you know?"

"Mrs. Schumacher," Brown said, "did you know your husband was planning a trip to Europe at the end of the month?"

"Yes, I did."

"Italy and France, wasn't it?"

"Yes, on business."

Coming up on it from the blind side, trying to find out if she'd known about those tickets in the safe-deposit box, if she had somehow *seen* those tickets . . .

"Leaving on the twenty-ninth for Milan . . ."

. . . or had learned in some other way, *any* other way, about the affair her husband was having with a beautiful, twenty-two . . .

"Yes."

". . . and returning from Lyons on the twelfth of August."

"Yes."

"Had you planned on going with him?"

"No, I just told you, it was a business trip."

"Did he often go on business trips alone?"

"Yes. Why? Do you think the trip had something to do with his murder?"

"Do *you* think it might have?" he asked.

"I don't see how. Are you saying someone . . . I mean, I just don't understand how the trip could have had anything to do with it."

"Are you sure he was going alone?" Carella asked.

"Yes, I think so," she said. "Or with one of his partners."

"Did he *say* he was going with one of his partners?"

"He didn't say either way. I don't understand. What are you . . . ?" and suddenly her eyes narrowed, and she looked sharply and suspiciously at Carella and then snapped the same look at Brown. "What is this?" she asked.

"Mrs. Schumacher," Carella said, "did you have any reason to believe your husband . . ."

"No, what is this?"

". . . might *not* be traveling alone?"

"What the hell is this?"

So there they were, at the crossroads.

And as Yogi Berra once remarked, "When you come to a crossroads, take it."

Carella glanced at Brown. Brown nodded imperceptibly, telling him to go ahead and bite the bullet. Carella's eyes flicked acceptance.

"Mrs. Schumacher," he said, "when we were here last Saturday, you told us your husband had *not* been involved with another woman. You seemed very definite about that."

"That's right, he wasn't. Would you mind . . . ?"

"We now have evidence that he *was*, in fact, involved with someone."

"What? What do you mean?"

"Evidence that links him to Susan Brauer."

Both of them alert now for whatever effect the revelation might have on her. Watching her intently. The eyes, the face, the entire body. They had just laid it on the line. If she'd known about the affair . . .

"*Links* him to her?" she said. "What does that mean, *links* him to her?"

"Intimately," Carella said.

What seemed like genuine surprise flashed in her eyes.

"Evidence?" she said.

"Yes, ma'am."

"What evidence?"

The surprise giving way to a look of almost scoffing disbelief.

"Letters she wrote to him," Carella said. "Letters we found in his safe-deposit . . ."

"Well, what does . . . ? Letters? Are you saying this woman wrote some *letters* to my husband?"

"Yes, ma'am."

"Even so, that doesn't mean . . ."

"We have *his* letters, too. The letters he wrote to her."

"*Arthur* wrote . . . ?"

"Yes, ma'am."

"Don't be ridiculous."

"We found the letters in her apartment."

"Letters *Arthur* wrote to her?"

"They weren't signed, but we feel certain . . ."

"Then how do you . . . ? Where *are* these letters? I want to see these letters."

"Mrs. Schumacher . . ."

"I have a right to see these letters. If you're saying my husband was involved with another woman . . ."

"Yes, ma'am, he was."

"Then I want to see proof. You're trying to . . . to . . . make it seem he was having an *affair* with . . . this . . . this *woman*, whatever her name was . . ."

"Susan Brauer."

"I don't *care* what it was! I don't believe a word of what you're saying. Arthur was *never* unfaithful to me in his life! Don't you think I'd have *known* if he was unfaithful? Are you deliberately trying to hurt me?" she shouted. "Is that it?" Eyes flashing now, entire body trembling. "I don't have to answer any more of your questions," she said, and went immediately to the phone. "My husband was a partner in one of the biggest law firms in this city, you can just go *fuck* yourself," she said, and began dialing.

"Mrs. Schumacher . . ."

"There's the door," she said, and then, into the phone, "Mr. Loeb, please."

Carella looked at Brown.

"Please *leave!*" Margaret shouted. Into the phone, in a quieter but still agitated voice, she said, "Lou, I have two detectives here who just violated my rights. What do I . . ."

They left.

In the hallway outside, while they waited for the elevator, Carella said, "What do you think?"

"Tough one to call," Brown said.

"This isn't new, you know."

"You're talking about last week, right?"

"Yeah, Saturday. I mean, she got angry from minute one, today isn't something new."

"Maybe we've got shitty bedside manners."

"I'm sure," Carella said.

The elevator doors slid open. They got into the car and hit the button for the lobby. They were both silent as the elevator hummed down the shaft, each of them separately thinking that Margaret Schumacher had just treated them to a fine display of surprise, shock, disbelief, indignation, anger, and hurt over the news of her husband's infidelity, but there was no way of knowing if any of it had been genuine.

As they stepped out of the building, the heat hit them like a closed fist.

"You think her lawyer's gonna call us?" Brown asked.

"Nope," Carella said.

He was wrong.

A detective named Mary Beth Mulhaney was working the door.

She normally worked out of the Three-One; Eileen had met her up there, oh, it must've been four years ago, when they'd called Special Forces for a decoy. Guy was beating up women on the street, running off into the night with their handbags. Eileen had run the job for a week straight without getting a single nibble. The hairbag lieutenant up there told her it was because she looked too much like a cop, S.F. should've sent him somebody else. Eileen suggested that maybe *he'd* like to go out there in basic black and pearls, see if *he* couldn't tempt the mugger to hit on him. The lieutenant told her not to get smart, young lady.

There was a lot of brass down here outside the lingerie shop. Emergency Service had contained the owner of the shop and the woman she was keeping hostage, barricading the front of the place and cordoning off the street. Mary Beth was working the back door, far from the Monday morning crowd that had gathered on the street side. The brass included Chief of Patrol Dylan Curran, whose picture Eileen had seen in police stations all over town, and Chief of Detectives Andrew Brogan, who all those years ago had reprimanded Eileen for talking back to the hairbag lieutenant at the Three-One, and Deputy Inspector John Di Santis who was in command of the Emergency Service and whom Eileen had seen on television only the other night at the Calm's Point Bridge where a guy who thought he was Superman was threatening to fly off into the River Dix. But Brady was the star.

A sergeant from Emergency Service was softly explaining to Eileen and the other trainees that the lady in there had a .357 Magnum in her fist and that she'd threatened to kill the only customer still in her shop if the police didn't back off. The reason the police were here to begin with was that the lady in there had already chased another customer out of her shop when she complained that the elastic waistband on a pair of panties she'd bought there had disintegrated in the wash.

The lady—whose name was Hildy Banks—had yanked the Magnum she kept under the counter for protection against armed robbers and such, and had fired two shots at the complaining customer, who'd run in terror out of the shop. Hildy had then turned the gun on the other terrified woman and told her to stop screaming or she'd kill her. The woman had not stopped screaming. Hildy had fired two more shots into the air, putting a hole in the ceiling and knocking a carton of half-slips off the topmost shelf in the store. The police were there by then. One of the responding blues yelled "Holy shit!" when Hildy slammed another shot through the front door. That was when Emergency Service was called. After which they'd beeped—

"Can we keep it down back there?"

Inspector Brady. Standing beside Mary Beth, who was talking calmly to the lady behind the door. Turning his head momentarily to scold the Emergency Service sergeant, and then giving Mary Beth his full attention again. Eileen wondered how long Mary Beth had been working with the unit. Brady seemed to be treating her like a rookie, whispering instructions to her, refusing to let her run with it. Mary Beth shot him an impatient look. He seemed not to catch it. He seemed to want to handle this one all by himself. Eileen guessed the only reason Mary Beth was outside the door was because the taker inside was a woman.

"Hildy?"

Mary Beth outside the door, cops everywhere you looked in that backyard. The rear door of the shop opened onto a small fenced-in courtyard. It was on the street-level floor of an apartment building, and clotheslines ran from the windows above to telephone poles spaced at irregular intervals all up and down the block. Trousers and shirts hung limply on the humid air, arms and legs dangling. Just in case Hildy in there decided to blow her head off, Mary Beth was crouched to one side of the door, well beyond the sight-lines of the single window on the brick wall. She was a round-faced woman with eyes as frosty blue as glare ice, wearing a blue shirt hanging open over a yellow T-shirt and gray slacks. No lipstick. No eye shadow. Cheeks rosy red from the heat. Perspiration dripping down her face. Eyes intent on that door. She was hoping nothing would come flying through it. Or the window, either.

"Hildy?" she said again.

"Go away! Get out of here! I'll kill her."

Voice on the edge of desperation. Eileen realized the woman in there was as terrified as her hostage. The cops outside here had to look like an army to her. Chief of Patrol Curran pacing back and forth, hands behind his back, a general wondering whether his troops would take this one or blow it. Chief of Detectives Brogan standing apart with two other beefy men in plainclothes, whispering softly, observing Mary Beth at the door. Uniformed policemen with rifles and handguns—out of sight, to be sure.

You promise them no guns, no shooting, Eileen thought. And you meant it. Unless or until. All these cops were here and ready to storm the joint the moment anyone got hurt. Kill the hostage in there, harm the hostage in there, you took the door. Hurt a cop outside here, same thing. You played the game until the rules changed. And then you went cop.

"Hildy, I'm getting that coffee you asked for," Mary Beth said.

"Taking long enough," Hildy said.

"We had to send someone down the street for it."

"That was an hour ago."

"No, only ten minutes, Hildy."

"Don't argue with her," Brady whispered.

"Should be here any second now," Mary Beth said.

"Who's that with you?" Hildy asked.

Voice touched with suspicion.

Mary Beth looked at Brady. Eyes questioning. What do I tell her, Boss?

Brady shook his head. Touched his index finger to his lips. Shook his head again.

"Nobody," Mary Beth said. "I'm all alone here."

"I thought I heard somebody talking to you."

Brady shook his head again.

"No, it's just me here," Mary Beth said.

Why is he asking her to *lie*? Eileen wondered.

"But there are cops out there, I know there are."

"Yes, there are."

"But not near the door, is that what you're saying?"

"That's it, Hildy. I'm all alone here at the door."

Brady nodded, pleased.

"Why don't you open the door just a little?" Mary Beth said.

This surprised Brady. His eyes popped open. As blue and as crisp as Mary Beth's, but clearly puzzled now. What was she doing? He shook his head.

"Then you can see I'm alone here," Mary Beth said, and waved Brady away with the back of her hand.

Brady was shaking his head more vigorously now. Standing just to Mary Beth's left, bald head gleaming in the sunshine, hawk nose cleaving the stiflingly hot air, head shaking No, no, no, what the hell are you *doing*?

Mary Beth shooed him away again.

"Open the door, Hildy. You'll see . . ."

Brady shook his head angrily.

". . . I'm alone here."

She lifted her head to Brady, shot him an angry glance. Their eyes locked. Blue on blue, flashing, clashing. Brady stomped off. Michael Goodman was standing with the trainees. Brady went directly to him. "I want her off that door," he said.

"Inspector . . ."

"She'll open the door when the coffee comes, Mulhaney's moving too fast."

"Maybe she senses something you don't," Goodman said. "She's the one talking, Inspector. Maybe she . . ."

"I was standing right there all along," Brady said. "I heard everything they said to each other. I'm telling you she's trying to get that door open too damn soon. The woman in there'll open it and start shooting, that's what'll happen."

He doesn't trust her, Eileen thought.

"Let's give her another few minutes," Goodman said.

"I think we should ease in another talker. Wait till the coffee comes, and then . . ."

"Look," Eileen said.

They turned to follow her gaze.

The door was opening. Just a crack, but it was opening.

"See?" Mary Beth said. "I'm all alone here."

They could not hear Hildy's reply. But whatever she'd said, it seemed to encourage Mary Beth.

"Why don't you leave it open?" she said. "I like to see who I'm talking to, don't you?"

Again, they could not hear her reply. But she did not close the door.

"Be careful with that gun now," Mary Beth said, and smiled. "I don't want to get hurt out here."

This time they heard Hildy's voice:

"Where's *your* gun?"

"I don't have one," Mary Beth said.

"You're a cop, aren't you?"

"Yes, I am. I told you that. I'm a Police Department negotiator. But I haven't got a gun. You can see for yourself, now that the door is open," Mary Beth said, and spread her hands wide. "No gun. Nothing. See?"

"How do I know you haven't got one under your shirt?"

"Well, here, I'll open the shirt, you can see for yourself."

Mary Beth opened the blue shirt wide, like a flasher, showing Hildy the yellow T-shirt under it.

"See?" she said.

"How about your pockets?"

"Would you like to put your hand in my pockets? Make sure I haven't got a gun?"

"No. You'll try something funny."

"Why would I do that? You think I want to get hurt?"

"No, but . . ."

"I don't want to hurt you, and I don't want to get hurt, either. I have a three-year-old son, Hildy. I don't think he'd want me getting shot out here."

"Do you really?"

"I really do, his name is Dennis," she said.

"Dennis the Menace, huh?"

"You said it," Mary Beth said, and laughed.

From inside the shop, they could hear the woman laughing, too.

"You got any children?" Mary Beth asked.

"I think she'll be all right," Goodman said.

"So the sexist bastard fires her," Eileen said. "Not from the *police* department, even *that* dictatorial son of a bitch couldn't swing that. But he kicked her off the team, sent her back full time to the Three-One. And you know why?"

"Why?" Karin asked.

They were in her office on the fifth floor of the building. Dr. Karin Lefkowitz. Five o'clock that afternoon, her last appointment of the day. A big-city Jewish girl who looked like Barbra Streisand, people told her, only much prettier. Brown hair cut in a flying wedge. Sharp intelligence in her blue eyes, something like anger in them, too, as she listened to Eileen's atrocity story about Inspector William Cullen Brady, commander of the hostage negotiating team. Good legs, crossed now, wearing her signature dark blue business suit and Reeboks, leaning forward intently, wanting to know why the son-of-a-bitch sexist bastard had fired Mary Beth Mulhaney.

"Because she wasn't doing it *exactly* his way," Eileen said. "You do it exactly his way, or so long, sister, it was nice knowing you. But Mary Beth's way was *working*, it *did* work, she got the hostage *and* the taker out of there without anyone getting hurt. You know what this is?"

"What is it?" Karin asked.

"It's the old-guard mentality of the police department," Eileen said. "They can say what they want about the gun on the hip making us all equal, but when push comes to shove, the old-timers still think of as *girls*. And us *girls* need a lot of help, don't we? Otherwise we might *endanger* all those hairy-chested *men* out there who are doing their best to maintain law and order. I say *fuck* law and order and fuck all thick-headed Irishmen like Brady who think sweet little Irish girls like me and Mary Beth should be in *church* saying novenas for all the brave *men* out there in the streets!"

"Wow," Karin said.

"Damn right," Eileen said.

"I've never seen you so angry."

"Yeah."

"Tell me why."

"Why do you think? If Brady can do that to Mary *Beth*, who was with the team for six months and who was doing an absolutely *great* job, then what's he going to do to *me* the first time *I* screw up?''

"Are you worried about screwing up?"

"I've never even worked the door yet, I'm just saying . . ."

"Do you want to work the door?"

"Well, that's the whole idea, isn't it? I mean, I'm in training as a hostage negotiator, that's what negotiators do. We work the door, we try to get the taker and the hostages . . ."

"Yes, but do you *want* to work the door? Are you looking forward to working the door?"

"I think I've learned enough now to give it a shot."

"You feel you're prepared now to . . ."

"Yes. We've simulated it dozens of times already, different kinds of takers, different kinds of situations. So, yes, I feel I'm prepared."

"Are you looking forward to your first time?"

"Yes."

"Your first *real* situation?"

"Yes. I'm a little nervous about it, of course, but there'll be supervision. Even if I was alone at the door, there'd be other people nearby."

"Nervous how?"

"Well, this isn't a game, you know. There are lives at stake."

"Of course."

"So I'd want to do it right."

"Are you afraid you might do it wrong?"

"I just wouldn't want anyone to get hurt."

"Of course not."

"I mean, the reason I hate *decoy* work . . ."

"I know."

". . . is because there's . . . there's always the possibility you'll have to . . ."

"Yes?"

"Put someone away."

"Yes. Kill someone."

"Kill someone. Yes."

"And you feel that would be a danger? When you're working the door?"

"Whenever there's a gun on the scene, there's a danger of that happening, yes."

"But in this situation, you wouldn't be the one with the gun, isn't that right."

'Well, yes, that's right."

"The taker would have the gun."

"The taker would have the gun, that's absolutely right."

"So there's no possibility that *you* would have to shoot anyone. Kill anyone."

"Well, you know, *I* don't want to get hurt, either, you know? The person in there has a *gun,* you know . . ."

"Yes, I know."

"And if I screw up . . ."

"What makes you think you'll screw up?"

"I *don't* think I'll screw up. I'm only saying *if* I should screw up . . ."

"Yes, what would happen?"

"Well, the person in there might use the gun."

"And then what?"

"We'd have to come down."

"You'd have to take the door by force."

"Yes. If the taker started shooting."

"And if the door was taken by force . . ."

"Well . . . yes."

"Yes *what,* Eileen?"

"The taker might get hurt."

"Might get killed."

"Yes. Might get killed."

"Which you wouldn't want to happen."

"I wouldn't want that to happen, no. That's why I want to get out of *decoy* work. Because . . ."

"Because you once had to kill a man."

"Bobby."

"Bobby Wilson, yes."

"I killed him, yes."

The women looked at each other. They had gone over this ground again and again and again. If Eileen heard herself telling this same story one more time, she would vomit all over her shoes. She looked at her watch. She knew Karin hated it when she did that. It was twenty minutes past five. Monday afternoon. Hot as hell outside and not much cooler here in this windowless room with faulty municipal-government air-conditioning.

"Why does Brady make you so angry?" Karin asked.

"Because he fired Mary Beth."

"But you're not Mary Beth."

"I'm a *woman*."

"He hasn't fired *you*, though."

"He might."

"Why?"

"Because he doesn't think women can do the job."

"Does he remind you of anyone you know?"

"No."

"Are you sure?"

"Positive."

"You can't think of a single other man who . . ."

"I'm not going to say Bert, if that's what you want me to say."

"I don't want you to say anything you don't want to say."

"It wasn't that Bert didn't think I could do the job."

"Then what was it?"

"He was trying to protect me."

"But he screwed up."

"That wasn't his fault."

"Whose was it?"

"He was trying to help me."

"You mean you no longer think . . . ?"

"I don't know *what* I think. *You* were the one who suggested I talk to Goodman about joining the team, *you* were the one who thought . . ."

"Yes, but we're talking about Bert Kling now."

"I don't want to talk about Bert."

"Why not? Last week you seemed to think he was responsible . . ."

"He *was*. If I hadn't lost my backups . . ."

"Yes, you wouldn't have had to shoot Bobby Wilson."

"*Fuck* Bobby Wilson! If I hear his name one more time . . ."

"Do you *still* think Bert was responsible for . . ."

"He was the one who made me lose my backups, yes."

"But was he responsible for your shooting Bobby Wilson? For your killing Bobby Wilson?"

Eileen was silent for a long time.

Then she said, "No."

Karin nodded.

"Maybe it's time we talked to Bert," she said.

Carella had spent his early adolescence and his young manhood in Riverhead. He had moved back to Riverhead after he married Teddy, and it was in Riverhead that his father had been killed. Tonight, he drove to a section of Riverhead some three miles from his own house, to talk to his brother-in-law, Tommy. He would rather have done almost anything else in the world.

Tommy had moved back to the house that used to be his parents' while he was away in the army. Nowadays, you did not have to say which war or police action or invasion a man had been in. If you were an American of any given age, you had been in at least one war. The irony was that Tommy had come through *his* particular war alive while his parents back home were getting killed in an automobile accident. He still owned the house, still rented it out. But there was a room over the garage, and he was living in that now.

Angela had told Carella that he'd moved out at the beginning of the month, after they'd had a terrible fight that caused their three-year-old daughter to run out of the room crying. Actually, Angela had *kicked* him out. Screamed at him to get the hell out of the house and not to come back till he got rid of his bimbo. That was the word she'd used. Bimbo. Tommy had packed some clothes and left. Two weeks ago, he'd called to tell her he had to go to California on business. Last night, he'd called to say he was back. Tonight, Carella was here to see him.

He had called first, he knew he was expected. He did not want to ring this doorbell. He did not want to be here asking Tommy questions, he did not want to be playing *cop* with his own brother-in-law. He climbed the steep flight of wooden steps that ran up the right hand side of the garage. He rang the bell. It sounded within.

"Steve?"

"Yeah."

"Just a sec."

He waited.

The door opened.

"Hey." Arms opening wide. "Steve." They embraced. "I didn't know about your father," Tommy said at once. "I would've come home in a minute, but Angela didn't call me. I didn't find out till last night. Steve, I'm sorry."

"Thank you."

"I really loved him."

"I know."

"Come in, come in. You ever think you'd see me living alone like this? Jesus," Tommy said, and stood aside to let him by. He had lost a little weight since Carella had last seen him. You get a little older, your face gets a look of weariness about the eyes. Just living did that to you, even if you weren't having troubles with your marriage.

The single room was furnished with a sofa that undoubtedly opened into a bed, a pair of overstuffed easy chairs with flowered slipcovers on them, a standing floor lamp, a television set on a rolling cart, a dresser with another lamp and a fan on top of it, and a coffee table between the sofa and the two easy chairs. On the wall over the sofa, there was a picture of Jesus Christ with an open heart in his chest radiating blinding rays of light, his hand held up in blessing. Carella had seen that same picture in Catholic homes all over the city. There was a partially open door to the left of the sofa, revealing a bathroom beyond.

"Something to drink?" Tommy asked.

"What've you got?" Carella asked.

"Scotch or gin, take your choice. I went down for fresh limes after you called, in case you feel like a gin and tonic. I've also got club soda, if you . . ."

"Gin and tonic sounds fine."

Tommy walked to where a sink, a row of cabinets, a Formica countertop, a range, and a refrigerator occupied one entire wall of the room. He cracked open an ice-cube tray, took down a fresh bottle of Gordon's gin from one of the cabinets, sliced a lime in half, squeezed and dropped the separate halves into two tall glasses decorated with cartoon characters Carella didn't recognize, and mixed two hefty drinks that he then carried back to where Carella was already sitting on the sofa.

They clinked glasses.

"Cheers," Tommy said.

"Cheers," Carella said.

The fan on top of the dresser wafted warm air across the room. The windows—one over the sink, the other on the wall right-angled to the sofa—were wide open, but there wasn't a breeze stirring. Both men were wearing jeans and short-sleeved shirts. It was insufferably hot.

"So?" Carella said.

"What'd she tell you?"

"About the fight. About kicking you out."

"Yeah," Tommy said, and shook his head. "Did she say why?"

"She said you had someone else."

"But I don't."

"She thinks you do."

"But she's got no *reason* to believe that. I love her to death, what's the *matter* with her?"

Carella could remember organ music swelling to drown out the sound of joyful weeping in the church, his father's arm supporting Angela's hand as he led her down the center aisle to the altar where Tommy stood waiting . . .

"I told her there's nobody else but her, she's the only woman I ever . . ."

. . . the priest saying a prayer and blessing the couple with holy water, Tommy sweating profusely, Angela's lips trembling behind her veil. It was the twenty-second day of June, Carella would never forget that day. Not only because it was the day his sister got married, but because it was also the day his twins were born. He remembered thinking he was the luckiest man alive. Twins!

". . . but she keeps saying she *knows* there's somebody else."

Teddy sitting beside him, watching the altar, the church expectantly still. He remembered thinking his little sister was getting married. He remembered thinking we all grow up. For everything there is a season . . .

Do you, Thomas Giordano, take this woman as your lawfully wedded wife to live together in the state of holy matrimony? Will you love, honor, and keep her as a faithful . . .

. . . a time to plant, and a time to pluck up what is planted . . .

"I've never cheated on her in my life," Tommy said. "Even when we were just going together . . . well, you know that, Steve. The minute I met her, I couldn't even *look* at another girl. So now she . . ."

. . . and forsaking all others keep you alone unto her 'til death do you part?

Yes. I do.

And do you, Angela Louise Carella, take this man as your lawfully wedded husband to live together in the state of holy matrimony? Will you love, honor, and cherish him as a faithful woman is bound to do, in health, sickness, prosperity, and adversity . . .

Tommy lifting his bride's veil and kissing her fleetingly and with much embarrassment. The organ music swelling again. Smiling, the veil pulled back onto the white crown nestled in her hair, eyes sparkling, Angela . . .

"Why does she think you're cheating, Tommy?"

"Steve, she's pregnant, she's expecting any day now, you know what I mean? I think it's because we aren't having sex just now is why she thinks I've got somebody else . . ."

. . . a time to embrace, and a time to refrain from embracing . . .

"I'm being completely honest with you. That's all I think it is."

"No other reason?"

"None."

"Nothing she could have got in her head . . . ?"

"Nothing."

"Something you did . . . ?"

"No."

"Something you said?"

"No."

"Tommy, look at me."

Their eyes met.

"Are you telling me the truth?"

"I swear to God," Tommy said.

5

Lieutenant Byrnes had advised him—*everyone* had advised him—to let the Four-Five run with it, stay out of it, he was too emotionally involved to do anything effective on the case. But this was now a week since his father had been shot and killed, and despite all the promises from the two detectives investigating the case, Carella hadn't heard a word from them. At nine o'clock that Tuesday morning, he called Riverhead.

The detective who answered the phone in the squadroom up there said his name was Haley. Carella told him who he was, and asked for either Detective Bent or Detective Wade.

"I think they're in the field already," Haley said.

"Can you beep them and ask them to give me a call?"

"What's this in reference to?"

"A case they're working."

"Sure, I'll beep them," Haley said.

But the way he said it made Carella think he had no intention of beeping anybody.

"Is your lieutenant in?" he asked.

"Yeah?"

"Would you put me through to him?"

"He's got somebody in with him just now."

"Just buzz him and tell him Detective Carella's on the line."

"I just told you . . ."

"Pal," Carella said, and the single word was ominous with weight. "Buzz your lieutenant."

There was a long silence.

Then Haley said, "Sure."

A different voice came on the line a moment later.

"Lieutenant Nelson. How are you, Carella?"

"Fine, thank you, Lieutenant. I was wond . . ."

"I got a call from Lieutenant Byrnes a few days ago, asking me to give this case special attention, which I would have done anyway. Bent and Wade are out on it right this minute."

"I was wondering how they made out with that witness."

"Well, he turned out not to be as good as we thought. All of a sudden he couldn't remember this, couldn't remember that, you know what I mean? We figure he thought it over and chickened out. Which happens lots of times."

"Yeah," Carella said.

"But they're out right this minute, like I told you, chasing down something they came up with yesterday. So don't worry, we're on this, we won't . . ."

"What was it they came up with?"

"Let me see, I had their report here a minute ago, what the hell did I do with it? Just a second, okay?"

Carella could hear him muttering as he shuffled papers. He visualized a mountain of papers. At last, Nelson came back on the line. "Yeah," he said, "they been looking for this kid who told his girlfriend he saw the punks who shot your father running out of the shop. They got his name and address . . ."

"Could I have those, sir? The name and . . ."

"Carella?"

"Yes, sir?"

"You want my advice?"

Carella said nothing.

"Let Bent and Wade handle it, okay? They're good cops. They'll get these guys, believe me. We won't disappoint you, believe me."

"Yes, sir."

"You hear me?"

"Yes, sir."

"Better this way."

"Yes, sir."

"I know how you feel."

"Thank you, sir."

"But it's better this way, believe me. They're out on it right this minute. They'll find those punks, believe me. Trust us, okay? We'll get 'em."

"I appreciate that."

"We'll stay in touch," Nelson said, and hung up.

Carella wondered why the hell they hadn't stayed in touch till now.

The kid began running the moment he saw them.

He was standing on the corner, talking to two other guys, when Wade and Bent pulled up in the unmarked car. It was as if the car had neon all over it, blaring POLICE in orange and green. Wade opened the door on the passenger side and was stepping out onto the curb when the kid spotted him and started running. Bent, who'd been driving the car and who was also out of it by this time, yelled, "He's going, Randy!" and both men shouted, almost simultaneously, "Police! Stop!"

Nobody was stopping.

Neither were any guns coming out.

In this city, police rules and regs strictly limited the circumstances in which a weapon could be unholstered or fired. There was no felony in progress here, nor did the detectives have a warrant authorizing the arrest of a person known to be armed. The kid pounding the pavement up ahead hadn't *done* anything, nor was he threatening them in any way that would have warranted using a firearm as a defensive weapon. The guns stayed holstered.

The kid was fast, but so were Wade and Bent. A lot of detectives in this city, they tended to run to flab. You rode around in a car all day long, you ate hamburgers and fries in greasy-spoon diners, you put on the pounds and you had a hell of a time taking them off again. But Wade and Bent worked out at the Headquarters gym twice a week, and chasing the kid hardly even made them breathe hard.

Bent was six-two and he weighed a hundred and ninety pounds, all of it sinew and muscle. Wade was five-eleven and he weighed a solid hundred and seventy, but the knife scar over his left eye made him look meaner and tougher than Bent, even though he was smaller and lighter. The kid up ahead was seventeen, eighteen years old, lean and swift, and white in the bargain. Just to make sure he hadn't mistaken them for a pair of bad black dudes looking to mug him, they yelled "Police!" again, "Stop!" again, and then one more time for good measure, "Police! Stop!," but the kid wasn't stopping for anybody.

Over the hills and dales they went, the kid leaping backyard fences where clothes hung listlessly on the sullen air, Wade and Bent right behind him, the kid leading the way and maintaining his lead because he *knew* where he was going whereas they were only following, and the guy paving the way usually had a slight edge over whoever was chasing him. But they were stronger than he was, and more determined besides— he had possibly seen the two people who'd killed the father of a cop. The operative word was *cop*.

"There he goes!" Wade yelled.

He was ducking into what had once been a somewhat elegant mid-rise apartment building bordering Riverhead Park but which had been abandoned for some ten to twelve years now. The windows had been boarded up and decorated with plastic stick-on panels made to resemble half-drawn window shades or open shutters or little potted plants sitting on windowsills, the *trompe-l'oeil* of a city in decline. There was no front door on the building. A bloated ceiling in the entryway dripped collected rainwater. It was dark in here. No thousand points of light in here. Just darkness and the sound of rats scurrying as the detectives came in.

"Hey!" Wade yelled. 'What are you running for?"

No answer.

The sound of the water dripping.

His voice echoing in the hollow shell of the building with the fake window shades and shutters and potted plants.

"We just want to talk to you!" Bent yelled.

Still no answer.

They looked at each other.

Silence.

And then a faint sound coming from upstairs. Not a rat this time, the rats had done all their scurrying, the rats were back inside the walls. Bent nodded. Together, they started up the stairs.

The kid broke into a run again when they reached the first floor. Wade took off after him and caught him as he was rounding the steps leading up to the second floor. Pulled him over and backward and flat on his back and then rolled him over and flashed his police shield in the kid's face and yelled as loud as he could, "Police, police, police! Got it?"

"I didn't do nothin'," the kid said.

"On your feet," Wade said, and in case he hadn't understood it, he yanked him to his feet and slammed him up against the wall and began tossing him as Bent walked over.

"Clean," Wade said.

"I didn't do nothin'," the kid said again.

"What's your name?" Bent asked.

"Dominick Assanti, I didn't do nothin'."

"Who said you did?"

"Nobody."

"Then why'd you run?"

"I figured you were cops," Assanti said, and shrugged.

He was five-ten or -eleven, they guessed, weighing about a

hundred and sixty, a good-looking kid with wavy black hair and brown eyes, wearing blue jeans, sneakers, and a T-shirt with a picture of Bart Simpson on it.

"Let's talk," Bent said.

"I didn't do nothin'," Assanti said again.

"Broken record," Wade said.

"Where were you last Tuesday night around nine-thirty?" Bent asked.

"Who remembers?"

"Your girlfriend does."

"Huh?"

"She told us you were near the A & L Bakery Shop on Harrison. Is that right?"

"How does she know where I was?"

"Because you told her."

"I didn't tell her nothin'."

"Were you there or weren't you?"

"I don't remember."

"Try remembering."

"I don't know *where* I was last Tuesday night."

"You went to a movie with your girlfriend . . ."

"You walked her home . . ."

"And you were heading back to your house when you passed the bakery shop."

"I don't know where you got all that."

"We got it from your girlfriend."

"I don't even have no girlfriend."

"She seems to think you're going steady."

"I don't know where you got all this, I swear."

"Dominick . . . pay attention," Wade said.

"Your girlfriend's name is Frankie," Bent said. "For Doris Franceschi."

"Got it?" Wade said.

"And you told her you were outside that bakery shop last Tuesday night at around nine-thirty. Now were you?"

"I don't want no trouble," Assanti said.

"What'd you see, Dominick?"

"I'm scared if I tell you . . ."

"No, no, we're gonna put these guys away," Bent said, "don't worry."

"What'd you see?" Wade asked. "Can you tell us what you saw?"

"I was walking home . . ."

He is walking home, he lives only six blocks from Frankie's house, his head is full of Frankie, he is dizzy with thoughts of Frankie. Wiping lipstick from his mouth, his handkerchief coming away with Frankie's lipstick, he can remember her tongue in his mouth, his hands on her breasts, he thinks they're backfires at first. The shots. But there are no cars on the street.

So he realizes these are shots he just heard, and he thinks Uh-oh, I better get out of here, and he's starting to turn, thinking he'll go back to Frankie's house, ring the doorbell, tell her some-body's shooting outside, can he come up for a minute, when all at once he sees this guy coming out of the liquor store with a brown paper bag in his hands, and he thinks maybe there's a holdup going on in the liquor store, the guy is walking in his direction, he thinks again I better get out of here.

Then . . .

Then there were . . .

"I . . . I can't tell you," Assanti said. "I'm scared."

"Tell us," Wade said.

"I'm scared."

"Please," Wade said.

"There were . . . two other guys. Coming out of the bakery next door."

"What'd they look like?"

Assanti hesitated.

"You can tell us if they were black," Bent said.

"They were black," Assanti said.

"Were they armed?"

"Only one of them."

"One of them had a gun?"

"Yes."

"What'd they look like?"

"They were both wearing jeans and black T-shirts."

"How tall?"

"Both very big."

"What kind of hair? Afro? Dreadlocks? Hi-top fade? Ramp? Tom?"

"I don't know what any of those things are," Assanti said.

"All right, what happened when they came out of the bakery?"

"They almost ran into the guy coming out of the liquor store. Under the streetlight there. Came face to face with him. Looked him dead in the eye. Told him to get the hell outta their way."

Bent looked at Wade knowingly. Their star witness, the guy coming out of the liquor store. Chickenhearted bastard.

"Then what?"

"They came running in my direction."

"Did you get a good look at them?"

"Yeah, but . . ."

"You don't have to worry, we're gonna send them away for a long time."

"What about all their *friends*? You gonna send *them* away, too?"

"We want you to look at some pictures, Dominick."

"I don't want to look at no pictures."

"Why not?"

"I'm scared."

"No, no."

"Don't tell me no, no. You didn't see this Sonny guy. He looked like a gorilla."

"What are you saying?"

"You saying a name?"

"You saying Sonny?"

"I don't want to look at no pictures," Assanti said.

"Are you saying Sonny?"

"Was that his name? Sonny?"

"You know these guys?"

"Was one of them named Sonny?"

"Nobody's gonna hurt you, Dominick."

"Was his name Sonny?"

"Sonny what?"

"We won't let anybody hurt you, Dominick."

"Sonny what?"

He looked at them for a long time. He was clearly frightened, and they thought for sure they were going to lose him just the way they'd lost the guy coming out of the liquor store. He did, in fact, shake his head as if to say he wasn't going to tell them anything else, but he was only shaking it in denial of something inside him that was telling him he'd be crazy to identify anyone who had killed a man.

"The one with the gun," he said softly.

"What about him, Dominick?"

"His name was Sonny."

"You know him?"

"No. I heard the other guy calling him Sonny. When they were running by. Come on, Sonny, *move* it. Something like that."

"Did you get a good look at them, Dominick?"

"I got a good look."

"Can we show you some pictures?"

He hesitated again. And again he shook his head, telling himself he was crazy to be doing this. But he sighed at last and said, "Yeah, okay."

"Thank you," Wade said.

The only white man he could trust with this was Carella. There were things you just knew.

"My goddamn skin," Brown said, as if Carella would understand immediately, which of course he didn't.

"All that *crap* I got to use," Brown said.

Carella turned to look at him, bewildered.

They were in the unmarked car, on their way downtown, Brown driving, Carella riding shotgun. So far, it had been an awful morning. First the disappointing promises-promises conversation with Lieutenant Nelson at the Four-Five and then Lieutenant Byrnes of their very own Eight-Seven asking them into his office and telling them he'd had a call from a lawyer named Louis Loeb, who'd wanted to know why a grieving widow named Margaret Schumacher had been harassed in her apartment yesterday morning by two detectives respectively named Carella and Brown.

"I realize you didn't harass her," Byrnes said at once. "The problem is this guy says he's personally going to the chief of detectives if he doesn't get written apologies from both of you."

"Boy," Carella said.

"You don't feel like writing apologies, I'll tell him to go to hell," Byrnes said.

"Yeah, do that," Brown said.

"Do it," Carella said, and nodded.

"How does the wife look, anyway?" Byrnes asked.

"Good as anybody else right now," Brown said.

But, of course, they hadn't yet talked to anyone else. They were on their way now to see Lois Stein, Schumacher's married daughter, Mrs. Marc with-a-c Stein. And Brown was telling Carella what a pain in the ass it was to be black. Not because being black made you immediately suspect, especially if you were *big* and black, because no white man ever figured you for a big, black *cop*, you always got figured for a big black *criminal*, with tattoos all over your body and muscles you got lifting weights in the prison gym.

The way Brown figured it—and this had nothing to do with why being black was such a very *real* pain in the ass—drugs were calling the tune in this America of ours, and the prime targets for the dealers were black ghetto kids who, rightly or wrongly (and

Brown figured they were right) had reason to believe they were being cheated out of the American dream and the only dream available to them was the sure one they could find in a crack pipe. But a drug habit was an expensive one even if you were a big account executive downtown, especially expensive *uptown* where if you were black and uneducated the best you could hope for was to serve hamburgers at McDonald's for four-and-a-quarter an hour, which wasn't even enough to support a heavy *cigarette* habit. To support a *crack* habit, you had to steal. And the people you stole from were mostly white people, because they were the ones had all the bread. So whenever you saw Arthur Brown coming down the street, you didn't think here comes a protector of the innocent sworn to uphold the laws of the city, state, and nation, what you thought was here comes a big black dope-addict criminal in this fine country of ours where the vicious circle was drugs-to-crime-to-racism-to-despair-to-drugs and once again around the mulberry bush. But none of this was why it was a supreme pain in the ass to be black.

"You know what happens when a black man's skin gets dry?" Brown asked.

"No, what?" Carella said.

He was still thinking about Brown's vicious circle.

"Aside from it being damn uncomfortable?"

"Uh-huh," Carella said.

"We turn gray is what happens."

"Uh-huh."

"Which is why we use a lot of oils and greases on our skin. Not only women, I'm talking about men, too."

"Uh-huh."

"To lubricate the skin, get rid of the scale. What was that address again?"

"314 South Dreyden."

"Cocoa butter, cold cream, Vaseline, all this crap. We have to use it to keep from turning gray like a ghost."

"You don't look gray to me," Carella said.

" 'Cause I use all this crap on my skin. But I got a tendency to acne, you know?"

"Uh-huh."

"From when I was a teenager. So if I use all this crap to keep my skin from turning gray, I bust out in pimples instead. It's another vicious circle. I'm thinking of growing a beard, I swear to God."

Carella didn't know what *that* meant, either.

"Up ahead," he said.

"I see it."

Brown turned the car into the curb, maneuvered it into a parking space in front of 322 South Dreyden, and then got out of the car, locked it, and walked around it to join Carella on the sidewalk.

"Ingrown hairs," he said

"Uh-huh," Carella said. "You see a boutique? It's supposed to be a boutique."

The shop was named Vanessa's, which Lois Stein explained had nothing to do with her own name, but which sounded very British and slightly snobbish and which, in fact, attracted the upscale sort of women to whom her shop catered. She herself looked upscale and elegantly groomed, the sort of honey blonde one usually saw in perfume commercials, staring moodily out to sea, tresses blowing in the wind, diaphanous skirts flattened against outrageously long legs. Margaret Schumacher had told them her stepdaughter was thirty-seven years old, but they never would have guessed it She looked to be in her late twenties, her complexion flawless, her grayish-blue eyes adding a look of mysterious serenity to her face.

In a voice as soft as her appearance—soft, gentle, these were the words Carella would have used to describe her—she explained at once how close she had been to her father, a relationship that had survived a bitter divorce and her father's remarriage. She could not now imagine how something like this could have happened to him. Her father the victim of a shooting? Even in this city, where law and order—

"Forgive me," she said, "I didn't mean to imply . . ."

A delicate, slender hand came up to her mouth, touched her lips as if to scold them. She wore no lipstick, Carella noticed. The faintest blue eye shadow tinted the lids above her blue-gray eyes. Her hair looked like spun gold. Here among the expensive baubles and threads she sold, she looked like an Alice who had inadvertently stumbled into the queen's closet.

"That's what we'd like to talk to you about," Carella said, "how something like this could've happened." He was lying only slightly in that on his block, at this particular time in space, anyone and everyone was still a suspect in this damn thing. But at the same time . . .

"When did you see him last?" he asked.

This because a victim—especially if something or someone had been troubling him—sometimes revealed to friends or relatives information that may have seemed unimportant at the time but that, in the light of traumatic death, could be relevant . . . good work, Carella, go to the head of the class. He waited. She seemed trying to remember when she'd last seen her own father. Who'd been killed last Friday night. Mysterious blue-gray eyes pensive. Thinking, thinking, when did I last see dear Daddy with whom I'd been so close, and with whom I'd survived a bitter divorce and subsequent remarriage? Brown waited, too. He was wondering if the Fragile Little Girl stuff was an act. He wasn't too familiar with very many white women, but he knew plenty of black women—some of them as blonde as this one—who could do the wispy, willowy bit to perfection.

"I had a drink with him last Thursday," she said.

The day before he'd caught it. Four in the face. And by the way, here's a couple for your mutt.

"What time would that have been?" Carella asked.

"Five-thirty. After I closed the shop. I met him down near his office. A place called Bits."

"Any special reason for the meeting?" Brown asked.

"No, we just hadn't seen each other in a while."

"Did you normally . . ."

"Yes."

". . . meet for drinks?"

"Yes."

"Rather than dinner or lunch?"

"Yes. Margaret . . ."

She stopped.

Carella waited. So did Brown.

"She didn't approve of Daddy seeing us. Margaret. The woman he married when he divorced Mother."

The woman he married. Unwilling to dignify the relationship by calling her his *wife*. Merely the woman he married.

"How'd you feel about that?"

Lois shrugged.

"She's a difficult woman," she said at last.

Which, of course, didn't answer the question.

"Difficult how?"

"Extremely possessive. Jealous to the point of insanity."

Strong word, Brown thought. Insanity.

"But how'd you feel about these restrictions she laid down?" Carella asked.

"I would have preferred seeing Daddy more often . . . I love him, I loved him," Lois said. "But if it meant causing problems for him, then I was willing to see him however and whenever it was possible."

"How'd *he* feel about that?"

"I have no idea."

"You never discussed it with him?"

"Never."

"Just went along with her wishes," Carella said.

"Yes. He was married to her," Lois said, and shrugged again.

"How'd your sister feel about all this?"

"He never saw Betsy at all."

"How come?"

"My sister took the divorce personally."

Doesn't everyone? Brown wondered.

"The whole sordid business beforehand . . ."

"What business was that?" Carella asked at once.

"Well, he was having an affair with her, you know. He left Mother *because* of her. This wasn't a matter of getting a divorce and then meeting someone *after* the divorce, this was getting a divorce because he wanted to marry Margaret. He already *had* Margaret, you see. There's a difference."

"Yes," Carella said.

"So . . . my sister wouldn't accept it. She stopped seeing him . . . oh, it must've been eight, nine months after he remarried. In effect, I became his only daughter. All he had, really."

All he had? Brown thought.

"What'd you talk about last Thursday?" Carella asked.

"Oh, this and that."

"Did he say anything was bothering him?"

"No."

"Didn't mention any kind of . . ."

"No."

". . . trouble or . . ."

"No."

". . . argument . . ."

"No."

". . . or personal matter that . . ."

"Nothing like that."

"Well, did he *seem* troubled by anything?"

"No."

"Or worried about anything?"

"No."

"Did he seem to be *avoiding* anything?"

"Avoiding?"

"Reluctant to *talk* about anything? *Hiding* anything?"

"No, he seemed like his usual self."

"Can you give us some idea of what you talked about?" Brown asked.

"It was just father-daughter talk," Lois said.

"About what?"

"I think we talked about his trip to Europe . . . he was going to Europe on business at the end of the month."

"Yes, what did he say about that?" Carella asked.

"Only that he was looking forward to it. He had a new client in Milan—a designer who's bringing his line of clothes here to the city—and then he had some business in France . . . Lyons, I think he said . . ."

"Yes, he was flying back from Lyons."

"Then you know."

"Did he say he was going alone?"

"I don't think Margaret was going with him."

"Did he mention who *might* be going with him?"

"No."

"What else did you talk about?"

"You know, really, this was just *talk*. I mean, we didn't discuss anything *special*, it was just . . . a nice friendly conversation between a father and his daughter."

"Yes, but about *what*?" Brown insisted.

Lois looked at him impatiently, squelching what appeared to be a formative sigh. She was silent for several seconds, thinking, and then she said, "I guess I told him I was going on a diet, and he said I was being ridiculous, I certainly didn't need to lose any weight . . . oh, and he told me he was thinking of taking piano lessons again, when he was young he used to play piano in a swing band . . ."

Blue-gray eyes looking skyward now, trying to pluck memory out of the air, corner of her lower lip caught between her teeth like a teenage girl doing homework . . .

". . . and I guess I said something about Marc's birthday . . . my husband, Marc, his birthday is next week, I *still* haven't bought him anything. You know, this is *really* very difficult, trying to remember every word we . . ."

"You're doing fine," Carella said.

Lois nodded skeptically.

"Your husband's birthday," Brown prompted.

"Yes. I think we talked about what would be a good gift, he's so hard to please . . . and Daddy suggested getting him one of those little computerized memo things that fit in your pocket, Marc loves hi-tech stuff, he's a dentist."

Carella remembered a dentist he had recently known. The man was now doing time at Castleview upstate. Lots of time. For playing around with poison on the side. He wondered what kind of dentist Marc Stein was. It occurred to him that he had never met a dentist he had liked.

". . . which Marc never even wore. That was last year. Daddy said you had to be careful with gifts like that. I told him I'd thought of getting Marc a dog, but he said dogs were a lot of trouble once you got past the cute puppy stage, and I ought to give that a little thought."

Two bullets in the dog, Brown thought. Who the hell would want to kill a man's *dog*?

"Did your father's dog ever bite anyone?" he asked.

"*Bite* anyone?"

"Or even *scare* anyone, *threaten* anyone?"

"Well . . . I really don't know. He never mentioned anything like that, but . . . I just don't know. You don't think . . . ?"

"Just curious," Brown said.

He was thinking there were all kinds in this city.

"Betsy hated that dog," Lois said.

Both detectives looked at her.

"She hates *all* dogs in general, but she had a particular animosity for Amos."

Amos, Brown thought.

"What kind of dog was he?" he asked.

"A black Lab," Lois said.

Figures, he thought.

"Why'd your sister hate him?" Carella asked.

"I think he symbolized the marriage. The dog was a gift from Margaret, she gave it to Daddy on their first Christmas together. This was when Betsy was still seeing him, before the rift. She hated the dog on sight. He was such a sweet dog, too, well, you know Labs. But Betsy's a very mixed-up girl. Hate Margaret, therefore you hate the dog Margaret bought. Simple."

"Is your sister still living on Rodman?" Carella asked, and showed her the page in his notebook where he'd jotted down Betsy Schumacher's address.

"Yes, that's her address," Lois said.

"When did you see her last?" Brown asked.

"Sunday. At the funeral."

"She went to the funeral?" Carella asked, surprised.

"Yes," Lois said. And then, wistfully, "Because she loved him, I guess."

"Nice view," the girl said.

"Yeah," Kling said.

They were standing at the single window in the room. In the near distance, the Calm's Point Bridge hurled its lights across the River Dix. Aside from the spectacular view of the bridge and the buildings on the opposite bank, there wasn't much else upon which to comment. Kling was renting what was euphemistically called a "studio" apartment. This made it sound as if an artist might live quite comfortably here, splashing paint on canvases or hurling clay at wire frames. Actually, the studio was a single small room with a kitchen the size of a closet and a bathroom tacked on as a seeming afterthought. There was a bed in the room, and a dresser, and an easy chair, and a television set and a lamp.

The girl's name was Melinda.

He had picked her up in a singles bar.

Almost the first thing she'd said to him was that she'd checked out negative for the AIDS virus. He felt this was promising. He told her that he did not have AIDS, either. Or herpes. Or any other sexually transmitted disease. She'd asked him whether he had any *non*sexually transmitted diseases, and they'd both laughed. Now they were in his studio apartment admiring the view, neither of them laughing.

"Can I fix you a drink?" he asked.

"That might be very nice," she said. "What do you have?"

At the bar, she'd been drinking something called a Devil's Fling. She told him there were four different kinds of rum in it, and that it was crème de menthe that gave the drink its greenish tint and its faint whiff of brimstone. She said this with a grin. This was when he began thinking she might be interesting to take home. Sort of a sharp big-city girl edge to her. Whiff of brimstone. He liked that. But he didn't have either crème de menthe or four different kinds of rum here in his magnificent studio apartment with its glorious view. All he had was scotch. Which, alone here on too many nights, he drank in the dark. He was not alone tonight. And somehow scotch seemed inadequate.

"Scotch?" he said tentatively.

"Uh-huh?"

"That's it," he said, and shrugged. "Scotch. But I can phone down for anything you like. There's a liquor store right around the . . ."

"Scotch will be fine," she said. "On the rocks, please. With just a splash of soda."

"I don't think I have any soda."

"Water will be fine then. Just a splash, please."

He poured scotch for both of them, and dropped ice cubes

into both glasses, and then let just a dribble of water from the tap splash into her glass. They clinked the glasses together in a silent toast, and then drank.

"Nice," she said, and smiled.

She had brown hair and brown eyes. Twenty-six or -seven years old, Kling guessed, around five-six or thereabouts, with a pert little figure and a secret little smile that made you think she knew things she wasn't sharing with you. He wondered what those things might be. He had not had another woman in this room since Eileen left him.

"Bet it looks even better in the dark," she said.

He looked at her.

"The view," she said.

Secret little smile on her mouth.

He went to the lamp, turned it off.

"There," she said.

Beyond the window, the bridge's span sparkled white against the night, dotted with red taillight flashes from the steady stream of traffic crossing to Calm's Point. He went to stand with her at the window, put his arms around her from behind. She lifted her head. He kissed her neck. She turned into his arms. Their lips met. His hands found her breasts. She caught her breath. And looked up at him. And smiled her secret smile.

"I'll only be a minute," she whispered, and moved out of his arms and toward the bathroom door, smiling again, over her shoulder this time. The door closed behind her. He heard water running in the sink. The only light in the room came from the bridge. He went to the bed and sat on the edge of it, looking through the window where the air conditioner hummed.

When the telephone rang, it startled him.

He picked up the receiver at once.

"Hello?" he said.

"Bert?" she said. "This is Eileen."

* * *

She could remember a telephone call a long time ago, when they were both strangers to each other. It had been difficult to make that call because she'd inadvertently offended him and she was calling to apologize, but it was more difficult to make this call tonight. She was not calling to apologize tonight, or perhaps she was, but either way she would have given anything in the world not to have to be making this call.

"Eileen?" he said.

Totally and completely surprised. It had been months and months.

"How are you?" she said.

She felt stupid. Absolutely stupid. Dumb and awkward and thoroughly idiotic.

"Eileen?" he said again.

"Is this a bad time for you?" she asked hopefully.

Looking for a reprieve. Call him back later or maybe not at all, once she'd had a chance to think this over. *Damn* Karin and her brilliant ideas.

"No, no," he said, "how are you?"

"Fine," she said. "Bert, the reason I'm calling . . ."

"Bert?" she heard someone say.

He must have covered the mouthpiece. Sudden silence on the other end of the line. There was someone with him. A woman? It had sounded like a woman.

Melinda was wearing only bikini panties and high-heeled pumps. She stood in partial silhouette just inside the bathroom door, her naked breasts larger than they'd seemed when she was fully dressed, the smile on her face again.

"Do you have a toothbrush I can use?" she asked.

"Uh . . . yes," he said, his left hand covering the mouthpiece, "there should be . . . I think there's an unopened one . . . uh . . . in the cabinet over the sink . . . there should be a new one in there."

She glanced at the phone in his hand. Arched an eyebrow.

Smiled again, secretly. Turned to show her pert little behind in the skimpy panties, posed there for a moment like Betty Grable in the famous World War II poster, and then closed the bathroom door again, blocking the wondrous sight of her from view.

"Eileen?" he said.

"Yes, hi," she said, "is there someone with you?"

"No," he said.

"I thought I heard someone."

"The television set is on," he said.

"I thought I heard someone say your name."

"No, I'm alone here."

"Anyway, I'll make this short," she said. "Karin . . ."

"You don't have to make it short," he said.

"Karin thinks it might be a good idea if the three of us . . ."

"Karin?"

"Letkowitz. My shrink."

"Oh. Right. How is she?"

"Fine. She thinks the three of us should get together sometime soon to talk things over, try to . . ."

"Okay. Whenever."

"Well, good, I was hoping you'd . . . I usually see her on Mondays and Wednesdays, how about . . . ?"

"Whenever."

"How about tomorrow then?"

"What time?"

"I've got a five o'clock . . ."

"Fine."

". . . appointment, would that be all right with you?"

"Yes, that'd be fine."

"You know where her office is, don't you?"

"Yes, I do."

"Headquarters Building, fifth floor."

"Yes."

"So I'll see you there at five tomorrow."

"I'll see you there," he said, and hesitated. "Been a long time."

"Yes, it has. Well, goodnight, Bert, I'll . . ."

"Maybe she can tell me what I did wrong," he said.

Eileen said nothing.

"Because I keep wondering what I did wrong," he said.

Her beeper went off. For a moment, she couldn't remember where she'd put it, and then she located it on the coffee table across the room, zeroed in on the sound as if she were a bat or something flitting around in the dark, reached for the bedside lamp and snapped it on—they used to talk to each other on the phone in the dark in their separate beds—the beeper still signaling urgently.

"Do *you* know what I did wrong?" he asked.

"Bert, I have to go," she said. "It's my beeper."

"Because if *someone* can tell me what I . . ."

"Bert, really, goodbye," she said, and hung up.

6

There were children in swimsuits.

The fire hydrant down the block was still open, its spray nozzle fanning a cascade of water into the street, and whereas not a moment earlier the kids had been splashing and running through the artificial waterfall, they had now drifted up the street to where the real action was. Outside the building where the blue-and-white Emergency Service truck and motor-patrol cars were angled into the curb, there were also men in tank tops and women in halters, most of them wearing shorts, milling around behind the barricades the police had set up. It was a hot summer night at the end of one of the hottest days this summer; the temperature at ten P.M. was still hovering in the mid-nineties. There would have been people in the streets even if there hadn't been the promise of vast and unexpected entertainment.

In this city, during the first six months of the year, a bit more than twelve hundred murders had been committed. Tonight, in a cluttered neighborhood that had once been almost exclusively Hispanic but that was now a volatile mix of Hispanic, Vietnamese, Korean, Afghani, and Iranian, an eighty-four-year-old man from Guayama, Puerto Rico, sat with his eight-year-old American-born

119

granddaughter on his knee, threatening to add yet another murder to the soaring total; a shotgun was in his right hand and the barrel of the gun rested on the little girl's shoulder, angled toward her ear.

Inspector William Cullen Brady had put a Spanish-speaking member of his team on the door, but so far the old man had said only five words and those in English: "Go away, I'll kill her." Accented English, to be sure, but plain and understandable nonetheless. If they did not get away from the door on the fifth-floor apartment where he lived with his son, his daughter-in-law, and their three children, he would blow the youngest of the three clear back to the Caribbean.

It was suffocatingly hot in the hallway where the negotiating team had "contained" the old man and his granddaughter. Eileen and the other trainees had been taught that the first objective in any hostage situation was to contain the taker in the smallest possible area, but she wondered now exactly *who* was doing the containing and who was being contained. It seemed to her that the old man had chosen his own turf and his own level of confrontation, and was now calling all the shots—no pun intended, God forbid! The narrow fifth-floor hallway with its admixture of exotic cooking smells now *contained* at least three dozen police officers, not counting those who had spilled over onto the fire stairs or those who were massed in the apartment down the hall, which the police had requisitioned as a command post, thank you, ma'am, we'll send you a receipt. There were cops all over the rooftops, too, and cops and firemen spreading safety nets below, just in case the old man decided to throw his granddaughter out the window, nothing ever surprised anybody in this city.

The cop working the door was an experienced member of the negotiating team who normally worked out of Burglary. His name was Emilio Garcia, and he spoke Spanish fluently, but the old man wasn't having any of it. The old man insisted on speaking English, a rather limited English at that, litanizing the same five words over and over again: "Go away, I'll kill her." This was a touchy situation here. The apartment was in a housing project where only last week the Tactical Narcotics Team had blown away four people in a raid, three of them known drug dealers, but the fourth—unfortunately—a fifteen-year-old boy who'd been in the apartment delivering a case of beer from the local supermarket.

The kid had been black.

This meant that one of the city's foremost agitators, a media hound who liked nothing better than to see his own beautiful face on television, had rounded up all the usual yellers and screamers and had picketed both the project and the local precinct, shouting police brutality and racism and no justice, no peace, and all the usual slogans designed to create more friction than already existed in a festering city on the edge of open warfare. The Preacher—as he was familiarly called—was here tonight, too, wearing a red fez and a purple shirt purchased in Nairobi and open to the waist, revealing a bold gold chain with a crucifix dangling from it; the man was a minister of God, after all, even if he preached only the doctrines of hate. He didn't *have* to be here tonight, though, shouting himself hoarse, nobody needed any help in the hate department tonight.

The guy inside the apartment was a Puerto Rican, which made him a member of the city's second-largest minority group, and if anything happened to him or that little girl sitting on his lap, if any of these policemen out here exercised the same bad judgment as had their colleagues from TNT, there would be bloody hell to pay. So anyone even remotely connected with the police department—including the Traffic Department people in their brown uniforms—was tiptoeing around outside that building and inside it, especially Emilio Garcia, who was afraid he might say something that would cause the little girl's head to explode into the hallway in a shower of gristle and blood.

"*Oigame,*" Garcia said. "*Solo quiero ayudarle.*"

"Go away," the old man said. "I'll kill her."

Down the hall, Michael Goodman was talking to the man's daughter-in-law, an attractive woman in her mid-forties, wearing sandals, a blue mini, and a red tube-top blouse, and speaking rapid accent-free English. She had been born in this country, and she resented the old man's presence here, which she felt reflected upon her own Americanism and strengthened the stereotyped image of herself as just another spic. Her husband was the youngest of his sons—the old man had four sons and three daughters—but even though all of them were living here in America, he was the one who'd had to take the old man in when he'd finally decided to come up from the island. She had insisted that the old man speak English now that he was here in America and living in her home. Eileen wondered if this was why he refused to speak Spanish with their talker at the door.

She was standing with the other trainees in a rough circle around the woman and Goodman, just outside the open door to the command post apartment, where Inspector Brady was in heavy discussion with Deputy Inspector Di Santis of the Emergency Service. Nobody wanted this one to flare out of control. They were debating whether they should pull Garcia off the door. They had thought that a Spanish-speaking negotiator would be their best bet, but now—

"Any reason why he's doing this?" Goodman asked the woman.

"Because he's crazy," the woman said.

Her name was Gerry Valdez, she had already told Goodman that her husband's name was Joey and the old man's name was Armando. Valdez, of course. All of them Valdez, including the little girl on the old man's lap, Pamela Valdez. And, by the way, when were they going to go in there and *get* her?

"We're trying to talk to your father-in-law right this minute," Goodman assured her.

"Never mind *talking* to him, why don't you just *shoot* him?"

"Well, Mrs. Valdez . . ."

"Before he hurts my daughter."

"That's what we're trying to make sure of," Goodman said. "That nobody gets hurt."

He was translating the jargon they'd had drummed into them for twelve hours a day for the past six days, Sunday included, time-and-a-half for sure. Never mind containment, never mind establishing lines of communication, or giving assurances of non-violence, just cut to the chase for the great unwashed, dish it out clean and fast, we're trying to talk to him, we're trying to make sure nobody gets hurt here.

"Not him, not *anybody*," Goodman said, just in case the woman didn't yet understand that nobody was going in there with guns blazing like Rambo.

Martha Halsted, the tight-assed little brunette with the Go-to-Hell look, seemed eager for a chance to work the door. She kept glancing down the hall to where Garcia kept pleading in Spanish with the old man, her brown eyes alive with anticipation, if you relieve Garcia, then choose me, pick me, I can do the job. Eileen guessed maybe she could.

She had asked Annie Rawles what she knew about her. Annie remembered her from when she was still working Robbery. She described her as a "specialist." This did not mean what Eileen at first thought it meant. A specialist in robbery or related crimes, right? Wasn't that what Annie meant? Annie explained that, well, no, the term as it was commonly used—hadn't Eileen ever heard the expression? Eileen said No, she hadn't, all eyes, all ears. Annie explained that a specialist was a woman who . . . well . . . a woman adept at oral sex, come on you're putting me on, you *know* what a specialist is. My, my, Eileen thought. Martha Halsted, a specialist. For all her hard, mean bearing and her distant manner, Martha Halsted was all heart, all mouth. Live and learn, Eileen thought, and never judge a book by its cover.

She figured Martha had as much chance of working the door on *this* one as she had of playing the flute with the Philharmonic. Unless she'd been blowing sweet music in the inspector's ear, so to speak, or perhaps even the good doctor's, who knew what evil lurked? Even so, neither of them would risk putting a trainee on the door a week after those Narcotics jerks had blown away a teenager. However much they taught that everything was theory until it was put into practice, and nothing was as valuable as actual experience in the field, nobody in his right mind was going to trust anyone but a skilled professional in a situation like this one. So eat your heart out, Martha. Tonight is a night for specialists of quite another sort.

From down the hall, Garcia was signaling.

Hand kept low at his side so that the old man in the apartment wouldn't see it, wouldn't spook and pull the shotgun trigger. But signaling distinctly and urgently, somebody get *over* here, *will* you please? Martha was the first one to spot the hand signal, busy as she was with watching the door and waiting for her golden opportunity. She told Goodman the guy at the door wanted something. Goodman went in to talk to Brady, and the inspector himself went down the hall to see what it was Garcia wanted. He had already decided to pull Garcia off the door. Now he had to decide who would replace him. A knowledge of Spanish was no longer a priority; the old man obviously spoke English and would speak nothing *but* English. In a situation as volatile as this one, Brady was thinking that he himself might be the right man for the job. Anyway, he went down the hall to see what the hell was happening.

Gerry Valdez was telling Goodman and the assembled trainees that her father-in-law was a sex maniac. She'd caught him several times fondling her daughters, or at least trying to fondle them. That was what had started it all today. She had caught him at it again, and she had threatened to ship him back to the goddamn island if he didn't quit bothering her daughters, and the old man had got the shotgun out of where Joey kept it in the closet, and had grabbed Pamela, the youngest one, the eight-year-old, and had yelled he was going to kill her unless everybody left them alone in the apartment.

Goodman was thinking they had a serious problem here.

Brady was coming back up the hall with Garcia. There was

no one at the door now. Just a lot of uniformed cops milling around down the hall, waiting for God only knew what.

"Mike?" Brady said. "Talk to you a minute?"

The three of them went inside the command-post apartment. Brady closed the door behind them.

Gerry Valdez began telling the trainees that she didn't *really* think the old man was a *sex* maniac, it was just that he was getting senile, you know? He was eighty-four years old, he sometimes forgot himself, forgot he wasn't still a little boy chasing little girls along the beach, you know? It was really a pity and a shame, but at the same time she didn't want him fooling around with her kids, that was child abuse, wasn't it?

Eileen guessed it was.

She wondered what they were talking about inside that apartment.

Were it not for the shotgun, it would have been comical. The old man wanted a girl.

"What do you mean, a girl?" Goodman said.

"He told me he'd trade his granddaughter for a girl," Garcia said.

"A girl?"

"He said if we send in a girl, he'd give us his grand-daughter."

"A girl?" Goodman said again.

This was unheard of. In all his years of hostage negotiation, Goodman had never had anyone request a girl. He'd had takers who'd asked for cigarettes or beer or a jet plane to Miami or in one instance spaghetti with red clam sauce, but he had never had anyone ask for a girl. This was something new in the annals of hostage negotiation. An eighty-four-year-old man asking them for a girl.

"You mean he wants a *girl*?" he said, shaking his head, still unwilling to believe it.

"A girl," Garcia said.

"Did he tell you this in Spanish or in English?" Brady asked.

"In Spanish."

"Then there was no mistake."

"No mistake. He wants a girl. *Una chiquita*, he said. I'm sure he meant a hooker."

"He wants a hooker."

"Yes."

"The old goat wants a hooker," Brady said.

"Yes."

"Mike?" Brady said. "What do you think?"

Goodman looked amused. But it wasn't funny.

"Can we send out for a hooker?" Brady said.

"And a dozen red roses," Goodman said, still looking amused.

"Mike," Brady said warningly.

"It's just I never heard of such a request," Goodman said.

"Can we get him a goddamn hooker or not?" Brady said. "Swap him a hooker for the little girl?"

"Absolutely not," Goodman said. "We never give them *another* hostage, that's a hard-and-fast rule. If we sent a hooker in there and she got blown away, you know what the media would do with *that*, don't you? Last week a fifteen-year-old kid, this week a hooker?"

"Yeah," Brady said glumly.

Garcia had been the talker on the door so far, and he didn't want anything to go wrong here, didn't want the old man to blow away either his granddaughter or anybody they might send in there. Garcia was only a Detective/Second, he didn't want any shit coming down on him. Do the job and do it right, but protect your ass at all times; he'd been a cop too long not to know this simple adage. So he waited for whatever Brady might come up with. Brady was the boss. Goodman was a civilian shrink who didn't matter, but Brady was rank. So Garcia waited for whatever he might decree.

"'We've got two girls right outside,'" Brady said.

He was referring to the two women police officers in his training program.

Apparently, the old man did not know that Martha Halsted was a specialist. He took one look at her and told Garcia, in Spanish, that if they didn't get a better-looking girl he would kill his granddaughter on the spot. He gave them ten minutes to get him a better-looking girl. Martha, supremely egotistical, felt his rejection of her had to do with the fact that she was wearing white sneakers, jeans, and a T-shirt; the old man had been expecting someone who looked more like a hooker. She suggested that Eileen—who was dressed almost identically, except for the sneakers—looked more like a hooker.

"So what do you say, Burke?" Brady asked.

"Sir?"

"You want to go in there or not?"

Decoy work all over again, Eileen thought. Either they put you on the street in hooker's threads or you go sit on an old man's lap in blue jeans and a T-shirt, and you try to talk him out of a shotgun. Or maybe you shoot him. She was not in this program because she wanted to shoot people.

"If the shotgun comes out, I go in," she said.

"That's not the deal we made with him," Brady said.

"What was the deal?"

"He sends out his granddaughter, we send in a girl."

"Then what?"

"Then the kid is safe," Brady said.

"How about me? Am I safe?"

Brady looked at her.

"We can't send in a real hooker," he said.

"I realize that. I'm asking if you're swapping my life for the kid's, sir. That's what I'm asking."

"It's up to you to calm him down, get that shotgun away from him."

"How do I calm him down?" Eileen asked.

"We've had run-throughs on situations like this one," Brady said.

"Not exactly, sir, no, sir. We didn't do any run-throughs on a man expecting a hooker and getting a talker instead."

"This is only a variation of a classic hostage situation," Brady said.

"I don't think so, sir. I think he may get very upset when he finds out I'm really a cop. I think he may decide to use that gun when he . . ."

"There's no reason for him to know you're a cop," Brady said.

"Oh? Do I lie to him, sir? I thought once we established communication, we told the truth all the way down the line."

"In this instance, we can bend the truth a little."

Goodman looked at him.

"Inspector," he said, "I think we may be confusing Detective Bur . . ."

"I'm certainly not trying to confuse her," Brady said. "But I've got an eight-year-old girl in there with a crazy old man who wants a hooker or he's going to blow her away. Now do I give him a hooker or don't I? That's the only pertinent question at this moment in time."

"I'm not a hooker, sir," Eileen said.

"I realize that. But you're a police officer who's impersonated hookers in the past."

"Yes, sir, I have. The point is . . ."

"Are you willing to do so now?" Brady asked reasonably. "That's the point, Detective Burke. Are you willing to impersonate a prostitute in order to save that little girl's life?"

How about *my* life? Eileen thought.

"Sir," she said, "how do you suggest I get that shotgun away from him? Once I'm inside that apartment, and he realizes I'm a police negotiator and not a hooker, how do I get him to give up that shotgun?"

"Detective Halsted was willing to go into that apartment within the parameters we've set up," Brady said, hurling down the gauntlet: Are you as good a man as Halsted? Do you have *cojones*, Detective Burke? "She was willing to accept the challenge of negotiating with him from a position of extreme vulnerability. Now I understand the risks involved here, don't you think I understand the risks? I've been in this game a long time now . . ."

Game, Eileen thought.

". . . and when I say I don't want *anyone* hurt, I mean *anyone*, not the taker, not his hostage, and certainly not any member of my team. I'm not asking you to do anything I wouldn't do myself . . ."

Then go *do* it yourself, Eileen thought.

". . . believe me, I'm as concerned for your safety as I would be for my own . . ."

Go in there in drag . . .

"But the situation has reached this point in time where we've got to make a decision. We've either got to satisfy the old man's desire or risk his killing that little girl. He's given us ten minutes, and eight of those minutes are already gone. So what would you like us to do, Detective?"

"Sir, you're asking me to go in there unarmed . . ."

"That's what we promised, that's what we always promise. No guns, no one gets hurt."

"But he *does* have a gun, sir."

He happens to have a goddamn *gun*, sir.

"They always have guns," Brady said. "Or knives. They always have weapons of some sort, yes."

"A double-barreled shotgun, sir."

"Yes, that's the situation here," Brady said.

"I'd have to be crazy, right?" Eileen said.

"Well, that's for you to decide, that's the nature of the work." Brady looked at his watch. "What do you say, Burke, we're almost out of time here. Yes or no? Believe me, there are plenty of female police officers in this city who'd be happy to work with this team.''

Female police officers, she thought.

Can you cut it or not, Detective Burke?

Are you a man or a mouse?

Bullshit, she thought.

"We negotiate *before* I go in," she said.

Brady looked at her.

"I work the door. The old man can believe what he wants, but nobody's going inside that apartment until he hands over the little girl *and* the shotgun. Take it or leave it."

He kept looking at her.

She figured whichever way this went, she'd be off the team tomorrow morning. Same as Mary Beth Mulhaney.

"Take it or *leave* it?" Brady said.

Or maybe off the team right this minute.

"Yes, sir," she said. "Take it or leave it."

Both you *and* the old man, she thought.

"If anything happens to that little girl . . ." Brady said, and let the sentence trail.

The old man thought the redhead was a vast improvement over the skinny one with the look of a mongrel. It was a pity she couldn't speak Spanish, but at his age he couldn't expect perfection. Enough that she had eyes as green as the sea and breasts as softly rolling as the hills of his native land. Freckles sprinkled like gold dust on her cheeks and across the bridge of her nose. A beauty. He was a very lucky man.

"We have to talk," she said. "My name is Eileen."

The door to apartment 5L was open just a crack, the night chain holding it. He could see her face and her body in the narrow opening. He knew she could see the shotgun against his grand-daughter's ear. His finger was inside the trigger guard. There were two shells in the shotgun. His son always kept the shotgun loaded in the closet. This was a bad neighborhood now that all the strangers had begun moving in.

"What is there to talk about?" he asked.

"About my coming in there," she said.

She had been taught not to lie to them. She would try not to lie to him now. She would not say she was a hooker. But neither would she say she wasn't. It was an omission she could live with. Unless someone got hurt. Then she would never be able to live with it again.

"I can't come in there as long as you have that gun in your hands," she said.

In the crack between the door and the doorjamb, she could see him smiling wisely. A wrinkled old man with a gray-white beard stubble, a terrified little dark-haired, dark-eyed girl on his lap, the double barrel of a shotgun against her head. If anything happened to that little girl . . .

"I'm afraid to come in there while you have that gun in your hands," Eileen said.

"Yes," the old man said.

What the hell does *that* mean? she wondered.

"But that is precisely why they've sent you to me, *verdad*?" he asked. "*Because* I have this gun in my hands."

Heavily accented English, but clearly understandable. And perfectly logical, too. The only reason they were submitting to the old man's wishes was that he had a gun. Give up the gun, he gave up his power to negotiate.

"Your granddaughter must be frightened, too," she said.

"I love my granddaughter," he said.

"Yes, but I'm sure she's terrified of that gun."

"No, she's all right. You're all right, aren't you, *querida*?" he said to the girl, and chucked her under the chin with his free hand. "Besides, I will let her go when you come in here," he said. "That is our understanding, eh? You come in, I let her go. Everybody's happy."

"Except me," she said, and smiled.

She knew she had a good smile.

"Well, I certainly don't want to make you unhappy," the old man said flirtatiously. "I will certainly do my best to make you happy."

"Not if you have a gun in your hands. I'm afraid of guns."

"Once you're in here," he said, "I'll let the little girl go. Then we can lock the door, and I'll put down the gun."

Oh, sure, she thought, Fat Chance Department.

"I'll make you very happy," he said.

Oh yes, she thought, I'm sure.

"Listen to me," she said. Her voice lowering conspiratorially. "Why don't you send out the little girl?"

Hostage first, weapon later.

All according to the book.

"When you come in, she goes out," he said. "That was the deal."

"Yes, but when they made the deal, they didn't know I'd be so afraid of guns."

"A pretty girl like you?" he said, flirtatiously again. "Afraid of a little gun like this one?"

Gently, he nudged his granddaughter's temple with the barrel of the shotgun. The girl winced.

Don't let it go off, Eileen thought. Please, God.

"I really am afraid," she said. "That's why, if you send her out, we can talk about the gun. Privately. Just the two of us."

"Tell me what else we will do privately."

"First send out the little girl," Eileen said.

"No. You come in here and then you can tell me what we'll do privately."

"Why don't you take the chain off the door?" she said.

"Why should I?"

"So I can see you better."

"Why do you want to see me?"

"It's just difficult to talk this way."

"I find it very easy to talk this way," he said.

You stubborn old bastard, she thought.

"Don't you want to see *me* better?" she asked.

"Yes, that would be nice."

"So take off the chain," she said. "Open the door a little wider."

"Are you a policeman?" he asked.

Flat out.

So what now?

"No, I'm not a policeman," she said.

The absolute truth. A police *woman*, yes. A police *person*, yes. But not a police *man*. She guessed she could live with that.

"Because if you're a policeman," he said, "I'll kill the little girl."

Which she could *not* live with.

"No," she said again, "I'm not a policeman. You said you wanted a woman . . ."

"Yes."

"Well, I'm a woman."

In the wedge between the door and the jamb, she saw him smile again.

"Come in here and show me what kind of woman you are," he said.

"For me to come in, you have to take the chain off the door."

"Will you come in then?"

"I'll come in if you take the chain off the door . . ."

She hesitated.

"And let the little girl come out . . ."

She hesitated again.

"And put down the gun."

Silence.

"Then I'll come in," she said.

Another silence.

"You want a lot," he said.

"Yes."

"I'll give you a lot," he said, and winked.

"I hope so," she said, and winked back.

Double meanings flying like spears on the sultry night air.

"Open your blouse," he said.

"No."

"Open your blouse for me."

"No."

"Let me see your breasts."

"No," she said. "Take off the chain."

Silence.

"All right," he said.

She waited. He leaned forward. Did not get out of the chair. The little girl still on his lap. The shotgun still to her head. His finger still inside the trigger guard. Leaned forward, reached out with his left hand, and slid the chain along its track until it fell free. She wondered if she should shove the door inward, try knocking him off the chair. He was so old, so frail. But the shotgun was young, the shotgun was a leveler of age.

Gently, with the toe of her foot, she eased the door open just a trifle wider. She could see the old man more completely now, a blue wall behind him deep inside the apartment, blue wall and blue eyes and gray hair and grizzled gray beard. He was looking directly into her eyes, an anticipatory smile on his face.

"Hello," she said.

"You're even prettier than I thought," he said.

"Thank you. Do you remember our deal?"

"Yes, you're coming in here."

"Only after you let the little girl go and put down the gun."

"Yes, I know."

"So do you want to let her go now?"

"How do I know . . . ?"

"You have my word."

"How do I know you'll come in here to me?"

"I said I would. I gave you my word."

"And are you a woman of your word?"

"I try to be."

Which meant she would break her word if he made the slightest move to harm either her or the little girl. She was unarmed . . .

That's what we promise. No guns, no one gets hurt . . .

. . . but there were backup cops to her right, and all she had to do was signal for them to storm the door. She hoped the old man would not do anything foolish.

"So let her come out now, okay?" she said.

"Pamela?" he said. And then in Spanish, "Do you want to go outside now, *querida*? Do you want to leave Grandpa here with the nice lady?"

Pamela nodded gravely. Too terrified to cry or to show relief. She knew this was her grandfather, but she also knew this was a gun. It was difficult for her to reconcile the two. She nodded. Yes, I want to go outside. Please let me go outside, Grandpa.

"Go on then," he said in English, and looked to Eileen for approval.

Eileen nodded.

"Come on, sweetheart," she said, and extended her arms to the little girl. "Come on out here before your grandfather changes his mind."

Pamela scrambled off his lap and out into the hall. Eileen clasped her into her arms, swung her around, and planted her securely in the arms of an Emergency Service cop, who swooped her up and hurried off down the hall with her.

Now there was only the old man and his gun.

No bargaining power anymore. If they wanted to blow him away, they could do so without any fear that a hostage was at risk. But that wasn't the name of the game. And she had given him her word.

"Now put down the gun," she said.

He had swung the shotgun toward the opening in the door. It sat in his lap, his finger still inside the trigger guard, the barrels angled up toward Eileen's head. From where he was sitting, he could not see the policemen in the hallway to her right. But he knew someone had taken the girl, he knew she had passed the girl on to someone, he knew she was not alone.

"Who's out there with you?" he asked.

"Policemen," she said. "Do you want to put down the gun, Mr. Valdez?"

"Do they have guns, these policemen?"

"Yes."

The truth. Tell him the truth.

"If I put down the gun, how do I know they won't shoot me?"

"I promise you we won't hurt you."

A slip.

We.

Identifying herself as a cop.

But he hadn't caught it.

Or had he?

"I promise you none of the policemen out here will hurt you."

Correcting it. Or compounding it. Which? How smart was he? Blue eyes studying her now, searching her face. Could he trust her?

"How do I know they won't shoot me? I made . . ."

"Because I . . ."

". . . a lot of trouble for everybody," he said.

"Yes, you did. But I promise they won't shoot you. No one will hurt you if you put down the gun. I promise you. I give you my word."

"Will they forget the trouble I made for everybody?"

She could not promise him this. There'd be the weapons charge, that wasn't a toy gun in there. And God knew what other charges there'd be on top of that. He wouldn't walk away from this clean, that wasn't the way it worked, the promises didn't extend that far. He was only a senile old man, true, who thought he was six years old and playing doctor under the coconut palms—

but he'd broken the law, broken several laws, in fact, and these were policemen here, sworn to uphold those laws.

"They'll help you," she said. "They'll try to help you."

Which was true. Psychiatric observation, therapy, the works, whatever seemed indicated.

But the shotgun was still in his lap, angled up at her.

"Come on," she said, "let's put down the gun, okay?"

"Tell them I want to see them. The policemen in the hall."

"I don't have any authority to tell policemen what to do."

"Ask them," he said. "Do you have authority to ask them?"

The smile on his face again.

Was he toying with her?

"He wants to see who's out here," she shouted down the hall to Brady, who was standing behind four Emergency Service cops with riot guns in their hands and sidearms strapped to their waists. The E.S. cops were all wearing ceramic vests. So what do you say, Inspector? she thought. Want to come in the water?

That's what we promise. No guns, no one gets hurt.

Except that now it was show time.

"Let him see you," Brady said to the E.S. men.

They lumbered down the hall in their heavy vests, toting their heavy guns, lining up against the wall behind Eileen, where the old man could see them.

"Are there any others?" he asked.

"Yes, but not right here," she said. "All the way down the hall."

"Tell them to put down their guns."

"I can't give them orders," Eileen said.

"Tell the other one. The one you were talking to."

Eileen nodded, turned away from the door, and shouted, "Inspector Brady!"

"Yes?"

"He wants them to put down their guns."

Silence.

"Or I'll shoot you," the old man said.

"Or he'll shoot me," she called to Brady, and then smiled and said to the old man, "You wouldn't do that, would you?"

"Yes, I would," he said, returning the smile.

"He means it," she shouted down the hall.

Behind her, the E.S. cops were beginning to fidget. Any one of them had a clear shot at the old bastard sitting there in full view with the shotgun in his lap. If they put down their guns, as he was now asking them to do, there was no guarantee that he wouldn't start blasting away. A ceramic vest was a very handy tool in a situation like this one, but you couldn't pull a ceramic vest over your head. If he cut loose at this range, nobody outside the door was safe. The E.S. cops were hoping this dizzy redhead and her boss knew what the hell they were doing.

"Put down your guns, men," Brady called.

"Now just a second, Bill!" another voice shouted.

Deputy Inspector John Di Santis, in command of the Emergency Service, and coming from behind Brady now to stand beside him in the hallway. Eileen could hear them arguing. She hoped the old man's ears weren't as good as hers. Di Santis was saying he was willing to go along with all this negotiating shit up to a point, but that point did not include standing four of his men against the wall for a firing squad. Brady answered him in a voice Eileen could not hear. Made aware, Di Santis lowered his voice, too. Eileen could not hear what either of them was saying now. Their whispers cascaded down the hallway. White-water whispers. Inside the apartment, the old man was watching her. She suddenly knew that he would in fact shoot her if the men behind her didn't put down their guns.

"What do you say, Inspector?" she called. "The man here's getting itchy."

Valdez smiled.

He knew what itchy meant.

She smiled back.

Little joke they were sharing here. The man's getting itchy, he's going to blow off my goddamn head, aren't you darling? Smiling.

"Inspector?"

The whispers stopped. Eileen waited. Somebody— either her or the old man or one or more of the cops standing behind her— was going to get hurt in the next few seconds, unless . . .

"All right, men, do what Inspector Brady says."

Di Santis.

Behind her, one of the E.S. cops muttered something Eileen couldn't understand, a word in Spanish that made the old man's smile widen. She heard the heavy weapons being placed on the floor . . .

"The other guns, too," the old man said.

"He wants the sidearms, too!" she yelled down the hall.

"All your weapons, men!" Di Santis shouted.

More muttering behind her, in English this time, soft grumbles of protest. They had been dealt a completely new hand, but the old man was still holding all the cards.

"Now you," Eileen told him.

"No," he said. "Come inside here."

"You promised me," she said.

"No," he said, smiling, "You're the one who made all the promises."

Which was true.

I promise they won't shoot you.

No one will hurt you . . .

"If you put down the gun," she reminded him.

"No."

Shaking his head.

"I promised that no one would hurt you if you put down the gun," she said.

"No one can hurt me, anyway," he said, smiling. "No one has a gun now but me."

Which was also true.

"Well, I thought I could trust you,"she said, "but I see I can't."

"You can trust me," he said. "Open your blouse."

"No," she said.

"Open your goddamn *blouse*," one of the E.S. cops whispered urgently.

She ignored him. "I'm going to leave now," she told the old man. "You broke your word, so I'm leaving. I can't promise what these men will do when I'm gone."

"They'll do nothing," he said. "I have the gun."

"There are others down the hall," she said. "I can't promise you anything anymore. I'm going now."

"No!" he said.

She hesitated.

"Please," he said.

Their eyes met.

"You promised," he said.

She knew what she'd promised. She'd promised that no one would be hurt. She'd promised she would go in to him if he put down the gun. She had given him her word. She was a woman of her word.

"Put down the gun," she said.

"I'll kill you if you don't come in here," he said.

"Put down the gun."

"I'll kill you."

"Then how will I be able to come in?"she asked, and the old man burst out laughing because the logic of the situation had suddenly become absurdly clear to him. If he killed her, she could not go in to him; it was as simple as that. She burst out laughing, too. Surprised, some of the E.S. cops behind her began laughing, tentatively at first, and then a bit more boldly. Down the hall, Eileen heard someone whisper, "They're laughing." Someone else whispered, "*What?*" This seemed funny, too. The cops in their ceramic vests began laughing harder, like armored knights who'd been told their powerful king was in fact impotent. Defenseless, their weapons and holsters and cartridge belts on the floor at their feet, contained here in this stifling hot hallway, they quaked with laughter, thinking how silly it would be if the old man actually *did* kill the redhead, thereby making it impossible for her to go in to him. The old man was thinking the same thing, how silly all of this had suddenly become, thinking too that maybe he should just put down the gun and get it over with, all the trouble he'd caused here, his blue eyes squinched up, tears of laughter running down his wrinkled face into his grizzled gray beard. Down the hall there were puzzled whispers again.

"Oh, dear," Eileen said, laughing.

"*¡Dios mío!*" the old man said, laughing.

Any one of the E.S. cops could have shot him in that moment. He had lowered the shotgun, it sat across his lap like a walking stick. No one was in danger from that gun. Eileen took a tentative step into the room, reaching for it.

"No!" the old man snapped, and the gun came up again, pointing at her head.

"Aw, come on," she said, and grimaced in disappointment like a little girl.

He looked at her. The tears were still streaming down his face, he could still remember how funny this had seemed a moment ago.

"Mr. Valdez?" she said.

He kept looking at her.

"Please let me have the gun."

Still looking at her. Weeping now. For all the laughter that was gone. For all those days on the beach long ago.

"Please?" she said.

For all the pretty little girls, gone now.

He nodded.

She held out her hands to him, palms up.

He put the gun into her hands.

Their eyes locked.

She went into the apartment, the gun hanging loose at her side, the barrels pointing toward the floor, and she leaned into the old man where he sat frail and weeping in the hardbacked chair, and she kissed his grizzled cheek and whispered, "Thank you," and wondered if she'd kept her promise to him after all.

Gloria Sanders was covered with blood.

This was ten o'clock on the morning of July twenty-fifth in the nurses' lounge at Farley General Hospital, downtown on Meriden Street. Her white uniform was covered with blood, and there were also flecks of blood in her blonde hair and on her face. They'd had a severe bleeder in the Emergency Room not ten minutes earlier, and Gloria had been part of the team of nurses who, working with the resident, had tried to stanch the flow of blood. There'd been blood all over the table, bed, blood on the walls, blood everywhere, she had never seen anyone spurting so much blood in her life.

"A stabbing victim," she told Carella and Brown. "He came in with a patch over the wound. The minute we peeled it off, he began gushing."

She was dying for a cigarette now, she told them, but smoking was against hospital rules, even though the people who'd *made* the rule had never worked in an emergency room or seen a gusher like the one they'd had this morning. Or the kid yesterday, who'd fallen under a subway car and had both his legs severed just above the knee. A miracle either of them was still alive. And they wouldn't let her smoke a goddamn cigarette.

Arthur Schumacher's taste for blue-eyed blondes seemed to go back a long way. His former wife's eyes were the color of cobalt, her hair an extravagant yellow that blatantly advertised its origins in a bottle. Slender and some five feet six or seven inches tall, Gloria strongly resembled the one daughter they'd already met, but there was a harder edge to her. She'd been around a while, her face said, her body said, her entire stance said. Life had done worse things to her than being bled on by a stabbing victim, her eyes said.

"So what can I do for you?" she asked, and the words sounded confrontational and openly challenging. I've seen it all and done it all, so watch out, boys. I'd as soon kick you in the groin as look at you. Blue eyes studying them warily. Blonde hair bright as brass, clipped short and neat around her head, giving her a stern, forbidding look. This was not the honey-blonde hair her daughter Lois had; if this woman were approaching you at night, you'd see her a block away. She reminded Carella of burned-out prison matrons he had known. So what can I do for you?

"Mrs. Sanders," he said, "we went . . ."

"*Ms*. Sanders," she corrected.

"Sorry," Carella said.

"Mm," she said.

It sounded like a grunt of disapproval.

"We went to your daughter's apartment on Rodman this morning . . ."

Eyes watching them.

"The address we have for her on Rodman," Brown said.

". . . and the super told us he hadn't seen her for the past several days."

"Betsy," she said, and nodded curtly.

"Yes."

"I'm not surprised. Betsy comes and goes like the wind."

"We're eager to talk to her," Carella said.

"Why?"

Leaning forward in the leather chair. The walls of the lounge painted white. She hadn't had a chance to wash before coming to talk to them; there were tiny flecks of blood in her yellow hair. Blood on the front of the white uniform. Blood on the white shoes, too, Brown noticed. He tried to visualize the bleeder. Most bleeders he'd seen were already dead.

"We understand she didn't get along with your former husband," Carella said.

"So what?" Gloria said. "Neither did I."

The challenge again. Is that why you're here? Because I didn't get along with my husband who's now dead from four bullets in the head?

"That *is* true, isn't it?" Carella said. "That your daughter . . ."

"She didn't kill him," Gloria said flatly.

"No one said she did," Carella said.

"Oh no?" she said, and pulled a face. "There are cops all over the E.R. every day of the week," she said, "uniformed cops, plainclothes cops, all kinds of cops. There isn't a cop in the world who doesn't first look to the family when there's any kind of trouble. I hear the questions they ask, they always want to know who got along with whom. Man's got a bullet in his belly, they're asking him did he get along with his wife. So don't lie to me about this, okay? Don't tell me we're not suspects. You know we are."

"Who do you mean, Ms. Sanders?"

"I mean Betsy, and me, and maybe even Lois, for all I know."

"Why would you think that?"

"I *don't* think that. *You're* the ones who think it."

"Why would *we* think it?"

"Let's not play games here, Officer. You told me a minute ago that you understood Betsy didn't get along with her father. So what does that mean? What are you, a social worker looking for a reconciliation? You're a cop, am I right? A detective investigating a murder. Arthur was killed, and his daughter didn't get along with him. So let's find her and ask her where she was last Friday night, Saturday night, whenever the hell it was, I don't know and I don't care. No games. Please. I'm too tired for games.''

"Okay, no games," Carella said. He was beginning to like her. "Where's your daughter? She was at her father's funeral on Sunday, and now she's gone. Where is she?''

"I don't know. I told you. She comes and goes.''

"Where does she go *to* or come *from*?" Brown asked. *He* didn't like her at all. He'd had a teacher like her in the fourth grade. She used to hit him on the hands with a ruler.

"This is the summertime. In the summer, hippies migrate. They cover the earth like locusts. Betsy is a thirty-nine-year-old hippie, and this is July. She could be anywhere.''

"Like *where* anywhere?" Brown insisted.

"How the hell should I know? You're the cop, you find her.''

"Ms. Sanders," Carella said, "no games, okay? Please. I'm too tired for games. Your daughter hated him, and she hated his dog, and now both of them are . . .''

"Who says so?''

"What do you mean?''

"That she hated the dog.''

"Lois. Your daughter Lois. Why? *Didn't* Betsy hate the dog?''

"Betsy seemed to hate the dog, yes.''

"Then why'd you question it?''

"I simply wanted to know who'd told you. I thought it might have been *her*." Almost snarling the word.

"Who do you mean?" Brown asked.

"Haven't you talked to her yet? His precious peroxide blonde?''

Pot calling the kettle, Carella thought.

"Do you mean Mrs. Schumacher?" Carella asked.

"*Mrs.* Schumacher, yes," she said, the word curling her upper lip into a sneer. She flushed red for a moment, as if containing anger, and then she said, "I thought she might have been the one who told you Betsy hated that dumb dog."

"How'd *you* feel about that dumb dog?" Carella asked.

"Never had the pleasure," Gloria said. "And I thought we weren't going to play games."

"We won't."

"Good. Look, let me make it easier for you, okay? I hated Arthur for what he did to me, but I didn't kill him. Betsy hated him for much the same reasons, but I'm sure she didn't kill him, either. I know you'll find out about the will, so I might as well tell you right now that I wouldn't grant a divorce until I made sure both my daughters were in his will for fifty percent of his estate. That's twenty-five percent each, which in Arthur's case comes to a hell of a lot of money."

"How much money?"

"I don't know the exact amount. A lot. But I know that neither of my daughters killed him for his money. Or for *any* reason at *all*, for that matter."

Both detectives were thinking that the only two reasons for murder were love or money. And hate was the other side of the love coin.

"How about you?" Brown asked. "Are *you* in that will?"

"No."

"Would you know if the present Mrs. Schumacher . . . ?"

"I have no idea. Why don't you ask *her*? Or better yet, ask Arthur's beloved partner, Lou Loeb. I'm sure he'll know all there is to know about it."

"Getting back to your daughter," Brown said. "Betsy. Did you talk to her after the funeral on Sunday?"

"No."

"When *did* you talk to her last?"

"I guess the day after he got killed."

"That would've been Saturday," Carella said.

"I suppose. It was on television, it was in all the papers. Betsy called and asked me what I thought about it."

"What'd you tell her?"

"I told her good riddance to bad rubbish."

"How'd *she* feel about it?"

"Ambivalent. She wanted to know whether she should go to the funeral. I told her she should do what she felt like doing."

"Apparently she decided to go."

"Apparently. But when we talked, she wasn't certain."

"Did she mention where she'd been the night before?" Carella asked.

"No games," Gloria reminded him.

He smiled.

"How about Lois?" he asked. "Did she call you, too?"

"Yes. Well, this was a shocking thing, a man gunned down right outside his apartment. Although in this city, it's starting to be the norm, isn't it?"

"*Any* city," Brown said, suddenly defensive.

"Not like here," Gloria said.

"Yes, like here," he said.

"When did Lois call you?" Carella asked.

"Saturday morning."

"To talk about her father?"

"Of course."

"How'd you feel about her continuing relationship with him?"

"I didn't like it. That doesn't mean I killed him."

"How'd she seem? When she called?"

"Seem?"

"Was she in tears, did she seem in . . ."

"No, she . . ."

". . . control of herself?"

"Yes."

"What'd she say?"

"She said she'd just read about it in the paper. She was surprised that her *stepmother*"—giving the word an angry spin—"hadn't called her about it, she was sure she must have known before then."

"You don't like Mrs. Schumacher very much, do you?"

"I loathe her. She stole my husband from me. She ruined my marriage and my life."

Carella nodded.

"But I didn't kill him," she said.

"Then you won't mind telling us where you were Friday night," he said, and smiled.

"Games again," she said, and did not return the smile. "I was home. Watching television."

"Anyone with you?"

"No, I was alone," she said. "I'm a sixty-year-old grass widow, a bitter, unpleasant woman who doesn't get invited out very often. Arthur did that to me. I never forgave him for it, and I'm glad he's dead. But I didn't kill him."

"What were you watching?" Brown asked.

"A baseball game."

"Who was playing?"

"The Yankees and the Minnesota Twins."

"Where?"

"In Minnesota."

"Who won?"

"The Twins. Two to one. I watched the news afterward. And then I went to bed."

"You still have no idea where we can find Betsy, huh?" Carella said.

"None."

"You'd tell us if you knew, right?"

"Absolutely."

"Then I guess that's it," he said. "Thank you very much, Ms. Sanders, we appreciate your time."

"I'll walk you out," she said, and rose ponderously and wearily. "Catch a cigarette in the alley," she added in a lower voice. And winked.

The trouble with a name like Sonny was that too many criminals seemed to favor it. This was a phenomenon neither Bent nor Wade quite understood. As kids growing up in the inner city, they had known their share of blacks named Sonny, but they hadn't realized till now just how popular the nickname was. Nor had they realized that its popularity crossed ethnic and racial barriers to create among criminals a widespread preference that was akin to an epidemic.

Bent and Wade were looking for a *black* Sonny.

This made their job a bit more difficult.

For whereas the computer spewed out a great many Sonnys who'd originally been Seymours or Stanislaws or Sandors, it appeared that blacks and people of Italian heritage led the pack in preferring the nickname Sonny to given names like Seward or Simmons or Salvatore or Silvano.

The detectives were further looking for a black Sonny who may or may not have had an armed-robbery arrest record. This made their job even more difficult in that the computer printed out a list of thirty-seven black Sonnys who within the past three years had done holdups in this city alone. As a sidelight, only six of those Sonnys were listed as wearing tattoos, a percentage much lower than that for the general armed-robber population, white, black, or indifferent. They did not bother with a nationwide search, which might have kept them sitting at the computer all day long.

Eight of the thirty-seven black armed robbers named Sonny were men who'd been born during the two years that Sonny Liston was the world's heavyweight boxing champion and considered a worthy role model. They were now all in their late twenties, and Wade and Bent were looking for a black Sonny who'd been described as being in his twenties. They knew that to most white men all black men looked alike. That was the difficulty in getting a white man to identify a black man from a photograph—especially a police photograph, which did not exactly qualify as a studio portrait. Dominick Assanti was no different from any other white man they'd ever known. To Dominick, only two black men were instantly recognizable: Eddie Murphy and Bill Cosby. All other black men, including Morgan Freeman and Danny Glover, looked alike. To Assanti, Bent and Wade probably looked alike, too.

First they showed him each of the eight mug shots one by one.

"Recognize any of them?" they asked.

Assanti did not recognize any of the men in the mug shots.

He commented once that he would not like to meet *this* guy in a dark alley.

Wade and Bent agreed.

Then they placed the mug shots on the table side by side, all eight of them, and asked him to pick out the three Sonnys who *most* resembled the Sonny who'd run past them with a gun in his fist on the night of the Carella murder.

Assanti said none of them looked like the man he'd seen.

"Are you sure?" Bent asked.

"I'm positive," Assanti said. "The one I seen had a scar on his face."

"Ah," Bent said.

So it was back to the computer again, this time with new information. Recognizing the difficulty of judging a man's age when he's rushing by you at night with a gun in his hand, the gun taking on more immediacy than the year of his birth, they dropped the age qualification. Recognizing, too, that the bakery shop holdup did not necessarily indicate a *history* of armed robbery, they dropped this qualification as well and ran a citywide search for any black man convicted of a felony within the past five years, provided he was named Sonny and had a scar on his face. They turned up sixty-four of them. This was not surprising.

It was almost impossible to grow up black in the inner city without one day acquiring a scar of one sort or another. And because keloids—scars that extended and spread beyond the original wound—were more prevalent in black skin than in white, these scars were usually highly visible. The knife scar over Wade's left eye was a keloid. He'd been told it could be treated with radiation therapy combined with surgery and injection of steroids into the lesion. He'd opted to wear the scar for the rest of his life. Actually, it didn't hurt in his line of work.

They now had sixty-four new mug shots to show Assanti. He pondered the photos long and hard. He was really trying to be cooperative, but he was severely limited in that he was white. In the long run, he simply gave up.

Bent and Wade hit the streets again.

Eileen was already there when Kling got to the office at five-ten that Wednesday afternoon. He apologized for being late and then took the chair Karin Lefkowitz offered him. He found it difficult to keep his eyes off Eileen. She was dressed casually— well, almost sloppily, in a faded denim skirt and a cotton sweater that matched her eyes—but she looked fresh and beautiful and radiantly happy. Karin explained that they'd just been talking about Eileen's first success with the hostage negotiating team. Last night, she'd . . .

"Well, it wasn't a major *triumph* or anything like that," Eileen said quickly.

"A baptism of fire, more or less," Karin said, and smiled.

"Bad word to use," Eileen said. "Fire."

Both of them were smiling now. Kling felt suddenly like an outsider. He didn't know how Eileen was using the word, and he felt somewhat like a foreigner here in his own country. Fire meant combustion. Fire meant to terminate someone's employment. Fire also meant to shoot. But Karin seemed to know exactly which meaning or meanings Eileen had intended, and this sense of shared intimacy was somehow unsettling to him.

"So," Karin said, "I'm glad you could make it."

But what had happened last night? Weren't they going to tell him?

"Happy to be here," he said, and smiled.

"I'll tell you where we are," Karin said. "Then maybe you can help us."

"Happy to," he said, and realized he'd repeated himself, or almost, and suddenly felt foolish. "If I can," he said lamely. Help them with what? he wondered.

Karin told him where they were.

Recounted the whole confusing tale of the Halloween night that had only been last year but that seemed centuries ago, when he'd stuck his nose into what was admittedly none of his business, causing Eileen to lose her two backups and placing her in an extremely dangerous and vulnerable position with a serial killer.

"Since that time," Karin explained, "Eileen has been blaming you for . . ."

"Well, you know," Kling started, "I was only trying to . . ."

"I know that," Eileen said.

"I mean, the *last* thing I wanted was to come between you and your backups. I know Annie Rawles," he said, turning back to Karin, "she's a good cop. And whereas this other guy . . ."

"Shanahan," Eileen said.

"Shanahan," he said, nodding to her in acknowledgment, "was a stranger to me . . ."

"Mike Shanahan."

"Which, by the way, is how the mixup came about. I didn't know him, he didn't know me . . ."

"I know," Eileen said.

"What I'm saying is I'd rather have cut off my right arm than put you in any kind of situation where you'd have to face down a killer."

The room went silent.

"I think Eileen knows that," Karin said.

"I hope so," Kling said.

"She also knows . . . don't you, Eileen? . . . that whereas you *were* to blame for losing her backups . . ."

"Well, as I told you . . ."

". . . you were *not* to blame for her having to kill Bobby Wilson."

"Well . . . who said I was?"

"Eileen thought you were."

"You didn't think that, did you?" he asked, turning to her.

"Yes, I did."

"That I was . . . how could you think that? I mean, the guy was coming at you . . ."

"I know."

". . . with a knife . . ."

"I know."

"So how could I have had anything to do with that? I mean, *anybody* . . . any police officer . . ."

"Yes, Bert, I know that now."

"Jesus, I really didn't think you were blaming me for that, Eileen."

"It's complicated," she said.

"Well, I know that. But you can't blame . . ."

"It's involved with the rape, too."

"Well, yeah, that," he said.

Eileen looked at him.

"Bert . . ." she said. "Don't just dismiss it."

"I'm not dismissing it, Eileen, you know that."

"Just don't fucking *dismiss* it, okay?"

He felt as if he'd been slapped in the face. He looked at her, stunned.

"It wasn't well, yeah, *that*," she said. "It was *rape*!"

"Eileen, I didn't mean it that way. I meant . . ."

He stopped dead, shaking his head.

"Yes, what did you mean, Mr. Kling?" Karin asked.

"Never mind, forget it."

"No, I think it may help us here."

"Help *who* here?" he asked. "Are you trying to help *me*, too, or are you trying to blame me for everything that happened since the rape? Or maybe even for the rape itself, who the hell knows, you're blaming me for everything else, why not the rape, too?"

"No one's blaming you for the rape," Eileen said.

"Thanks a lot."

"But, yes, I think you did have a lot to do . . ."

"Oh, listen . . ."

". . . with what happened *since* the rape, yes."

"Okay, I lost your backups, I admit it. I shouldn't have been there, I should have let them handle it. But that's not the crime of the cent . . ."

"You're *still* doing it," Eileen said.

"Doing *what*, for Christ's sake?"

"He doesn't even realize it," she said to Karin.

"What is it I don't realize? What do you want me to say? That *I'm* the one who really killed that cocks . . . ?"

He cut himself short.

"Yes?" Karin said.

"I didn't kill Bobby Wilson," he said. "But if it makes you happier to think I was responsible for it, I'll take the rap, okay?"

"What were you about to call him?"

Kling hesitated.

"Go ahead," Karin said.

"A cocksucker," he said.

"Why'd you stop?"

"Because I don't know you well enough to use such language in your presence."

Eileen started laughing.

"What's funny?" he said.

"You never used that word in *my* presence, either," she said.

"Well, I guess that's a sin, too," he said, "watching my language when there's a lady around."

"If only you could hear yourself," Eileen said, still laughing.

"I don't know what's so funny here," he said, beginning to get angry again. "Do you know what's so funny?" he asked Karin.

"Why'd you go to the Canal Zone that night?" Karin asked.

"I told you."

"No, you didn't," Eileen said.

"I went there because I didn't think Annie and Shanahan could handle it."

"No," Eileen said.

"Then why'd I . . . ?"

"You thought *I* couldn't handle it."

He looked at her.

"Yes," she said.

"No. I didn't want to trust your safety to two people . . ."

"You didn't want to trust my safety to *me*."

"Eileen, *no* cop trusts himself alone in a situation . . ."

"I know that."

"That's why there are backups . . ."

"Yes, yes . . ."

"The *more* backups the better."

"But you didn't trust *me*, Bert. Ever since the rape . . ."

"Oh, Jesus, here's the *rape* again! Ever since the rape, ever since the *rape* . . ."

"*Yes*, goddamn it!"

"*No*, goddamn it! You're talking about *trust*? Well, who didn't trust *who*? I don't like being blamed for something I . . ."

"I blame you for losing faith in me!"

"No. You blame me for wanting to protect you!"

"I didn't *need* your protection! I needed your understanding!"

"Oh, come on, Eileen. If I'd been any more understanding, I'd have qualified for the priesthood."

"What does that mean?"

"Well, you figure it out, okay?"

"No, what does it mean?"

"It means who wouldn't let me touch her after the rape?"

"Oh, is *that* what it gets down to?"

"I guess it gets down to I'm not the one who raped you, Eileen. I didn't rape you, and I didn't come at you with a knife, either, and if you've got me mixed up in your head with *either* of those two . . . *cocksuckers*, okay? . . . then there's nothing I can do to help you."

"Who asked for your help?"

"I thought I was here to . . ."

"Nobody asked for your help."

"She said maybe I could . . ."

"Nobody needs your goddamn help."

"Well, okay, I guess I misunderstood."

"And let's get one thing straight, okay?" Eileen said. "I didn't *ask* to be a victim."

"Neither did I," he said.

She looked at him.

"The only difference is I haven't made a career of it," he said.

"I'm sorry," Karin said, "our time is up."

The house Tommy was now living in was not quite a mile from the church Carella used to attend when they moved up here to Riverhead. Our Lady of Sorrows, it was called. He'd stopped going to mass when he was fifteen, sixteen, he could hardly remember now, because of something stupid one of the priests had said to him, but that hadn't kept him from attending the Friday night dances in the church basement. Thinking back on it now, it seemed to him that most of his early sex life was defined by those dances in the church basement. Had God known what was happening on that dance floor? All that steamy adolescent activity, had God known what was going on? If so, why hadn't He sent down a lightning bolt or something?

And if God Himself wasn't noticing, if He was busy someplace else, visiting plagues or something, then couldn't the *priest* see all that feverishly covert grinding, all that surreptitious clutching of buttock and breast, all that secret dry-humping there in the semi-dark? Standing there beaming at his flock while they slow-danced their way to virtual orgasm, didn't the priest at least *suspect* that no one was silently saying five Hail Marys? Father Giacomello, his name was. The younger priest. Always smiling. The older one was the one who'd scolded Carella for coming to confession at the busiest time of the year.

Not a smile from where he stood tonight, watching the garage from the shadow of the trees across the street, waiting for Tommy to come out, *if* he was coming out. Angela had told Carella that her husband had a bimbo. Well, okay, if there was a bimbo, this was as good a time as any to be seeing her. He'd been kicked out of the nest, this was as good a time as any to seek comfort and solace. *If* there was a bimbo.

He waited in the dark.

Playing cop with his own brother-in-law.

He shook his head.

There were roses in bloom, he could smell the roses on the still night air. They used to walk home from those Friday night dances, roses blooming in the soft summer night, he and his sister when she got old enough, walking home together, talking about things, talking about everything. At the time, he was closer to her than to any other human being on earth, he guessed, but he hated it nonetheless when she came to the dances because he felt she was intruding on his sexual freedom. How could a person dry-hump Margie Gannon when a person's own sister was dancing with some guy not four feet away? And, also, how could you keep an eye on your sister to make sure some sex fiend wasn't dry-humping *her* while you were busy trying to dry-hump Margie Gannon? It got complicated sometimes. Adolescence was complicated.

He remembered talking things over with his father.

So many things.

He remembered telling his father one time—the two of them alone in the shop late at night, the aroma of good things baking in the oven, breads and cakes and pastries and muffins and rolls, he would never forget those smells as long as he lived—he remembered telling him that the longest walk he ever had to make in his life was across a dance floor to ask some girl to dance, any girl, a pretty one, an ugly one, just taking that walk across the floor to where she was sitting, that was the longest walk in the world.

"It's like torture," he said. "I feel like I'm walking a mile across the desert, you know?"

"I know."

"Over hot sand, you know?"

"Yes, of course."

"To where she's sitting, Pop. And I hold out my hand, and I say Would you like to dance, or How about the next dance, or whatever, standing there, everybody watching me, everybody knowing that in the next ten seconds she's gonna say Get lost, jerk . . ."

"No, no," his father said.

"Sometimes, Pop, yeah, I mean it. Well, not those exact words, but you know they'll say like I'm sorry or I'm tired just now or I already promised this one, whatever, but all it means is Get lost, jerk. And then, Pop, you have to walk *back* to where you came from, only now everybody *knows* she turned you down . . ."

"Terrible," his father said, shaking his head.

". . . and the walk *back* is even longer than the walk when you were coming over, the desert is now a hundred miles long, and the sun is scorching hot, and you're gonna drop dead before you reach the shade, and everybody's laughing at you . . ."

"Terrible, terrible," his father said, and began laughing himself.

"Don't they *know*?" Carella said. "Pop, don't they *realize*?"

"They don't know," his father said, shaking his head. "But they're so beautiful, even the ugly ones."

There was activity across the street. The door to the room over the garage opening, a rectangle of light spilling onto the platform just outside the door. Tommy. Reaching inside to snap off the interior lights. Only the spot over the steps shining now. He locked the door and then came down the steps. He was wearing jeans and a striped polo shirt. Head bent, watching the steps as he came down. Carella ducked deeper into the shadows.

Was there a bimbo?

He gave him a decent lead, and then fell in behind him. Not too close to be spotted, not too distant to lose him. Tailing his own brother-in-law, he thought, and shook his head again.

He'd once talked to his father about faithfulness. Or rather *listened* to his father talking about it, listened carefully to every word because by then Carella was old enough to realize that his father had come through many of these same things himself and was able to discourse on them without sounding like the wise old man of the world. Without sounding like—a father. Sounding like just another man you happened to like a lot. A friend. Possibly the best friend Carella had or ever would have.

This was just before he married Teddy. A week before the wedding. He and his father were in the bakery shop—all of their important conversations seemed to take place near the ovens, the aroma of baking bread wafting on the air—and Carella was experiencing what he guessed could be defined as prenuptial jitters, wondering out loud whether or not he was about to enter a contract that might be, well, too limiting. Too restrictive, you know what I mean, Pop?

He guessed he felt the way he had when Angela started coming to those Friday night dances with him, that his *turf* was being invaded, his *space* threatened. He'd never told his father that he used to dry-hump Margie Gannon on the dance floor, or that his sister's presence had cramped his style somewhat. Neither had he ever mentioned that he'd later moved onward and upward to the blissful actuality of *truly* humping Margie in the backseat of the family Dodge, but he suspected his father knew all this, understood that his only son had been leading a fairly active sex life with a wide variety of women before he'd met Teddy Franklin, the woman he was now about to marry, the woman to whom he was about to commit the rest of his life.

He was troubled, and his father realized it.

He'd never signed any kind of contract in his entire life, not for a car, not for an apartment, not for anything, and here he was about to sign a contract that would be binding forever. He'd never sworn to anything in public except to uphold the laws of the city, state, and country when he took his oath as a policeman, but now he was about to swear before his relatives and friends and her relatives and friends that he would love her and keep her and all that jazz so long as they both should live. It was scary. In fact, it was terrifying.

"Do you love her?" his father asked.

"Yes, I love her, Pop," he said. "I love her very much."

"Then there's nothing to be scared of. I'll tell you something, Steve. The only time a man considers taking another woman is when he no longer loves the woman he already has. Do you think that's going to happen? Are you afraid the time will come when you won't love Teddy anymore?"

"How can I know that, Pop?"

"You can know it. You can feel it in your bones and in your blood. You can know you'll love this woman till the day you die, and you'll never want another woman but her. And if you don't know this *now* . . . don't marry her."

"Now isn't tomorrow," he said.

"Yes, now is tomorrow. Now is forever," his father said. The shop fell silent.

"Listen to me," his father said.

"Yes, Pop."

His father put his hands on Carella's shoulders. Big hands covered with flour. He looked into Carella's eyes.

"How do you feel about anyone else touching her?" he asked.

"I would kill him," Carella said.

"Yes," his father said, and nodded. "You have nothing to worry about. Marry her. Love her. Stay with her and no one else. Or I'll break your head," he said, and grinned.

And now, all these years later, Carella was following his sister's husband because the possibility existed that a time had come when he didn't love her anymore. He supposed that time could come to anyone. He did not think it would ever come to him. But he wondered now if that was because he truly loved Teddy to death or only because his father had threatened to break his head. In the darkness, quickening his pace as Tommy rounded a corner ahead, he smiled to himself.

He must have been trailing Tommy for at least half a mile, ten blocks or so, the area changing from strictly residential to commercial, elevated train tracks overhead now, stores still open on this gaudy summer night, July still flaunting her passion, men and women in the streets—was he planning to take a train? Was he heading for the platform on the next . . .?

No, he walked right past the stairway leading up to the platform and the tracks, staying on the avenue, his stride deliberate, his step that of a man who knew where he was going, a man with a destination. A little past nine o'clock now, the earlier lingering dusk now snuffed, the moonless sky black, the only illumination coming from store lights and sidewalk lamps and the red and green traffic lights on the tracks above and the streets below. Tommy was moving at a pretty fast clip, looking at his watch every now and then, continuing on up the avenue until he reached Brandon, and then turning left, off the avenue, down to Willow where the brick library Carella used as a kid stood on the southern side of the street, mantled in darkness now.

A car was parked up the street, some short distance from the library.

Tommy walked directly to the car.

He opened the door on the passenger side, triggering the interior light, the light going out again the instant he slammed the door behind him. The headlights came on. Carella ducked away from their sudden glare. The driver gunned the engine into life and set the car in motion. Carella moved deeper into the shadows as it approached the corner. A red Honda Accord sped by.

A woman was at the wheel.

8

"**H**e wanted to fire you," Goodman said. "I talked him into a thirty-day probation period."

"*Fire* me?" Eileen said. "But why?"

They were having lunch together in a seafood joint down near the Headquarters Building. Special Forces was on the tenth floor, Goodman's office was on the fourth. It was convenient. But she'd believed, until this moment, that he'd asked her to lunch to offer congratulations.

"You have to understand him," Goodman said.

"Oh, I understand him, all right."

"Well, yes, that," he said.

She loved the way men brushed off matters of enormous concern to women. Bert yesterday with his *Well, yeah, that* in reference to what had merely been the most traumatic experience in her life, and now Goodman with his *Well, yes, that*, when he knew she'd been referring to Brady's blatantly sexist attitude.

"He just *adores* the class clown," she said, "and he . . ."

"Well, you have to admit Materasso's a pretty funny guy."

"How about Pellegrino? Or Riley? They're not too comical,

and Brady treats them like long-lost brothers. He's got two women on the team only because . . ."

"Give credit where it's due, Eileen. He's the one who *put* women on the team in the first place."

"I wonder why."

"Certainly not because he's sexist."

"Then what was the 'Well, yes, that' all about?"

"I thought you knew."

"No, Mike, I'm sorry, I don't."

Using the name for the first time, realizing she hadn't called him *anything* until now, not Dr. Goodman, not Michael, and certainly not Mike. But there it was. Mike.

"I'm willing to bet he's never trusted a woman in his life."

"You'd lose."

"Would I?"

"I'm starved," he said, suddenly peering at her from behind his eyeglasses, raising his eyebrows and looking very much like a hungry little boy. "Aren't you?"

"I can eat," she said.

"Good, let's order."

They both ordered the steamed lobster. Eileen ordered a baked potato, he ordered fries. Eileen asked for Roquefort on her salad, he asked for creamy Italian. The salads came first. He ate ravenously. It was almost comical watching him. No manners at all. Just dug in. She wondered if he'd come from a large family.

"So tell me," she said.

"He lost one," Goodman said.

"What does that mean?"

"A negotiator. A woman."

"What are you saying?"

"Early on. The first woman he put on the team."

"You're kidding me."

"No, no. This was a long time ago, you probably weren't even on the job at the time. Woman named Julie Gunnison, worked out of Auto Theft, good cop, a Detective/Second. It was summertime, same as now. First time she worked the door. Woman in an apartment with her three kids, suddenly went bananas, threw one kid out the window before the police got there, was threatening to do the same with the other two if they didn't pull back. He put Julie on the door because it was a woman in there. There was a theory at the time that women confided more freely in other women, we now know it doesn't always work that way. But that was the thinking back then. Hostage negotiation was a new thing. You got a woman taker, you gave her a woman talker.''

"What happened?" Eileen asked.

"Who gets the baked?' the waitress asked.

"I do.''

The waitress put down their plates.

"Anything to drink?" she asked.

"Eileen, some wine? Beer?''

"I'm working,'' she said.

"Right. Coke? Pepsi?''

"Coke.''

"I'll have a Heineken beer,'' Goodman said.

"One Coke, one Heineken,'' the waitress said, and rushed off looking harried.

"I'm listening,'' Eileen said.

"Julie was on that door for six hours straight, performing a high-wire act that defied all the laws of gravity. Every five minutes, the lady inside there grabbed one of her kids and rushed to the window and hung the kid outside it, upside down, holding him by the ankles, swinging him, yelling she was going to let go if the cops didn't back off. Cops and firemen all over the street, trying to figure out where to run with the net, which way she was going to swing that kid before she dropped him. Julie at the door, talking her out of it each time, telling them all they wanted to do was help her, help the kids, help each other, come on out of there and we'll talk it over. Woman had a meat cleaver in her hands. Her husband was a butcher. The kid she dropped out the window before they got there, she'd cut off his hands at the wrist."

"Wow," Eileen said.

"Heineken and a Coke," the waitress said, and put down the drinks, and rushed off again

"Anyway," Goodman said, "Julie started to think she was making some progress. For the past hour—this was now eight o'clock at night, she'd been on the door since two in the afternoon, they'd already sent out for pizza and sodas. The woman had asked for beer, but you know we never let them have anything alcoholic . . ."

Eileen nodded.

". . . and she'd already fed herself and the kids and was beginning to feel chatty and at least for the past hour she hadn't tried to throw anyone out the window. So Julie starts telling her about her own kids, the way Mary Beth did with that woman in the lingerie shop last week, and they're getting along fine, and Julie's got her convinced she isn't armed, takes off her jacket, pats herself down . . . no guns, see? Nobody gets hurt, right? And then she takes a chance, she asks the lady to send out one of the kids, nobody's going to hurt her, the kids must be sleepy, they've got a cot set up down the hall, why doesn't she send out one of the kids? And the lady says Let me see again that you don't have a gun, and Julie shows her she doesn't have a gun, which is the truth, and the lady says Okay, I'll let you have one of the kids, and she opens the door and splits Julie's head in two with the cleaver."

"Jesus!" Eileen said.

"Yeah. So the E.S. cops stormed the door and killed the lady and that was the end of the story. Except that Brady got called on the carpet downtown, the Commish wanting to know what had happened there, a kid dead, a woman dead, a police officer dead, what the hell had gone wrong? If there was already a person dead when the hostage team *got* there, why didn't they just storm the door to begin with? Brady explained that we didn't work that way, whatever had happened *before* we got there didn't matter, it was a clean slate, our job was to make sure nobody got hurt *after* we were on the scene. Which the Commish must have thought was ridiculous because people *had* got hurt, there were three people dead and television was having a field day.

"The TV people were angry because Brady wouldn't let any of them near where the lady was contained—well, that's still a rule, no television cameras. So they began questioning the entire validity of the program. Almost wrecked it, in fact. All the hard work Chief McCleary had done getting it started, all the advances Brady had made when he took over, all of it almost went down the drain. The newspapers went after him, too. They'd all endorsed the incumbent mayor, who'd lost the election, and the new mayor had appointed a new commissioner and now the Commish was being blamed for what Brady had done, and naturally the buck stopped at Brady, it was his program, he was in command of the team. It was a hell of a mess, believe me."

Goodman was working on his lobster as he said all this. Delicately taking it apart with nutcracker, fingers, and fork, dipping the succulent meat into the butter sauce, chewing, popping a fry into his mouth, back to the lobster, working on the claws now, a gulp of beer, another fry, eating, talking.

"Brady blamed himself, of course, he's that kind of man. Got it into his head that he hadn't adequately trained Julie . . . which wasn't true, we've since learned there's only so much you can teach in a classroom. And, anyway, she was really a top-notch negotiator with a great deal of experience. Played it just the way she should have, in fact. Her bad luck was to come up against a lady who'd've snapped under any circumstances."

Goodman fell silent. Eileen watched him demolishing the rest of the lobster. Huge gulp of beer now. Another fry.

"Big family?" she asked.

"Just the three kids," he said.

"I meant you."

"No, I'm . . . huh?"

"The way you're eating."

"Oh. No, I've always eaten this way," he said, and shrugged. "I get hungry."

"I see that."

"Yeah," he said, and shrugged again, and drained what was left of his beer. "Took him a long time to get over it," he said. "For a while there, he wouldn't have any women on the team at all. Then he hired Georgia . . . I don't think you've met her . . . and Mary Beth. I don't know why he fired her, I thought she was doing a good job. Maybe he began feeling helpless again. A woman working the door, another woman contained, the entire situation a volatile one. Maybe he fired Mary Beth because he was afraid something would happen to her."

"Mike . . ."

Using the name again, getting used to the name.

". . . however you slice it, that's a sexist attitude. Has he fired any *men*?"

"One. But the guy had a drinking problem."

"Well, there you are."

"I'm not sure it's that simple."

"Do you think he'll fire me?"

"I don't know."

"Well . . . did he feel I was in danger yesterday?"

"You *were* in danger. He shouldn't have put you on the door. I argued against it, in fact. Sending in either you or Martha."

"Why?"

"Too early. Not enough observation yet, not enough training."

"But it worked out."

"Luckily. I don't think Martha would have been successful, by the way. It's a good thing the old man turned her down."

"Why do you say that?"

"Too eager, too aggressive. I'm not sure she'll *ever* make a good negotiator, for that matter."

"Have you told that to Brady?"

"I have."

"How about me? Do you think I'll make a good one?"

"You're already a pretty good one. You handled some things clumsily, but it was an enormously difficult situation. I like to call a spade a spade, Eileen. A police negotiator is a police negotiator and we should *never* lie about that, *whatever* the taker may want. Pretending to be a hooker . . ." He shook his head. "I told Brady I didn't like the idea. When he insisted we go ahead with it, I told him we should call Georgia, get her to come in. If we were going to lie to the taker, then we needed an experienced negotiator to pull it off. Georgia's done undercover work, by the way, decoy work, too. I'm surprised you don't know her."

"What's her last name?"

"Mobry. M-O-B-R-Y. Georgia Mobry."

"Doesn't ring a bell."

"She works mostly with Narcotics."

"No."

"Anyway, she could've handled it nicely yesterday. Trouble is she's on vacation. But . . . as you said . . . it worked out."

"Luckily. As *you* said."

"Well . . . however."

"I *was* lucky, wasn't I?"

"I think it could have gone either way. We shouldn't have lied to him. If he'd found out . . ."

"I tried to keep it ambiguous. If that's the word."

"That's the word. But the fact is we were passing you off as a hooker. And if he once discovered we were deceiving him . . ." Goodman nodded knowingly. "There was a little girl in that apartment. And a shotgun."

"Why'd Brady take the chance?"

"On you? Or the whole deception?"

"Both."

"You because the old man turned down Martha. Brady preferred her, she was his first choice. The deception? I don't know.

He probably thought it would work. And if it might save that little girl's life . . .''

"It *did* save her life."

"As it turned out."

"So why'd he want to fire me?"

"I'm not sure how his mind works. I've been with him for ten years now . . .''

"That long?"

"Yes. Why?"

"You look younger."

"I'm thirty-eight."

"You still look younger. Why'd he want to fire me?"

"I don't know. It came as a total surprise to me. First he picks Martha over you, and then he agrees to your terms for working the door. So you get the old man *and* the kid out without anybody getting hurt, and he decides to fire you. *Meshugge*, do you understand Yiddish?"

"I know what *meshugge* means. And I think I know why he wanted to fire me, too."

"Why?"

"Because I didn't do it *his* way."

"He knew you weren't going to do it his way when you told him nobody went in till the old man let go of the kid *and* the gun. That wasn't Brady's way, that was *your* way. His way was the kid comes out and you go in, an even trade."

"That's exactly what I'm . . .''

"You're missing my point. If he wanted to fire you because you didn't do it his way, then why didn't he fire you on the spot? When you *refused* to do it his way?"

"I don't know. Why didn't he?"

"Maybe he realized you were right. But then, after it was all over, he *had* to fire you to show he's still the boss."

"But he *didn't* fire me."

"Only because I talked him out of it."

"How'd you do that?"

"I told him you were fearless and honest and sympathetic and smart and that you'd probably turn out to be the best negotiator the team ever had, male *or* female."

"Fearless, huh? You should only know."

"Fearless," he said. "And all those other things, too."

"And that's why he gave me the thirty-day probation."

"Well, I also told him you were beautiful."

"You didn't,' she said.

"I did," he said. "Want to go to a movie tonight?"

She looked at him.

"What do you say?"

"What's playing?" she asked.

Louis Loeb told Carella on the telephone that his partner's will had already been filed and was a matter of record and he had neither the time nor the inclination to discuss it in detail with the detectives investigating his murder, certainly not after they had violated the civil rights of Mr. Schumacher's widow, an offense for which he—Mr. Loeb and not Mr. Schumacher—was still awaiting an apology. Carella said, "Thank you, Mr. Loeb," and hung up.

At two o'clock that afternoon—after having spent an hour and a half poring over the will in what was called Surrogate's Court in this city but which in many other cities was called Probate Court—he and Brown drove uptown onto Jefferson Avenue and parked the car in a neighborhood sprinkled with antiques shops, boutiques, beauty salons, and art galleries. Nestled between two of these galleries was a shop called Bide-A-Wee Pets. The woman who owned the shop was named Pauline Weed. She had sold a black Labrador retriever puppy to Margaret Schumacher for her to give to her husband on the occasion of their first Christmas together—and now she'd been named in Arthur Schumacher's will as the legatee of ten thousand dollars.

The woman was astonished.

Blonde and beautiful, in her early thirties, Carella guessed, slender and tall in black dancer's tights, black pumps, and a blue smock that matched her eyes, she accepted the news with disbelief at first, asking them if they were playing a joke on her, and then taking a closer look at the gold, blue-enameled shields they showed yet another time, and then bringing her hand up to her mouth and giggling behind it and shaking her head, all in what appeared to be a genuine display of surprise and delight.

"I can't believe this," she said, "it's so impossible."

"You had no idea, huh?" Brown said.

"None at all," she said, "this is a total and unimaginable surprise! Ten thousand dollars, that's a *fortune*! For *what*? I hardly *knew* the man. Are you sure this isn't a mistake?"

They assured her it was not a mistake.

They showed her the paragraph they had copied from the will:

In appreciation of the excellent medical services provided to my beloved Labrador retriever, Amos, by the NBB Veterinary Hospital at 731 Derwood Street, Isola, I give to Dr. Martin Robert Osgood the sum of Ten Thousand Dollars ($10,000.00) to further his work with animals. In similar appreciation of the excellent consultation and advice she gave to me regarding the care of the aforesaid Amos, I leave to Pauline Byerly Weed, owner of Bide-A-Wee Pets at 602 Jefferson Avenue, Isola, the sum of Ten Thousand Dollars ($10,000.00). Inasmuch as I have made prior arrangements with the Hollybrook Pet Cemetery and Crematory at 4712 Liberty Road in Pinesdale for the burial and perpetual graveside care of the aforementioned Amos, I request that my wife Margaret, should she survive me, or my daughter Lois Stein, should she survive my said wife, determine that Hollybrook Pet Cemetery and Crematory honors its contractual obligations.

Of the rest, residue and remainder of my estate ...

"This is amazing," she said, "truly. I don't know what to say. I haven't seen him in . . . God, it must be six, seven months since he last came in. This is incredible. Excuse me, but I can't get over it."

"What sort of 'consultation and advice' did you give him?" Carella asked. "About the dog?"

"Well, the first time he called . . . gee, this had to've been at *least* a year ago. Listen, are you *positive* this isn't a gag? I mean, all I did was sell his wife a *dog*."

"You do remember the dog?"

"Amos? Oh, sure, an adorable puppy. Well, you know Labs, they're the gentlest dogs on earth. I've got some back here now, come take a look."

She led them through the shop, past cages of puppies and kittens, past hanging cages of brightly colored birds and tanks of tropical fish, yet more cages with hamsters in them, endlessly paddling their wheels. There was the aroma of feathers and fur and an almost indiscernible aroma of what might have been cat piss disguised by litter. The Labrador retriever pups were in a cage at the back of the shop, two of them, looking up expectantly and . . . well, yes, *cheerfully* at Pauline as she approached them.

"Hello, babies," she said, "here're two people who brought me some very good news today."

She poked her forefinger between the strands of the cage and waggled it at the dogs, scratching first one puppy's head and then the other's, and then allowing them to nip and lick at her finger. The puppies were still frisking around the cage as she led the detectives back to the front of the shop again, explaining that she didn't like to stray too far from the cash register when she was alone in the shop . . . well, she guessed they knew what this city was like.

"So this first time he called . . ." Carella prompted.

"It was about a flea collar, actually. He wanted to know how old the dog should be before he put a flea collar on him. He'd named the dog by then, on the phone he kept calling him Amos, a cute name actually . . .''

Brown frowned.

''. . . Amos this and Amos that, and I told him if he planned to take the dog out to the beach—they had a house at the beach, Mr. and Mrs. Schumacher—or any place where there'd be plant life and ergo fleas or ticks—then he ought to put a collar on him right away, the dog was already three months old. So he came in sometime that week, and I sold him a collar specifically designed for puppies, there are different strengths, you know, this was a Zodiac puppy collar. I still can't get over this, forgive me,'' she said, shaking her head. ''Just *telling* you about it—I mean, I hardly *knew* the man.''

''And you say he came in every so often . . .''

''Yes, oh, once a month, once every six weeks, something like that. He'd be passing by . . . there are wonderful shops in the neighborhood, you know . . . and he'd stop in and buy a little something for Amos, a rawhide bone, or some kind of toy, we're always getting new shipments of toys, and we'd talk about the dog, he'd tell me stories about the dog, how Amos did this, how Amos did that . . .''

''In his will, he says you gave him consultation and advice . . .''

''Well, hardly *consultation*. But advice, yes, I guess so. I mean, well, yeah, I'd give him little tips I'd picked up, things to make a dog happy, well, *any* animal. Animals are like people, you know. They're all individuals, you have to treat them all differently. He'd bring Amos in every now and then, I'd look him over, tell him what a good dog he was, like that. I remember once . . . well, I really shouldn't take any credit for this because I'm sure the vet would've discovered it anyway the next time Mr. Schumacher took him in. But I was patting Amos on the head, and he had his tongue hanging out, panting, you know, and looking up at me, and I don't know what made me look in his mouth, I guess I wanted to see how his teeth looked, you can tell a lot about a dog's health by looking at his teeth and his gums. And I saw—I didn't know *what* it was at first—this sort of *ridge* across the roof of his mouth, like a narrow ridge on his palette. And I reached in there and it was . . . you won't believe this . . . he'd bitten down on a twig, and it had got wedged in there across his mouth, running from one side of his mouth to the other, where his teeth had bitten it off, wedged up there on the roof of his mouth with his teeth holding it in place on either side. And I yanked that out of there . . . *Jesus!* He didn't even bleed. The thing just came free in my hand and that dog looked as if he was going to get up on his hind legs and kiss me! Can you imagine the pain that must've been causing him? Wedged up there like that? Like a toothache day and night, can you imagine? That poor dog. But, you know . . . that wasn't worth ten thousand dollars. I mean, *nothing* I did was worth ten thousand dollars.''

"Apparently Mr. Schumacher thought so," Carella said.

"But you didn't know you were in the will, is that right?" Brown asked.

"Oh my God, *no*! Wait'll I tell my mother! She'll die."

"He never mentioned it to you."

"Never."

"Not any of the times he stopped by . . ."

"Never."

"When did you say the last time was?" Brown asked.

"That he came in? January? February? At *least* that long ago. I really can't believe this!"

"How about his wife? Did she ever come into the shop?"

"Not after she bought the dog, no."

"You never talked to her after that?"

"Never."

"Or saw her?"

"Never. Look at me, I'm shaking. I am positively shocked!"

Brown was wondering how come *he* didn't know any people who might want to leave *him* ten thousand smackers.

* * *

Arthur Schumacher had really loved that dog.

He could not have known they would die together in the same angry fusillade, but nonetheless he had made provision in his will for "the burial and perpetual graveside care of the aforementioned Amos," in addition to the ten grand each he'd left to Dr. Martin Osgood and Miss Pauline Weed for remembered little courtesies and services.

Of the rest, residue, and remainder of his estate, of whatsoever nature and wheresoever situated, he had given, devised, and bequeathed fifty percent to his wife, Margaret Schumacher, twenty-five percent to his daughter Lois Stein, and twenty-five percent to his daughter Betsy Schumacher. The detectives still didn't know the total worth of the estate, but according to Gloria Sanders, his embittered grass widow, it came to a considerable sum of money.

There was no mention of Susan Brauer in the will.

But in addition to the safe-deposit box Schumacher had kept at Union Savings downtown near his office, there was also a checking account in his name. A perusal of his statements—after obtaining a court order granting the privilege—revealed that he had, in fact, been taking five thousand dollars in cash from this account at the beginning of every month, and there now seemed little doubt that this money found its way into Susan's personal checking account. Unaccounted for, however, was the twelve thousand dollars they'd found in her closet cash box. Had Schumacher been giving her additional money? If so, where had it come from?

Maybe he was stealing it, Teddy signed.

Carella looked at her, wondering how such a generous and lovely person could come up with thoughts that attributed such devious machinations to human beings.

From his firm, she signed. *Or from his wife's account, if she had one.*

"I don't think he was stealing," Carella said, talking and signing at the same time.

But where *had* the money come from?

"Maybe he had some other bank accounts," he said. "He was keeping *this* one from his wife, so why not some others? I mean, the guy wasn't exactly what you'd call trustworthy, was he? Divorced Gloria to marry *one* blonde and then started carrying on with yet another one. So maybe he kept secret bank accounts as a life-style. In preparation, you know?"

Teddy watched his hands as if she were watching a television mini-series, his words conjuring banks all over town, tall granite pillars and brass tellers' cages, long black limousines and beautiful blonde women, champagne chilling in silver buckets, clandestine passion on red silk sheets.

But he was kind to his dog, she signed, her hands somehow managing to convey the dryness of her words.

"Oh *yes*," Carella said. "*And* the vet who took care of the dog, *and* the woman who'd sold Margaret the dog. Ten thousand each, can you imagine? Margaret," he said, seeing her puzzlement, and signing the name letter by letter. "The *first* blonde. Susan was the *second* one. Susan. S-U-S-A-N."

Maybe I should open a pet shop, Teddy signed. *Or become a vet.*

"Good idea, we can use the money. She was pretty foresighted, wasn't she? Gloria, I mean, the first wife. The bleached blonde, Gloria. G-L-O-R-I-A. Getting it put in their settlement agreement, I mean. That he'd leave the daughters fifty percent of the estate? Lots of guys remarry, they forget they ever *had* kids. Speaking of which . . . Mark!" he yelled. "April! Five minutes."

"Aw, shit!" Mark yelled from down the hall.

"We still can't find the hippie daughter," Carella said. "Remember I was telling you . . . ?"

Teddy nodded.

"She disappeared," Carella said. "Let me go tuck them in, I'll be right back. There's something else I have to tell you."

She looked up at him.

"When they're asleep."

She frowned, puzzled.

He mouthed the word *Tommy*.

Teddy sighed.

The twins were in the bathroom brushing their teeth. Eleven years old already, my how the time flew by.

"Mark said shit," April said.

"I heard him."

"You're supposed to fine him."

"I will. That's ten cents, Mark."

"Did Mom hear it?"

"No."

"Then it's only a nickel."

"Who says?"

"If only one of you hears it, it's half the price."

"He's making that up, Dad."

"I know he is. Ten cents, Mark."

"Shit," Mark said, and spat into the sink.

"That's twenty," Carella said. "Go kiss your mother, then bedtime."

"Why don't *you* ever curse?" Mark asked his sister as they went out of the bathroom.

"I do," she said. "I know even dirtier words than you."

"So how come I never hear you saying them?"

"I say them in the dark."

"That's ridiculous," Mark said.

"Maybe, but it doesn't cost me any money."

He could hear them in the living room, saying goodnight to Teddy. He waited in the hallway, very tired all at once, remembering his father all at once. When he and Angela were small, his father used to read them to sleep every night. He sometimes thought his father got a bigger kick out of the bedtime stories than either of the kids did. Now there was only television.

"See you in the morning!" April called. A ritual with her. Saying it would make it true. She would see them in the morning if only she said it each night. He took them to their rooms, separate rooms now, they were getting older, separate prayers. He tucked Mark in first.

"I like swearing," Mark said.

"Okay, so pay for it."

"It isn't fair."

"Nothing is."

"Grandpa said to always be fair."

"He was right. You should."

"Do you miss him?"

"Yes. Very much."

"I do, too."

Carella kissed him on the forehead.

"Goodnight, son," he said.

"G'night, Dad."

"I love you."

"Love you too."

He went into the room next door and listened to April's prayers and at last said, "Goodnight, angel, sleep well."

"See you in the morning," she said.

"See you in the morning."

"I don't really, you know," she said. "Curse in the dark."

"Much better to light a single candle," Carella said, and smiled.

"Huh?" she said.

"I love you," he said, and kissed her on the forehead.

"I love you, too. See you in the morning," she said.

"See you in the morning," he said.

Teddy was waiting in the living room. Sitting under the Tiffany-style lamp, reading. She put down the book the moment he came in. Her hands signed *Tell me*.

He told her about following Tommy the night before. Told

her he'd seen Tommy getting into a red Honda Accord driven by
a woman.

"I don't know what to tell Angela," he said.

Just be sure, Teddy signed.

Their informant told them he'd seen these two dudes from
Washington, D.C., one of them named Sonny and the other named
Dick, in an abandoned building off Ritter. There was a girl with
them, but he didn't know the name of the girl at all; she wasn't
from Washington, she was from right here in this city. All three
of them were crackheads.

This was the information Wade and Bent had.

They had got it at a little after nine o'clock that night from a
man who himself was a crackhead and who had volunteered the
information because they had him on a week-old pharmacy break-
in. He said word was out they was looking for a dude named
Sonny and that's who he'd seen earlier tonight, Sonny and this
other dude and a girl couldn't be older than sixteen, he was being
cooperative, wasn't he? They told him he was being real cooperative, and then they clapped him in a holding cell downstairs to
wait for the ten o'clock van pickup.

The building was around the corner from Ritter Avenue, on
a street that had once been lined with elegant apartment buildings,
most of them occupied by Jews who'd moved up here a generation
after their parents made the long journey from Poland and Russia
to settle in the side streets of Lower Isola. The Jews had long since
left this section of Riverhead. The area became Puerto Rican until
they, too, left because landlords found it cheaper to abandon
rent-controlled buildings than to maintain them. Ritter Avenue
and its surrounding side streets now looked the way London or
Tokyo or Berlin had looked after World War II—but America had
never suffered any bombing raids. What had once been a thriving
commercial and residential community was now as barren as a
moonscape. Here there was only an unsteady mix of rubble and

buildings about to fall into rubble. Here there was no pretense of rescue, no fancy plastic flowerpot decals promising later reconstruction; the jungle had already reclaimed what had once been a rich and vibrant community.

Sonny and Dick and the sixteen-year-old girl were presumably holed up at 3341 Sloane, the only building still standing in a field of jagged brick and concrete, strewn mattresses and rubbish, roaming dogs and skittering rats. Clouds scudded across a thin-mooned sky as the detectives got out of their car and looked up at the building. Something flickered in one of the gutted windows.

Third floor up.

Wade gestured.

Bent nodded.

They both figured it was a candle flickering up there. Too hot for a fire unless they were cooking food. Probably just sitting around a candle, smoking dope. Sonny and Dick and the sixteen-year-old girl. Sonny who had been carrying a gun on the night Anthony Carella got killed. Sonny who was maybe still carrying that same gun unless he'd sold it to buy more crack.

Neither Wade nor Bent said a word. Both of them drew their guns and entered the building. The shots came as they rounded the second-floor landing. Four shots in a row, cracking on the night air, sundering the silence, sending the cops flying off in either direction, one to the right, one to the left of the staircase, throwing themselves out of the line of fire. Someone was standing at the top of the stairs. A cloud passed, uncovering a remnant moon, revealing a man in silhouette on the roofless floor above, huge against the sky, gun in hand, but only for an instant. The figure ducked away. There was noise up there, some frantic scrambling around, a girl's nervous giggle, a hushed whisper, and then rapid footfalls on the night—but no one coming down this way. Wade stepped out. Bent covered him, firing three shots in rapid succession up the stairwell. Both men pounded up the steps, guns fanning the air ahead of them. The apartment to the right of the stairwell was vacant save for a handful of empty crack vials and a guttering votive candle in a red glass holder. It took the detectives only a moment to realize where everyone had gone; there was a fire escape at the rear of the building.

But there were spent cartridge cases at the top of the staircase, and they now had something they could compare with what they'd found on the floor of the A & L Bakery on the night Anthony Carella was killed.

9

Friday could not make up its mind. It had been threatening rain since early morning, the sky a dishwater gray that changed occasionally to a pale mustard yellow that promised sunshine and then dissipated again into the drabs. At six that evening, the heat and humidity were still with the suffering populace, but nothing else was constant. There was not the slightest breeze to indicate an oncoming storm, and yet the sky seemed roiling with the promise of rain.

Outside the old gray stone Headquarters Building downtown on High Street, Kling waited on the sidewalk in front of the low flat steps, watching the homeward-bound troops coming out of the building; invariably, they looked up at the sky the moment they came through the big bronze doors at the top of the steps. Karin Lefkowitz emerged at twenty minutes past the hour. She did not look up at the sky. She was carrying one of those small folding umbrellas and probably didn't give a damn *what* the weather did. She was also carrying a shoulder bag in which she'd undoubtedly placed her Reeboks; in their place, she was wearing high-heeled blue leather pumps to match her blue linen suit. He fell into step beside her.

"Hi," he said.

She turned to him in surprise, hand tightening on the umbrella as if she were getting ready to swing it.

"Oh, hi," she said, recognizing him. "You startled me."

"Sorry. Have you got time for a cup of coffee?"

She looked at him.

"Mr. Kling . . ." she said.

"Bert," he said, and smiled.

"Does this have to do with the meeting we had on Wednesday?"

"Yes, it does."

"Then I'd prefer two things. One, whatever this is, I'd like to discuss it in my office . . ."

"Okay, wherever you . . ."

". . . and I'd like Eileen to be present."

"Well, I came down here alone because I didn't *want* Eileen to be present."

"Discussing anything that concerns Eileen . . ."

"Yes, it does concern . . ."

". . . would be inappropriate."

"Is it inappropriate for you and Eileen to discuss *me*?"

"You're not my client, Mr. Kling."

"I just want to tell *my* side of it."

She looked at him again.

"A cup of coffee, okay?" he said. "Ten minutes of your time."

"Well . . ."

"Please," he said.

"Ten minutes," she said, and looked at her watch.

Carella had been waiting outside the bank since three o'clock, wondering if and when it would rain, and it was now six-thirty but it still hadn't rained. He hadn't expected Tommy to come out at three, because Tommy was an executive who went to meetings that sometimes lasted well into the night. Tommy's job was trying to rescue loans the bank had made. If the bank made a three-million-dollar loan to someone who ran a ball-bearing company in Pittsburgh, and the guy started to miss his payments, Tommy got sent out to see how they could help the guy make good on the loan. The bank didn't want to own a ball-bearing company; the bank was in the money business. So if they could work something out with the guy, everybody would be happy. That was Tommy's job, and it took him all over the country, sometimes even to Europe. Carella could see how such a job might allow for the opportunity to fool around, if a man was so-inclined to begin with.

Tommy came out of the bank at twenty minutes to seven. There was a woman with him, an attractive brunette who appeared to be in her late twenties, smartly dressed in a tailored suit and high-heeled pumps, and carrying a briefcase. From across the street, Carella could not tell whether she was the same woman who'd been in the car last night. He gave them a lead, and then began following them, staying on the opposite side of the street, walking parallel and almost abreast of them.

They seemed to have nothing to hide. Carella guessed she was a business associate. They walked past the subway kiosk up the street; neither of them was planning to take a train anyplace. They continued on up the street toward a parking garage, and then walked past that as well, and continued walking some several blocks until they came to a second garage. The woman turned in off the sidewalk, Tommy at her side. She opened her handbag and handed him a yellow ticket. Carella immediately hailed a taxi.

He got in and showed the driver his shield.

"Just sit here," he said.

The driver sighed heavily. Cops, he was thinking.

Tommy was at the cashier's booth, paying to retrieve the parked car. He came back to where the woman was standing, and the two fell into conversation again. From the backseat of the taxi across the street, Carella watched.

Some two minutes later a red Honda Accord came up the ramp.

It was the same car Tommy had got into last night.

In this area of courthouses and state and municipal buildings, there were not many eating establishments that stayed open beyond five, six o'clock, when the streets down here became as deserted as those in any ghost town. But there was a delicatessen on the cusp of the area, closer to a genuine neighborhood, and it had a sign in its window that announced it was open till 9:00 P.M.

Kling urged Karin to have something to eat.

The smells coming from the kitchen were hugely tempting.

She admitted that she was starving and said it would take her an hour or more to get home; she lived across the river, in the next state.

Kling suggested the hot pastrami.

She told him she *loved* hot pastrami. She said that when she was a kid her mother used to take her for walks around the neighborhood . . .

"I'm Jewish, you know."

"Gee, really?"

". . . past all these wonderful delis. But she wouldn't let me eat anything they served, I was only allowed to stand outside and *smell* the food. 'Take a sniff,' she would say, 'take a good sniff, Karin.' "

She smiled with the memory now, though to Kling it seemed like extraordinarily cruel and unusual punishment.

"So what'll it be?" he asked.

She ordered the hot pastrami on rye. He ordered it on a seeded roll. They both ordered draft beer. There was a big bowl of sour pickles on the table. They sat eating their sandwiches. Reaching for pickles. Sipping beer. There was only a handful of other diners in the place, men in short-sleeved shirts, women wearing summer dresses. The air was hushed with the expectation of rain.

"So why'd you want to see me?" Karin asked.

"I don't like what happened on Wednesday," he said.

"What didn't you like?"

"You and Eileen ganging up on me."

"Neither of us . . ."

"Because it just isn't true, you see. That whatever happened to Eileen is all my fault."

"No one says it was, Mr. Kling . . ."

"And I wish to hell you'd call me Bert."

"I don't think that would be appropriate."

"What do you call Eileen?"

"Eileen."

"Then why isn't it appropriate to call me Bert?"

"I told you. Eileen is my client. You're not. And whereas it may not be true that you were responsible for . . ."

"Never mind the buts. It *isn't* true."

"I'm not suggesting it was. I'm saying that Eileen *perceived* it as the truth. Which, by the way, she no longer does."

"Well, I hope not. If she wants to think of herself as some kind of damsel in dis . . ."

"I'm sure she doesn't. In fact, she never did."

"I think she did, where it concerns that night, where it concerns her having to put that guy away. Damsel in distress, woman in jeopardy, whatever you want to call it. When the plain truth of the matter is she was a *cop* in a showdown with a serial killer. It was her *job* to put him away. She was only doing her goddamn job."

"It would be nice if it were that simple," Karin said, and bit into her sandwich again. "But it isn't. Eileen was raped. And unfortunately, the rapist resembled you. So when you later step into a situation that . . ."

"I didn't know that."

"He had blond hair. The rapist. Like yours."

"I really didn't know."

"Yes. And he was armed with a knife . . ."

"Yes."

". . . was threatening her with a knife. Cut her, in fact. Thoroughly terrified her."

"Yes, I know."

"So now there's a *second* man with a knife, coming at her again, and she's alone with him because *you* caused her to lose her backups."

"I didn't deliberately . . ."

"But you *did*. This isn't merely her perception, it's reality. If you had stayed home that night, Eileen would have had two capable and experienced detectives following her, and chances are she wouldn't have found herself in a confrontational situation with a serial killer. But there she was. Because of you."

"Okay. I'm sorry it happened. But . . ."

"And you're wrong when you say she *had* to put him away. She didn't have to. Her perception—and, again, the reality as well—was that this man was going to cut her if she didn't stop him, she was going to get cut again if she didn't stop this man. But she didn't have to *kill* him in order to stop him. The man was armed only with a knife, and she had her service revolver—a .44-caliber Smith & Wesson—*plus* a .25-caliber Astra Firecat in a holster strapped to her ankle, *and* a switchblade knife in her handbag. She certainly did not have to kill him. She could have shot him in the shoulder or the leg, wherever, anything of the sort would have effectively stopped him. The point is she *wanted* to kill him."

Kling was shaking his head.

"Yes," Karin said. "She wanted to kill him. Even though he wasn't the man she *really* wanted to kill. The man she *really* wanted to kill was the man who'd raped her and cut her, and who—I say 'unfortunately' again—looked somewhat like you. If it weren't for the blond rapist, she wouldn't have to kill this man. If it weren't for *you* . . ."

Shaking his head, no, no, no.

"Yes, this is what her *mind* was telling her. If it weren't for *you,* she wouldn't have to kill this man. I gave you a chance, she told him, meanwhile pumping bullets into his back, I gave you a chance. Meaning she gave *you* a chance. To prove yourself, to show you still believed in her . . ."

"I *did* believe in her, I *do* believe in her."

"But you didn't. You followed her to the Canal Zone . . ."

"Yes, but only . . ."

"Because you didn't trust her, Bert, you didn't think she could take care of herself. It was your failure of confidence that caused the mixup, caused the confrontation, and eventually caused the murder."

"It wasn't murder, it was self . . ."

"It was murder."

"Justified then."

"Perhaps."

There was the soft sound of rain pattering the sidewalk outside. They both looked up.

"Rain," he said.

"Yes," she said.

"Heading uptown," the cabdriver said.

"Stay with them," Carella said.

Windshield wipers snicked at the lightly falling rain. Tires hissed against the pavement. Up ahead, the red Honda Accord moved steadily through the gray curtain of drizzle and dusk. Carella leaned over the back of the front seat, peering through the windshield.

"Pulling in," the driver said.

"Go past them to the corner."

He turned his head away as they passed the other car and then he looked back through the rear window to keep the car in sight. The woman was maneuvering it into the curb now, across the street from a playground where children stood under the trees looking out at the rain.

Carella paid and tipped the driver, got out of the cab, and ducked into a doorway just as Tommy climbed out of the Accord on the passenger side. A moment later, the woman joined him on the sidewalk. Together, they ran through the rain to a brownstone some twenty feet up from where she'd parked the car. Carella watched them entering the building. He walked up the street.

He was copying down the address on the brownstone when his beeper went off.

Brown was waiting for him in the rain.

The woman lay on the sidewalk under the trees. Blood seeping from her, mingling with the rain, diluted by the rain, running in rivulets into the gutter. Long blonde hair fanned out around her head. Raindrops striking her wide-open blue eyes. When Carella's father was taken to the hospital with his heart attack three years ago, it was raining. One of the nurses walking alongside the stretcher as he came out of the ambulance said, "He doesn't like it." The other nurse said, "It's raining on his face," and tented a newspaper over it. His father had always recounted that story with amusement. The idea that he was suffering a massive heart attack and the nurses were discussing rain in his face. Big Chief Rain in the Face, he'd called himself.

Lying on her back with her blonde hair spread on the slick gray pavement and her blood-drenched face shattered by the impact of the bullets that had entered it, Margaret Schumacher wasn't concerned about the rain in her face.

"When?" Carella asked.

"Boy One called it in an hour ago."

"Who found her?"

"Kid over there under the awning."

Carella looked up the street to where a white sixteen-year-old boy was standing with the doorman.

"He saw the whole thing," Brown said, "yelled at the perp, got shot at himself. He ran inside the building, got the doorman to call nine-one-one. Boy One responded."

"Homicide here yet?"

"No, thank God," Brown said, and rolled his eyes.

"Let's talk to him some more," Carella said.

They walked through the rain to where the doorman was counseling the kid on how to handle interviews with cops. This was the same doorman who'd been on duty the night Arthur Schumacher and his dog were killed. Now Schumacher's wife was lying dead on the sidewalk in almost the identical spot; it was getting to be a regular epidemic. Carella introduced himself and then said, "We'd like to ask a few more questions, if that's all right with you."

He wasn't talking to the doorman, but the doorman immediately said, "I called nine-eleven the minute he ran in here."

"Thanks, we appreciate it," Carella said, and then to the kid, "What's your name, son?"

"Penn Halligan," the kid said.

"Can you tell us what happened?"

The kid was handsome enough to appear delicate, almost feminine, large brown eyes fringed with long black lashes, a high-cheekboned porcelain face with a cupid's bow mouth, long black hair hanging lank with rain on his forehead. Tall and slender, he stood under the awning with the doorman and the detectives, hands in the pockets of a blue nylon windbreaker. He was visibly trembling; he'd had a close call.

"I was coming home from class," he said. "I take acting lessons."

Carella nodded. He was thinking Halligan was handsome enough to be a movie star. Though nowadays that certainly wasn't a prerequisite.

"On The Stem," he said, gesturing with his head. "Upstairs from the RKO Orpheum. I go every Monday, Wednesday, and Friday afternoons. Five o'clock to seven o'clock. I was on my way home when . . ." He shook his head. The memory caused him to shiver again.

"Where do you live?" Brown asked.

"Just up the block. 1149 Selby."

"Okay, what happened?"

"I was coming around the corner when I saw this guy running across the street from under the trees there," he said, turning to point. "There was this blonde lady walking toward me on *this* side of the street, and the guy just crossed sort of diagonally, running from under the trees to where the blonde was walking, like on a collision course with her. I was just coming around the corner, I saw it all."

"Tell us everything you saw," Carella said. "Don't leave anything out."

"I was walking fast because of the rain . . ."

Head ducked against the rain, a gentle rain but you can still get pretty wet if you're coming from eight blocks away on Stemmler. He has walked all the way down to Butterworth and is continuing on down the four blocks to Selby, and is turning the corner onto his own street when he sees this blonde lady walking toward him. Tall good-looking blonde wearing a short, tight mini and rushing through the rain even though she's got this bright orange-and-white umbrella over her head, one of these huge things that looks like it should be covering a hot-dog stand. High heels clicking on the sidewalk, rain pattering everywhere around her, he's thinking here comes a sexy young mother, which he's been told is the most passionate woman you can find, a young mother . . .

Carella suddenly wonders if the kid's delicate good looks have ever raised questions about his masculinity. Else why the gratuitous comment about a woman lying dead on the sidewalk not twenty feet away?

. . . coming at him in the rain, long legs flying through the rain, when all of a sudden he sees this movement from the corner of his eye, on his left, just a blur at first, almost a shadow, a black shadow moving from the deeper black shadow of the trees across the street, flitting across the wet black pavement merging with the blackness of the asphalt and the grayness of the rain, there is a gun in the man's hand.

The man is dressed entirely in black, wearing like black mechanic's overalls, you know? Like what you see mechanics wearing all covered with grease, except it's entirely black, and he's wearing black socks and shoes, running shoes, and a black woolen hat pulled down over his forehead, almost down onto his eyes, he's got the gun sticking out ahead of him, did you ever see *Psycho*? Do you remember when Tony Perkins comes out of that doorway upstairs with the big bread knife raised high over his head, just rushes out in the hallway to stab Marty Balsam? He's in drag, do you remember, we're supposed to think it's his crazy mother running out, but it's the knife held high over his head in that stiff-armed way that scares you half to death. Well, this guy all in black . . .

And Carella suddenly knows it's a *woman* this kid saw.

. . . is rushing across the street with the gun already pointing at the blonde, the arm straight out and stiff, the gun like following the blonde's progress, like tracking her on radar, like a compass needle or something, rushing across the street in the rain, with the gun zeroing in on her. She doesn't see the guy, he's moving very fast, like a dancer, no, like a bullfighter, I guess, more like a bullfighter . . .

And Carella is positive now that this is a *woman* the kid is talking about . . .

. . . coming at her, she's under the orange-and-white umbrella, she doesn't even *see* him. I'm the only one who sees them both, the blonde coming toward me where I'm already around the corner, the guy rushing across the street with this gun in his hand, I'm the only one who knows what's about to happen, I'm like the camera, you know, I'm like *seeing* this through the wide-angle viewfinder on a camera. My first reaction is to yell . . .

"Hey!" he yells. "Hey!"

The guy keeps coming. The blonde looks up because she hears the yell, she thinks at first Halligan is the one to worry about, Halligan is the one yelling, Halligan is the crazy lunatic in this city full of crazy lunatics, Halligan is coming at her from the corner, yelling at her, Hey, hey, hey! She hasn't yet seen the guy in black, she doesn't yet know that a gun is pointed at her head, she doesn't yet realize that the threat is angling in on her from diagonally across the street, ten feet away from her now, eight feet . . .

"Hey!" he yells again. "Stop!"

. . . six feet away, four feet . . .

And the gun goes off. Bam, bam on the wet night air, bam again, and again, four shots shattering the steady patter of the rain. "Hey!" he yells, and the man turns to face him squarely, the blonde tumbling in slow motion to the sidewalk behind him, the man turning in slow motion, everything suddenly in slow motion, the blonde falling, crumbling in slow motion, the rain coming down in slow motion, each silvery streak sharp and clear against the blackness of the night, the gun swinging around in slow motion, a yellow flash at its muzzle as it goes off, the explosion following it in seeming slow motion, reverberating on the rain-laden air, he thinks Jesus *Christ!* and the gun goes off again.

He is already hurling himself to the sidewalk and rolling away, he has seen a lot of movies, not for nothing is he a drama student. He rolls away toward the opposite side of the gun hand, the gunman is right-handed, the pistol is in his right hand, he does not roll *into* the gun, he rolls away from it, you have to watch movies carefully. He expects another shot, he has not been counting, when you are about to wet your pants you don't count shots exploding on the night. He knows he will be dead in the next ten seconds, suspects that the blonde lying in a bleeding crumpled heap on the sidewalk is already dead, hears the man's footfalls in the rain, pattering through the pattering rain . . .

A woman, Carella thinks.

. . . to where he is lying against the brick wall of the building now, waiting for the fatal shot, it's a miracle he hasn't been shot yet, it's a miracle he isn't already dead.

He hears a *click* and another *click* and the word *Shit!* whispered on the night, hissing on the night, and the man turns and runs, he does not see the man running, he only hears the footfalls on the night, in the rain, rushing away, fading, fading, and finally gone. He lies against the wall trembling, and then at last he gets to his feet and realizes that he has in fact either wet his pants or else he was lying in a puddle against the wall. He looks into the darkness, into the rain. The man is gone.

"Could it have been a woman?" Carella asked.

"No, it was very definitely a man," Halligan said.

"Are you sure he was right-handed?" Brown asked.

"Positive."

"The gun was in his right hand?"

"Yes."

"What'd you do then?" Brown asked. "After he was gone."

"I came over here and told the doorman what I'd just seen."

"I called nine-eleven right away," the doorman said.

"You're sure this wasn't a woman, huh?" Carella asked.

"Positive."

"Okay," Carella said, and thought maybe it was only the reference to Tony Perkins in drag.

"I called nine-eleven right away," the doorman said again.

They found Betsy Schumacher the very next day.

Or rather, she found them.

It was still raining.

Brown and Carella were just about to leave for the day. The shift had been relieved at a quarter to four, and it was a quarter past when she came into the squadroom, dripping wet in a yellow rain slicker and a yellow rain hat, straight blonde hair cascading down on either side of her face.

"I'm Betsy Schumacher," she said. "I understand you've been looking for me."

Betsy Schumacher. Arthur Schumacher's alienated daughter. Whom they'd been trying to locate ever since her father's murder, because—for one reason—she'd been named in his will as the legatee of twenty-five percent of his estate.

So here she was.

As blue-eyed as the blue out of which she'd appeared.

"I read about Margaret in the newspaper," she said.

So had everyone else in this city. The newspapers were clearly having a ball with this one. First a beautiful blonde bimbo in a love nest, then her elderly lover, and then the elderly lover's equally beautiful and equally blonde wife. Such was the stuff of which American headlines were made. But when you're in love, the whole world's blonde, Carella figured, because here was yet another beauty wearing neither lipstick nor eye shadow, the slicker and hat a brighter yellow than her honey-colored hair, cornflower eyes wide in a face the shape of her sister's and—come to think of it—her mother's as well. Betsy Schumacher, how do you do?

"I figured I'd better come up here," she said, and shrugged elaborately. "Before you started getting ideas."

The shrug seemed all the more girlish in that she was thirty-nine years old. This was no teenager standing here, despite the dewy complexion and the freshness of her looks. Her own father had called her an aging hippie, and her mother had corroborated the description: *Betsy is a thirty-nine-year-old hippie, and this is July. She could be anywhere.*

"Where've you been, Miss Schumacher?" Carella asked.

"Vermont," she said.

"When did you go up there?"

"Last Sunday. Right after the funeral. I had some heavy thinking to do."

He wondered if she'd been thinking about how she would spend her money.

"How'd you learn we were looking for you?"

"Mom told me."

"Did she call you, or what?" Brown asked.

A trick question. Gloria Sanders had told them she didn't know where her daughter was.

"I called *her*," Betsy said. "When I read about Margaret."

"When was that?"

"Yesterday."

"How'd your mother feel about it?"

"Gleeful," Betsy said, and grinned mischievously. "So did I, in fact."

"And she told you we wanted to see you?"

"Yeah. So I figured I'd better come on down. Okay to take off my coat?"

"Sure," Carella said.

She unclipped the fasteners on the front of the slicker and slipped it off her shoulders and arms. She was wearing a faded denim mini, somewhat tattered sandals, and a thin, white cotton T-shirt with the words SAVE THE WHALES printed across its front. She wasn't wearing a bra. Her nipples puckered the words SAVE on her right breast and WHALE on her left breast, the word THE falling someplace on her neutral sternum. She did not take off the hat. It sat floppily on her head, like a wilted wet sunflower, its petals framing her face. She looked around for a place to hang the slicker, spotted a coatrack near the water cooler in the corner, carried the slicker to it, hung it on one of the pegs, had herself a drink of water while she was at it—bending over the fountain, denim skirt tightening over her buttocks—and then came back to where the detectives were waiting for her. There was a faint secret smile on her face, as if she knew they'd been admiring her ass, which in fact they had been doing, married men though they both were.

"So what would you like to know?" she asked, sitting in the chair beside Carella's desk and crossing her legs, the skirt riding up recklessly. "I didn't kill the bimbo, and I didn't kill *Mrs*. Schumacher, either . . ."

Same malicious twist to the dead woman's true and courteous title . . .

"And I *certainly* didn't kill the fucking mutt."

Poor Amos, Brown thought.

"So who else is left?" she asked, and grinned in what Carella could only interpret as a wise-ass hippie challenge of the sort she'd extended all too often when the world was young and nobody wore a bra and everybody had long blonde hair and all cops were pigs.

"Nobody, I guess," he said, and turned to Brown. "Can you think of anybody else, Artie?"

"Gee, no," Brown said. "Unless maybe her father."

"Oh, right, right," Carella said. "*He* was killed, too, wasn't he? Your father."

Betsy scowled at him.

"But let's start with the first one," Carella said. "The bimbo. Susan Brauer. That would've been Tuesday night, the seventeenth. Can you tell us . . .?"

"Am I going to need a lawyer here?" she asked.

"Not unless you want one," Carella said. "But that's entirely up to you."

"Because if you're going to ask me where I was and all that shit . . ."

"Yes, we're going to ask you where you were," Brown said.

And all that shit, he thought.

"Then maybe I need one," she said.

"Why? Were you someplace you shouldn't have been?"

"I don't remember where I was. I don't even know *when* that was."

"Today's Saturday, the twenty-eighth," Carella said. "This would've been eleven days ago."

"A Tuesday night," Brown said.

"The seventeenth," Carella said.

"Then I was in Vermont."

"I thought you went up to Vermont after your father's funeral."

"I went *back* up. I've been there since the beginning of July."

"Did your mother know this?"

"I don't tell my mother everything I do."

"Where do you go up there?" Brown asked.

"I have a little place my father gave me after the divorce. I think he was trying to win me over. He gave me this little house up there."

"Where?"

"Vermont. I told you."

"*Where* in Vermont?"

"Green River. It's a little house in the woods, I think one of his clients gave it to him years ago, instead of a fee. This was even before he married Mom. So it was just sitting there in the woods, practically falling apart, and he asked me if I wanted it. I said sure. Never look a gift horse, right?"

Carella was thinking she wouldn't even give her father the time of day, but she accepted a little house from him.

"Anyway, I go up there a lot," she said. "Get away from the rat race."

"And your mother doesn't know this, huh?" Brown said. "That you go up to Vermont a lot to get away from the rat race."

"I'm sure my mother knows I go up to Vermont."

"But she didn't know you went up there on the first day of July . . ."

"The *beginning* of July. The *fifth*, actually. And I don't remember whether I told her or not."

"But you were up there when Susan Brauer was killed, is that right?"

"If she was killed on the seventeenth, then I was up there, yes."

"Anybody with you?"

"No, I go up there alone."

"How do you get there?" Carella asked.

"By car."

"Your own car? Or do you rent one?"

"I have my own car."

"So you drive up there to Vermont in your own car."

"Yes."

"All alone?"

"Yes."

"How long does it take you to get there?"

"Three, three-and-a-half hours, depending on traffic."

"And it takes the same amount of time to get back, I suppose."

"Yes."

"When did you come back down again?"

"What do you mean?"

"You said you went up on the fifth . . ."

"Oh. Yes. I came down again right after my sister called me."

"When was that?"

"The day after my father got killed. She called to give me the news."

"That he'd been murdered."

"Yes."

"Then your sister also knew you were in Vermont."

"Yes."

"Both your mother *and* your sister have the number up there."

"Yes, they both have the number."

"So the day after your father got killed . . ."

"Yes."

"Your sister called you."

"Yes."

"That would've been Saturday, the twenty-first."

"Whenever."

"What time would that have been?"

"She called early in the morning."

"And you say you came back to the city right after she called?"

"Well, I called my mother first. After I spoke to my sister."

Which checked with what Gloria Sanders had told them.

"What'd you talk about?"

"About whether or not I should go to the funeral."

Which also checked.

"And what'd you decide?"

"That I'd go."

"So what time would you say you left Vermont?"

"I had breakfast, and I dressed and packed some things . . . it must've been eleven o'clock or so before I got out of there."

"Drove straight back to the city, did you?"

"Yes."

"Took you three, three-and-a-half hours, right?" Brown said.

"About that, yes."

They were both thinking that Vermont wasn't the end of the world. You could get up there in three hours. You could be here in the city killing somebody the night before and you could be back in Vermont taking a telephone call the next morning. People could see you coming and going in Vermont, into a grocery story, into a bakery, into a bookshop, into a bar, and no one would know whether you were in residence in your little house in the woods or commuting back and forth to the city to do murder.

"Did you know that under the provisions of your father's will, you would inherit twenty-five percent of his estate?" Carella asked.

"Yes, I knew that."

"How'd you happen to know?"

"Mom constantly told us."

"What do you mean by constantly?"

"Well, all the time. *Certainly* while they were negotiating the settlement . . . we weren't children, you know, this was only two years ago. Mom told us she wouldn't give him a divorce unless he agreed to put both of us in the will. Me and Lois. For half the estate. Together, that is. Sharing half the estate. So we knew about it at the time, and since then she's repeated the story again and again, with a great deal of pleasure and pride. Because she felt she'd done something very good for us. Which she had.''

''Where were you on Friday night, Miss Schumacher?'' Brown asked.

''Vermont. I told you.''

The hippie grin again. Her mother's daughter for sure. No tricks, please. Just the facts, ma'am.

''You weren't down here in the city?''

''No. I was in Vermont.''

''Anyone with you?''

''I told you. I go up there alone.''

''I didn't ask if you went up there with anyone,'' Brown said pleasantly. ''I asked if anyone was with you on the night Margaret Schumacher was killed.''

''No. I was home alone. Reading.''

''Reading what?'' Carella asked.

''I don't remember. I read a lot.''

''What kind of books?''

''Fiction mostly.''

''Do you read murder mysteries?''

''No. I *hate* murder mysteries.''

''You said you read about Margaret Schumacher's murder in the newspaper . . .''

''Yes.''

''Local Vermont paper?''

''No. I picked up one of our papers at the . . .''

''*Our* papers?''

''Yes. From here in the city. We *do* get them up there, you know.''

''And that's when you saw the headline . . .''

''It wasn't a headline. Not in the paper I bought. It was on page four of the metropolitan section.''

''A story about Mrs. Schumacher's murder.''

"Yes. *Mrs*. Schumacher's murder."

Repeating the title scornfully, so that it sounded dirty somehow.

"And you say you felt gleeful . . ."

"Well, perhaps that was too strong a word to use."

"What word would you use now?"

"Happy. The story made me happy."

"Reading about a woman's brutal murder . . ."

"Yes."

" . . made you happy."

"Yes."

"She'd been shot repeatedly in the head and chest . . ."

"Right."

"And reading about this made you happy."

"Yes," Betsy said. "I'm glad someone killed her."

Both detectives looked at her.

"She was a rotten bitch who wrecked our lives. I used to pray she'd fall out a window or get run over by a bus, but it never happened. Well, now someone got her. Someone gave it to her good. And yes, that makes me happy. In fact, it makes me *gleeful*, yes, that *is* the right word, I'm overflowing with *glee* because she's dead. I only wish she'd been shot a *dozen* times instead of just four."

There was a satisfied smile on her face.

You couldn't argue with a smile like that.

You could only wonder whether the newspapers had mentioned that Margaret Schumacher had been shot four times.

It was getting late.

They'd been talking in the living room of the house Angela had shared with Tommy until just recently, three-year-old Tess asleep in the back room, Angela telling her brother she was dying for a cigarette but her doctor had forbidden her to smoke while she was pregnant. Carella thought suddenly of Gloria Sanders, who'd been dying for a smoke when they'd talked to her at the hospital.

He could not shake the persistent feeling that Penn Halligan had been describing a *woman* running through the rain. Or had the image been created by the foreknowledge that three women had survived Arthur Schumacher: two daughters, and an ex-wife who hated him.

"But it won't be long now," Angela said.

"You should *stay* off them," Carella said.

"Tough habit to kick," she said, and shrugged.

His father hadn't known that Angela smoked. Or at least had *pretended* not to know. Carella could remember one Sunday afternoon when all the family was gathered together . . . this was when he himself still smoked. A long time ago. Shortly after Angela and Tommy got married. An Easter Sunday, was it? A Christmas? The entire family gathered. They'd just finished the big afternoon meal—with Italian families, every meal was a feast—and he patted down his pockets, and realized he was out of cigarettes, and he went across the room to where Angela was sitting at the old upright piano, playing all the songs she'd learned as a little girl, a grown woman now with a husband, and he'd said, "Sis? Have you got a cigarette?" And Tony Carella, sitting in an easy chair listening to his daughter playing, suddenly shook his head and put his finger to his lips, shushing Carella, letting Carella know that his father wasn't supposed to know his darling daughter smoked, the sly old hypocrite.

Carella smiled with the memory.

"They say it's easier to kick heroin than nicotine," Angela said.

"But you've *already* kicked it," Carella said. "Eight, nine months now, that's kicking it."

"I *still* want a cigarette."

"So do I."

"And I'm gonna *have* one. As soon as the baby's born . . ."

"I wish you wouldn't," he said.

"Why the hell *not*?" she asked.

And suddenly she was crying.

"Hey," he said.

She shook her head.

"Hey, come on."

Raised her hand in mild protest, still shaking her head, no, please leave me alone. He went to her, anyway. Put his arm around her. Handed her his handkerchief.

"Here," he said. "Dry your eyes."

"Thanks," she said.

She dried her eyes.

"Okay to blow in it?" she asked.

"Since when do you ask?"

She blew her nose. She sniffed some more. She dried her eyes again.

"Thanks," she said again, and handed the handkerchief back to him.

"Cigarettes mean that much to you, huh?"

"Not cigarettes," she said, and shook her head.

"Tell me," he said.

"I just figured what the hell's the use? Smoke my brains out, die of cancer, who cares?"

"Me, for one."

"Yeah, you," she said. She seemed on the edge of tears again.

"Why do you think Tommy's having an affair?" he asked.

"Because I know he is."

"*How* do you know?"

"Just by the way he's been acting lately. I haven't found any handkerchiefs with lipstick on them, and he doesn't stink of perfume when he comes home, but . . . ."

"Yes, but what?"

"I just *know*, Steve. He *behaves* differently. His mind is someplace else, he's got another woman, I just know it."

"How is he behaving differently?"

"He's just *different*. He tosses and turns all night long . . . as if he's thinking of someone else, can't get her out of his mind, can't fall asleep . . ."

"What else?"

"I'll be talking to him and his mind starts wandering. And I look at him and I just know he can't concentrate on what I'm saying because he's thinking of *her*."

Carella nodded.

"And he . . . well, I don't want to talk about it."

"Talk about it," Carella said.

"No, really, I don't want to, Steve."

"Angela . . ."

"All right, he doesn't want to make love anymore, all right?" she said. "Oh!" she said and suddenly grabbed for her belly. "Oh!" she said again.

"Sis?" he said.

"Oh!"

"What is it?"

"I think . . . oh!"

"Is it the baby?"

"Yes, I . . . oh!" she said, and clutched for her middle again.

"Which hospital?" he said at once.

From the squadroom, he'd have used the TDD on his desk, "talking" to Teddy directly, tapping out the letters of his message on the machine's keyboard, hitting the GA key for Go Ahead, reading her message in return. But he was calling home from the hospital waiting room, and public telephones hadn't yet caught up with state-of-the-art technology. Fanny Knowles answered the phone.

"Carella household," she said.

He visualized her standing at the kitchen counter, fiftyish and feisty, hair tinted a fiery red, wearing a pince-nez and standing with one hand on her hip as if challenging whoever was calling to say this was police business that would intrude on the sanctity of the home.

"Fanny, it's me," he said.

"Yes, Steve," she said.

"I'm at Twin Oaks, Teddy knows the hospital, it's where the twins were born."

"Yes, Steve."

"Can you tell her to catch a cab and come on over? Angela's already in the delivery room."

"Do you want me to call your mother?"

"No, I'll do that now. Twin Oaks, the maternity wing."

"I've got it."

"Thank you, Fanny. Everything all right?"

"Yes, fine. I'll tell her right now."

"Thanks," he said, and hung up, and fished in his pocket for another quarter, and then dialed his mother's number.

"Hello?" she said.

Her voice the same dull monotone he'd heard ever since his father's death.

"Mama, it's me," he said. "Steve."

"Yes, honey."

"I'm here with Angela at the hospital . . ."

"Oh my God!" she said.

"Everything's all right, she's in the delivery room now, do you want to . . .?"

"I'll be right there," she said.

"Twin Oaks Hospital, the maternity wing," he said. "Call a taxi."

"Right away," she said, and hung up.

He put the receiver back on the hook and went to sit next to a balding man who looked extremely worried.

"Your first one?" the man asked.

"It's my sister," Carella said.

"Oh," the man said. "It's my first one."

"It'll be all right, don't worry," Carella said. "This is a good hospital."

"Yeah," the man said.

"My twins were born here," Carella said.

"Yeah," the man said.

All those years ago, Carella thought. Meyer and Hawes pacing the floor with him, Meyer consoling him, telling him he'd been through it three times already, not to worry. Teddy up there in the delivery room for almost an hour. Twins. Nowadays . . .

"We're having a boy," the balding man said.

"That's nice," Carella said.

"*She* wanted a girl."

"Well, boys are nice, too," Carella said.

"What do you have?"

"One of each," Carella said.

"We're going to call him Stanley," the man said. "After my father."

"That's nice," Carella said.

"*She* wanted to call him Evan."

"Stanley is a very nice name," Carella said.

"I think so," the man said.

Carella looked up at the clock.

Up there for twenty minutes already. He suddenly remembered Tommy. Tommy should be here. Whatever problems they were having, Tommy should be here. He went to the phone again, took out his notebook, found the number for the room over the garage, and dialed it. He let it ring a dozen times. No answer. He hung up and went to sit with the worried balding man again.

"What's she having? Your sister."

"I don't know."

"Didn't she have all the tests?"

"I guess so. But she didn't tell me what . . ."

"She should have had the tests. The tests tell you everything."

"I'm sure she must have had them."

"Is she married?"

"Yes."

"Where's her husband?"

"I just tried to reach him," Carella said.

"Oh," the man said, and looked at him suspiciously.

Teddy got there some ten minutes later. The man watched them as they exchanged information in sign language, fingers moving swiftly. Signing always attracted a crowd. You could get a crocodile coming out of a sewer in downtown Isola, it wouldn't attract as big a crowd as signing did. The man watched, fascinated.

She was asking him if he'd called his mother.

He told her he had.

I could have picked her up on the way, she signed.

"Easier this way," he said, signing at the same time.

The man watched goggle-eyed. All those flying fingers had taken his mind off his worries about his imminent son Stanley.

Carella's mother came into the waiting room a few minutes later. She looked concerned. She had come to this same hospital eleven days earlier, to identify her husband in the morgue. Now her daughter was here in the delivery room—and sometimes things went wrong in the delivery room.

"How is she?" she asked. "Hello, sweetie," she said to Teddy, and kissed her on the cheek.

"She went up about forty minutes ago," Carella said, looking at the wall clock.

"Where's Tommy?" his mother said.

"I've been trying to reach him," Carella said.

A look passed between him and Teddy, but his mother missed it.

Teddy signed *Forty minutes isn't very long.*

"She says forty minutes isn't very long," he repeated for his mother.

"I know," his mother said, and patted Teddy on the arm.

"Did Angela tell you what it would be?" Carella asked.

"No. Did she tell you?"

"No."

"Secrets," his mother said, and rolled her eyes. "With her, everything's always a secret. From when she was a little girl, remember?"

"I remember," he said.

"Secrets," she said, repeating the word for Teddy, turning to face her so she could read her lips. "My daughter. Always secrets."

Teddy nodded.

"Mr. Gordon?"

They all turned.

A doctor was standing there in a bloodstained surgical gown. The worried balding man jumped to his feet.

"Yes?" he said.

"Everything's fine," the doctor said.

"Yes?"

"Your wife's fine . . ."

"Yes?"

"You have a fine, healthy boy."

"Thank you," the man said, beaming.

"You'll be able to see them both in ten minutes or so, I'll send a nurse down for you."

"Thank you," the man said.

Angela's doctor came down half an hour later. He looked very tired.

"Everything's fine," he said.

They always started with those words . . .

"Angela's fine," he said.

Always assured you about the mother first . . .

"And the twins are fine, too."

"Twins?" Carella said.

"Two fine healthy little girls," the doctor said.

"Secrets," his mother said knowingly. And then, to Carella, "Where's Tommy?"

"I'll try to find him," Carella said.

He drove first to the house Tommy had inherited when his parents died. No lights were showing in the room over the garage. He climbed the steps, anyway, and knocked on the door. It was only a quarter past eleven, but perhaps Tommy was already in bed. There was no answer. Carella went back down to the car, thought for a moment before he started the engine, and then started the long drive downtown.

He hoped Tommy would not be with his girlfriend on the night his twin daughters were born.

The playground across the street from the brownstone was deserted. Raindrops plinked on the metal swings and slides. This was an alternate-side-of-the-street parking zone. Water ran in sheets off the streamlined surfaces of the cars lining the curb that bordered the fenced-in playground. Carella found a spot dangerously close to a fire hydrant, threw down the visor with its police department logo, locked the car, and began running up the street in the rain.

He'd been a cop too long a time not to have noticed and recognized at once the two men sitting in a sedan parked across the street from the brownstone. He went over to the car, knocked on the passenger-side window. The window rolled down.

"Yeah?" the man sitting there said.

"Carella, the Eight-Seven," he said, showing his shield, shoulders hunched against the rain. "What's happening?"

"Get in," the man said.

Carella opened the rear door and climbed in out of the rain. Rain beat on the roof of the car. Rainsnakes trailed down the windows.

"Peters, the Two-One," the man behind the wheel said.

"Macmillen," his partner said.

Both men were unshaven. It was a look detectives cultivated when they were on a plant. Made them look overworked and underpaid. Which they were, anyway, even without the beard stubbles.

"We got cameras rolling in the van up ahead," Peters said, nodding with his head toward the windshield. Through the falling rain, Carella could make out a green van parked just ahead of the car. The words HI-HAT DRY CLEANING were lettered across the back panel, just below the painted-over rear window.

"Been sitting the building for a week now," Macmillen said.

"Which one?"

"The brownstone," Peters said.

"Why? What's going on over there?" Carella asked.

"Cocaine's going on over there," Macmillen said.

10

It was Monday morning, and all the Monday-morning quarterbacks were out. Or at least one of them. His name was Lieutenant Peter Byrnes, and he was telling his assembled detectives what he hoped they should have known by now.

"When you're stuck," he said, "you go back to the beginning. *You* start where *it* started."

He was sitting behind his desk in the corner office he warranted as commander of the 87th Squad, a compact man with silvering hair and no-nonsense flinty-blue eyes. There were six detectives in the office with him. Four of them had already given him rundowns on the various cases they were investigating. The *big* case had waited patiently in the wings till now. The big case was multiple murder, the tap-dancing, singing, piano-playing star of this here little follies. Like a network television executive lecturing six veteran screenwriters on basics like motivation and such, the lieutenant was telling his men how to conduct their business.

"This case started with the dead girl," he said.

Susan Brauer. The dead girl. Twenty-two years old, a girl for sure, though Arthur Schumacher had considered her a woman for sure.

"And that's where *you* gotta start all over again," Byrnes said. "With the dead girl."

"You want my opinion," Andy Parker said, "you already *got* your perp."

Carella was thinking the same thing.

"Your perp's the hippie daughter," Parker said.

Exactly, Carella thought.

Looking at Parker in his rumpled suit, wrinkled shirt, and stained tie, his cheeks and jowls unshaven, Carella remembered for the hundredth time the two cops planted outside that brownstone downtown. He still hadn't talked to his brother-in-law because he hadn't yet figured out how the hell to handle this. Nor had he yet told Angela that her husband's sudden behavioral changes had nothing whatever to do with sex with a perfect stranger, but were instead attributable to what most cocaine addicts considered far more satisfying than even the *best* sex. He was hoping neither Peters nor Macmillen had pictures of Tommy marching in and out of a house under surveillance for drugs; how could he have been so goddamn dumb?

". . . the will for a quarter of the estate to begin with," Parker was saying. "Reason enough to kill the old . . ."

"That isn't starting with the dead girl," Byrnes reminded him.

"The dead girl was a smoke screen, pure and simple," Parker said breezily and confidently.

"Was *she* in the will?" Kling asked. "The dead girl?"

His mind was on Eileen Burke. On Monday mornings, it was sometimes difficult to get back to the business at hand, especially when the business happened to be crime every day of the year.

"No," Brown said. "Only people in the will are the two daughters, the present wife . . ."

"Now dead *herself*," Parker said knowingly.

". . . the vet, and the pet-shop lady," Brown concluded.

"For *how* much?" Hawes asked. "Those two?"

"Ten grand each," Carella said.

Hawes nodded in dismissal.

"The point is," Parker said, "between them, the two kids are up for fifty percent of the estate. If *that* ain't a good-enough motive . . ."

"*How* much did you say?" Hawes asked again. "The estate?"

"What the hell are *you* this morning?" Parker asked. "An accountant?"

"I want to know what the estate was, okay?" Hawes said.

"Supposed to be a lot of money," Carella said. "We don't have an exact figure."

"*Whatever* it is," Parker said, and again nodded knowingly, "it's enough to get the hippie daughter salivating."

This was a big word for him, *salivating*. He looked around as if expecting approval for having used it.

"What's this about she knew four bullets did the wife?" Willis asked.

"Yeah," Carella said.

"Was that in the papers?"

"No, but it was on one of the television shows."

"Who gave it out?" Byrnes asked.

"We're trying to find out now," Brown said. "It might've been the M&M's. Or *anybody* from Homicide, for that matter."

"Homicide," Byrnes said, and shook his head sourly.

"That don't mean *she* didn't put those four slugs in the wife herself," Parker said. "Get rid of her, too, make it a clean sweep. She kills the old man to get her quarter of the pot . . ."

"Assuming she knew that," Byrnes said.

"She knew it, Pete."

"From when she was on her mother's knee," Parker said.

"Well, both daughters were grown at the time of the divorce, this was only two years ago. But they knew they were in the will for a quarter."

"Who gets the wife's share of the estate?" Kling asked. "Now that she's dead."

"Her will leaves it to a brother in London."

"Sole heir?"

"Yeah. But we called him and that's where he is, London. Hasn't visited the States in four years."

"Forget him," Parker said, "London's a million miles away. The hippie daughter was after the money, case closed."

"Then why'd she kill the other two?" Kling asked.

"Hatred, pure and simple," Parker said.

"You should hear the way she says, '*Mrs.* Schumacher,' " Carella said.

"The *first* wife, too," Brown said. "She says it the same way. *Mrs.* Schumacher. She hated both of them. The old man, the new wife . . ."

"So'd the hippie daughter," Parker said, defending his case.

"No, wait a minute, don't let go of that so fast," Willis said. "The old lady hates Schumacher . . ."

"Right," Kling said, nodding.

"So she not only wipes out *him,* but also all the women in his life."

"Kills two birds with one stone," Kling said. "Gets the mistress *and* the present wife . . ."

"*Three* birds," Hawes corrected. "When you count Schumacher himself."

"Well, yeah, but I'm not talking body count. What I mean is she knocks over the women, and at the same time she puts her daughters in line for the cash."

"Yeah, but she has to kill Schumacher to do that."

"Well, sure."

"Is all I'm saying," Hawes said.

"Sure."

"How about the three of them did it in *concert,*" Willis suggested. "Maybe we're looking at *three* killers instead of just one. Like the Orient Express."

"What the fuck's the Orient Express?" Parker asked.

"You know, Agatha Christie."

"Who the fuck's that, Agatha Christie?" Parker asked.

"Forget it," Willis said.

"Anyway, that was more than three people," Hawes said.

"And the younger daughter loved him," Carella said. "I don't think she'd have . . ."

"*Claims* she loved him," Willis said.

"Well, that's true, but . . ."

"Butter wouldn't melt," Brown said.

"Those are sometimes the worst kind," Willis said. "And I *know* it was more than three people, Cotton. I was just using it as an example."

"What is this, the public library?" Byrnes asked.

"Huh?" Parker said, looking bewildered.

"What about this pet-shop lady?" Kling asked.

"What about her?"

"Did *she* know she was in the will?"

"Claims she knew nothing about it," Carella said.

"Seemed genuinely surprised," Brown said.

"Anyway," Hawes said, "who'd kill somebody for a lousy ten grand?"

"*Me,*" Parker said, and everyone laughed.

"Besides, she hardly knew the guy," Brown said.

"Just gave him occasional advice on the pooch," Carella said.

"Also she knew the dog from when he was a pup," Hawes said. "Whoever blew away that mutt was somebody who hated him."

"Right, the hippie daughter," Parker said, nodding. "I was you, I'd pick her up, work her over with a rubber hose."

Everybody laughed again. Except Byrnes.

"Where'd that twelve grand come from?" he asked.

"What twelve grand?" Hawes said.

"The twelve grand in the cash box in her closet," Byrnes said. "And how'd the killer get in the apartment?"

"Well, we don't actually . . ."

"Anybody talk to the doorman who was on?"

"Yes, sir," Kling said. "Me and Artie."

"So what'd he say?"

"He didn't see anybody suspicious."

"Did he or did he not let anyone in that apartment?"

"He said there's deliveries all the time, he couldn't remember whether anyone went upstairs or not."

"He couldn't remember," Byrnes repeated flatly.

"Yes, sir."

"He couldn't remember."

"Yes, sir, that's what he said. He couldn't remember."

"Did you try to *prod* his memory?"

"Yes, sir, we spent an hour, maybe more, talking to him. His statement's in the file."

"He could hardly speak English," Brown said. "He's from the Middle East someplace."

"Talk to him again," Byrnes said. "Go back to the beginning."

The beginning was the dead girl.

Blue eyes open. Throat slit. Face repeatedly slashed. Nineteen, twenty years old, long blonde hair and startling blue eyes, wide open. Young beautiful body under the slashed black kimono with poppies the color of blood.

They were in the penthouse apartment again, just as they'd been on the night of July seventeenth, standing in the same room where the girl had lain before the coffee table—martini on the table, lemon twist curled on the bottom of the glass, paring knife on the floor beside her, blade covered with blood—bleeding from what appeared to be a hundred cuts and gashes.

This time the doorman was with them.

His name was Ahmad Something. Carella had written down the last name, but he couldn't pronounce it. Short and squat and dust-colored, narrow mustache over his upper lip, looking like a member of the palace guard in his gray uniform with its red trim. Squinting, straining hard to understand what they were saying.

"Did you let anyone into the apartment?"

"Dunn remembah," he said.

Thick Middle Eastern accent. They had not asked him where he was from. Carella was wondering if they'd need a translator here.

"*Try* to remember," he said.

"Many peckages always," he said, and shrugged helplessly.

"This would've been sometime in the late afternoon, early evening."

The medical examiner had set the postmortem interval at two to three hours. That would've put the stabbing at sometime between five and six o'clock. The doorman looked only puzzled. Carella guessed he was unfamiliar with the words "afternoon" and "evening."

"Five o'clock," he said. "Six o'clock. Were you working then?"

"Yes, working," the doorman said.

"Okay, did anyone come to the door and ask for Miss Brauer?"

"Dunn remembah."

"This is important," Brown said.

"Yes."

"This woman was killed."

"Yes."

"We're trying to find whoever killed her."

"Yes."

"So will you help us, please? Will you try to remember whether you let anyone go up?"

There was something in his eyes. Carella caught it first, Brown caught it a split second later.

"What are you afraid of?" Carella asked.

The doorman shook his head.

"Tell us."

"Saw nobody," he said.

But he had. They knew he had.

"What is it?" Carella asked.

The doorman shook his head again.

"You want to come to the station house with us?" Brown said.

"Hold off a second, Artie," Carella said.

Good Cop/Bad Cop. No need to signal for the curtain to go up, they both knew the act by heart.

"Hold off, *sheeee*-it," Brown said, doing his Big Bad Leroy imitation. "The man here is lying in his teeth."

"The man's afraid, is all," Carella said. "Isn't that right, sir?"

The doorman nodded. Then he shook his head. Then he nodded again.

"Let's go, mister," Brown said, and reached for the handcuffs hanging from his belt.

"Hold off, Artie," Carella said. "What is it, sir?" he asked gently. "Please tell me why you're so afraid."

The doorman looked as if he might burst into tears at any moment. His little mustache quivered, his brown eyes moistened.

"Sit down, sir," Carella said. "Artie, put those goddamn cuffs away!"

The doorman sat on the black leather sofa. Carella sat beside him. Brown scowled and hung the cuffs on his belt again.

"Now tell me," Carella said gently. "Please."

What it was, the doorman was an illegal alien. He had purchased a phony green card and social-security card for twenty bucks each, and he was scared to death that if he got involved in any of this, the authorities would find out about him and send him back home. Back home was Iran. He knew how Americans felt about Iranians. If he got involved in this, they would start blaming him for what had happened to the girl. He just didn't want to get involved. All of this in a broken English on the edge of tears. Carella was thinking that for an illegal alien, Ahmad was learning very fast; *nobody* in this city wanted to get involved.

"So tell me," he said, "*did* you send someone up to Miss Brauer's apartment?"

Ahmad had said everything he was going to say. Now he stared off into space like a mystic.

"We won't bother you about the green card," Carella said. "You don't have to worry about the green card. Just tell us what happened that afternoon, okay?"

Ahmad kept staring.

"Okay, you little shit," Brown said, "off we go," and he reached for the cuffs again.

"Well, I did my best," Carella said, and sighed heavily. "He's all yours, Artie."

"Vittoria," Ahmad said.

"What?" Carella said.

"Her name," Ahmad said.

"Whose name?"

"The woman who comes."

"What woman who comes?" Brown asked.

"That day."

"A woman came that day?"

"Yes."

"Say her name again."

"Vittoria."

"Are you saying Victoria?"

"Yes. Vittoria."

"Her name was Victoria?"

"Yes."

"Victoria *what*?"

"Seegah."

"What?"

"Seegah."

"How are you spelling that?"

Ahmad looked at them blankly.

"How's he spelling that, Steve?"

"Is that an *S*?" Carella asked.

Ahmad shrugged. "Seegah," he said.

"What'd she look like?"

"Tall," Ahmad said. "Tin."

"Thin?"

"Tin, yes."

"White or black?"

"White?"

"What color hair?"

"I dunn know. She is wearing . . ."

He searched for the word, gave up, mimed pulling a kerchief over his head and tying it under his chin.

"A scarf?" Brown asked.

"Yes."

"What color eyes?" Carella asked.

"She has glasses."

"She was wearing glasses?"

"Yes."

"Well, couldn't you see the color of . . .?"

"Dark glasses."

"Sunglasses? She was wearing sunglasses?"

"Yes."

"What else was she wearing?"

"Pants. Shirt."

"What color?"

"Sand color."

"What'd she say?"

"Says Vittoria Seegah. Tell Miss Brauer."

"Tell her what?"

"Vittoria Seegah here."

"*Did* you tell her?"

"Tell her, yes."

"Then what?"

"She tell me send up."

"And *did* she go up?"

"Yes. Go elevator."

"How are you spelling that?" Brown asked again. "S-E-E-G?"

"Seegah," Ahmad said.

"What time was this?" Carella asked. "That she went upstairs?"

"Five. Little more."

"A little past five?"

"Yes. Little past."

"Did you see her when she came down?"

"Yes."

"When was that?"

"Six."

"Exactly six?"

"Little past."

"So she was up there a full hour, huh?"

Ahmad went blank.

"Did you look at your watch?"

"No."

"You're just estimating?"

The blank look.

"Any blood on her clothes?"

"No."

"What else do you remember about her?"

"Bag. Market bag."

"She was carrying a bag?"

"Yes."

"A *what* bag?" Brown asked.

"Market bag."

"You mean a shopping bag?"

"Yes. Shopping bag."

"Did you see what was in the bag?"

"No."

"Went upstairs with it?"

"Yes."

"Came back down with it?"

"Yes."

"Can you try spelling that name for us?" Carella asked.

Ahmad went blank again.

Brown shook his head. "Seeger," he said.

Which was close, but—as they say—no see-gah.

There were thirty-eight Seegers, Seigers, and Siegers listed in the telephone directories for all five sections of the city, but none of them was a Victoria. There were eight Seagers and eleven Seagrams. Again, no Victorias. There were hundreds and hundreds of Seegals and Segals and Segels and Seigals and Scigels and Siegels and Slegles and Sigals and Sigalls. One of them was a Victoria and seven of them were listed as merely V's. But the possibility existed that a Victoria might be residing at any one of the addresses listed for a Mark or a Harry or an Isabel or a Whoever.

"It'll take forty cops working round the clock for six months to track down all those people," Byrnes said. "And we don't even know if the Arab was saying the name right."

As a matter of fact, the doorman was an Iranian of the Turkic and not the Arabian ethnic stock—but people in America rarely made such fine distinctions.

They went back to the apartment again that Monday afternoon. Stood there in the living room where Susan Brauer had lain with her wounds shrieking silently to the night, slash and stab marks on her breasts and her belly and the insides of her thighs, blood everywhere, torn white flesh and bright red blood. Shrieking.

The apartment was silent now.

Early-afternoon sunlight slanted through the living room windows.

They had checked her personal address book and had found no listing for any of the Seeger or Seigel variations, Victoria or otherwise. No Seagrams, either. No nothing. No help.

They were now looking for . . .

Anything.

It had come down to that.

They'd been told to go back to the beginning, and that's exactly where they were. Square one. Zero elevation. The lockbox had been found in her bedroom closet. Twelve thousand dollars in that box. In hundred-dollar bills. Now they went back to the closet again, and searched again through the fripperies and furs, the satins and silks, the feathers and frills, the designer dresses and monogrammed suitcases, the rows of high-heeled shoes in patent and lizard and crocodile. They found nothing that Kling and Brown hadn't found the first time around.

So they went through the desk again, and the trash basket under the desk, unwrapping balled pieces of paper, studying each scrap carefully for something they might have missed, yanking a piece of paper free from where it was stuck to a wad of chewing gum, reading the scribbling on it, discarding it as unimportant.

The kitchen was still ahead of them.

The garbage was waiting for them in the pail under the sink. It didn't smell any better than it had thirteen days ago. They dumped it out onto the open newspapers again, and they began going through it bit by bit, the whole noisome lot of it, the moldy bread and rotten bananas, the empty oat-bran box, the coffee grinds and milk container, the soup cans, the crumpled paper towels, the soft smelly melon, the rancid slab of butter, the wilted vegetables and wrinkled summer fruit, the old . . .

"What's that?" Brown asked.

"Where?"

"In the container there."

A flash of white. A piece of crumpled white paper. Lying on the bottom of a round white container that once had held yogurt. The container stank to high heaven. By proximity, so did the crumpled ball of paper, perfectly camouflaged, white on white. It was easy to see how it could have been missed on the first pass. But they weren't missing it this time around.

Carella picked it up.

White as the driven snow.

He unfolded it, smoothed out the wrinkles and creases, transformed it from the wadded ball it had been an instant earlier into a strip of paper some seven inches long and perhaps an inch-and-a-half wide. White. Nothing on it. A plain white strip of paper. He turned it over. There were narrow violet borders on each side of the strip. Printed boldly from border to border across the strip was the figure $2000, repeated some five times over at regularly spaced intervals along its length. Ink-stamped between two of these bold figures were what at first appeared to be cryptic markings:

Is. Bk. & Tr. Co., N.A.
Jeff. Ave. Br.

JUL 09
WL

They were looking at what banks call a currency strap.

The manager of the Jefferson Avenue Branch of the Isola Bank & Trust Company was a man named Avery Granville, fiftyish and balding, wearing a brown, tropical-weight suit, a beige button-down shirt, and an outrageous green-and-orange striped tie. With all the intensity of an archeologist studying a suspect papyrus scroll, he scrutinized the narrow violet-bordered strip of paper and then looked up at last and said, "Yes, that's one of our straps," and smiled pleasantly, as if he'd just approved a loan application.

"What does the 'N.A.' stand for?" Brown asked.

"National Association," Granville said.

"And the WL?"

"Wendell Lawton. He's one of our tellers. Each teller has his own stamp."

"Why's that?" Brown asked.

"Why, because he's accountable for whatever's printed on the strap," Granville said, looking surprised. "The teller's personal stamp is saying he's counted that money and there's fifty dollars in the strap, a hundred dollars, five hundred, whatever's printed on the strap."

"So if this one says two thousand dollars . . ."

"Yes, that's what's printed there. And the violet border confirms the amount. Violet is two thousand dollars."

"Then this wrapper . . ."

"Well, a strap, we call it."

"This strap at one time was wrapped around two thousand dollars."

"Yes. We've got straps for smaller amounts, of course, but this one's a two-thousand-dollar strap."

"How high do they go? The straps?"

"That's the highest, two thousand, usually in hundred-dollar bills. All the straps have different colors, you see. Here at IBT, a thousand-dollar strap is yellow and a five-hundred-dollar one is red, and so on. It varies at different banks, they all have their own color-coding."

"And the date here . . ."

"That's stamped by the teller, too. First he puts his personal stamp on the currency strap, and then he uses a revolving stamp to mark the date."

"I'm assuming this means . . ."

"July ninth, yes. The straps are temporal and disposable, we just stamp in the month and the day, easier that way."

"Is Mr. Lawton here now?"

"I believe so," Granville said, and looked at his watch. "But it's getting late, you know, and he's balancing out right now."

The clock on the wall read ten minutes to four.

"What we're interested in knowing, sir," Brown said, "is just who might have withdrawn that two thousand dollars on the ninth of July. Would there be any record of such a cash transaction? Two thousand dollars withdrawn in cash?"

"Really, gentlemen . . ."

"This is very important to us," Brown said.

"It may be related to the murder of a young woman," Carella said.

"Well, believe me, I'd be happy to help. But . . ."

He looked at his watch again.

"This would mean checking Wendell's teller tape for that day, and . . ."

"What's that?" Carella asked. "A teller tape?"

"A computer printout for all the transactions at his window. It looks somewhat like an adding-machine tape."

"Would this tape show such a withdrawal? Two thousand dollars in cash?"

"Well, yes, if in fact it was made. But, you see . . ."

Another look at his watch.

"A teller can handle as many as two hundred and fifty transactions on any given day of the week. To go through all those . . ."

"Yes, but a two-thousand-dollar cash withdrawal would be unusual, wouldn't it?"

"No, not necessarily. There could be any number of those on any given day."

"Exactly two thousand dollars?" Carella said skeptically. "In cash?"

"Well . . ."

"Could we have a look at the tape, Mr. Granville?" Brown asked. "When your teller's finished with his tally?"

"His balancing out," Granville corrected, and sighed. "I suppose so, yes."

Wendell Lawton was a man in his early thirties, wearing a lightweight blue blazer, a white shirt, and a red tie that made him look like either a television news commentator or a member of the White House staff. He confirmed that this was indeed his stamp on the two-thousand-dollar strap, but he told them that he handled many such bundles of currency every day of the week, and he couldn't possibly be expected to recall whether this particular strap had been handed over the counter to anyone in par—

"But we understand there's a teller's tape," Carella said.

"Well, a *teller* tape, yes," Lawton said, correcting him, and then looking up at the clock; Carella figured it must have have been a long, hard day.

"So perhaps if we looked at that tape . . ."

"Well," he said again.

"This is a homicide we're investigating," Brown said, and fixed Lawton with a scowl that was in itself homicidal.

Lawton's teller tapes were kept in a locked drawer under the counter. His stamp was in that same locked drawer. He unlocked it now, and searched through what he called his proof sheets, looking for and finding at last the one dated the ninth of July. A tape that did indeed look like an adding-machine tape was stapled to it. Lawton had handled a hundred and thirty-seven counter transactions on that day. None of them was for an exact two-thousand-dollar withdrawal in cash. But one of the recorded transactions rang a bell.

The computer printout on the tape showed the date, and then the time, and then:

```
113-807-40    162    772521
SW $2400
```

"The first number is the account number," Lawton explained. "The next number is the number of the IBT branch here, one-sixty-two. The last number is my teller's number."

"What's the SW stand for?" Brown asked.

"Savings withdrawal. Twenty-four hundred is what the customer took out of his account. It's likely that I gave it to him in a two-thousand-dollar strap and four hundred in loose bills outside the strap."

"Can you trace that account number . . ."

"Yes."

". . . and give us the customer's name?"

"If Mr. Granville says it's okay."

Mr. Granville said it was okay to give them the customer's name.

When the computer punched it up, Lawton said, "Oh yes."

"Oh yes what?" Brown asked.

"He's been withdrawing twenty-four hundred in cash every month since March."

The customer's name was Thomas Mott.

He didn't know what they were talking about.

"There must be some mistake," he said.

They always said that.

"No, there's no mistake," Carella said.

They were standing in the center aisle of his antiques shop on Drittel Avenue. A German grandfather clock bonged the hour: six P.M. again. It was always six P.M. here. Mott seemed annoyed that they'd arrived just as he was about to close. Everyone seemed annoyed at having to work a long day today. But the cops had been on the job since seven forty-five this morning.

"You *do* remember withdrawing twenty-four hundred dollars in cash on the ninth of *this* month, don't you?" Carella asked.

"Well, yes, but that was a very special circumstance. A man came to me with a rare William and Mary tankard, and he would accept only cash for it. He didn't know what he had, it was truly a steal. I went to the bank . . ."

"At twelve twenty-seven P.M.," Brown said, showing off.

"Around then," Mott said.

"That's what the teller tape says," Brown said.

"Then that's what it must have been."

"Who's this man with the rare William and Mary tankard?" Carella asked.

"I'm sure I have his name in the file somewhere."

"Then I wish you'd find it for us," Carella said. "And while you're at it, maybe you can look through your records for the withdrawals you made on June first, which was a Friday, and May first, which was a Tuesday, and April second, which was a Monday, and March . . ."

"I don't recall any of those withdrawals," Mott said.

"The teller tapes," Brown reminded him, and smiled pleasantly. "That's when the withdrawals started. In March."

"Twenty-four hundred every month."

"For a total of twelve thousand dollars."

"Remember?"

"Yes, now that you mention it . . ."

They always said that, too.

". . . I do remember withdrawing that amount each month. Against just such an opportunity as the rare William and Mary."

"Ahhh," Brown said.

"Then that explains it," Carella said.

"What it *doesn't* explain," Brown said, "is how that twelve thousand dollars ended up in Susan Brauer's cash box."

Mott blinked.

"Susan Brauer," Brown said, and smiled pleasantly again.

"Remember her?" Carella asked.

"Yes, but . . ."

"She came to your shop every now and then, remember?"

"She was in here on the ninth, remember?"

"To look at a butler's table you'd told her about . . ."

"Yes, of *course* I remember."

"Do you remember giving her twenty-four hundred dollars in cash every month?"

"I never did such a thing."

"Since March," Brown said.

232

"Of course not. Why *would* I have done such a thing?"

"Gee, I don't know," Brown said. "Why would you?"

"The woman was a customer, why would . . .?"

"Mr. Mott . . . we found a currency strap in her apartment . . ."

"I don't know what that is, a currency . . ."

". . . and we've traced it back to your account. The money came from your account, Mr. Mott, there's no question about that. Now do you want to tell us why you were paying Susan Brauer twenty-four hundred dollars a month?"

"For the past five months . . ."

"Two thousand in a strap . . ."

"The rest in loose hundreds . . ."

"Why, Mr. Mott?"

"I didn't kill her," Mott said.

He'd met Susan . . .

He'd called her Susan in deference to her wishes; *Nobody calls me Suzie,* she'd said.

. . . here at the shop when she came in one day in January, just browsing, she'd told him. She was renting an apartment up on Silvermine Oval, and whereas it was furnished, she missed the little touches that made a house a home, and was always on the lookout for anything that might personalize the place. He asked her what sort of things she had in mind, and she told him Oh, nothing *big,* no sideboards or dining-room tables or Welsh dressers or anything like that. But if there was a small footstool, for example, or a beautiful little lamp that she could take with her when she moved out— she was hoping to move to a bigger apartment as soon as certain arrangements had been made, she told him, but apartments were soooo expensive these days, weren't they?

He'd called her one day toward the end of the month, he'd just got a new shipment from England, this was the end of January. He and his wife had spent a week in Jamaica, he remembered calling Susan as soon as they got back because there was a beautiful set of Sheffield candlesticks in the shipment, none of the copper showing through, rare for Sheffields, and they were reasonably priced, and he thought she might like to take a look at them. She came to the shop that afternoon, and fell in love with them, of course, they *were* truly beautiful, but then expressed some doubt as to whether or not they'd fit in with the decor of the apartment, which was essentially modern, leather and stainless, you know, huge throw pillows on the floor, abstract paintings, and so on. So he said he'd be happy to lend her the candlesticks until she made up her mind, and she'd said Ohhh, *would* you? and he had them sent around the very next day.

She called him on a Saturday, this was sometime during the first week in February, and asked if he could possibly stop by to take a look at the candlesticks himself. She'd put them on the dining-room table, which was all glass and stainless, and she thought maybe the brass clashed with the steel, and she really would appreciate his opinion. So he went by at the end of the day.

She had mixed a pitcherful of martinis, she was fond of martinis.

He told her frankly that he thought the candlesticks *did* look out of place on that table, and she thanked him for his honesty and thanked him again for coming all the way uptown, and then she offered him a drink, which he accepted. It was close to six-thirty, he guessed. A very cold Saturday afternoon in February. She put on some music. They had a few drinks. They danced. That's how it started. It all seemed so natural.

Toward the end of February . . .

This was after they'd been to bed together at least half a dozen times . . .

Toward the end of the month, she told him she was having trouble meeting the rent on the apartment and that the owner was threatening to throw her out on the street. She told him the rent was twenty-four hundred a month, which he found absolutely shocking in view of the fact that the mortgage on his house in Locksdale was only *three* thousand and some change a month, and she said it would be a shame if she lost the apartment because it was such a wonderful way for the two of them to be together in such lovely surroundings. She wasn't asking him to *give* her the money . . .

"I didn't know what she meant at first," Mott said.

. . . but only to *lend* it to her, you see.

Temporarily.

The twenty-four hundred.

Just for the March rent, you see. Because she had these modeling jobs coming up, and she'd get paid for them before the April rent was due, and then she'd have enough to pay him back and then some. If he could just lend her the twenty-four hundred. Because she just *loved* being with him and doing all the things they did together, didn't he love the things they did together?

"She was so beautiful," Mott said.

So very beautiful. And remarkably . . .

"Well, in fact, *amazingly* . . ."

He could not find the word. Or perhaps he knew the word and refused to share it with the detectives.

"I gave her the money," he said. "Drew it out of a savings account, handed it over to her. She asked if I wanted a written I.O.U., and I told her of *course* not, don't be ridiculous. Then . . ."

When it came time to pay the April rent, she didn't have the money for that, either, so he'd loaned her another twenty-four hundred, and then another twenty-four in May, and when June came around, he realized this had become a regular thing, he was paying for the rent on her apartment, he was *keeping* her, she was in effect his . . .

"Well, never mind in effect," he said. "That's what she was. My mistress."

Yours and Shumacher's both, Carella thought.

"God, I loved her so much," Mott said.

In July, he and his wife went away for the Fourth . . . well, actually, they'd left the city on the thirtieth of June, which was a Saturday, and spent the whole next week in Baltimore with her sister, didn't get back until the following Sunday. Susan came into the shop the very next day. Monday. The ninth. Came in around lunchtime, wanted to know if he hadn't forgotten a little something? He didn't know what she meant at first. Oh? she said. You don't know? You really don't know? Maybe you think a girl like me just comes along every day of the week, huh? Maybe next time you want me to . . .

"Well, she made a reference to . . . to what we . . . to what we . . . well, what she . . . uh. She said I might . . . she said I ought to think about that the next time I asked her to . . . you know. Because if I was going to forget all about the *rent* coming due, then maybe she should start looking for someone who might enjoy being with her and taking advantage of her that way. She was furious. I'd never seen her like that. I hadn't really thought I was taking advantage of her, I thought she *enjoyed* it. I tried to explain . . ."

He'd tried to explain. It had been the holiday, you see, the Fourth of July, the bank would be closed on Wednesday, anyway, and he'd had to go away with his wife, she *knew* he was married, she *knew* he had a wife. She said did he know how humiliating it was for her to receive a call from the woman who was renting her the apartment, asking her where the *rent* was, did he *realize*? He'd gone to the bank while she waited in the shop . . .

"This *was* around twelve-thirty, the bank's record is correct," he said.

. . . and he'd brought the money back, and all of a sudden she was a different person, the same Susan he'd always known. In fact, right there in the shop she'd . . .

"Well," he said.

They did not ask him what she'd done right there in the shop.

Instead, Carella said, "Where were you on the night she was killed?"

"Home with my wife," Mott said.

Isabelle Mott was a woman in her mid-to-late forties, some five feet seven or eight inches tall, with long straight black hair and dark brown eyes, which combined with the silver-and-turquoise jewelry she was wearing to give her the strikingly attractive look of a native American Indian, which she was not. She was, in fact, of Scotch-Irish ancestry, go figure.

They did not tell her that her husband, Thomas, had been enjoying of late an affair with a beautiful twenty-two-year-old blonde who'd been murdered only eight days after he'd last seen her. They figured there was no sense causing more trouble than already existed. They simply asked if she knew where he'd been on the night of July seventeenth, that would've been a Tuesday night, ma'am. When she asked why they wanted to know, they said what they said to any civilian who wanted to know why certain questions were being asked: Routine investigation, ma'am.

"He was here," she said.

"How do you happen to remember that?" Carella asked.

She had not looked at a calendar, she had not consulted an appointment—

"I was sick in bed that night," she said.

"Uh-huh," Carella said.

"Sick with what, ma'am?" Brown asked.

"Actually, I was recovering from surgery," she said.

"Uh-huh," Carella said.

"What kind of surgery, ma'am?" Brown asked.

"Minor surgery," she said.

"Had you been hospitalized?" Carella asked.

"No. The surgery was done that morning, Tommy came to pick me up that afternoon."

"Where was this surgery done, ma'am?" Brown asked.

Both cops were thinking abortion. It sounded like abortion.

"At Hollingsworth," she said.

A hospital not far from here, in the Three-Two Precinct.

"And what was the nature of the surgery?" Carella asked.

"If you *must* know," Isabelle said, "I had a D and C, okay?"

"I see," Carella said, and nodded.

Brown was thinking that's what they used to call abortions before *Roe* v. *Wade*.

"What time did you get home from the hospital?" Carella asked.

"Around four, four-thirty."

"And you say your husband was with you?"

"Yes."

"Did he leave the house at any time after that?"

"That night, do you mean?"

"Yes. The night of the seventeenth. After you got home from the hospital, did he leave the house at any time?"

"No."

Firm and emphatic.

"He was home all night long?"

"Yes," she said, positively nailing it to the wall.

"Well, thank you," Carella said.

Brown nodded glumly.

The signs on the corner lamppost read respectively Meriden St and Cooper St, white lettering on green, one sign running horizontally in an east-west direction, the other running north-south. Below these, white on blue, was a larger sign that read:

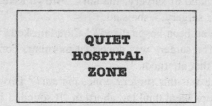

**QUIET
HOSPITAL
ZONE**

Across the street, Farley General's huge illuminated windows glared a harsh yellow-white against a black moonless sky. It was fifteen minutes to midnight, and the street was silent and deserted. An occasional automobile passed, but for the most part the traffic was light; motorists tended to avoid this street because the speed limit here was only twenty miles an hour, and they preferred Averill as an approach to the bridge.

Standing in the shadows of the trees across the street, you could almost hear your own heartbeat, it was that still. Hand around the butt of the gun in the right-hand pocket of the long black coat, black again, wearing black again, the gun butt warm now, though it had felt cool earlier, there in the cool dark of the coat pocket. Warmer now. Palm of the hand somewhat moist on the walnut stock of the gun, but not from nervousness, you did this often enough it didn't make you nervous anymore. Moist with anticipation, the honest sweat of anticipation, expectation. Shoot her dead the moment she came through those doors. *Empty* it in her. *Kill* her.

She would be coming out at midnight.

Monday was when she worked the four-to-midnight shift, it was important to check such things, make sure you knew who would be where when. Otherwise you made mistakes. There'd been no mistakes so far. All the questions they'd asked, but no mistakes. Too smart for them, was what it was. All you had to do was show them whatever they wanted to see, tell them whatever they expected to hear, and they were satisfied. Well, sure, look what you were dealing with here. So easy to fool them, so very easy. Just play the person they *thought* you were, never mind what was inside, never mind the pain and the suffering inside, just show them the surface. Play back the image they themselves had created, the stereotype of whoever they *thought* you were, this is me, right? Isn't this who I am? Whoever you *think* I am? Whatever idea of me you had in your heads even before you met me, isn't that right? Isn't that me?

No, it's *not* me. No. I'm sorry, but no.

This is me.

This *gun* is me.

Hard and cold and wet and hot in my hand.

Five minutes to midnight.

Coming out in your starched white uniform soon, never

change before you go home, do you? March right out in your whites, Madam Nurse, his first and *foremost* choice, the pattern for all the rest, how *dumb*, how essentially stupidly *dumb*! Slender, beautiful, your basic American blonde, the man has a decided weakness for blondes, *had*. But not quite so beautiful *now*, are you, Miss Nightingale? And blonde only with a little help from your friends, isn't that correct? Little help from Miss Clairol, hmm? Little help from me, too, tonight, little help from Miss *Cobra* here in my pocket, little *spit* from Miss Cobra, *empty* it in you! Bloody the image of yourself as *nurse*, confirm *my* image as whatever you *wish* me to be, whatever you've constructed in your mind as the true and only *image* of me, again all in black tonight, hidden in mourning, shrouded in black, only my face showing white in the dark, who *am* I, *tell* me!

Red light over the door across the street.

Employees entrance.

Sign says employees entrance.

Three minutes to midnight.

Door opening now.

Nurses spilling out. Orderlies. Interns. Scattering on the night. Some in uniform, some in street clothes. Dispersing. But where are *you*, Madam Nurse? You mustn't keep us waiting, you know. Miss Cobra and I become extremely irritated when. . .

There!

Coming out now. Saying goodnight to a man wearing a blue jacket over his white hospital pants. Calling something to him. See you tomorrow, voice carrying on the still night air, oh, no, you won't see *anyone* tomorrow. Turning away now. Smiling. Moving left toward the subway kiosk on the next corner. Pair of nurses ahead of her. *Now!*

Step out. Fast. Cross the street. Gun out. Move in. Fast. Behind her. Here! Here! Here! Here! Here!

Someone screaming.

Run.

Run!

11

She could not have appeared more fearsome had she ridden into the squadroom on a broomstick. Her blonde hair a tangled mare's nest, blue eyes flashing, lips curled back over teeth on the biting edge of anger, she flung open the gate in the slatted-rail divider and strode directly to where Brown and Carella were sitting at his desk.

"Okay, let's hear it!" she said.

Both detectives blinked. Since they'd just been looking over the report that had arrived from Ballistics not five minutes earlier, they could have told her that they now had a positive match on the .22-caliber bullets that had slain her mother last night. But she did not appear in the mood to hear that the same gun had also killed her father and stepmother. They had seen this look on indignant citizens before, but rarely quite so close to flash point. Fists clenched, it seemed as if Betsy Schumacher would at any moment strike out at either or both of the detectives. They wondered what they had done. She told them.

"Why didn't you call me?"

"We didn't have your number in Vermont," Carella said. "Your sister said she would . . ."

"Never mind my *sister*! It was *your* responsibility to inform me that my mother was dead!'

Actually, it hadn't been their responsibility at all. Nothing in the law or in any of the instructional guides required an investigating detective to notify the family of a murder victim. Moreover, in this day and age police notification was often a redundancy; in most cases, the family had already been informed by television. In a manual prepared by a former chief of detectives, family and friends ranked only sixth in importance on his suggested list of procedures:

Start worksheet . . .

Determine personnel needs . . .

Assign personnel to clerical duties . . .

Arrange for additional telephone lines . . .

Carefully question all witnesses and suspects . . .

Interview family and friends of the deceased for background information.

Only after rounding up all the usual suspects was it considered necessary to talk to the family and friends. And then only to gather background information. But nowhere did the chief, or anyone else, insist that a detective *had* to call the family *first*, even if—in working practice—this often proved to be the case. Last night, they had notified Lois Stein at once, and had in fact asked her for Betsy's number in Vermont. She'd told them she would call her sister personally. Apparently she had. Because here was Betsy now, fuming and ranting and threatening to have them brought up on charges or hanged by their thumbs in Scotland Yard, whichever punishment most fitted their heinous crime. Carella was thinking that the *true* heinous crime was yet another murder, and he was wondering if the lady might not be protesting a bit too much about an imaginary oversight. Brown had already carried this a step further: he was wondering if Betsy hadn't boxed her own mother. Done the round-trip number from Vermont to here and back again. So long, Mama.

"We're very sorry, Miss Schumacher," he said, sounding

genuinely sorry, "but it was very late when we finally got to your sister . . ."

"So many things to do at the scene . . ." Carella said.

"And we *did* ask her for your number, truly."

"She called me at four in the morning," Betsy said.

"Which was just a bit after we left her," Brown said.

Letting her know that these hardworking underpaid minions of the law had been on the job all night long, doing their crime-scene canvass, typing up re . . .

"It was still your responsibility," Betsy said petulantly, but she was beginning to soften. "Lois told me Mother was shot around midnight, and I didn't hear till . . ."

"Yes, according to the witnesses, that's when . . ."

"You mean there are witnesses?" Betsy said, surprised.

"Yes, two of them."

"People who saw the shooting?"

"Well, *heard* it, actually," Carella said. "Two nurses heading down the steps to the subway. They turned when they heard the shots, saw the killer running off."

"Then you have a description."

"Not exactly. They saw a *person*. But they couldn't tell us what that person looked like except that he . . ."

"Or she," Brown said.

"Or she," Carella repeated, nodding, "was dressed entirely in black."

"Then you don't really know . . ."

"No, Miss Schumacher, we don't," Carella said. "Not yet."

"Uh-huh, not yet," she said. "When do you think you *will* know?"

"We're doing our . . ."

"This is the fourth *one*, for Christ's sake!"

"Yes, we . . ."

"It *is* the same person, isn't it? Who killed Daddy and now . . ."

"We have good reason to believe it's the same person, yes."

"I don't give a *damn* about his bimbos, I wish someone had killed them both a long *time* ago. But if you want my opinion . . ."

Which they truly didn't.

". . . this person is after the whole family. The bimbos were a smoke screen . . ."

Which theory they had considered, too. And rejected.

" . . to hide the *real* targets, who were my mother and father. And that means maybe Lois and I are next." She hesitated for just an instant and then said, "While you do nothing."

"We're doing all we can," Carella said.

"No, I don't think so. Not if four people can get killed in the space of two weeks, three weeks, whatever the hell it is."

"It's exactly two weeks today," Brown said.

"So, sure, that's doing something. That's doing *nothing* is what it's doing. Where the hell were you last night when my mother was getting killed?"

The detectives said nothing.

"You can see there's a goddamn pattern, can't you?"

"What pattern do you see, Miss Schumacher?" Carella asked patiently.

"I see Daddy's bimbo getting killed, and then Daddy himself. So we'll think this is something that has to do exclusively with him and her. But then the *other* bimbo gets killed . . ."

"By the *other* bimbo . . ."

"*Mrs*. Schumacher, his beloved *wife*," she said mockingly. "Margaret, the very *first* bimbo. Come September, they'd have been married for two years. But isn't the irony wonderful? By last June—even before the wedding meats were cold—he'd already found himself *another* girlfriend. The point is . . ."

No, your timing is off, Brown thought.

". . . this person, whoever he is, first kills the new bimbo and then my father . . ."

He didn't start with the Brauer girl till *this* year.

". . . in an attempt to make it seem as if there's a link between them . . ."

"Well, there *was* a link," Carella said. "Your father was having an . . ."

"I *know* what he was doing, I can read the papers, thank you. My point is the killer goes after Margaret *next*, so we'll think he's after *all* my father's little dollies when instead what he's going after is the whole damn Schumacher *family*. It doesn't take a genius to recognize that. I thought you were supposed to be policemen. Who would you like to see killed next? My sister? Me?"

"You've got that wrong, by the way," Brown said.

"Oh, have I?" she said, turning to him. "Then how do *you* see it? The first three murders were . . ."

"I mean about when he started with the Brauer girl."

"I don't know when he *started* with her, whatever that means, but I know he was intimately *involved* with her last June."

"Couldn't have been."

"I'm telling you . . ."

"Miss, we've got a letter from your father saying he met her on New Year's Day . . ."

"*Her* letter is dated last June."

Both detectives looked at her.

"Whose letter?" Carella said.

"Well, who do you think? The woman he was keeping, the woman who was all over the newspapers, Little Suzie Sunshine."

"You have a letter Susan Brauer wrote to your father?"

"Yes."

"How'd you get it?"

"I found it."

"Where?"

"In Vermont."

"In the house your father gave you?"

"Not the house, the garage. A shoe box in the garage. I was cleaning out the garage when I moved in, and I . . ."

"Just that one letter in the box?"

"Yes."

"What kind of letter?" Brown asked.

"*Hi!*" she said, and put her hands alongside her face, and spread her fingers like fans. Blue eyes wide, smiling like Shirley Temple, she chirped in a tiny little voice, "I sure would love to suck your cock, baby!" and then snapped her hands shut and said in the same little voice, "*Bye!*"

Brown nodded.

"*That* kind of letter," she said.

"And you found this when?" Carella asked.

"Last July. When I moved into the house up there."

"Can't be," Brown said again. "Him and Susan . . ."

"Don't tell *me* what can't be!" Betsy said. "I know damn *well* when it was! It was the most important day of my life!"

"We have his letters to her," Carella said, "all dated this year . . ."

". . . and hers to him," Brown said.

"Well, I found that letter a year ago," Betsy insisted, "and it's dated Friday, June thirtieth."

"Has to be this year," Brown said.

"Are you telling me I don't know when I . . . look, where's a calendar?"

Carella looked at Brown, stifled a sigh, and reached into his desk drawer. He took out his appointment book, flipped through the pages till he came to the calendar for June of this year, glanced at it briefly, looked up, and said, "The thirtieth fell on a Saturday."

"See what you got for last year," Brown said softly.

At the back of the book, facing a map showing time zones and postal area codes for the entire United States, Carella found three reduced calendars printed on the same page, the current calendar flanked above and below by calendars for the preceding year and the one following. Squinting at the smaller numerals, he studied last year's calendar, looked up, and said to Brown, "She's right, June thirtieth fell on a Friday."

Brown nodded.

"You still got that letter?" he asked.

Friday, June 30

Hi!

I like this game. I'm only sorry you didn't
think of it sooner. But the next time I see
you, you'll have to explain the rules again. Am
I allowed to write whatever comes into my mind?
Oh dear, I'll be so naughty, you won't be able
to stand it.

It's raining today. Want to go splash in the
rain with me? Want me to play with you in the
rain?

You always ask me what I'm wearing. Right now I
have on a push-up black lace bra, cut so low it
exposes my nipples. Black silk stockings, held
up by a garter belt. Black crotchless panties.
Black spiked heels. These silk stockings feel
so smooth. I think you'd like to run your hand
over them, run your hand up along my thigh
until you reach the rim of the hose. Maybe then
you'd like to move your hand over to my moist,
eager cunt. My legs are spread so wide for you.
But maybe, since you know I'm ready and aching
for you, you'd just like to slide your cock
inside me and start fucking me right this
minute.

Do you think of me when you're fucking your
wife?

I'm getting so hot sitting here, thinking of you and your big hard cock. Why aren't you here with me? What am I supposed to do without you here? Maybe I'll just put my own hand between my legs, do you think I should do that? Start rubbing my middle finger against my clitoris? Yes, that's what I'll do, I think that's just what I'll do. Just touch myself and think of you and think of your cock in my mouth. Close my eyes and see that cock in my mouth, feel it in my cunt, hear you say all those things to me, oh God I wish it was your mouth down here between my legs, wish it was your tongue licking me, licking me, licking me, this can't be me talking. I would never say to you that thinking of you makes my breasts swell and grow and ache with desire, that thinking of you fucking me makes my cunt drool a river. I love the way you caress my breasts, it makes them feel red hot with desire. My wet cunt is more than ready for you, come to me, come slip your cock inside me. Fuck me real slow at first—it's so sexy to feel a cock almost pull all the way out, and then go in again as deep as it can—faster and faster, fuck me, come fuck me, I love it, I love it, oh Jesus I'm coming and you're not even here.

What an evil man you are to make me do such things.

Stop by and I'll give you a new toy.

Bye!

The same typewriter had been used on this letter as on the letters they'd found in Arthur Schumacher's safe-deposit box; the typeface was unmistakably identical. Like the seventeen other letters, this one began with first the typewritten day of the week . . .

Friday.

Then the month . . .

June.

And then the date in numerals.

30.

June thirtieth last year had fallen on a Friday. A call to the morning newspaper's morgue confirmed that it had been raining that day. In all of the letters, there was no year following the date. There was only Wednesday, June 28, and Friday, June 30, and Tuesday, July 4, and Saturday, July 15, and so on—eighteen letters in all, including the one Betsy had found at the bottom of an otherwise empty shoe box in a dusty garage in Vermont. All of the dates corresponded to last year's calendar; there was no doubt now as to when they'd been written.

But if anyone at all . . .

Well, all the indications . . .

But still . . .

If any of the master sleuths on the 87th Squad had taken the trouble to check a calendar against the dates on the letters they'd found, *when* they found them . . .

Well, the letters seemed absolutely related to . . .

Then they'd have realized at once that none of the dates on the letters in Schumacher's box corresponded to the days in this year's calendar.

Still, it was easy to see how . . .

No, damn it, they should have checked.

"We should have checked," Brown said.

"Nobody's perfect," Carella said.

Which was true.

Nonetheless, if Arthur Schumacher had not met Susan Brauer until January of this year, then she could not have written those letters dated in June and July of last year.

Which was elementary.

In which case, who *had* written them?

None of them were signed. Each began with the salutation "Hi!" and ended with the complimentary close "Bye!" The contents were similar and so was the style—if such it could be called. Whoever had written any one of those letters had written all of them.

"What do you think she means here?" Brown asked.

"Where?" Carella said.

"Here. About the toy."

"I don't know."

Brown looked at him.

"What is it?" Carella said.

"I don't *know*. Something just seems to be ringing some kind of bell."

"Are you talking about the toy?"

"I don't know if it's the toy."

"Then . . ."

"Just something," Brown said.

"Stop by and I'll give you a new toy," Carella said, prompting him.

Both men looked at each other. Both men shrugged.

"Some kind of sex toy?" Carella said.

"Could be, but . . ."

"Or maybe she meant a three-way."

"Uh-huh."

"A new *toy*, you know?"

"Uh-huh."

"Another *girl*. A three-way. Stop by and I'll give you a new toy."

"Uh-huh," Brown said. "But doesn't that ring some kind of bell with you?"

"No. The toy, you mean?"

"The *new* toy. Didn't somebody . . . wasn't there something about *new* toys?"

"No, I don't . . ."

"About getting a new toy . . ."

"No . . ."

". . . or buying a new toy . . . or . . . some kind of *shipment* of toys . . ."

"Oh God the dog!" Carella said.

The place used to be called Wally's Soul, and it still served soul food, but the owner had renamed it the Viva Mandela Deli shortly after the South African leader's triumphant visit to the city. At seven o'clock that Tuesday night, it was fairly crowded. Bent was eating country fried steak with mashed potatoes and gravy, green beans cooked with fatback and hot buttered biscuits. Wade was eating fried chicken with mashed rutabaga, fried okra, and hot buttered corn bread. They were not here primarily to eat, but every cop in this city knew you grabbed a bite whenever you could because you never knew when the shit might hit the fan.

They were here to talk to a sixteen-year-old white girl named Dolly Simms.

"No racial bullshit about old Dolly, huh?" Wade said.

"None a'tall. Jus' no *taste* is the problem," Bent said. "Shackin' up with two crackheads from D.C."

"*If* Smiley was talkin' the Book."

Smiley was a sour-faced stoolie they sometimes used; they were holding over his head a five-and-dime for armed robbery. The Book was the Bible. Bent was wondering out loud if Smiley'd been telling them the truth when he said Dolly Simms was living with the two black dudes from Washington. Dolly was a hooker.

"You think she *really* comes in here to eat?" Bent asked.

"You heard Smiley. Every night before she heads out."

"I mean, *I* can hardly eat this shit, and I'm black."

Both men laughed.

"Fried chicken's pretty good, though," Wade said.

Bent looked over at his partner's plate.

"Changed the name, shoulda changed the food, too," he said sourly.

"Shouldn'ta changed the name, either," Wade said. "Cost two-point-nine mill to throw the man a party, he tells us to rise up and kill Whitey."

"He didn't say that," Bent said.

"His wife did. Up there in Diamondback. Said all us black Americans should join their brothers in the bush when it comes time to fight the white man in South Africa. Now what kinda shit is *that*, Charlie?"

"We got ties to Africa," Bent said.

"Oh, yeah, must be *millions* of blacks in this city got brothers all *over* the South African bush."

"Well, there are ties," Bent said again.

"You identify with some African got flies in his eyes, drinkin' goat's milk and blood?"

"Well, no, but still . . . we're talkin' roots here."

"What roots? *My* roots are in South Carolina where my Mama and Daddy were born," Wade said, "and my Gran'daddy and Gran'ma before 'em. And you know where *their* roots were? You know where *their* Mama and Daddy came from? Ghana— what used to be called the Gold Coast. And *that* ain't nowhere *near* South Africa."

"Plenty of slaves came from South Africa, though," Bent said.

"No, plenty of slaves did *not* come from South Africa, nossir. The slave trade was with *West* Africa, go look it up, Charlie. Places like Dahomey and the Ivory Coast and Ghana and Nigeria, all of them around the Gulf of Guinea, *that's* where the slave trade was. Or sometimes the Congo or Gambia, don't you know *nothin'* about Africa?"

"I know where those places are," Bent said, offended.

"Mandela wakes up after twenty-seven years in jail," Wade said, gathering steam, "he comes here walkin' in his sleep an' talkin' like a man who don't know the whole world's already thrown *off* Communism. An' he tells us to join hands with our black brothers in South Africa, where none of our brothers come from in the first place, what kind of dumb niggers does he think he's talkin' to?"

"I think he done some good here," Bent said.

"I think he made things worse," Wade said flatly. "We got serious problems of our own here, and parades for foreigners ain't gonna solve 'em."

"So how come you eatin' fried chicken?" Bent asked. "You so fuckin' white, whyn't you have a slice of Wonder Bread with cholesterol-free margarine on it?"

"I'm black," Wade said, nodding, "you can bet your ass on that. But I ain't South African, and you can bet your ass on *that*, too. Here she comes now."

He was facing the entrance door. Bent turned to look over his shoulder. What they both saw was a teenaged girl who looked anorexic, standing some five feet six or seven inches tall and weighing maybe a hundred pounds. She was wearing fringed, purple suede boots with a black mini and a lavender silk blouse scooped low over tiny breasts and a narrow chest. Her frizzed hair was the color of the boots. She had hooker stamped on her forehead and junkie stamped all over her face. Both cops got up and swung toward the door. They weren't going to let this one get away.

"Miss Simms?" Wade said.

Moving in on her right and stepping slightly behind her so she wouldn't go right out the door again.

Bent was on her left. "Police officers," he said, and flashed the tin.

Didn't faze her a bit. Blinked at the shield, and then looked up into Bent's face and then turned to look at Wade. They figured she was stoned out of her mind. Little past seven o'clock, a long hard night ahead of her, and she was already completely out of it.

"Few questions we'd like to ask you," Wade said.

"What about?" she asked.

Pale eyes somewhat out of focus. Faint smile on her mouth. They wondered what she was on. Bent's eyes went automatically to her naked arms. He could not see any tracks on the pale white flesh. And her skirt was short enough to have revealed any hit marks on her thighs.

"Let's have a seat," he said.

"Sure," she said.

Nothing to hide here, all very open and casual, they figured she wasn't holding. This was merely a stoned-out hooker and two cops, all of them walking the same street but on opposite sides.

They sat at a table at the back of the place. There was a steady stream of traffic to the rest rooms. Wade and Bent figured people were going in there to snort a few lines, but they were after a killer here, they didn't give a damn about arresting any penny-ante noses. That was the trouble when a city started sliding south. You couldn't bother about the little things anymore. When people were getting killed, you couldn't go chasing kids spraying graffiti on walls. You couldn't ticket a truck driver for blowing his horn. You couldn't bust people who were jumping subway turnstiles. When you had murder and rape and armed robbery to worry about, the rest was merely civilization.

"Tell us all about Sonny and Dick," Wade said.

"I don't know them," Dolly said. "Can I get something to eat? I came in here to get something to eat."

"Sure. What would you like, Dolly?"

"Ice cream," she said. "Chocolate, please."

They ordered a dish of chocolate ice cream for her. At the last minute, she decided she wanted sprinkles on it. The waiter carried the dish of ice cream to the counter and put sprinkles on it. When he came back to the table, she picked up a spoon and began eating at once.

"Yum," she said.

"Sonny and Dick," Bent said. "Two men, both black."

"I like black men," she said, and winked at them and licked her lips.

"So we've been told."

"Yum," she said, and spooned up more ice cream.

"Where are they now?" Wade asked.

"Don't know them," she said.

"Sonny what?" Bent said.

"Nope. Sorry," she said. Eating. Licking her lips. Licking the spoon.

"Dick what?" Wade asked.

"Don't know him, either."

"Remember Thursday night?"

"Nope."

"Remember where you were Thursday night?"

"Sorry, nope. Where was I?"

"Around ten o'clock, a little later?"

"Sorry."

"Remember Sloane Street?"

"Nope."

"3341 Sloane?"

"This is very good," she said. "You should try some. Want a taste?" she asked Bent and held out the spoon to him.

"Third floor," Wade said. "You and Sonny and Dick, cooking dope over a candle in a red holder."

"I don't do dope," she said. "I'm clean."

"Remember the shooting?"

"I don't remember anything like that. Could I have some more ice cream?"

They ordered another dish of chocolate ice cream with sprinkles on it.

"You really should try some of this," she told them, "it's yummy."

"One of your pals was packing a nine-millimeter Uzi," Wade said.

"Gee, what's that?" she said.

"It's a big pistol with a twenty-bullet clip in it. He fired down the stairs at us, remember?"

"I don't even know where Sloane Street is," Dolly said, and shrugged.

"Dolly, listen carefully," Wade said. "Put down your spoon and listen."

"I can listen while I'm eating," she said.

"Put down the spoon, honey."

"I told you, I can . . ."

"Or I'll break your fucking arm," he said.

She put down the spoon.

"One of your pals killed somebody," he said.

She said nothing. Just kept watching him, a sullen, angry look on her face because he wouldn't let her eat her ice cream.

"Did you know that one of your pals killed somebody?"

"No, I didn't know that."

"We think it was Sonny, but it could have been Dick. Either way . . ."

"I don't know these people, so it don't mean a fuck to me," she said.

"He killed a cop's father," Wade said.

Dolly blinked.

He leaned in closer to her, giving her a good look at the knife scar that stretched tight and pink over his left eye. You dig black men, honey? Okay, how you feel about *this* one with his bad-ass scar?

"A *cop's* father," he repeated, coming down hard on the word.

She may have been stoned senseless not ten minutes ago, and maybe she was still flying, it was hard to tell. But now there was a faint flicker in those pale dead eyes. She was allowing the words to register, allowing the key words to penetrate, they were talking about a cop's father getting killed.

"You know what that means?" Bent asked. "Somebody killing a cop's father?"

"I don't know anybody named Sonny."

"It means every cop in this city's gonna be trackin' the man till they catch him. An' then he be lucky he makes it alive to jail."

"Don't matter shit to me," she said, "I don't know anybody named Sonny."

"That's good," Wade said, "because if you *do* know him . . ."

"I told you I don't."

". . . and it turns out you were *protecting* him . . ."

"Nor Diz neither."

"Diz?" Wade asked at once. "Is *that* his name? *Diz*?"

Dolly still didn't realize she'd tripped herself.

"Diz *what*?" Bent asked.

"If I don't know him, how would I know Diz what?"

"But you *do* know him, don't you, Dolly?"

"No, I . . ."

"You know *both* of them, don't you?"

And now they came at her from either side, hurling words at her, not waiting for answers, battering her with words, Wade on her right and Bent on her left, Dolly sitting between them with her spoon on the table and her chocolate ice cream melting fast.

"Sonny and Diz."

"Two black killers from D.C."

"What're their last names, Dolly?"

"Tell us their last names."

"Sonny what?"

"Diz what?"

"They killed a cop's father!"

"You want to go down with them?"

"You want to keep on protecting two strangers?"

"Two killers?"

"You want every cop in this city on your ass?"

"You won't be able to breathe."

"You'll go down with them, Dolly."

"A cop's father, Dolly!"

"You want that on your back for the rest of your life?"

"I . . ."

They both shut up.

Waiting.

She was staring down at the melting ice cream.

They kept waiting.

"I don't know anything about them," she said.

"Okay," Wade said, nodding.

"That's the only time I ever saw them, Thursday night."

"Uh-huh."

"I haven't seen them since. I don't know any . . ."

"Honey, you want big trouble, don't you?" Wade said.

"But I'm telling you the *truth*!"

"No, you're shitting us!" Bent said. "We know you're living with them . . ."

"I'm not!"

"Okay, have it your way," Bent said, and shoved back his chair. "Let's go, Randy."

"Expect heat, baby," Wade said, and got up. "Lots of heat. From every cop walkin' this city. Heat till you die. This is *cop* business you're messin' with, this is a cop's *father*."

"Sleep tight," Bent said, and they started walking out.

"Hold it," she said.

They stopped, turned to her again.

"Could I have some more ice cream?" she said.

They were waiting for her when she got back to the shop that night. They were standing near a tankful of tropical fish. Water bubbling behind them. Fish gliding. They were talking about a James Bond movie where a tank of fish explodes or something. They were trying to remember the name of the movie.

They'd called first and spoken to Pauline Weed's assistant, a young girl who'd told them she was out getting something to eat, expected her back in half an hour or so. They'd driven directly downtown to Bide-A-Wee Pets on Jefferson, where they'd learned that the girl's name was Hannah Kemp, that she was sixteen years old and wanted to be a veterinarian when she grew up, and that she worked here after school every Tuesday and Friday, when the shop was open till eight o'clock. She was with a customer up front when Pauline walked in some five minutes later. She pointed to where the detectives were standing near the gliding tropical fish, and said something they couldn't hear. Pauline looked up the aisle at them in surprise, and then walked to where they stood trying to remember the name of that movie.

"Hey, hi," she said.

"Hello, Miss Weed," Carella said.

"Can I sell you some fish?" she asked, and smiled.

Blonde and beautiful and blue-eyed, the type the man favored. Smile a bit wavering, though.

"Miss Weed," Carella said, "when we called here earlier tonight, your assistant . . ."

"Hannah," she said. "Great girl."

"Yes, she told us you were out getting something to eat . . ."

"Uh-huh."

"And you'd be back in half an hour or so."

"And here I am," she said, and grinned.

"Miss Weed, have you ever been married?" Brown asked.

"No, I haven't," she said, looking surprised.

"I thought the middle name might be . . ,"

"Oh. No, that was my mother's maiden name. It's where I got the name of the shop, actually. The Bide and the Wee. From my middle name and my last name."

"Byerly and Weed," Brown said.

"Yes. Bide-A-Wee."

"Miss Weed," Carella said, "when we called here, we asked to speak to you, and Hannah said . . ."

"Great girl," she said again.

But she looked nervous now.

"She said . . . these are her exact words . . . she said, 'Bye's out getting something to eat.' "

"Uh-huh."

"She called you Bye."

"Uh-huh."

"Do a lot of people call you that?"

"Fair amount, I guess."

"Short for Byerly, is that it?"

"Well, my first name's Pauline, that's not such great shakes, is it?"

"Do *you* call yourself Bye?"

"Yes."

"How do you *sign* yourself?"

"Pauline Byerly Weed."

"You sign all your . . . ?"

"I sign everything Pauline Byerly Weed, yes."

"How about personal correspondence?" Brown asked.

She turned to him.

"Yes," she said. "That, too. Everything."

"You call yourself Bye, but you sign yourself Pauline Byerly Weed."

"Yes."

"Miss Weed," Carella said, "do you own a typewriter?"

Her eyes flashed. Danger. Careful. That's what her eyes were saying.

"We can get a search warrant," Brown said.

"I own a typewriter," she said, "yes."

"Did you own this same typewriter in June of last year?"

"Yes."

"July of last year?"

"Yes."

"May we see it, please?"

"Why?"

"Because we think you wrote some letters to Arthur Schumacher," Brown said.

"I may very well have written . . ."

"Erotic letters," Carella said.

"Can we see that typewriter, please?" Brown said.

"I didn't kill him," she said.

"What it was," Dolly said, "they started out as tricks, you know? I was working Casper . . . you know Casper and the Fields, up there near the old cemetery? St. Augustus Cemetery? Where there used to be like this little stone building got knocked down? Just inside the gates? Well, a lot of girls line up there at night because cars come through to pick up the Expressway, the Casper Avenue entrance, you know where I mean? Anyway, that's where I met them, they came walkin' up the street, lookin' over the merchandise, there's lot of girls along that cemetery stretch, well, I guess I don't have to tell you. I'm tryin' explain I don't want to take a rap for a cop's old man got killed. I hardly *know* these guys, they started out as tricks."

"When was this?" Wade asked.

"Last Sunday night."

"Almost a week ago."

"Almost."

"What does that make it, Charlie?"

Bent took a little celluloid bank calendar from his notebook.

"The twenty-second," he said.

Five days after Carella's father got killed.

"So they came up to you . . ."

"Yeah, and they told me they kind of liked my looks," she said, and shrugged modestly, "and would I be interested in a three-way. So I told them I usually get more for a three-way, and they asked me how much, and I told them a hun' fifty and they said that sounded okay, and we went to this little hot-bed place the girls use, it's near that big hall on Casper, where they cater weddings and things? Right next door to it? So that's how it started,'' she said, and shrugged again.

"How'd you end up in an abandoned building on Sloane?"

"Well, it turns out these guys were loaded . . ."

There'd been twelve hundred dollars in Tony Carella's cash register.

". . . and they liked crack as much as I do. Well, I mean, who don't? I had my way, I'd *marry* crack. So we had a nice little arrangement, you know what I mean? I'd do whatever they wanted me to do, and they supplied me with crack."

A simple business arrangement. Basic barter. A usual arrangement at that. Sex for dope. And because everyone was stoned or about to *get* stoned, it was rarely if ever safe sex. When crack's on the scene, nobody's worrying about a rubber. Which is why you had a lot of crack addicts getting pregnant. Which is why you had a lot of tormented crack babies crying for cocaine. What goes around comes around.

"I don't know where they got all that money . . ." she said.

Killed a man for it, Wade thought.

". . . but listen, who cares?"

Twelve hundred dollars, he thought.

"I do you, you do me, one hand washes the other, am I right? No questions asked, just beam me up, Scottie."

Just beam you up, he thought.

"How'd you end up on Sloane Street?" he asked.

"I think they were on the run."

"What do you mean?"

"I think they done a job that night. They called me up, told me they didn't want to come home. They were afraid . . ."

"Which is where?"

"So we like went to this crack house, you know, but the guy on the door looks at us through the peephole, he says 'How the fuck *I* know who you are?' Like we're *cops*, right?" she said sarcastically. "I been hookin' since I was thirteen, I suddenly look like I'm undercover, right? Sonny and Diz, too, you ain't gonna mistake either one of them for nothing but an ex-con. So the guy at the door gives us all this bullshit and we're forced to score on the street. Which is no big deal, I mean I do it all the time, you can buy crack on any street corner, look who I'm tellin'. But it would've been easier we could've smoked there in private without having to find a place to go. 'Cause we couldn't go back to the pad, you know. 'Cause Sonny and Diz thought the cops would come lookin' for them there."

"And where's that?" Bent asked.

"So that's how we ended up on Sloane, in that building, Jesus, what a place! Rats the size of alligators, I swear to God. So that was you guys, huh?"

"Yeah, that was us," Wade said.

"Scared the shit out of us," Dolly said, and giggled the way she had that night. "We went down the fire escape."

"We figured."

"I almost broke my neck."

"Where're Sonny and Diz now?"

"I already told you everything I know about them."

"Except where they are."

"I don't know where they are."

"You said you were living together . . ."

"But not no more."

"You said you had a pad . . ."

"Yeah, that was then."

"Dolly . . ." Wade said warningly.

"I mean it," she said. "I don't know."

"Okay," he said, "let's go up the station house, okay?"

"No, wait a minute," she said. "Please."

The Q&A took place in Lieutenant Byrnes's office at twenty minutes to ten that night. That was how long it took everyone to assemble. Nellie Brand had to come all the way uptown from her apartment on Everetts. The police stenographer with his video camera had to come all the way uptown, too, from the Headquarters Building on High Street. Pauline Weed's attorney, a man named Henry Kahn, had to come all the way crosstown from his office on Stockton. Brown, Carella, and Byrnes were the only ones who'd just had to walk down the hall from the squadroom to the Interrogation Room.

Nellie was here to find out if this was real meat. It had sounded that way when they'd filled her in on the initial interrogation, but you never knew. She was wearing a lightweight beige suit with a straw-colored handbag and pumps. She still wore her tawny hair in a wedge that gave an impression of speed, someone on the move, windswept, almost airborne. She knew that as assistant D.A. she'd be asking most of the questions unless she needed Carella or Brown to fill in something specific. She wasn't expecting any problems; Pauline's lawyer looked like a dip—but, again, you never knew. Tall and thin and wearing a wrinkled brown suit that matched his watery eyes, he sat alongside Pauline at the far end of the long table, whispering something Nellie couldn't hear. The stack of steamy letters were on the table in front of her. She had read them when she'd got here. *Some* letters. From a woman who looked as if butter wouldn't melt.

Carella started to read Pauline her rights again, but Kahn interrupted with a curt, "We've been through all that already, Detective," to which Carella replied, "Just for the record, Counselor," each of them using the respective titles in a way that made them sound derogative and somewhat dishonorable. Kahn gave his permission with an impatient patting of his hand on the air, and Pauline listened and affirmed that she knew her rights and that she was willing to answer the questions about to be put to her.

Carella looked up at the clock, and—for the videotape and the stenographer—announced that it was now nine-fifty P.M. Nellie began her questioning:

Q: Can you tell me your name, please?

A: Pauline Weed.

Q: Is that your full name?

A: Yes.

Q: What I'm asking you, Miss Weed ...

A: (from Mr. Kahn) She's answered the question.

Q: I don't believe she has. I'm asking if that's the name on her birth certificate.

A: (from Mr. Kahn) All right, go ahead then.

Q: Is that the name on your birth certificate? Pauline Weed?

A: No.

Q: What *is* the name on your birth certificate?

A: Pauline Byerly Weed.

Q: Then *that's* your full name?

A: Yes.

Q: Thank you. Where does the Byerly come from?

A: It was my mother's maiden

A: (from Mr. Kahn) Excuse me, but what's any of this got to do with ...?

Q: I think you'll see where I'm going, Mr. Kahn.

A: Well, I wish I knew where you were going *now*. You drag my client down here in the middle of the night ...

Q: Excuse me, Mr. Kahn. If your client doesn't want to answer my questions, all she has to do is ...

A: Oh, please, spare me First-Year Law, will you please?

Q: Just tell me what you want to do, Mr. Kahn. Do you want the questions stopped? That's your prerogative, your client said she understood her rights. Does she wish me to stop? If not, please let me ask my questions, okay?

A: Go ahead, go ahead, it's always the same old story.

Q: Miss Weed, are you ever known by the nickname Bye?

A: Sometimes.

Q: Wouldn't you say it's more than just sometimes?

A: Occasionally. I would say occasionally.

Q: Well, do you *answer* to that name? Bye?

A: Yes.

Q: If I called you Bye, you'd answer to it, wouldn't you?

A: Yes.

Q: What does that stand for? Bye?

A: Byerly.

Q: Which, of course, is your middle name.

A: Yes.

Q: So it's really a common thing, isn't it? Your being called Bye, your answering to the name Bye.

A: I sometimes use the name Bye. But I'm also called Pauline. And Byerly, too, sometimes.

Q: Do you ever sign your letters with that name?

A: Byerly, do you mean?

Q: No, I mean *Bye*. Do you ever sign your letters with the name Bye?

A: Sometimes.

Q: Miss Weed, I show you copies of letters ...

A: (from Mr. Kahn) May I see those, please?

Q: They're copies of letters Detectives Brown and Carella recovered from Arthur Schumacher's safe-deposit box. We don't want the originals handled any more than they've already been.

A: Let me see them, please.

Q: Sure. Don't burn your fingers.

(Questioning resumed at 10:05 P.M.)

Q: Miss Weed, did you write these letters?

A: No.

Q: You did not sign the name Bye to these letters?

A: *Nobody* signed a name to those letters.

Q: Yes, excuse me, you're absolutely right. Did you *type* the name Bye to these letters?

A: No, I didn't. I didn't write those letters.

Q: We have a typewriter the detectives recovered at your shop ...

A: (from Mr. Kahn) What typewriter? I don't see any typewriter.

Q: It's on the way to the lab, Mr. Kahn. It was recovered at Bide-A-Wee Pets at 602 Jefferson Avenue and is now being examined as possible evidence ...

A: Evidence? Of *what*?

Q: Evidence in the crime of murder.

A: I don't see the connection, Ms. Brand, I'm sorry. Even if Miss Weed *did* write those letters ... and I certainly hope you have proof of that since the letters in themselves would appear damaging to her reputation ...

Q: That's why the typewriter's at the lab, Mr. Kahn. But if you'll excuse me, we're not trying a case here, we're simply trying to question a suspect, aren't we? So may I be permitted to do that? Or, as I suggested earlier, do you want me to stop the questioning right now?

A: (from Miss Weed) I have nothing to hide.

Q: Mr. Kahn? May I take that as permission to continue?

A: Sure, go ahead, it's always the same old story.

Q: Miss Weed, when did you first meet Arthur Schumacher?

A: January a year ago.

Q: That would've been ... what's this?

A: (from Mr. Carella) July thirty-first.

Q: So that would've been ... what does that come to? Eighteen, nineteen months?

A: (from Mr. Carella) Eighteen.

Q: Is that right, Miss Weed?

A: A bit more.

Q: How did you happen to meet him?

A: His wife bought a dog from me. For a Christmas present. He came in a month later to ask about a collar.

Q: And that was the start of your relationship.

A: I didn't have a *relationship* with him. He was a *customer*.

Q: Nothing more than that.

A: Nothing.

Q: Then how do you explain these letters?

A: I didn't write those letters.

Q: You do know, do you not, that under the Miranda guidelines . . .

A: (from Mr. Kahn) Here comes First-Year Law again!

Q: We are permitted to take your fingerprints, for example . . .

A: (from Mr. Kahn) I would strenuously object to that.

Q: Yes, but it wouldn't change the law. Are you aware of that, Miss Weed?

A: If you say that's the law . . .

Q: I say so.

A: Then I guess it's the law.

Q: Are you also aware that whereas a great many people have already handled the originals of these letters . . .

A: I didn't write those letters.

Q: *Whoever* wrote them, the writer's fingerprints may still be on the originals, are you aware of that?

A: I don't know anything about those letters. I don't know whose fingerprints are on those letters.

Q: Have you ever *seen* the originals of these letters?

A: No.

Q: You're sure about that.

A: (Silence)

Q: Miss Weed?

A: Yes. I'm sure I never saw them.

Q: Then your fingerprints couldn't *possibly* be on them, isn't that so?

A: They couldn't.

Q: What if they *are?* What if we find fingerprints on the letters and they match yours? How would you explain that, Miss Weed?

A: (Silence)

Q: Miss Weed?

A: (Silence)

Q: Miss Weed? Would you please answer my question?

A: (Silence)

Q: Lieutenant, I'd like this prisoner's fingerprints taken, please.

A: (from Mr. Kahn) Hey now, wait just a minute. There's nothing in Miranda that says you can ...

Q: Can someone please get him a copy of the guidelines?

A: (from Mr. Kahn) Now wait just a minute!

A: (from Lt. Byrnes) Somebody go down to the desk, see if there's a copy of the Miranda book behind it. Miss, you want to come along now? Steve, take her prints for me, will you?

A: (from Mr. Carella) Let's go, Miss.

Q: (from Ms. Brand) Miss Weed?

A: (Silence)

Q: Miss Weed?

A: I loved him so much.

I didn't know he'd found someone else. I thought he'd just lost interest. That happens, you know. People fall out of love. And I was willing to accept that. If a person doesn't love you anymore, then he just doesn't. It had been a year—well a little less than a year, actually. He came into the shop that first time on the twenty-third, that was our anniversary, the twenty-third of January. So we'd had a good run. Nowadays, a year is a long time, believe me. I have girlfriends, if a man stays with them for six months they consider themselves lucky. This was almost a year. The day he told me he wanted to end it was the fifteenth of January. I'm good on dates. That was almost a year. So . . .

You know.

I . . .

I said okay.

I mean, what can you do? If a man doesn't love you anymore, you just have to let him go, don't you?

I kept remembering the things we did together.

The letters were fun, but that only lasted a little while, it was a hot summer.

Every now and then I'd get this other girl for him. Well, for us. I used to go to college with her. Marian. A blonde, like me . . . well, he liked blondes. But that was when I was still sure of him. I mean, it was the *three* of us, sure, but it was still really just the *two* of us, do you know what I mean? It was him and me calling the tune. Marian was just there to please us.

We had good times together.

But when something's over, it's over, am I right? I mean, I'm not a child, I know when to call it a day. And even though I was lonely . . .

I was very lonely.

I loved him so much.

Still I . . . I figured I could live with it. I had the shop, I love animals, you know. I kept myself busy. And I guess I would have been able to manage if I hadn't . . .

It was one of those things where I thought I was looking at myself in a mirror, a younger version of myself, walking up the street toward me, hanging on Arthur's arm, head thrown back in a laugh, long blonde hair and blue eyes, it was me and Arthur all over again. Only it wasn't me. It was another woman, a girl really, she couldn't have been older than twenty, reaching up to kiss him on the cheek, I turned away before he could see me. Turned my back. Started to cross the street against traffic. Horns blowing, it was terrible. When I turned back again, they were gone. Lost in the crowd. Lost.

I thought Well well.

I thought The son of a bitch already has somebody new.

It's only a month . . .

This was February the twelfth, I'm very good on dates . . .

It was only a month and already he had himself a new woman, a new *girl*, really, she looked so young. And then I wondered if . . .

I mean, was it possible he could have found someone else so *fast*? I mean, only a month after we'd said goodbye? Wasn't that awfully fast? And then it occurred to me that he'd maybe had her all along, maybe he'd had her *before* he called it quits with me. And that bothered me. It really did. I guess I should have said the hell with it, but it really bothered me. You know how some things can just *eat* at you? Well, that's what this did to me. It just *ate* at my insides.

I mean, all the things we did together.

Jesus.

So I . . .

I guess I began following him. Because I wanted to find out how long this had been going on, you see. I mean, had he been making a fool of me all along? Did he have this girl on the side while I was writing all those letters to him, and getting other women for him . . . well, just Marian, but we did it a lot with her, we must have done it a dozen times with her at least. Had he been making a goddamn fool of me all along?

She lived in this fancy apartment building on Silvermine Oval . . . well, you know where she lived. He would go to see her maybe two, three times a week. I followed him up there. One day I asked one of the doormen, not the Saudi, whatever he is, the little one who can't speak English, this was another doorman. I told him I was sure I knew the girl who'd just gone in, a girl named Helen King, I was sure I used to work with her, and he said no, that wasn't her name, and I said I'm sure that was her, can you tell me her name, please, and he gave me that look doormen always give you, as if you're going to go in and kill somebody in their precious fucking building, and he said, No, I can't give out names, so you see it wasn't so easy getting her name.

I began following her around, too. Not just when he was with her, Arthur, but when she was alone. Trying to find out her name, you know. It's not easy to find out somebody's name in this city, everybody's so suspicious. I finally got it at the supermarket. From following her around I knew she got all her groceries from the Food Emporium up on The Stem, filled out this little slip to have the stuff delivered. So I just made sure I got in line at the checkout behind her, and I watched while she wrote down her name and the address on the order pad, Susan Brauer, 301 Silvermine Oval, PH, bingo.

Not that I was planning to do anything. I just wanted to know about her.

Because it kept eating at me that maybe he'd been seeing her at the same time he was telling me how much he loved me.

And then one day, I saw the other man.

Saw her and this other man together.

This was right after Easter, the eighteenth of April, it was raining. It was the daytime. Raining hard. They came out of the building together, he'd obviously been up there with her. He had white hair, I thought he was an old man at first. I couldn't understand what she saw in him. After Arthur? This skinny little bullfighter?

They went to lunch together in an Italian restaurant on Culver. Then they went back to the apartment. They were up there all afternoon. Arthur went there later that night. She was seeing *both* of them, I couldn't believe it! Mott, his name was. Thomas Mott. I followed him to an antiques shop he owns on Drittel. I went in the shop one day, just to see him up close. He was younger than I'd thought, in his fifties, I guessed. Dark brown eyes in a very pale face. I told him I was interested in a Tiffany lamp. He seemed pleasant.

But you see, she'd made her one big mistake.

This was how I could get Arthur back. By telling him she was cheating on him. I mean, in all the time I knew Arthur—it was almost a year, don't forget—I never once cheated on him. Never. But here was someone he'd known since . . . well, I really didn't *know* how long because it could have been going on forever, for all I knew . . . but it had to have been since January at least, and here it was only April, and she was already cheating on him. So I thought I'd go talk to her. Tell her I was going to blow the whistle unless she quit seeing Arthur. Reason with her. She had one man, why did she need two? Talk to her. Reason with her. The day I went there . . .

The weather on Tuesday, the seventeenth of July, is swelteringly hot, the three horsemen of haze, heat, and humidity riding roughshod over a city already trampled into submission. She is going there only to talk to her. She has called first to say she is holding some lingerie here for delivery, would it be all right if one of the girls stopped by with it later this afternoon? He *had* to have gifted her with sexy lingerie in the past, no? The whole garter-belt-and-panties routine? The bra with the cutout nipple holes? Oh sure.

Little Suzie says, "Oh, yes, please, just leave it with the doorman, please."

Little Minnie Mouse voice. First time she's ever heard the voice.

"The gentleman asked us to make sure you got it personally," she says into the phone. "The gentleman insisted that you sign for delivery."

"What gentleman?" Little Suzie asks in her little Minnie Mouse voice. "May I have his name, please?"

"Arthur Schumacher," she says.

"Oh well then all right," Suzie says in the same rushed, breathless voice, "can you send it by at the end of the day?"

"What time would be most convenient for you, Miss?"

"I just *said* the end of the *day*, didn't I? The end of the day is five o'*clock*!"

Q: How'd you feel about that? The way she answered you?

A: I thought what a little bitch she was.

Q: Yes, but did her response have anything to do with what happened later? The impatience of her response?

A: No, I just thought what a bitch she was, but I was still planning to go up there only to talk to her.

Q: All right, what happened next?

A: There was a doorman to contend with, but I knew there'd be a doorman. I was wearing ...

She is wearing a beige silk scarf to hide her blonde hair, dark glasses to hide the color of her eyes, dressed entirely in the same indeterminate beige, a color—or *lack* of color—she hates and rarely wears. She is wearing it today only because it matches the color of the store's shopping bag. She wants to pass for someone delivering from the store. Beige polyester slacks and a beige cotton blouse, gold leather belt, the temperature hovering in the high eighties, approaching the doorman in his gray uniform with its red trim, carrying in her right hand the big beige shopping bag with its gold lettering. She has spoken to this doorman before, he is the short, fat one with the accent. She tells him now . . .

Q: When was that?

A: I'm sorry?

Q: That you'd spoken to him?

A: Oh. When I was still trying to find out her name. But he can barely speak English, so I finally gave up on him. He was the one on duty that day. I stated my business ...

"Miss Brauer, please."

"You are who, please?"

Looking her up and down, she *hates* when they do that.

"Just tell her Victoria's Secret is here," she says.

"Moment," he says, and buzzes the apartment upstairs.

"Yes?"

Her voice on the intercom.

"Lady?" he says.

"Yes, Ahmad?"

"Vittoria Seegah here," he says.

"Yes, send it right up, please."

Bingo.

Still wanting only to talk to her.

But, of course, there is no talking to some people.

Little Suzie is annoyed that she's been tricked. Two black leather sofas in the living room, one on the long wall opposite the door that led into it, the other on the shorter window wall at the far end of the room. Glass-topped coffee table in front of the closest sofa, martini glass sitting on it, lemon twist floating, the little lady has been drinking. She stands before the sofa, all annoyed and utterly beautiful, all blonde and blue-eyed in a black silk kimono that has itself probably come from Victoria's Secret, patterned with red poppies, naked beneath it judging from the angry pucker of her nipples.

"You had no right coming here," she says.

"I only want to talk to you."

"I'm going to call him right this minute, tell him you're here."

"Go ahead, call him."

"I will," she says.

"It'll take him at least half an hour to get here. By then, we'll be finished."

"By then *you'll* be finished."

"I really would like to talk to you. Can't we please talk?"

"No."

"Please. Please, Susan."

Perhaps it is the note of entreaty in her voice. Whatever it is, it stops Little Suzie cold on her way to the phone and brings her back to the coffee table, where she picks up her martini glass and drains it. She goes back to the bar then, bare feet padding on the thick pile rug, and—charming hostess that she is—pours herself and only herself another drink. There is a whole lemon sitting on the bartop, so yellow. There is a walnut-handled bottle opener. There is a paring knife with a matching walnut handle. Late-afternoon sunlight streams through the sheer white drapes behind the black leather sofa on the far wall. Little Suzie Doll walks back to the coffee table, stands posed and pretty beside it, barefoot and petulant, the kimono loosely belted at her waist. There is a hint of blonde pubic hair.

"What is it you want?" she asks.

"I want you to stop seeing him."

"No."

"Hear me out."

"No."

"Listen to me, Suzie . . ."

"Don't call me Suzie. No one calls me Suzie."

"Do you want me to tell him?"

"Tell him what?"

"I think you know what."

"No, I don't. And, anyway, I don't care. I'd like you to go now."

"You want me to tell him, right?"

"I want you to get out of here," Suzie says, and turns to put the martini glass on the table behind her, as if in dismissal—end of the party, sister, no more cocktails, even though I haven't yet offered you a drink.

"Okay, fine, I'll tell him what's been going on between you and . . ."

"So tell him," Suzie says, and turns again to face her, grinning now, hands on her hips, legs widespread, pubic patch blatantly defiant. "He won't believe you," she says, and the grin widens, mocking her.

Which is only the truth. He will not believe her, that is the plain truth. He will think this is something she's invented. A lie to break them apart. And facing the truth, feeling helpless in the cruel and bitter glare of the truth, she becomes suddenly furious. She does not know what she says in the very next instant, perhaps she says nothing at all, or perhaps she says something so softly that it isn't even heard. She knows only that the paring knife is suddenly in her hand.

Q: Did you stab and kill Susan Brauer?

A: Yes.

Q: How many times did you stab her?

A: I don't remember.

Q: Do you know there were thirty-two stab and slash wounds?

A: Good.

Q: Miss Weed ...

A: My clothes were covered with blood. I took a raincoat from her closet and put it on. So the doorman wouldn't see all that blood when I was going out.

Q: Miss Weed, did you also kill Arthur Schumacher?

A: Yes. I shouldn't have, it was a dumb move. I wasn't thinking properly.

Q: How do you mean?

A: Well, she was gone, you see. I had him all to myself again.

Q: I see.

A: But, of course, I didn't, did I?

Q: Didn't what, Miss Weed?

A: Didn't have him all to myself again. Not really. Because he was the one who'd ended it, you see, not me. And if he'd found somebody else so quickly, well, he'd just find somebody again, it was as simple as that, wasn't it? He was finished with me, he'd never come back to me, it was as simple as that. He'd find himself another little cutie, maybe even younger this time—he'd once asked me to set up something with Hannah from the shop, can you believe it? She was fifteen at the time, he asked me to set up a three-way with her. So I ... I guess I realized I'd lost him forever. And that was when I began getting angry all over again. About what he'd done. About leaving me like that and then starting up with her. About *using* me. I don't like to be used. It infuriates me to be used. So I ... he'd given me this gun as a gift. I went up there and waited outside ...

Q: Up where, Miss Weed?

* * *

Nellie's voice almost hushed. Wanting to pin down the address for later, for when this thing came to trial. Getting all her ducks in a row in this day and age when even videotaped confessions sometimes didn't mean a thing to a jury.

A: His apartment. On Selby Place.

Q: When was this, can you remember?

A: Yes, it was the twentieth. A Friday night.

Q: And you say you went there and waited outside his building ...

A: Yes, and shot him.

Q: How many times did you shoot him? Do you remember?

A: Four.

Q: Did you also shoot the dog?

A: Yes. I was sorry about that. But the dog was a gift from her, you see.

Q: From ...?

A: Margaret. His wife. I knew all about Margaret, of course, Margaret was no secret, we talked about Margaret all the time.

Q: Did you kill her, too?

A: Yes.

Q: Why?

A: All of them.

Q: I'm sorry, what ...?

A: Any woman he'd ever had anything to do with.

Q: Are you saying ...?

A: All of them, yes. Did you see his will? The *insult* of it!

Q: No, I haven't seen it. Tell me what ...

A: Well, you should take a look at it. I was never so insulted in my life! Ten thousand dollars! Is that a slap in the face, or what is it? After all we meant to each other, after all we *did* together? He left the same amount to his fucking veterinarian! Jesus, that was *infuriating!* What did he leave the *other* ones, that was the question? How much did he leave his beloved Margaret, or his *first* wife, who by the way used to go with him to bars to pick up hookers, he told me they'd once had three of them in the apartment at the same time, three black hookers, this was when his precious daughters were away at camp one summer. Or how about *them*? The Goody-Two-Shoes dentist's wife and the stupid hippie he gave that house in Vermont to? How much did he leave *them* in his will? Oh, Jesus, I was furious! Did he take me for a fool? I'm no fool, you know. I showed him.

Q: How did you show him?

A: I went after all of them. I wanted to get all of them. To show him.

Q: When you say 'all of them ...'

A: All of them. Margaret and the first wife and the two darling daughters, *all* of them, what do you think all of them means? His *women*! His fucking *women*!

Q: Did you, in fact, kill Gloria Sanders?

A: Yes, I did. I said so, didn't I?

Q: No, not until this ...

A: Well, I did. Yes. And I'm not sorry, either. Not for her, not for any of them. Unless ... well, I suppose maybe ...

Q: Yes?

A: No, never mind.

Q: Please tell me.

A: I guess I'm sorry about ... about hurting ...

Q: Yes?

A: Hurting Arthur.

Q: Why is that?

A: He was such a wonderful person.

A knock sounded on the door.

"Busy in here!" Byrnes shouted.

"Excuse me, sir, but . . ."

"I said we're *busy* in here!"

The door opened cautiously. Miscolo from the Clerical Office poked his head into the room.

"I'm sorry, sir," he said, "but this is urgent."

"What is it?" Byrnes snapped.

"It's for you, Steve," Miscolo said. "Detective Wade from the Four-Five."

12

The cars nosed through the night like surfaced submarines, two big sedans with five detectives in each of them. The detectives were all wearing bulletproof vests. Carella was riding in the lead car, with Wade and Bent and two cops they'd introduced as Tonto and the Lone Ranger. Tonto didn't look the slightest bit Indian. Carella had suited up with the others at the Four-Five, and was sitting on the backseat between Wade and Bent. They were all big men. Wearing the vests made them even bigger. The car felt crowded.

"The one done the shooting is named Sonny Cole," Wade said. "He's packing a nine-millimeter for sure, and from the way the girl described it, it's the Uzi we're looking for."

"Okay," Carella said, and nodded. Sonny Cole, he thought. Who killed my father.

"The other one's named Diz Whittaker. I think his square handle is Desmond, we're running computer checks on both of them right this minute. From what she told us, Diz is the brains of the operation."

"Some brains," Bent said sourly.

"Anyway, he's the one planned the holdup in your father's

shop and also another one last Thursday night, when we almost got them.''

"A liquor store," Bent said. "This is how they keep themselves in dope, they do these shitty little holdups.''

Wade looked at him sharply.

Carella was thinking A shitty little holdup. My father got killed for twelve hundred dollars. He was thinking he was going to enjoy meeting these two punks. He was going to enjoy it a lot.

"Girl's been living with them a coupla weeks now, they picked her up on Cemetery Row one night, she's a hooker," Wade said.

"A junkie, too," Bent said.

"An all-around straight arrow," Wade said.

"The house is on Talley Road, in the Four-Six, mostly black and Hispanic, they're renting a room on the second floor. Two-family house, wide open, bulldozed lots on either side of it, getting ready for another project.''

"Means they can see us coming a mile away."

"Yeah, well, that's life," Bent said.

The house was a two-story clapboard building with an asphalt shingle roof. Empty sandlots on either side of it, looked like somebody had built it in the middle of a desert. New low-cost housing project just up the street, not a block away, looking as though it had already been taken over by a marauding army, graffiti all over the brick walls, benches torn up, windows broken.

There were eight detectives waiting across the street under the trees, all of them from the Four-Six, all of them wearing bulletproof vests. This was a big one; a cop's father had been shot. A slender moon hung over the trees, casting a silvery glow on the scraggly lawn in front of the house. Night insects were singing. It was almost midnight. There was not a police vehicle in sight yet. They were all up the street in the project's parking lot, out of sight and just a radio call away; nobody wanted to spook the perps. The two cars from the Four-Five dropped eight of the ten detectives into the silent dark and moved off into the night. Under the trees, the sixteen detectives huddled, whispering like summer insects, planning their strategy.

"I want the door," Carella said.

"No," Wade said.

"He was *my* . . ."

"The door's mine."

None of the other cops argued with him. What they were discussing here was something called taking the door, and that meant they were discussing sudden death. Taking the door was the most dangerous thirty seconds in any policeman's life. Whoever was the point of the attacking wedge could be next in line for a halo and a harp because you never knew what was inside any apartment, and with today's weaponry bullets could come flying through even a metal-clad door. In this case, they *knew* what was inside that house across the street. What was in there was a killer with a nine-millimeter semiautomatic weapon. Nobody in his right mind wanted to take that door. Except Carella. And Wade.

"We'll take it together," Carella said.

"Can't but one man kick in a door," Wade said, and grinned in the moonlight. "It's mine, Carella. Be nice."

The hands on Carella's watch were standing straight up. Tonto put in a call to the patrol sergeant waiting in his car in the project's parking lot. There were six other cars with him. He told the sergeant they were going in. The sergeant said, "Ten-four."

The detectives all looked at each other.

Wade nodded and they started across the street.

The eight detectives from the Four-Six and four of the detectives from the Four-Five split into teams of six each and headed around to cover the sides and back of the house. Carella and Wade started up the walkway with the Lone Ranger and Tonto close behind them.

There was a low, virtually flat flight of steps leading up to a railed porch on the front of the house. This looked like a house on the prairie someplace. You expected to see tumbleweeds rolling by. Dolly had told them they were renting a room on the second floor front, right-hand side of the house. But there were no lights showing anywhere. Four black windows on the upper level, two black windows to the left of the blue entrance door. The walkway was dark, too, except for pale moonlight; someone had knocked out the street lamp. The walkway was covered with gravel.

They'd have preferred sand or snow or even mud; the goddamn gravel went off like firecrackers under their feet. They moved up the walk two abreast, swiftly, silently except for the crunching of the gravel, wincing at each rattle of stone, heading in a straight line for that blue front door. Wade and Carella had just gained the porch steps when the shots came.

They went flying off the steps like startled bats, throwing themselves into the low bushes on either side, one to the left, one to the right, three more shots on the night, the Lone Ranger and Tonto hurling themselves off the path and rolling away onto the patchy lawn, bracing themselves for whatever might come next.

The next shot came almost at once, but this time they saw where it was coming from, a yellow flash in one of the pitch-black windows on the left-hand side of the porch, followed by the immediate roar of a high-powered pistol slamming slugs into the night, and then yellow and *bam*, and yellow and *bam*, and four and five—and silence again.

Either Dolly had been wrong about which room she and her pals were renting, or Sonny and Diz had moved downstairs to another room.

That's what they were thinking.

It never crossed their minds that Dolly might have—

"Don't shoot!" she yelled. "They got me in here!"

"Shit," Wade said.

Three minutes into the job and they already had a hostage situation.

The people from the nearby project all came out to watch the Late Night Show. This was either *Die Hard* or *Die Harder* on a summer's night at the very top of August. Except that this wasn't a high rise in L.A. or an airport in D.C. What this was here was a shitty little house scheduled for the bulldozer to make room for another project exactly like the one these people lived in. And there weren't thousands of trapped airport people involved here or even hundreds of trapped skyscraper people, there were only two punks from the nation's capital—which had the highest per capita murder rate in the entire world—and a sixteen-year-old hostage who happened to be both a Cemetery Row hooker and a certified crackhead. Whose life was at stake. Carella knew that. Dolly Simms hadn't killed his father. Sonny Cole and Diz Whittaker, acting in concert, had done that. But because Dolly was in there now with the two killers—how the hell had she managed to get herself in there, damn it!—the police couldn't just go in and bust up the place.

It was amazing how the crowd grew. This might turn out to be merely *Little House on the Prairie*, but who could tell? Meanwhile, it was better being out here on the street, where there was at least the semblance of a breeze, than inside a sweltering brick tower eighteen stories high. By one o'clock that morning of the first day of August, the house was surrounded on all four sides and police barricades had been thrown up in a haphazard rectangle in a vain attempt to keep some order among the spectators. Both Emergency Service trucks were on the scene, and there were some three dozen blue-and-white patrol cars arranged like war chariots around the besieged building, with uniformed cops and detectives behind each car. A generator had been set up and spotlights illuminated all four sides of the house, but particularly the front of it, where Inspector Brady's fourth hostage negotiator crouched low behind the bushes lining the porch and tried to talk to either of the two men inside the room. Brady had used up three negotiators so far. The first two had almost had their heads blown off. None of them had dared venture onto the porch.

Dolly Simms sat in one of the windows, staring straight out at the glaring lights.

She was all you could see.

The two men were deep inside the room, far from the window.

Getting them to the window would be the first job.

It was Dolly who kept telling the negotiators that nobody better start shooting. She didn't look scared at all. One of the negotiators reported that she seemed stoned—which was not a surprise.

The Preacher was in the streets already, doing what he did best, doing in fact the only thing he knew how to do, which was to agitate people into a frenzy. Pacing behind the barricades, long hair slicked back, gold chains gleaming in the reflected light of the spots, bullhorn in hand, he kept telling the crowd that whenever a *white* girl yelled rape, then the nearest African-American males were always accused of it . . .

"But take a pure innocent young virgin like Tawana Brawley, who gets raped by a screaming mob of white men who then scrawl the word *nigger* . . ."

Yuh, yuh, from the handful of men in dark suits and red ties standing behind him.

". . . on her body, scrawl this word in *excrement* on her young violated body, and of course the white system of justice finds these rapists and bigots innocent of any crime and labels young Tawana a liar and a whore!"

The police could hardly hear themselves talking over the blare of the bullhorn.

"Well, brothers and sisters, what we've got in there tonight is a *true* whore, a bona fide and verified one-hundred-percent white purveyor of flesh who has enticed two young African-American brothers into a situation not of their own making! And that is why we have the whole mighty police force of this great city out here tonight, that is why we have this circus out here tonight, it is to once again persecute and pillory the youth of male black America!"

Young kids bobbed in and out of television-camera range, angling for a shot, big grins on their faces, this was the big chance to be on tee-vee, wow, see myself on the news tomorrow morning. The Preacher had been right in that respect, there *was* a circus atmosphere out here tonight, but not because anyone wanted to see a pair of killers safely apprehended. Instead, the air was charged with an excitement akin to what might have been felt in the Roman arena where nobody had a chance but the lions. Nobody in these mean streets believed that anybody in that building was coming out of there alive, not with the cops lined up out here like an army. Black or white, whoever was in there was already dead meat, that's what all these people in the streets were thinking, whatever their color or religion, whatever their stripe or persuasion. The only pertinent question was *when* it was going to happen. And so, like Roman spectators waiting for a lion or a tiger to bite off someone's arm or preferably his head, the crowd milled about patiently behind the sawhorses, hoping to be in on the moment of the kill, hoping to see all those fake die hard/die harder fireworks erupting here in real life on their tired tawdry turf. Hardly anybody was listening to The Preacher ranting and raving except the guys in the suits and red ties who stood behind him yuh-yuhing his every word. Everyone's eyes were on the woman crouched in the bushes, talking to the girl with the purple hair who sat in the window with the glare of the spotlights on her.

The problem here was that nobody could establish contact with the takers. There was no telephone in the room, and so the police couldn't ask the phone company to seize the line and give them control if it, which would have allowed them—and them alone—to talk with either Sonny or Diz or whoever was calling the tune in there. The further problem was that this was what the hostage team called a two-and-one, which meant there were two takers and only one hostage, which was a hell of a lot better than a four-and-twelve, but which still meant you were dealing with group dynamics, however small the group. Nobody knew who was in charge inside that house. Dolly had told Wade and Bent that Diz was the brains of the outfit, a supposition belied by his nickname, which they guessed was short for Dizzy. But since neither of the two were willing to talk to anyone, the negotiators had no idea who was running the show. A gun—or perhaps several guns—had so far done all the talking, with shots ringing out from somewhere deep in the room whenever a negotiator so much as lifted his head above the porch's floorboards. Four negotiators thus far. None of them making so much as a dent.

The Tac Team observers with their night-vision binocs couldn't see far enough into the room to determine whether there was just that single nine-millimeter gun in there or other weaponry as well. There were five observers in all, one each on the back and both sides of the building, two at the front, where all the action was. The observers had reported that all the windows on the sides of the house were boarded over: Sonny and Diz had been expecting company.

This was the first bit of important news Georgia Mobry got out of Dolly sitting there in the window.

Georgia was Brady's top female negotiator, back from her vacation only yesterday, and right in the thick of it now. She was the fourth one working the window, or working the porch perhaps, or more accurately working the bushes, because that's where she was crouched some six feet from the window in which Dolly sat all pale and purple in the lights. They'd all been wondering how Dolly had allowed herself to get into a situation like this one. She had told the detectives where they could find Sonny and Diz and so it would have seemed only sensible for her to stay as far away from there as possible.

But she now revealed to Georgia—who was truly expert at milking cream even from a toad—that she'd begun feeling guilty right after the two black cops left her, and so she'd come back here and told Sonny and Diz what was about to come down, and instead of getting out of there, they gave her some crack to smoke and told her she was their ticket to Jamaica. That was the *second* bit of important information.

"So please don't do any shooting," she said, "because they'll kill me, they told me they'd kill me."

Which is what she'd said many times before to the other three negotiators who'd been pulled out of the ball game. But now Georgia knew that Dolly herself had caused her present predicament, and the price of her release was a ticket to the Caribbean.

"Do they want to go to Jamaica?" she asked, checking it. "Is that it, honey?"

Accent as gentle and as thick as her name and her native state.

"Well, I'm only telling you what they said."

"That you were their ticket to Jamaica?"

"Yeah."

"Gee, I wish I could talk to them personally," Georgia said.

"Yeah, but they don't wanna."

" 'Cause I'm thinking maybe we can work something out here."

Like getting you out of there and then blowing these suckers away, Georgia was thinking. To her mind—and she'd been trained by Brady—what they were looking at here was a nonnegotiable hostage situation. Sooner or later, somebody was going to order an assault. The computer make on Sonny Cole had come in not ten minutes ago, and it revealed that he'd done some time on the West Coast for killing a man during the commission of a grocery-store holdup in Pasadena. So what they had here was not only a man who'd *maybe* killed a cop's father, but a man who'd been convicted once of having taken a life and who was now armed with a weapon and firing indiscriminately through an open window whenever the spirit moved him.

Desmond Whittaker was no sweetheart, either. In Louisiana, he'd done five years at hard labor for the crime of manslaughter, which would have been murder under subdivision (1) of Article 30 in the state's Criminal Code, except that it was committed "in sudden passion or heat of blood." How the pair had come together in D.C. was a mystery. So was how they'd ended up here in this city. But they were both extremely dangerous, and if they showed no signs soon of willingness to enter even the earliest stages of negotiation, then somebody was going to ask for a green light for either a direct assault or the use of chemical agents. A sharp-shooter was out of the question; nobody could see where the hell they *were* in that room. The only target was the girl in the window. And she was the one they wanted to save.

So Georgia didn't have much hope of success here.

"Why don't you ask one of them to talk to me directly?" she said.

"Well, they don't wanna," Dolly said again.

"Ask them, okay?"

"They'll shoot me," she said.

"Just for asking them? No, they wouldn't do that, would they?"

"Yes, they would," Dolly said. "I think they might."

No two hostage situations were alike, but a hostage serving as mediator was something Georgia had come across at least a dozen times before. Sometimes the taker even gave one of his hostages safe passage to go outside and talk to the police, with the understanding that if he or she didn't come back, somebody else would be going out of the building—*dead*. Georgia didn't want that to happen here. The pathetic little creature mediating in the window seemed stoned enough not to realize that there were hordes of policemen out here ready and in fact aching to storm that house and shoot anything in there that moved. But she wasn't so stoned that she couldn't smell the immediate danger behind her in that room, an armed man, or perhaps two armed men, threatening to kill her unless—

Unless *what*?

"You see," Georgia said, "we're not sure what the problem is here."

You never defined the problem for them. You let them do that.

"If we knew what the problem was, I'm sure we could work something out. We'd like to help here, but nobody wants to talk to us."

You always suggested help. The taker or takers were usually panicked in there. The political terrorists, the trapped criminals, even the psychotics, were usually panicked. If you told them you wanted to help . . .

"So why don't you ask them how we can help?" Georgia said.

"Well . . ."

"Go ahead. Just ask them, okay? Maybe we can work this out right away. Give it a try, okay?"

"Well . . ."

"Go ahead."

Dolly turned her head from the window. Georgia couldn't hear what she was saying. Nor could she hear what someone in the room behind her said. She heard only the deep rumble of a masculine voice. Dolly turned back again.

"He said he ain't got no problem, *you* got the problem."

"Who's that? Who told you that?"

"Diz."

Okay, Diz was the honcho, Diz was the one they wanted to reach.

"What does he say our problem is?" Georgia asked. "Maybe we can help him with it."

Dolly turned away from the window again.

In the distance, beyond the barricades that defined the outer perimeter, Georgia could hear The Preacher's voice extolling the merits of Tawana Brawley, "a priestess of honor and truth," he was calling her, "in an age of political lies and paramilitary deceit. And we have the same thing here tonight, we have a fierce and mighty demonstration of white police power against two young African-Americans as innocent as were the Scottsboro . . ."

Dolly turned back to the window.

"He says the problem is getting a chopper to the airport and a jet to Jamaica, that's the problem."

"Is that what he wants? Look, can't he come to the window? He's got the gun, I'm unarmed, nobody's going to hurt him if he comes to the window. Ask him to come to the window, okay?''

Georgia was truly unarmed. She was wearing light body armor, but that was a nine-millimeter gun in there. Red cotton T-shirt. Blue jacket with the word POLICE on it in white letters across the back. Walkie-talkie hanging on her belt.

''Dolly?''

''Mm?''

''Ask him, okay, honey? Nobody's gonna hurt him, I promise him.''

Dolly turned away again. The deep rumble of the voice inside again. She turned back to the window.

''He says you're full of shit, they killed a man,'' Dolly said.

''That was then, this is now. Let's see if we can work out the problem we got now, okay? Just ask him to . . .''

He appeared at the window suddenly, huge and black in the glare of the spotlights. It was like that scene in *Jaws* where Roy Scheider was throwing the bait off the back of the boat and the great white suddenly came up with his jaws wide, it was as heart-stopping as that. Georgia ducked. She had spotted an AK-47 in his hand.

''Who're you?'' he said.

''My name's Georgia Mobry,'' she said, ''I'm a Police Department negotiator. Who are you?''

Negotiator was the word you used. You were here to *deal*, get the people out before anybody got hurt. You never used the word *hostage* to define the people any taker had in there with him. You never used the word *surrender,* either. You asked a taker to send the people out, come on out yourself, let us help you, nobody's gonna hurt you, soothing words, neutral words. *Hostage* was a word that gave the taker even bigger ideas, made him think he was the Ayatollah Khomeini. *Surrender* was an insulting kill word that only triggered further defiance.

''I'm Diz Whittaker,'' he said, ''an' there's nothin' to negotiate here. Georgia, huh?''

She was looking up toward the window, eyes barely showing

above the deck. She saw a big muscular man with a close-shaved skull, wearing a white T-shirt, that was all she could see of him in the window frame. AK-47 in his right hand. Just the sight of that gun always sent a shiver up her spine. The illegal, Chinese-made assault rifle—a replica of the gun used by the Viet Cong—was a semiautomatic, which meant that it required a separate pull of the trigger for each shot. But it could fire up to seventy-five shots without reloading, and its curved clip gave it the lethal look of a weapon of *war*, no matter *how* many claims the National Rifle Association made for its legitimate use as a hunting rifle.

"Stan' up, Georgia," he said.

She didn't like the way he was saying her name. Almost a snarl. Georgia. Like she was Georgia the whole damn state instead of Georgia the person. Made her nervous the way he was saying the name.

"I don't want to get hurt," she said.

"Lemmee see you, Georgia." Snarling it again. "You fum Georgia? That where you fum?"

"Yes," she said.

"Stan' up lemmee see you, Georgia."

"First promise me you won't hurt me."

"You strapped?"

"Nossir."

"How do I know that?"

"Because I'm telling you. And I don't lie."

"Be the firs' cop *I* ever met dinn lie like a thief," he said. "Stan' up an' lemmee see you ain't strapped."

"I can't do that, Mr. Whittaker. Not till you promise . . ."

"Don't give me no *Mr.* Whittaker shit," he said. "How much you know about me, Georgia?"

"My superior told me who you and your friend are, I know a little bit about both of you. I can't help you without knowing something about . . ."

"What'd your boss tell you *exactly*, Georgia?"

You always told them you weren't in this alone, you didn't

have sole authority to do whatever it was they wanted you to do, you had to check first with your superior, or your boss, or your people, whatever you chose to call the person above you. You wanted them to believe you were their partner in working this out. You and them against this vague controller offstage, this unseen person who had the power to say yea or nay to their requests. Most people had bosses. Even criminals understood how bosses worked.

"He said you'd done some time."

"Uh-huh."

"You and your friend both."

"Uh-huh. He tell you Sonny killed that man in the bak'ry shop?"

"He said that's what they're thinking, yeah."

"An' I was with him, he tell you that, Georgia?"

"Yes."

"Makes me a 'complice, doan it?"

"It looks that way. But why don't we talk about the problem we have right now, Mr. Whittaker? I'd like to help you, but unless we . . ."

He suddenly opened fire.

The semiautomatic weapon trimmed the bushes over her head as effectively as a hedge-clipper might have. She hugged the ground and prayed he wouldn't fire through the wooden deck of the porch because then one of those highpowered slugs might somehow find her; eyes closed, she hugged the ground and prayed for the first time since she was fifteen, the bullets raging over her head.

The firing stopped.

She waited.

"Tell yo' boss send me somebody ain't a lyin' redneck bitch," Whittaker said. "You go tell him *that*, Georgia."

She waited.

She was afraid to move.

She took the walkie-talkie from her belt, pressed the Talk button.

"Observer Two," she said, "what've you . . . what've you got at the window?"

Her voice was shaking. She cursed her traitor voice.

There was a long pause.

"Hello, Observ . . ."

"Shooter's gone," a man's voice said. "Just the girl in it."

"You sure?"

"Got my glasses on it. Window's clear."

"Inspector?" she said.

"Yeah, Georgia?"

"I think I'd better come in. I'm not gonna do any more good here."

"Come on in," he said.

From where Mike Goodman stood with Brady and the assorted brass, he saw the Tac Team come up into firing position behind the inner-perimeter cars, saw Georgia sprinting back like a broken field runner toward the cover of Truck One, which Brady had set up as his command post. She was clearly frightened. Her face was a pasty white, and her hands were trembling. One of the E.S. cops handed her a cup of coffee when what she really needed was a swig of bourbon, and she sipped it with the cup shaking in her hands, and told Brady and the E.S. commander and the chief of detectives and the chief of patrol that there were now at least two weapons in there, the nine-millimeter and an AK-47 that had almost taken off her head. She also told them the takers wanted a chopper and a jet to Jamaica . . .

"Jamaica?" Brady said.

. . . and that Whittaker didn't appreciate Southern belles doing the police negotiating, witness him having called her a redneck when her mother was a librarian and her father a doctor in Macon. The brass listened gravely and then talked quietly among themselves about the use of force. Georgia merely listened; she was out of it now.

Di Santis was of the opinion that they had probable cause for an assault. Given the priors on both perps and the strong possibility that they were the men who'd murdered the bakery-shop owner, he was willing to take his chances with a grand jury and a coroner's inquest if either of the perps got killed. Brady was concerned about the girl in there. So was Brogan.

Curran thought they should try a chemical assault, there being no gas-carrying vents to worry about the way there'd be in an apartment building, and anyway who cared if a fire started in an already condemned building? Brady and Brogan were still worried about the girl in there. Suppose those two punks began shooting the minute they let loose with the gas? Two assault weapons in there? The girl would be a dead duck. They decided to try another negotiator in the bushes there, see if they couldn't get somebody on that porch, talk some sense into those bastards.

Trouble was, Brady had already used up all his skilled negotiators who weren't on vacation, and the only people he had left were himself and his trainees. Ever ready to step into the role of fearless leader, Brady was willing to risk the AK-47 and whatever else they might throw at him, but Di Santis pointed out that the three negotiators who'd made the least headway there in the bushes had all been men and that it might be advisable to try another woman. Georgia agreed that a woman might have better luck with the young girl up there who, like it or not, was the mediator of choice until the two shitheads came around. That left either Martha Halsted or Eileen Burke. And since Eileen, through no choice of her own, had had previous experience on the door, it was decided they'd let her have another go at it. Brady sent Goodman over to Truck Two to fetch her.

"Inspector wants you to talk to you," he said.

"Okay," she said.

"You blowing him or what?" Martha asked.

"Stick it," Eileen said.

But as she walked away, she could hear Martha and the other trainees whispering. It didn't bother her anymore. Cops had been whispering behind her back ever since the rape. Whispering cops were more dangerous than The Preacher and his bullhorn.

The crowd was silent now, waiting for the next technical effect, this here movie was beginning to sag a little, ho-hum.

Even The Preacher seemed bored. He kept rattling his gold chains and scowling.

Brady and all the brass looked extremely solemn.

"Hello, Burke," he said.

"Sir."

"Feel like working?" he asked, and smiled.

"No, sir," Eileen said.

The smile dropped from his mouth.

"Why not?" he said.

"Personal matter, sir."

"Are you a goddamn police officer, or what are you?" Brady said, flaring.

"Steve Carella's a personal friend," she said. "I know him . . ."

"What the hell . . .?"

". . . I know his wife, I know his . . ."

"What the hell has *that* got to . . . ?"

"I'm afraid I'll screw up, sir. If those men get away . . ."

"Inspector?"

They all turned.

Carella and Wade were standing there.

"Sir," Carella said, "we have an idea."

The crowd had begun chanting, "Do the hook-er, do the hook-er, do the hook-er," breaking the word in two, "Do the hook-er, do the hook-er, do the hook-er," urging the two men trapped in that house to break Dolly in half the way they'd broken the word, "Do the hook-er, do the hook-er, do the hook-er."

If Dolly heard what the crowd was chanting, she showed no

sign of it. She sat in the window like some pale and distant Lily Maid of Astolat, waiting for a knight to come carry her away. There were no knights out here tonight, there were no blue centurions, either. There was only a group of trained policemen hoping that their organization, discipline, teamwork—and above all patience—would resolve the situation before somebody inside that house exploded.

The two men in there were criminals, and in Brady's experience criminal takers were easier to handle than either political terrorists or psychotics. Criminals understood the art of the deal; their entire lives were premised on trade-offs. Criminals knew that if you said you couldn't trade for weapons, you meant it. If the taker had a .45 in there, for example, he knew you weren't going to trade him an MP83 for one of the hostages. And if you told him you'd never let him have *another* hostage, he knew you meant that, too. If he said, for example, he wouldn't hurt anybody if only you'd send somebody in to cook his meals or wash his clothes, he knew you wouldn't do that. There was a bottom line, and he knew exactly what it was, and he knew he'd look stupid or unprofessional if he tried to trade beyond that line. A criminal could even understand why his request for beer or wine or whiskey would be refused; he knew as well as you did that this was a dangerous situation here, and alcohol never made a bad situation better. A criminal understood all this.

And probably, somewhere deep inside, he also knew this wasn't going to end on a desert island with native girls playing ukeleles and stringing flowers in his hair. He knew this was going to end with him either dead or apprehended. Those were the only two choices open to him. Deep down, he knew this. So the longer a negotiation dragged on, the better the chances were that a criminal's common sense would eventually prevail. Make the deal, go back to the joint, it was better than being carried out in a body bag. But the situation here was volatile, and Brady had no real conviction that the men inside there would *ever* be ready to talk sense. The best he was hoping for was that Eileen would be able to make a little more progress than any of the other negotiators had.

"Dolly?"

Blank stare, looking out at the lights as if hypnotized by them, the chanting wafting on the night air from across the street, "Do the hook-er, do the hook-er, do the hook-er," urging men who needed no urging at all.

"My name is Eileen Burke, I'm a Police Department negotiator," she said.

No answer.

"Dolly? Could you please tell Mr. Whittaker I'd like to talk to him?"

"He don't wanna," Dolly said.

"Yes, but that was when the other negotiator was here. Tell him there's a new . . ."

"He still don't wanna."

"If you could please tell him . . ."

"Tell me yourself."

Looming in the window again. Tall and glowering, the white T-shirt stained with sweat, the AK-47 in his hands.

"Mr. Whittaker," she said, "I'm Eileen Burke, a Police De . . ."

"The fuck you want, Burke?"

"You were talking earlier about a helicopter . . ."

"Tha's right. Stan' up an' lemmee see you. Can't see nothin' but the top of your head and your eyes."

"You know I can't do that, Mr. Whittaker."

"How come I know that, huh?"

"Well, you've been shooting at anything that moves out here . . ."

"You got somebody trainin' in on me?" he asked, and suddenly ducked behind the window frame.

On the walkie-talkie to Brady, a sharpshooter in position said, "Lost him."

"You wanna talk some more," Whittaker said, "you come up here on the porch, stan' here front of the winnder."

"Maybe later," she said.

" 'Cause I ain't givin' nobody a clear shot at me, tha's for sure."

"Nobody's going to hurt you, I can promise you that," Eileen said.

"You can promise me *shit,* Red."

"I don't like being called Red," she said.

"Tough *shit* what you like or don't like."

She wondered if she'd made a mistake. She decided to pursue it. At least they were talking. At least there was the beginning of a dialogue.

"When I was a kid, everybody called me Red," she said.

He said nothing. Face half-hidden behind the window frame. Dolly sitting there all eyes and all ears, this was the first interesting story she'd heard all night long.

"One day, I cut off all my hair and went to school that way . . ."

"Oh Jeez!" Dolly said, and brought her hand to her mouth.

"Told the kids to call me Baldy," Eileen said, "told them I preferred that to Red."

Behind the window frame, she could hear Whittaker chuckling. The story was a true one, she hadn't made it up. Cut off all her goddamn red hair, wrapped it in newspaper, her mother was shocked, Eileen, what have you *done*?

"Cut off all my hair," she said now, just as she'd said all those years ago.

"You must've looked somethin'," Dolly said.

"I just didn't like being called Red," she said reasonably.

"Cut off all your hair, wow."

"Cut it all off."

"Boy oh boy," Dolly said.

Whittaker still hadn't said anything. She figured she'd lost him. Got a few chuckles from him, and then it was right back to business.

"So whut you *like* bein' called?" he asked suddenly, surprising her.

"Eileen," she said, "how about you? What shall I call you?"

"You can call me a chopper," he said, and burst out laughing.

Good, he'd made his own joke. Variation on the old "You can call me a taxi" line, but at least he hadn't said "You can call me anything you like so long as you don't call me late for dinner." And they were back to the chopper again. Good. Trade-off time. Maybe.

"A chopper's possible," she said, "but I'd have to talk to my boss about it."

"Then you go talk to him, Eileen."

"I feel pretty sure he can arrange it . . ."

"I sure hope so, Eileen."

"But I know he'd expect . . ."

" 'Cause I'm gettin' pretty goddamn impatient here . . ."

"Well, this is really the first time . . ."

". . . an' I'd hate to see anythin' happen to this little girl here, hmm?"

"I'd hate to see anything happen to *anybody*, believe me. But this is the first time you and I have really talked, you know, and . . ."

"Why don't you come up here on the porch?" he said.

"You think I'm crazy?" she said.

He laughed again.

"No, come on, I won't hurt you. I mean it, come on."

"Well . . ."

"Come on."

"How about I just stand up first?"

"Okay."

"But you'll have to show me your hands. Show me there's nothing in your hands, and I'll stand up."

"How I know what you got in *your* hands?"

"I'll show you my hands, too. Here, see?" she said, and raised both hands above the porch deck and waggled all the fingers. "Nothing in my hands, okay?"

"How you know I won't show you my hands and then dust you anyway? Jus' pick up the piece again an' . . ."

"Well, I don't think you'd do that. Not if you promise me."

The first time she'd heard this in class, she'd thought it was ridiculous. You asked a terrorist to promise he wouldn't blow you away? You asked some nut just out of the loony bin to promise he wouldn't hurt you? She had been assured over and over again that it worked. If they *really* promised you, if you got them to say the words "I promise you," then they really wouldn't hurt you.

"So can I see your hands?" she asked.

"Here's my hands," he said, and stepped around the window frame for just an instant, waggling his fingers the way she just had, and then ducking back out of sight again. She thought she'd seen a grin, too. "Now stan' up," he said.

"If I stand up, will you promise you won't hurt me?"

"I promise."

"You won't hurt me?"

"I promise I won't hurt you."

"All right," she said, and stood up.

He was silent for a moment, looking her over. Fine, she thought, look me over. But this isn't the old man all over again, you aren't eighty-four years old and senile, you're a killer. So look me over all you like but . . .

"Put your hands on the windowsill where I can see them, okay?" she said.

"Matter, don't trust me?" he said.

"I trust you, yes, because you promised me. But I'd feel a lot better if I could see your hands. You can see mine," she said, holding them out in front of her and turning them this way and that like a model for Revlon nail polish, "so you know I'm not going to hurt you, isn't that right?"

"It is."

Still not stepping out from where he was hidden.

"So how about showing me the same consideration?" she said.

"Okay, here's my hands," he said, and moved into the window frame beside Dolly and grabbed the sill with both huge hands.

"Clear shot," the sharpshooter said into his walkie-talkie. "Shall I take him out?"

"Negative," Brady told him.

"What I'd like to do now," Eileen said, "is go back to my boss and ask him about that helicopter."

"Sure is *red*," Whittaker said, grinning.

"Yeah, I know," Eileen said, shaking her head and smiling back at him. "I'm pretty sure he can get you what you want, but it might take some time. And I know he'll expect something from you in return.

"Whutchoo mean?"

"I'm just saying I know what he's like. He'll get you that helicopter, but one hand washes the other is what he's going to tell me. But let me go talk to him, okay? See what he says."

"If he o'pects me to let go Dolly, he's dreamin'. Dolly stayin' with us till we on that jet."

"What jet?"

"Dolly tole you we . . ."

"No, not me. Maybe she told the other negotiator."

"We want a jet to take us to Jamaica."

Eileen was thinking he'd been standing there in the window for the past three, four minutes now, a clean shot for any of the Tac Team sharpshooters. But Sonny was still somewhere in the darkness of that room. And Sonny was strapped with a nine-millimeter auto.

"Why Jamaica?" she asked.

"Nice down there," he said vaguely.

"Well, let me talk to him, okay? You're asking for *two* things in a row now, and that's gonna make it a little harder for me. Let me see what I can do, okay?"

"Yeah, go ahead. An' tell him we ain't foolin' aroun' here."

"I will. Now Mr. Whittaker, I'm gonna turn my back on you and walk over to the truck there. Do I still have your promise?"

"You have my promise."

"You won't hurt me."

"I won't hurt you."

"I have your promise then," she said, and nodded. "I'll be back as soon as I talk to him."

"Go ahead."

She turned away, giving him no reason to believe she was frightened or even apprehensive, turned and began walking swiftly and deliberately toward the emergency service truck, the word POLICE in white across the back of her blue poplin jacket, trying not to pull her head into her shoulders, thinking nonetheless that any minute now a spray of bullets would come crashing into her spine.

But Whittaker kept his promise.

It was Carella who'd realized the perps had blindsided themselves. Boarded up the windows on three sides of the house. And if all those windows were boarded, they couldn't see out. Which meant that three sides of the house were accessible to the police. This was what he'd told Brady.

They had finally got a floor plan from the realty company that had sold the house to a Mr. and Mrs. Borden some twelve years ago, long before a housing development had been planned for the area. It looked like this:

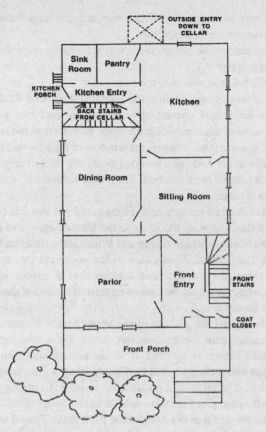

According to Dolly, when the owners of the house converted from a private residence to a rooming house, the living room and dining room were both refurnished as bedrooms, and what had once been the sitting room was now a sort of public room with a sofa, two easy chairs, and a television set on a stand. The kitchen and its adjoining pantry and laundry room—what had originally been called the sink room—were the only rooms on this floor of the house that remained as they'd been since its construction back before the turn of the century. There was only one large bathroom in the house, on the second floor.

At the rear of the house, there was an outside entry that led down to the cellar.

Carella pointed this out, too.

One of those sloping things that kids just loved to slide down, two doors on it that opened upward and outward like wings. Observer number four, working the inner perimeter at the rear of the house, reported that whereas the window to the left—*his* left— of the cellar doors had been boarded over, the doors themselves seemed not to have been touched. They were fastened by a simple padlock in a hasp.

It was Carella's thought that if they could get into that cellar, they could then come up the stairs to the kitchen entry and move through the house to where Sonny and Whittaker were holding the girl in the front room. From either of the doorways that opened into that room, they would have a clean shot at anyone inside, including whoever might be backed against the rear wall, as they suspected Sonny was.

Brady wanted the girl out of the house first.

No assault until the girl was out.

He told Eileen to go back to Whittaker and tell him they couldn't get him a chopper, but they could bring a limo around to the back door if he let the girl go at the same time. His thinking was to split up the pair. Get Whittaker to send Sonny back to the kitchen entry while the girl was coming out the front door. Time it so that Carella and Wade would be at the top of the cellar stairs when Sonny came back to check on the limo. No assault until they knew for certain Dolly was out of the house. Position themselves in the cellar, get themselves in place, but no assault till the girl was clear.

It could work.

Maybe.

"I'm sorry," Eileen said, "but he can't get a chopper for you."

"You tole me . . ."

"I know, but . . ."

"Tell him I'll kill the fuckin' girl! He wants to play games here, I'll kill the fuckin' girl!"

"Can I come up there on the porch?" Eileen asked.

You always asked for permission to approach. You always asked for assurances that there'd be no accidents, no slipups. You didn't want anyone to get hurt here. Not you, not him, not anyone.

"Okay?" she said. "Can I come up?"

"No," Whittaker said. "What'd you do, Red? Pick up a gun while you were back there with your pals?"

"No, I didn't. I'm not armed, I'll show you if you like. Is it okay to stand up?"

"You got to be crazy, you know that? You come back with *shit* from him, and you 'spect me to . . ."

"You promised you wouldn't hurt me. Have I still got your promise?"

"Why should I promise you anything?"

" 'Cause I think I've got a way out of this. If we can just talk it over . . ."

"I'm not givin' him anythin' till he gives *me* somethin'!"

"That's just what I want to talk about. Can I stand up? Will you promise not to hurt me if I stand up?"

"Go on, stan' up," he said.

"I didn't hear your promise."

"You got my fuckin' *promise*, okay?"

She wondered if she should ask to see his hands again. She decided that would be pushing it. He'd given her his promise, and she had to trust him. Pretending a confidence she didn't quite feel, she stood up, opened her jacket wide, and said, "Nothing under it, Mr. Whittaker. I'm unarmed."

"Turn aroun', liff up the back of the jacket."

She turned to show her back to him and the assault rifle in his hands. Lifted the jacket, showed him the back of the yellow shirt under it. Nothing strapped to her. No gun and holster. Nothing.

"Okay?" she said.

"What's that on your belt?" he asked.

"A walkie-talkie. Don't worry, it isn't some kind of trick gun or anything."

"Throw it up here on the porch."

"No, I can't do that. I have to stay in touch. In case they want me to pass on a message. Okay?"

"Yeah, okay."

"Okay to put my jacket down now?"

"Yeah, go on, Red."

"You want me to cut off all my hair again?"

She thought she heard a chuckle in there.

"So stop calling me Red, okay?"

No answer.

"Okay for me to turn around again?" she asked.

"Yeah, okay."

She turned to face the window again. She still could not see him. Only Dolly sat in the window. Blank stare on her face.

"Can I come up on the porch?"

"Why?"

"So we can talk without having to yell."

"Come on up."

"Do I still have your promise?"

"I ain't shot you yet, have I?"

"I'd like your promise that you won't."

"I won't. I promise you."

"Okay, so I'm coming up there, right?"

"I said okay."

"I just don't want any accidents. I want you to know what I'm doing, so there won't be any slipups."

"Yeah, come on up."

She went up the low flat steps that led to the front door of the house, and then she moved left toward the nearest window and was moving along the porch toward . . .

"Hold it right there," he said.

"Okay."

"That's fine right where you are."

"Okay."

"So what's your idea?"

"He says no chopper, he can't get one. There's been a big accident on the Harb . . ."

"The *what*?"

"The Harb, the river, don't you—that's right, you're from Washington."

"How you know that?"

"Well, we have your . . ."

"Yeah, what kine a accident?"

"A pleasure boat hit the ferry to Bethtown. We've got all our choppers out in a big rescue operation."

A flat-out lie. But the game had changed. Two men with a bolt cutter would soon be dancing around back to that cellar door. And once the girl was clear—

"So tell your boss t'get me a *commercial* chopper."

"I'll ask him, if you want me to. But you know what I think?"

"Whut?"

"I think you'd be better off with a limo. Time the jet gets out there . . ."

"Whut jet? He gettin' me a jet?"

"I thought I told you. A jet's being fueled right this minute."

"No, all you said was no chopper."

"It'll be ready in . . ."

"Be ready *where*?"

"Spindlerift. In an hour or so. If I can get him to send a limo for you, you'd be there in plenty of time. Might be *quicker* than a chopper, matter of fact, the way air-traffic control is out there."

She could see his face now. She had lured him closer to the window. He was thinking it over.

"I'll ask my boss to give you a motorcycle escort," she said, "get you to the airport in forty minutes."

The idea was beginning to appeal to him. Big-shot ambassador from Washington, D.C., in his own stretch limo with a motorcycle escort taking him to his private jet plane. She could almost hear the wheels grinding in the dark there inside the house and inside his head.

"I'll let go the girl when we're inside the jet," he said.

"Aw, come on, Mr. Whittaker, how can I tell my boss that?"

"I don't give a shit *whut* you tell him . . ."

Easy now, she thought.

". . . I'm the one got a gun pointin' at her *head*!"

"I know that," she said. Her heart was pounding. "And I don't want her to get hurt, Mr. Whittaker, I don't want *anybody* to get hurt. But I've got to go back to him with something reasonable, I'm sure you can understand that. He's giving you a limo and a jet, I've got to tell him you're willing to give him something in return." Talking a mile a minute now, dazzling him with the brilliance of her logic. "I *know* I can get the limo for you, I've already discussed that with him. And he's got the jet being fueled right this minute, he's getting you everything you asked for, he's being cooperative all the way down the line, isn't he? It's just a chopper's out of the question because of that freak accident on the river, which was something none of us could control, am I right? So if I can go to him and say, Look, Mr. Whittaker'll let the girl go, but he wants certain assurances, whatever those may be, you tell me what you want and I'll pass it on. And if we can work it out, get you what you want, make sure the girl's safe and you're safe, we can have you on your way in five, ten minutes, be there in time to meet the jet, what do you say?"

"How do I know this ain't a *trick* is whut I say."

"That's why I asked you to tell me what assurances you want for your safety. Just tell me what guarantees you want, and I'll pass them on. We don't want any slipups here. You tell us what you want, we'll tell you what we're going to do. That way *you'll* know what we're doing and *we'll* know what you're doing and nobody'll get hurt, what do you say?''

Come *on,* she thought.

"How do I know there'll even *be* a limo. I let the girl go, you come in here with a fuckin' army . . .''

"No, we'll bring the limo up before you send the girl out. You can check to see it's there.''

"Where?''

"Wherever you want it. I thought outside the door on the left side of the house. Where there's that little porch there. Would that be okay?''

"Tell your boss I want whiskey in the limo.''

Good, she thought, he's ready to cut a deal.

"No,'' she said, "I can't get you whiskey.''

"Why not?'' he said.

"Well, we don't want anybody getting hurt. I know you'll keep *your* promise, Mr. Whittaker, but whiskey doesn't know how to keep promises.''

Inside the house, she thought she heard him chuckle again.

"So what shall I tell him?'' she asked. "If I get you the limo, will you send the girl out?''

"Suppose I see the limo out there . . .''

"We'll bring it right up to the door there. All you have to do is step down from the porch there, and get right in the car.''

"But suppose I *see* the car out there, and I let the girl go, like you said, and you blow me away 'fore I even get a chance to climb *in* that car?''

Working out all the details. Knowing in his heart of hearts that no one was going to let him board a jet to Jamaica, no one was going to let him sip piña coladas in the sun on a tropical beach. But bargaining anyway. Hoping against hope that maybe this *would* be the big payoff, after all. Let the girl go, climb in the limo . . .

"Well, how would you *like* us to work it?'' she asked. "The bottom line is my boss is going to want to make sure the girl's safe before he lets that limo . . ."

"Ain't no way a limo's gonna be safe," he said. "I get in that limo, you blow me *an'* Sonny *an'* the car to hell and gone. No way, Red. Tell your fuckin' boss I want a chopper. I don't care where he gets it, but that's what I want. Tell him the girl comes out with me to the chopper, I let her go *after* Sonny's inside an' I'm climbin' in. That's when you get the girl. Tell your boss he's got five minutes to make up his mind. Otherwise he gets the girl, all right, but he gets her *dead*. Five minutes. Tell him."

On the street outside, the crowd behind the barricade was getting restless. This was already three o'clock in the morning, but no one was thinking of sleep. The only thing on anyone's mind was Showdown at the O.K. Corral. Toward that end, and with the seeming purpose of rattling everyone in sight so that the only possible outcome *would* be a loss of blood, a loss of life, further fuel for the inevitable fire to come, The Preacher took up his bullhorn yet another time and started a catchy little chant that had nothing whatever to do with the circumstances at hand.

"No More Jogger Justice!" he shouted in a voice worn and ragged and hoarse. "No More Jogger Justice!"

He was referring to the raped and brutally beaten young woman who had captured the attention of the entire world. He was referring to the guilty verdicts brought in against her attackers. It didn't matter that the young white hooker and the two black killers inside that house could not by the remotest stretch of anyone's imagination, least of all The Preacher's, be identified with the jogger and her brutal assailants. What mattered to The Preacher was that he place himself at the heart of wherever the action was, creating action if there didn't happen to be any, and presenting himself on television as the lone and lonely voice of black sensibility—whereas in reality most black people knew he was nothing but a rabble-rouser dedicated exclusively to self-promotion.

"No More Jogger Justice!" he shouted into the bullhorn. "No More Jogger Justice!"

And the crowd—not a moment earlier lulled almost to sleep by this endless chess game with its black and white pieces being maneuvered on a black-and-white board that seemed to stretch off to a vanishing point somewhere all too far in the infinite distance— the crowd picked up the catchy little chant, "No More Jogger Justice!" and amplied it without benefit of bullhorns, "No More Jogger Justice!," beating out the words in a four-four tempo that all but cried for foot-stomping, "No More Jogger Justice!," the litany spilling out over the barricades to cascade onto the front porch of the house where Dolly Simms sat white-faced and stunned at the window.

She could hear the subtle rhythm of the chant under the steady roar of the police chopper circling overhead. Sonny and Diz were deep inside the room now, whispering, Sonny with the nine-millimeter pointed at her head where she sat in silhouette against the glare of the lights. Dolly figured they were talking about killing her. She knew they were crazy enough to kill her. Somehow, she didn't seem to care anymore.

"Mr. Whittaker?"

The redhead. Out there in the bushes again, some people never gave up. Imagine her cutting off all her hair. Maybe *she* was crazy, too. Maybe the whole world was crazy except Dolly herself, who would be dead in five, ten minutes, the way she figured it, which would probably be an easier life after all was said and done.

"Mr. Whittaker? It's me again. Eil . . ."

"They can't hear you," Dolly said.

"What?"

"They can't hear you," she repeated. "The chopper's too loud."

"Go back and tell Mr. Whittaker I have to talk to him."

"He'll shoot me if I move from this window."

"Just tell him we have to talk some more."

"I can't."

Eileen reached for her walkie-talkie.

"Inspector?" she said.

"Here," Brady said.

"Lose the goddamn chopper, I can't hear myself think."

"Ten-four," he said.

From where Wade worked with the bolt cutter, he could hear the chopper moving off, the steady clatter of its blades succumbing to the chant that rose now as if to call the aircraft back, insistent voices reaching to the blackness of the sky overhead, "No More Jogger Justice! No More Jogger Justice!"

"Dumb assholes," he said, and closed the jaws of the cutter onto the steel shackle of the padlock. The steel snapped. He tossed the cutter aside and yanked the lock free of its hasp. In three seconds flat, Carella had both cellar doors raised and was starting down the steps, Wade behind him. The sound of the chopper was all but gone now. There was only the sound of the chanting.

It was pitch-black in the cellar.

There was the smell of coal and the smell of dust.

They figured the steps were straight ahead and slightly to their left.

They dared not turn on a light.

"Where's it going?" Sonny asked.

"Shut up," Whittaker said.

"It's *leavin'*, man, can't you hear it?"

"I hear it, shut up," Whittaker said, and went to the window. "Red!" he yelled. "The hell are you?"

"Right here," she said.

"Where? Stan' up so I can see you."

"Nope," she said.

"Whutchoo mean *nope*? You want me to . . ."

"Mr. Whittaker, it's time we talked turkey here. You know there's a . . ."

"Don't you tell me whut I gotta talk, woman! I'm the one got the girl in here. You ain't got . . ."

"Okay, you want to stay in there forever with her? Is that what you want? Or do you want to settle this thing, get on your way to the airport, which is it? The chopper's here, I got the damn chopper for you, so how about lending me a hand here? I've been busting my ass for you, Mr. Whittaker . . ."

She heard him chuckling.

"Yeah, very funny," she said. "And you're making me look like a fool in front of my boss. Do you want that chopper to land, or do you want to keep me running back and forth all night? I've got the walkie-talkie right here, look at it," she said, and held her hand up over her head, over the porch deck so he could see her hand and the walkie-talkie sticking up out of the bushes. "Just tell me what you want and I'll call him. I'm trying to facilitate this operation, I'm trying to get you on that chopper and the girl outside that house without anybody getting hurt. So will you help me do that, Mr. Whittaker? I'm trying my best here, really, I am. All I need is a little help from you."

There was a deep silence inside there.

At last, he said, "Okay, here's the deal."

They had found the cellar steps.

The walkie-talkie volume control was at its lowest setting, and they were listening to what Eileen was relaying back to the inspector. The way they understood the deal, the chopper would land in the vacant lot on the left-hand side of the house, some fifty feet from what was marked on the floor plan as the kitchen porch. The pilot of the helicopter would be alone, and he would step out of the aircraft and down onto the ground and raise his hands above his head before they came out of the house. Whittaker would come out of the house first, with Sonny remaining behind in the kitchen entry, his pistol to the girl's head. When Whittaker was safely behind the pilot, the muzzle of the AK-47 angled up against the pilot's neck, he would signal for Sonny to let the girl loose. As the girl began her run back to the E.S. truck, Eileen would be waiting to lead her in. By that time, Sonny should have reached the helicopter. If anyone tried to harm Sonny as he ran over from the house, Whittaker would kill the pilot.

"Sounds to me like they're making an exchange," Wade whispered. "The girl for the pilot."

"They don't make exchanges," Carella said. "That's one of their rules."

"Then what does it sound like to you?"

"It sounds like an exchange," Carella said. "But the pilot is a cop."

"Does that make it okay to kill him?"

"No, but . . ."

"What's the plan once they get to the airport?"

"I don't know," Carella said. "I just work here."

They listened outside the door at the top of the steps. In just a little while, if all went well, Sonny and Whittaker would be coming down the hallway outside that door. The minute Sonny turned the girl loose, Carella would be face to face with the man who'd killed his father.

The sharpshooter crouched low in the cabin on the right-hand side of the aircraft. Below, a lone police officer wearing luminous orange trousers and jacket was running out from the inner police perimeter.

"Who's that?" Whittaker asked at once.

"He's unarmed," Eileen assured him. "He'll be signaling to the pilot, telling him where to put the ship down. We don't want any mistakes."

"I want him out of there as soon as it lands."

"Inspector?" Eileen said into the walkie-talkie.

"Here," Brady said.

"He wants that man out of there as soon as the chopper touches down."

"He's got it," Brady said.

"Did you hear that?" she asked Whittaker.

"No."

"He'll get out of there as soon as the ship lands."

"He better."

Dolly was still sitting alone in the open window. The other two were somewhere in the darkness of the room beyond. Eileen was talking to no one she could see. But she was certain Whittaker could see out of the room; he had spotted the man in orange running toward the cleared sandlot on the side of the house.

"Ain't nobody leavin' this house till that man's back where he belongs," he said from out of the blackness.

"Don't worry about it. He's signaling now," she said. "You can't see him from where you are, but he's signaling to the chopper."

The sharpshooter could see the man below swinging a red torchlight in a circle over his head. The sliding door on the right-hand side of the ship was open. The pilot would bring the ship down with that side facing the house. The moment Whittaker was in place, using the pilot as a shield, facing the police line out there, the sharpshooter should have a clean shot at the back of his head. The pilot *hoped*.

"Hedgehog, this is Firefly, over," the pilot said.

"Come in, Firefly."

"We've got your man sighted, ready to take her down."

"Take her down, Firefly."

"Ten-four."

A police code sign-off, even though this was air-to-ground radio traffic and a wilco might have been more appropriate. Neither the pilot up there preparing to land and be seized by an armed killer whose head the sharpshooter might or might not succeed in blowing from his body, nor Chief of Patrol Curran, talking to him from the ground, had exchanged anything but landing instruc-.

tions. These days, nobody knew who was listening on what frequency, and there was still a sixteen-year-old girl in that house.

"Coming in," Eileen said.

"I'm sending Sonny back to the kitchen with the girl," Whittaker said. "He yells loud enough, I can hear him from back there. Minute he tells me the chopper's down, I'm headin' back myself. Ress is up to you whether anybody gets hurt or not."

"Just about down," she said.

"You hear me?"

"I heard you."

"Move it on out, Sonny."

The leaves on the bushes outside the house shook violently as the chopper skids came closer to the ground. Over the roar of the ship and the rush of the wind, Eileen said into her walkie-talkie, "Sonny's heading toward the kitchen now." With all that clamor, she hadn't expected Whittaker to hear her, but he had.

"Why you tellin' him that?" Whittaker shouted over the noise.

"We don't want any mistakes, you know that." Into the walkie-talkie, she said, "Chopper's down, Inspector, better get that man out of there," but this was really for the benefit of Carella and Wade, who were standing on the landing just inside the cellar door.

"Diz!"

Jesus!

His voice sounded as if it was right at Carella's elbow, just outside the door!

"*Move* it, bitch!"

Running by in the corridor now, past the door.

"Ow!"

The girl's voice.

"I said *move* it! Diz! Can you hear me, Diz?"

"You don't have to poke me with the damn . . ."

"Diz!"

A bit further away now. Yelling from the kitchen, Carella guessed. Visualizing the floor plan in his head, the narrow corridor running from the outside porch to the kitchen. Sonny Cole, his father's murderer, standing in the kitchen, yelling to his partner at the front of the house.

"Diz! It's down, I can see it! It's on the ground! Diz, can you hear me?"

They could not hear anyone answering him.

But there were footsteps again, coming back toward them in the corridor outside. Carella kept the walkie-talkie pressed to his ear, fearful of a sound leak that would give away their position. There was sudden laughter just outside the door, startling him again.

"We goin' to *Jamaica*," Sonny told the girl, laughing, his voice high and shrill.

That's what *you* think, Carella thought.

"That was Sonny jus' then," Whittaker said. "He says the chopper's down."

"He's right, it is," Eileen said.

"So I'm headin' back there now." He sounded almost sad to be leaving. "You sure you got this all straight in your head?"

"I hope so," Eileen said.

"Me, too," Whittaker said, "otherwise somebody goan *die*, you know? Minute I see the pilot standin' out there, I'm headin' for the chopper. You know the ress."

"I do."

"Better be no tricks."

"There won't be," she said.

"No surprises," he said, and suddenly appeared in the window. "So long, Red," he said, and grinned, and was gone into the darkness again.

"It's *Eileen*," she muttered under her breath, and then, immediately, into the walkie-talkie, "Whittaker's moving back."

* * *

Carella would have been blind without Eileen's voice coming over the walkie-talkie. The voice of a good cop and a good friend filling him in, giving him updates on when it would be all right to come out and say hello to his father's killer.

"Chopper's down . . ."

And then:

"Whittaker's moving back . . ."

And now:

"Pilot's out of the ship . . ."

Carella waited. Wade stood tensely beside him, his ear pressed to the cellar door, listening for any sound from outside there in the corridor.

Both of them had drawn their guns long ago.

Now they simply waited.

"Putting his hands up over his head . . ." Eileen said.

She was standing midway between Truck One and the helicopter, the flaps of her blue jacket dancing in the wind produced by the whirling blades, watching the pilot as he came to a stop just beyond the ladder leading down from the ship, sliding door open above him and behind him, his hair flapping wildly, his hands high over his head. She could not see anyone inside the ship.

"Kitchen door's opening," she said into the walkie-talkie.

She caught her breath.

"Whittaker's poking his head out, looking around . . ."

She waved to him. Let him know she was here. Everything according to plan, right? Soon as you've got the pilot, you let the girl go, and I'm waiting here for her. He did not wave back. Come on, she thought, acknowledge my presence. Let me know you see me. She waved again, bigger movements this time, more exaggerated. He still did not wave back. Just took a last look all around to make sure nobody was waiting out here to ambush him, and then began running for the helicopter.

"He's on his way to the chopper!" she shouted into the

walkie-talkie. "Girl's still inside the house, hold steady. Inspector?"

"Yes."

"Who calls the play?"

"I do. Just tell me when the girl is clear."

"Yes, sir."

Silence.

"He's just about there now."

More silence.

"He's behind the pilot now. Signaling to the door. The girl's out! *Dolly!*" she yelled. "This way! Over here!"

"Assault One, *go!*" Brady shouted.

They would later, in a diner near Headquarters downtown, over coffee and doughnuts as another hot day dawned over the city, try to piece together what had happened next, assemble it as they might have a jigsaw puzzle, pulling in separate pieces of the action from various perspectives, trying to make a comprehensive whole out of what seemed at first to be merely a scattering of confused and jagged pieces.

The girl was running toward her.

Purple hair like a beacon in the night.

"Dolly!" she shouted again.

"Hey! Red!"

She was startled for a moment, his voice coming out of the darkness near the helicopter where he stood behind the pilot. She turned to locate his voice, taking her eyes off the girl for just an instant.

"I *lied!*" he shouted.

And the girl exploded in blood.

They broke out of the cellar the instant Brady gave them the green light. Sonny had just released the girl and was poised for flight inside the side door, like a runner toeing his mark while waiting for the starting gun. The starting gun came from behind him, a shot fired from Wade's .38, catching Sonny in the right leg and knocking him off his feet before he could step out onto the porch. They were all over him in the next ten seconds, Wade kicking the nine-millimeter out of his hand as Sonny tried to sit up and raise the gun into a firing position, Carella kneeing him under the chin and slamming him onto his back on the linoleum-covered floor in the narrow corridor. Green linoleum, he would remember later. Yellow flowers in the pattern. Green and yellow and Sonny's wide-open brown eyes as Carella put the muzzle of his gun in the hollow of his throat. Jagged pink knife scar down one side of his face.

"Do it," Wade whispered.

The girl came stumbling forward, rosebud breasts in the lavender blouse erupting in larger red flowers as the slugs from the assault rifle ripped into her back and exited in a shower of lung and blood and gristle and tissue, spattering Eileen in gore as the girl fell forward into her arms.

"Oh dear God," Eileen murmured, and heard the shots from inside the helicopter as the sharpshooter fired twice and only twice, but twice was more than enough. The first bullet took Whittaker at the back of his neck, ripping out his trachea as it exited. The second shot caught him just above his right cheek as the force of the first bullet spun him around and away from the pilot. He was dead even before the shattered cheek sent slivers of bone ricocheting up into his brain.

Behind the barricades, even The Preacher stopped chanting.

"Do it!" Wade whispered urgently.

There was sweat in that narrow corridor, and fear, and anger, and every sweet thought Carella had ever had for his father, every emotion he'd ever felt for him, all of these burning his eyes and causing his gun hand to shake violently, the muzzle of the Police Special trembling in the hollow of Sonny's throat, great gobs of sweat oozing on Sonny's face, Wade's face close to Carella's now, all three of them sweating in that suffocating corridor where murder was just the tick of an instant away. "Do it," Wade whispered again, "we all *alone* here."

He almost did it.

Almost squeezed the trigger, almost pulled off the shot that would have ended it for Sonny and might have ended it for himself as well, all the anger, all the sorrow, all the hatred.

But he knew that if he heeded those whispered words *Do it*—and oh how easy to do it here in this secret place—he would be doing it not only to Sonny, he would be doing it to himself as well. And to anyone in this city who had ever hoped for justice under law.

He swung himself off the man who had killed his father.

"Up!" he said.

"You *shot* me, you mother-fucker!" Sonny yelled at Wade.

"*Up!*" Carella said again, and yanked him to his feet and clamped the cuffs onto his wrists, squeezing them shut hard and tight. Wade was looking at him, a puzzled expression on his face.

"I'm gonna bring charges," Sonny said. "*Shootin'* me, you mother-fucker."

"Yeah, you bring charges," Wade said. He was still looking at Carella. "I don't understand you," he said.

"Well," Carella said, and let it go at that.

13

He called his brother-in-law from the diner and told him he'd be picking him up on the way home. When Tommy asked why, he said, "Because you have twin daughters, and I think you ought to go see them."

Tommy said Wow, gee, twin *girls,* holy moley, wow.

In the car on the way to the hospital, Carella told him he knew Tommy was doing cocaine.

Tommy said Wow, gee, cocaine, holy moley, wow, where'd you get *that* idea?

Carella said he'd got the idea by following him to a house on Laramie Street, which incidentally the police had under camera surveillance, *that's* how he'd got the idea.

Tommy was about to do the wow-gee number a third time, but Carella cut him short by asking, "Who's the woman?"

Tommy debated lying. The car was moving slowly through heavy early-morning traffic, Carella at the wheel, Tommy beside him. He took a long time to answer. Trying to decide whether he should wow-gee it through or come clean. He knew his brother-in-law was a detective. This wasn't going to be easy.

"She works in the bank with me," he said at last.

"I'm listening."

"It goes back a couple of months."

"We've got time."

Tommy wanted him to understand straight off that there wasn't any sex involved here, this wasn't any kind of an affair, Angela had been wrong about that, although she'd been right about there being another woman. The other woman's name was Fran Harrington, and this all started when they'd traveled out to Minneapolis together, this must've been shortly after Labor Day last year . . .

"I thought you said a couple of months," Carella said, turning from the wheel.

"Well, yeah."

"Labor Day is the beginning of September. That isn't a couple of months. That's almost a *year*."

"Well, yeah."

"You've been doing coke for almost a year."

"Yeah."

"You goddamn jackass."

"I'm sorry."

"You ought to be, you jackass."

He was furious. He gripped the wheel tightly and concentrated on the traffic ahead. The automobiles were moving through a shimmering miragelike haze. The first day of August, and summer seemed intent on proving that July hadn't been just a fluke. Tommy was telling him how he and Fran had gone out there to deal with a customer who was on the edge of defaulting and how they'd been able to work out a method of payment that was satisfactory to both him and the bank. This was a huge loan; the man leased snow-removal equipment, which in the state of Minnesota was as essential as bread. So both he and Fran were tickled they'd been able to work it out, and Tommy suggested they go have a drink in celebration. Fran said she didn't drink, but maybe they could scare up something better. He didn't know what she meant at first.

You wouldn't think you could get cocaine in Minneapolis, Minnesota, which Tommy had always thought of as some kind of hick city in the middle of nowhere. But Fran knew a place they could go to, and it wasn't the kind of sleazy joint you saw on television where the cops are knocking down doors and yelling freeze. The one thing Tommy had learned since last September . . . well, yeah, that's right, it *had* been almost a year now . . . was that it wasn't only black kids doing crack in the ghettos, it was white people, too, doing coke *uptown*—coke didn't know about racial inequality, coke was the great emancipator. Just the way you used to have slum kids rolling marijuana joints on the street while rich people out in Malibu were offering you tailor-mades in silver cigarette boxes, it was the same thing now with cocaine. You didn't have to go smoke a five-dollar vial of crack in some shitty tenement apartment, there were places where people just like yourself could sit around in pleasant, sometimes luxurious surroundings, snorting really terrific stuff, socializing at the same time . . .

"You stupid jackass," Carella said.

"Anyway, that's how it started," Tommy said. "In Minnesota that time. And we've been doing it together since. She travels with me a lot, she knows all the places. The dangerous thing is getting caught with it, you know . . ."

Tell me about it, Carella thought.

". . . so if you don't make a buy and *carry* the stuff away, if instead you go to where the stuff *is,* one of these upscale apartments with people just like yourself . . ."

Noses just like yourself, Carella thought.

". . . like the one here on Laramie, for example, is really nice, we go there a lot."

"You better *quit* going there," Carella said. "You're already a movie star."

"Do you think you could . . .?"

"Don't even ask. Just stay away from that place. Or anyplace like it."

"I'll try."

"Never mind *trying*, you dumb jackass. You quit or I'll bust you myself, I promise you."

Tommy nodded.

"You hear me? You get psychiatric help, and you *quit*. Period."

"Yeah." He was silent for a moment. Then he said, "Does . . . did you tell Angela?"

"No."

"Are you going to?"

"That's your job."

"How do I . . . what do I . . .?"

"That's entirely up to you. You got yourself into this, you get yourself out."

"I just want you to understand," Tommy said again, "this had nothing to do with sex. Angela was wrong. This isn't like sex at all."

Yes it is, Carella thought.

Sitting here by the river, waiting for him to arrive, Eileen looked out over the water at the tugs moving slowly under the distant bridge. The place she'd chosen was a plain, unadorned seafood joint perched somewhat precariously on the end of the dock, all brown shingles and blue shutters and walls and floors that weren't plumb. Brown sheets of wrapping paper served as tablecloths, and waiters ran around frantically in stained white aprons. At dinnertime, the place was a madhouse. She was only meeting him for a drink, but even now, at ten past five, there was a sense of hyperkinetic preparation.

She sat at a table on the deck and breathed in deeply of air that smelled vaguely of the sea, activity swarming behind her, the river roiling below. She was feeling pretty good about herself. The minutes passed serenely.

At a quarter past five, Kling came rushing out onto the deck. "I'm sorry I'm late," he said, "we had a . . ."

"I just got here myself," she said.

"Gee, I really *am* late," he said, looking at his watch. "I'm sorry, have you ordered yet?"

"I was waiting for you."

"So what would you like?" he asked, and turned to signal to one of the peripatetic waiters.

"A white wine, please," she said.

"I saw you on television," Kling said, grinning. "We'll have a white wine and a Dewar's on the rocks, please, with a twist," he told the waiter.

"White wine, Dewar's rocks, a twist," the waiter said and went off.

"You look a little tired," he said.

"It was a long night."

"Worked out okay, though."

"Yeah, it went pretty . . ."

"The girl getting killed wasn't your fault," he said quickly.

"I know it wasn't," she said.

In fact, until this very moment, she thought she'd handled the situation in a completely pro . . .

"It was the bad guy . . . what was his name, Whitman . . . ?"

"Whittaker," she said.

"Whittaker, who killed the girl, you had nothing to do with it, Eileen. Even that guy interviewing you on television mentioned right on the air that the girl was within minutes of safety when she got shot in the back. So don't start blaming yourself for . . ."

"But I'm not," she said.

"Good, for something you didn't do. Otherwise you'll mess up a real opportunity here to start a whole new line of police work you might be very good at."

She looked at him.

"I *am* good at it," she said.

"I'm sure you are."

"I'm *already* good at it."

Who needs this? she thought.

"Bert," she said, "let's end it once and for all, okay?"

The Monday-night poker game was composed of off-duty detectives from precincts all over the city. There were usually seven players in the game, but in any case there were never fewer than six or more than eight. Eight made the game unwieldy. Also, with eight players and only fifty-two cards, you couldn't play a lot of the wild-card games the detectives favored. Playing poker was a form of release for them. The stakes weren't high—if you had bad luck all night long, you could maybe lose fifty, sixty dollars— and the sense of gambling in a situation where the risks weren't frightening had a certain appeal for men who sometimes had to put their lives on the line.

Meyer Meyer was debating whether or not to bet into what looked like a straight flush, but which might be only a seven-high straight, if it was a straight at all.

He decided to take the risk.

"See the buck and raise it a buck," he said.

Morris Goldstein, a detective from the Seven-Three, raised his eyebrows and puffed on his pipe. He was the one sitting there with a three, four, five, and six of clubs in front of him and maybe a deuce or a seven of clubs in the hole. He seemed surprised now that Meyer had not only seen his bet but raised it as well.

There were only three players still in the pot. Meyer, who had a full house composed of three kings and a pair of aces; Goldstein with what appeared to be a straight flush but which perhaps wasn't; and Rudy Gonsowski from the One-Oh-Three, a sure loser even if he'd tripped one of his low pairs. Goldstein puffed on his pipe and casually raised the ante another buck. He was a lousy poker player, and Meyer figured he was still trying to bluff his phony straight flush. Gonsowski dropped out, no big surprise. Meyer thought it over.

"Let's go, ladies," Parker said, "this ain't mah-jongg night."

They were playing in his apartment tonight. The two other players in the game were a detective named Henry Flannery from Headquarters Command downtown and Leo Palladino from Midtown South. They were both very good players who usually went home winners. Tonight, though, both of them were suffering losing streaks. They sat back with the impatient, bored looks of losers on their faces, waiting for Meyer to make up his mind.

"One more time," Meyer said, and threw four fifty-cent chips into the pot.

Goldstein raised his eyebrows yet again.

He puffed solemnly on his pipe.

"And again," he said, and threw another two bucks into the pot.

Meyer figured it was time to start believing him.

"See you," he said.

Goldstein showed his deuce of clubs.

"Yeah," Meyer said, and tossed in his cards.

"You should'a known all along he had it," Parker said, sweeping in the cards and beginning to shuffle.

"He didn't start raising till the fourth card," Meyer said in defense.

"What the hell were *you* doing in the game, Gonsowski?" This from Flannery, who was so far losing thirty bucks.

"I had two pair in the first four cards," Gonsowski said.

"You can shove two pair up your ass, a straight flush," Palladino said.

"He coulda been bluffing," Gonsowski said.

"You're still looking at aces over kings," Flannery said. "Meyer had you beat on the board."

"This is called Widows," Parker said, and began dealing.

"What the hell's Widows?" Palladino asked.

"A new game."

"Another crazy new game," Flannery said.

Neither of them enjoyed losing.

"What I do, I deal two extra hands . . ."

"I hate these dumb crazy games," Flannery said.

". . . facedown. One of them has three cards in it, the other has five cards. Facedown. Two hands, facedown."

"Is this a five-card game?" Gonsowski asked.

"What the hell you think it is?" Palladino said.

"It could be a seven-card game, how do I know what it is? I never played it in my life. I never even *heard* of it till tonight."

"It stinks already," Flannery said.

"Two hands facedown," Parker said. "They're called widows, the hands. One, two, three," he said, dealing, "that's the first widow . . . and one, two, three, four, five," still dealing, "that's the second widow."

"Why're they called widows?"

"I don't know why. That's what they're called, and that's the name of the game. Widows."

"I still don't get it," Gonsowski said. "what's the basic game here?"

"Five-card stud," Parker said, dealing all around the table now. "One card down, four up, we bet after each card."

"Then what?" Meyer asked.

"After the third card, if you don't like your hand, you can bid on the three-card widow. Whoever bids highest, the money goes in the pot, and he tosses in his hand and gets a whole *new* hand, those three cards in the widow."

"Sounds shittier and shittier every minute," Palladino said.

"It's a good game," Parker said, "wait and see."

"What about that other hand?" Goldstein asked. "The five-card hand?"

"Well," Parker said, beaming like a magician about to pull a rabbit from a hat, "after the *fifth* card is dealt, if you *still* don't like your hand, you can bid on that second widow, and if you're the highest bidder, you get a whole new *five*-card hand."

"You serving drinks here?" Flannery asked, "or did Prohibition come back?"

"Help yourself, it's in the kitchen," Parker said. "Rudy, you're high."

Gonsowski looked around the table, surprised that his eight of diamonds was high on the board.

"I need *both* those other hands," Meyer said.

"Widows," Palladino said sourly.

"Another dumb game," Flannery said.

"Relax," Goldstein said. "It'll come and go in the night."

"Like all the others," Palladino said sourly.

"Bet fifty cents," Gonsowski said.

The following is a selection from
KISS
Ed McBain's next novel in the
87TH PRECINCT series
coming soon

She was standing at the center of the subway platform, waiting for the uptown train to come in, when the man stepped up to her and punched her.

She felt shocking pain and then immediate outrage, how *dare* he? And then she remembered that this was the city in which she'd been born and bred, and in this city crazy things happened, and when they happened you tried to protect yourself. So she stepped back and away from him—a glimpse of red, he was wearing a red woolen hat—and was swinging her handbag at his head when he shoved her toward the edge of the platform.

He's crazy, she thought, he's a lunatic, and she said out loud, "*Stop* it, are you crazy?" but he grabbed her arm and pulled her toward the very edge of the platform, trying to throw her over, struggling with her. She screamed, she pulled away, tried to pull away, heard her coat tearing up the back when he reached for her again. Each time she moved away from the edge of the platform, he shoved her back again. The red hat, a brown jacket, blue jeans—she saw all these in almost subliminal flashes. He was only an inch or so taller than she was, but he was much stronger, and when finally he put all his strength into what seemed a last desperate shove, she lost her balance and fell backward onto the tracks. In the moment before she went over, she saw his boots. Brown leather boots with a white—

A train was coming.

She heard its thunder up the track, and from where she was crouched on her knees she turned to see its lights in the distance. She scrambled to her feet, tried to get back onto the platform, it was almost waist high, put her hands flat onto it, and tried to hoist herself up as if she were in a swimming pool and bouncing up out of the water. But there was no water here, there was no buoyancy to help her, there was only the high platform and the rattling sound of the train coming closer, Help me, she said to no one, Oh dear God help me, and grabbed the edge of the platform with both hands, the train rumbling closer, thrusting herself up from the elbows, swinging one leg over the rim, scrabbling for purchase, the other leg over and up now, she was on the platform now, the train not thirty feet away and screeching out of the darkness.

Her pantyhose were laddered, her coat split up the back seam. She was wearing only a light wool dress under the coat. Shivering from the cold, or her fear, or perhaps both, her eye throbbing where the man had punched her, both hands bruised from trying to cushion her fall to the tracks, knees scraped raw and bleeding, she lay flat on the platform, hugging the platform, sobbing, sucking in great gobs of air.

She did not know how long it was before a Transit Authority policeman came to her.

Five feet eight inches tall, blonde and buxom and blue-eyed and bursting with red-cheeked health, Birgitta Rundqvist marched into the station house at three o'clock on the afternoon of December 28, the Friday before the big New Year's Eve weekend. It was eight degrees Fahrenheit outside, but she was wearing only a lightweight red parka over a red reindeer patterned sweater, a short black mini, red pantyhose, and little cuffed black boots. The desk sergeant thought she looked like Little Red Riding Hood. Birgitta told him she wanted to talk to a detective. When he asked her why, she said she had just witnessed a murder attempt.

This was a rarity. Someone in this city actually coming to the police to report having witnessed a crime. The desk sergeant figured if you lived long enough you saw everything. He buzzed the squadroom.

Upstairs, Detective Meyer Meyer was sitting at his desk, minding his own business, typing up a report. Across the room, Andy Parker and Fat Ollie Weeks were talking about the new police commissioner. Parker and Weeks got along fine together. That's because they were both bigots. Weeks was perhaps a bigger bigot than Parker, but nobody can be only a little bit pregnant, although Weeks did in fact look a little bit pregnant—in fact about three months gone.

Obese and a trifle smelly, his belly hanging over his belt buckle, his fat round face set with little pig eyes, Weeks was here visiting his good old buddies at the Eight-Seven, his own bailiwick being the Eight-Three, all the way uptown in Diamondback. Parker was always happy to see him. In Weeks's presence, and by comparison, Parker seemed nattily dressed—even though he was sporting a three-day beard stubble and a wrinkled suit. Whenever anyone questioned Parker's appearance, he told them he was on a stakeout. Whenever anyone questioned Weeks's appearance, he told them to go fuck themselves. Parker liked him a lot.

"The new commissioner's a scholar," Weeks said.

"A professor," Parker said, nodding in agreement.

"Used to teach criminology down there in that shitty little town the mayor snatched him from."

"He always refers to himself as *we*, you notice that? *We* this, *we* that. *We* feel the number of policemen on the street has nothing to do with crime prevention . . ."

"*We* have learned over the years that community interaction is paramount . . ."

"*We* this, *we* that."

"Like he's two people," Weeks said, and turned suddenly to look at Meyer. "You listening to this?" he asked.

"No," Meyer said.

"You ought to," Weeks said. "You might learn a few things about this new commissioner we got."

"I know enough about the new commissioner," Meyer said.

"Without your people," Weeks said, "there wouldn't *be* this new commissioner."

The new police commissioner was black.

So was the new mayor.

Weeks was saying that if it hadn't been for the Jews in this city, a black mayor wouldn't have been elected, and if a black mayor hadn't been elected, there wouldn't now be a black police commissioner. Meyer himself hadn't voted for the new mayor, but neither the new mayor nor the new commissioner was on anyone's Top Ten list at the moment, and it was always easy to blame the failings of one minority group on yet another minority group. Crouched behind his typewriter, pecking out his report with the index fingers of both hands, blue eyes squinting at the page in the roller, bald head gleaming in the late afternoon light that streamed through the grilled windows, Meyer wanted nothing less than an argument about either the new commissioner *or* the new mayor. He busied himself with indifference.

"Maybe the new commissioner can show your people where Bethtown is," Weeks said, and nudged Parker with his elbow.

Bethtown was the city's smallest sector, across the River Harb and reached either by ferry or bridge. Weeks was making a joke. The new commissioner had been quoted in yesterday's papers as asking his driver where Calm's Point, one of the city's *largest* sectors, was located. Meyer agreed that the man was a small-town hick in bib overalls, so why was Weeks virtually *insisting* that Meyer defend him? He was about to tell Weeks to stuff the new commissioner up his ass when the telephone rang.

"Eighty-Seventh Squad," he said, "Detective Meyer." He listened for a moment, raised his eyebrows in surprise, said, "Send her up," and then put the receiver back on the cradle. Birgitta came into the squadroom some three minutes later. Weeks looked her up and down. So did Parker. Meyer offered her the chair alongside his desk.

She told him who she was, told him she worked as a nanny for a Mrs. David Feinstein on Barber Street in Smoke Rise . . .

"I'm from Stockholm," she said.

Which was why she was dressed for the tropics, Meyer supposed.

. . . told him she was just wheeling the baby into the house when she saw this automobile come roaring around the corner . . .

Across the room, Parker burst out laughing at something Weeks had just said. What Weeks had just said was that he loved eating Danish. He had overheard the girl's faint accent and had mistaken her for Danish. Parker found this hysterical.

". . . aiming straight for this woman," she said.

"What woman?" Meyer asked.

"This woman walking on the sidewalk."

"The car was *aiming* for her?"

"Yes, sir," Birgitta said. "It jumped onto the curb, it tried to run her over."

"When was this?"

"Just before lunch. I had to wait for Mrs. Feinstein to get back before I could come here."

"What kind of car was it?"

"A Ford Taurus."

"What color?"

"Gray. A sort of metallic gray."

"Did you notice the license plate number?"

"I did."

A proud little nod. She watched television a lot, Meyer guessed. He supposed they had television in Sweden, didn't they? They certainly had it in Smoke Rise.

"Can you tell me the number, please?" he said.

"DB 37 612," Birgitta said.

He wrote it down, showed it to her, and said, "Is this it?"

"Yes," she said. "Exactly."

"It wasn't an out-of-state plate, was it?"

"No, no."

He wondered if they had states in Sweden. Sweden had Volvos, that he knew.

"Did you see who was driving the car?"

"I did."

"Man or woman?"

"A man."

"Can you tell me what he looked like?"

"Not really. It all happened very fast. He turned the corner, and aimed the car at her, and tried to hit her. And she threw herself over this low wall in front of the house next door to ours, and he just drove off."

"Was he white or black, did you notice?"

"White."

"Can you tell me anything else about him?"

"He was wearing a red woolen hat."

Big day for red, Meyer thought.

"How about the woman?" he said. "Anyone you know?"

"No."

"Not anyone you might have seen in the neighborhood? Before this, I mean."

"No, I'm sorry."

"Did you talk to her at all?"

"No. I took the baby inside the house, and when I came out again she was gone."

"What'd she look like, can you tell me that?"

"She had blonde hair. Like mine. But longer. And she was a little shorter than I am."

"How old would you say she was?"

"In her thirties."

"Did you notice the color of her eyes?"

"I'm sorry."

"What was she wearing?"

"A mink coat. No hat. Dark boots. We still have snow on the ground up there."

Smoke Rise. Like the country up there. Hard to believe it was part of the Eight-Seven, but it was. Big expensive houses, rolling woodlands, even a stream running through some of the choicer lots. Smoke Rise. Where a man driving a gray Ford Taurus had tried to run down a blonde woman in a mink coat.

"Anything else you can tell me?" Meyer said.

"That's all," Birgitta said. "He was trying to kill her. Will you do something about it?"

"Of course," he said.

The first thing he did was call Motor Vehicles to request a computer check on the license plate number Birgitta had given him. The MVB reported that the car in question was registered to a Dr. Peter Gundler who lived downtown in the Quarter. Meyer wrote down the doctor's address and then called Auto Theft. The detective he spoke to there took down the license plate number, the name and address of the registered owner, asked for the year and make of the car, settled for the make alone, and told Meyer he'd get back to him in ten minutes. He got back in seven to report that the good doctor's car had been reported stolen on Christmas day, nice present, huh? Meyer thanked him and hung up.

Easy come, easy go, he thought.

There were times when Detective Steve Carella looked positively Chinese. Sitting in the sunlight that angled through the grilled squadroom windows, the light touching his face in a way that made his dark eyes appear more slanted, pondering the Ballistics report on his desk like a Buddhist monk studying a prayer scroll, it seemed conceivable that he'd been left on his parents' doorstep by a silk merchant from the Orient. He looked up from the report, glanced at the clock. Five minutes to eleven. Ballistics wouldn't be out to lunch yet. He was picking up the phone to dial, when she came down the corridor and stopped just outside the gate in the slatted-rail divider.

His first impression was one of paleness.

A tall slender blonde woman wearing a long gray cavalry officer's coat. Taking a crumpled tissue from her pocket now, blowing her nose, returning the tissue to the pocket, hesitating outside the gate.

"Mrs. Bowles?" he said.

"Yes?"

"Come in, please," he said, and put the phone back on its cradle.

She had found the latch on the gate. She opened it and walked to his desk. Long firm strides, pale horse, pale rider. He asked if he could take her coat . . .

"Yes, please."

. . . and then carried it to the rack in the corner, near the water cooler. Under the coat, she was wearing a black sweater, a pleated watch-plaid skirt, and black stockings. She resembled a student at a private girl's school.

"Please sit down," he said, and offered her the chair alongside his desk. She looked very grave. Straight blonde hair sitting on her head like a burnished helmet. Dark eyes solemn. Face raw from the wind outside.

"Someone's trying to kill me," she said.

"Yes," he said, and nodded.

She had called not a half-hour earlier. When a woman on the phone tells you someone has made two attempts on her life, you ask her to come in immediately. She was here now. And now she was telling him how she'd been coming from a baby shower on Silvermine Oval and was waiting on the subway platform at Culver and Ninth to take a train uptown to Smoke Rise, the Barber Street station up there, do you know it? In Smoke Rise? Waiting for the train when a man pushed her onto the tracks. This was two weeks ago, a little more than two weeks ago. And then, yesterday, he'd tried to kill her again. Tried to run her over with an automobile. The same man. Closer to home this time.

This was all news to Carella.

The Transit Authority cop to whom Emma Bowles had sobbingly poured out the information on the night of December twelfth hadn't filed a report with the Eight-Seven, and Meyer hadn't told Carella about his visit from the Swedish nanny yesterday. So he listened now while Emma told him that she'd gone out for a little walk before lunch yesterday, strolling up Barber Street and into Smoke Rise, and suddenly this gray car that might have been a Lincoln Continental came tooling around the corner and climbed the sidewalk chasing her, and would have hit her if she hadn't jumped over this little stone wall bordering one of the houses.

"The same man was driving the car," she said. "The one who pushed me off the platform."

"Are you sure?"

"Positive," she said. "And I know who he is."

Carella looked at her.

"It came to me yesterday, when he tried to run me over," Emma said. "I suddenly remembered."

"Who is he?" Carella asked.

"He used to drive my husband."

"Drive him?"

"Martin is a stockbroker. He works all the way downtown, a car picks him up in the morning and takes him home again at night."

"When you say this man *used* to drive him . . ."

"Yes. He doesn't any longer."

"When did he stop?"

"Last spring. I don't know what happened then, but Martin got another driver."

"You're sure this is the same man?"

"Yes, he drove us to the theater once. I *know* it's the same man."

"But you didn't recognize him when he shoved you off that subway platform."

"No, I didn't make the connection. But yesterday he was in a *car*. And it rang a bell."

"Good," Carella said. "What's his name?"

Martin Bowles was a man in his late thirties, tall and slender, with thick dark hair, deep brown eyes, and the solid build of someone who worked out regularly. Every New Year's Eve, he wore a dinner jacket. Didn't matter where they were going, big party, small one, private home, restaurant, didn't even matter if they were going anywhere at *all*. They could be staying home, just the two of them, enjoying a quiet candlelit dinner, Bowles would nonetheless put on a dinner jacket. To him, New Year's Eve was an occasion. To Emma, it was like any other day of the year. She therefore found it mystifying that her husband went through the ritual of dressing up each year, and she was somewhat amused by the way he preened before a mirror each time he put on his ruffled shirt and black tie. His posturing might have appeared foolish on any other man, but he was truly strikingly handsome, and never as good-looking as when he was wearing formal attire. Tonight, he looked spectacularly elegant.

"I've hired a private detective," he said.

She was sitting at the bedroom vanity, fastening a pearl earring to her ear. She almost dropped it.

"A private detective?" she said. "What for?"

"To get to the bottom of this," he said.

She looked at him. He had to be kidding. The bottom of this was Roger Turner Tilly, the man who used to drive him to and from work. Once the police found him . . .

"The police don't seem to be doing anything about this,"

he said. "A man pushes you off a subway platform, and the same man . . ."

"Well, yes," she said. "But I know who he is, I told you who he . . ."

"Well, you don't know for certain," he said.

"But I *do* know," she said. "It was Tilly."

"The thing is, the police are treating these two incidents . . ."

"Incidents?" she said. "He tried to *kill* me."

"I know that. Why do you think I'm so concerned? The thing is they're treating attempted murder like any ordinary occurrence. When was the first time? How long ago was that?"

"The twelfth."

"Exactly. And again last week. So what have they done, Emma? Nothing. Man tries to push you under a subway train," he said, and shook his head in disbelief. "Same man tries to run you over. Well, I don't want to wait for a *third* attempt. I've hired a private detective."

"I really don't think we need . . ."

"Man named Andrew Darrow, supposed to be excellent."

"A private detective," she said, and shook her head. "Really, Martin, let's leave this to the police, okay? The man I spoke to up there seemed . . ."

"The police are underpaid and overworked," Bowles said, as if quoting from an editorial he'd read. "I don't want to trust your life to them."

"That's very sweet of you, darling, really," she said, and stood up and turned to him. "But . . ."

"You look beautiful," he said.

She was wearing a shimmering white gown cut low over her breasts. Her long blonde hair was piled on top of her head. Drop pearl earrings dangled from her ears.

"Thank you," she said. "But, Martin, what would this man *do*? I mean . . ."

"Stay with you. Protect you. Try to get to the bottom of this."

"Let's go on a vacation instead," she said. "Use the money you're paying him . . ."

"We can do both," he said. "Soon as we resolve this thing, we'll take a nice long trip to the Caribbean, how does that sound?"

"I can taste it," she said.

Smiling, he put his arm around her and walked her out to the entrance foyer. He took her mink from the closet, helped her into it, put on his own coat, and draped a white silk scarf around his neck.

"I don't want anything to happen to you," he said.

"Nothing will happen to me," she said.

"I love you too much."

"I love you, too."

"He'll be starting next week," Bowles said. "Case closed."

The intercom buzzer sounded from the lobby downstairs. He went to the wall speaker, pressed the TALK button.

"Yes?"

"Your car's here, Mr. Bowles."

"Thank you," he said. "We'll be right down."

"The car," he said, and came back to her and took her in his arms, and offered her his lips.

"Kiss?" he said.

When Carella was a kid, his mother used to serve lentils shortly after midnight on New Year's Day. It had something to do with an Italian tradition her grandparents had brought over from the Old Country. Louise Carella didn't know what the tradition was—"Something to do with good luck," she explained to her son with a shrug—and neither did Carella's father. For that matter, Carella's grandparents couldn't remember, either. His mother and father, his grandparents on both sides of the family, had all been born here; the ties to forebears who had arrived at the turn of the century were already dim and uncertain. But after midnight, when the New Year was scarcely minutes long and everyone had already banged away to his heart's content on pots and pans at open windows, his mother used to serve cold lentils. She didn't know why they had to be cold, either. Cold lentils with a little olive oil. "For good luck," she said.

And on New Year's Day, they would all go over to Grandma's house for the big feast prepared by all the women in the family. There'd be Grandpa and Grandma and his mother's sister Josie and her husband Mike, and his mother's brother Salvatore, who everybody called Salvie, and his wife Dorothy, whom Carella loved to death. And the kids, all Carella's cousins, and sometimes Uncle Freddie who lived in Las Vegas and who was a casino dealer who occasionally came east on the holidays and who once gave Carella a silver ring with a turquoise stone which he said he'd won from a wild Apache Indian in a poker game. This was the old neighborhood— Carella's parents had already moved out of it to Riverhead, but Grandma and Grandpa refused to leave, even though more and more often you saw signs announcing *bodega* or *lecheria* rather than *salumeria* or *pasticceria*.

Carella's father used to bring the pastry.

Baked in his own shop.

The meal would start with antipasto—sweet red peppers his grandmother had roasted over the gas jets on the kitchen stove, and ripe black olives, and anchovies and eggplant and crisp celery stalks and imported olive oil into which you dipped the crusty bread his grandfather sliced from a big round loaf. And then there was the pasta, always with a delicate tomato sauce, either spaghetti or rigatoni or penne which he loved to smother with the grated parmesan cheese he spooned from the bowl passed around the table—"Take a little more cheese, Stevie," his grandmother used to say sarcastically, scowling at him with a smile, he always wondered how she managed that trick.

And then there'd be the roast chicken and the roast beef and the potatoes and the green beans and the fresh peas he'd seen the women shelling in the kitchen, the Italian part of the meal magically seguing into what was essentially American, the way the immigrants had magically segued into their new lives here, I pledge allegiance. And there'd be fruit and cheese and coffee—and the pastries his father had baked in his own shop and carried downtown in little white thin cardboard boxes fastened with white string.

His Uncle Salvie was a great storyteller. He used to drive a cab all over the city, and he had a thousand stories about all the crazy passengers he carried. Grandma kept saying he should have been a writer. Salvie used to shrug this aside, though Carella suspected this was really a secret ambition of his, the stories he told. It was Carella's sister, Angela, who was always scribbling away. She seemed to have more homework than anybody in the entire world. Any holiday they spent at Grandma's house, Angela had books with her. All the cousins would be running around the apartment chasing each other and yelling at each other and laughing and Angela would be curled up in a chair in the living room, reading a book, and then writing into her notebooks. "The Homework Kid," Uncle Mike called her. She always smiled shyly when he said this, he was her favorite.

Aunt Dorothy had a ribald and bawdy sense of humor. She was always telling jokes Carella at first suspected, and later realized, were sexual in content. Everytime she started to tell one, Grandma would warn, "*I creaturi, i creaturi*," scowling at her without a smile, gesturing with her head in the direction of the children. Aunt Dorothy would wave aside Grandma's warnings and plunge right ahead with whatever joke she'd started. When Carella turned twelve, thirteen, whenever it was that he began seriously noticing girls and realizing what his aunt's jokes were all about, he would grin in knowledgable embarrassment whenever she delivered a punch line, and she would wink at him in defiance of Grandma's disapproving scowl.

He never could understand how she'd learned about Margie Gannon. But she'd sensed unerringly—or perhaps his mother had tipped her to the fact—that he was enjoying what to him at the time was a wildly erotic relationship with the little Irish girl who lived across the street from him in Riverhead, and she teased him mercilessly about her, referring to her as Sweet Rosie O'Grady, God alone knew why.

The family would sit around the table, joking and laughing, drinking coffee and eating the pastries his father had baked. The *cannoli* and the *sfogliatelli* and the *zeppoli* and the *strufoli* and the *Napolitani* and the *sfingi di San Giuseppe*.

Aunt Josie was the one who always suggested, "Why don't we play a little poker?"

"Good idea," Uncle Freddie would say.

Uncle Freddie always won, even though they only played for pennies. Aunt Josie was a sore loser, Louise could never understand how her sister had developed such a temper. If she drew to an inside straight and failed to pull the card she was looking for, she'd throw her cards on the table and start swearing at whoever was dealing. "*Vergogna, vergogna*," Grandma would scold, another of the few Italian expressions she had picked up from her mother, long dead. Grandma herself was dead now. Grandpa, too. Aunt Josie and Uncle Mike had moved to Florida and they never came north anymore. Uncle Salvie died of cancer shortly after Carella joined the force. Aunt Dorothy remarried almost immediately afterward and the family lost touch with her. Carella missed her and her dirty jokes.

At his father's funeral last July, there were no uncles or aunts who'd known Carella when he was small. There were a handful of cousins he hardly remembered, all of them expressing condolences over this terrible thing that had happened, one of them asking if Carella could fix a speeding ticket for him, the jackass. Behind their sad countenances, there lurked the unspoken thought that if such a thing could happen to a *cop's* father . . .

On New Year's Day this year, there were no pastries baked by Tony Carella. Tony Carella had been gunned down in his shop on the night of July seventeenth, and never again would there be pastries baked by him. Carella's mother was still in mourning. Black dress, black stockings, black shoes, honoring a tradition virtually gone in the land from which it had come; except in the most remote sections of Italy, widows rarely wore black for very long. But Louise was a woman who still served cold lentils after midnight on New Year's Day.

This was not a joyous Tuesday. The weather, chill and bleak and gray, seemed to echo the sense of loss that pervaded the house in which Carella and his sister had both grown up. A fierce and icy wind rattled the windows in the old house. There were cooking smells, yes, just as there had been on all the holidays Carella could remember, but there was no laughter and even the children seemed oddly hushed. Only the immediate family—and not even all of it—was here today. The feast seemed somehow paltry; you did not celebrate when the funeral meats were not yet cold upon the table.

His mother was a blunt, plain-spoken woman.

"I want to come to the trial," she said.

This was after the midday meal. Carella was due in the squadroom at a quarter to four; the police department had no respect for holidays. The family was sitting at the dining room table under which he and Angela used to hide when they were children. Long tablecloth hanging almost to the floor. Giggling because they thought the grown-ups didn't know they were listening. *I creaturi*. The dishes had been cleared, they were drinking coffee. His mother dressed in black, her hands folded on the table, her slender gold wedding band tight on the ring finger of her left hand. Carella and his sister sitting side by side, both of them dark haired and dark eyed, the eyes slanting downward, their father's legacy. Teddy Carella sat beside her mother-in-law, raising her eyes from the knitting needles in her hands; she was knitting sweaters for the new twins in the family. Cynthia and Melinda, Angela's daughters, born on the twenty-eighth of July last year, eleven days after his father's murder;

what the Lord taketh away, the Lord giveth back. Carella didn't much care for either name. He visualized one of them growing up as Cindy and the other as Mindy. He knew that his sister had unilaterally named them. His brother-in-law Tommy was conspicuously absent today. There were problems here, too. Carella sometimes felt overwhelmed.

Louise was waiting for an answer. She saw her son's eyes click with her daughter's, brown against brown, in the secret communication she recognized from when they were children. Teddy was watching Carella's lips.

"I don't think that's such a good idea," he said.

"Why not?"

"Mom, there's going to be testimony . . ."

"I want them to know he had a wife. I want the jury to know that."

"They'll know that anyway, Mom."

Teddy's eyes flashed from lips to lips, reading the words on them. Her world was a silent one. She had been born deaf and had never uttered a word in her life. Carella knew how to sign, but her mother-in-law tried it only occasionally, both she and Angela preferring to speak with exaggerated lip motions they hoped Teddy could decipher. Except at times like now, when they were intent on the urgency of their own messages.

"Mom," Angela said, "Steve's . . ."

"No, don't *Mom* me . . ,"

"But he's right. There's going to be stuff you won't want to hear."

"I want to hear it all. want them to know I'm there listening to it all."

"Mom . . ."

"Especially that *sfasciume* who killed him."

Carella automatically looked to see where the children were. He was never quite certain what the word *sfasciume* meant, but he suspected it was obscene and something *i creaturi* shouldn't hear coming from their grandmother's lips. His daughter was curled up with a book, reminding him of Angela at that age, and in fact resembling her somewhat. His son was working intently on a model airplane that had been a Christmas gift. Mark and April. Sensible names for twins, never mind Miffy and Muffy or whatever his sister's kids would grow up to be called. Angela's three-year-old, Tess, her brow furrowed in concentration, was working on a coloring book.

Bringing Teddy more completely into the conversation, signing as he spoke, Carella said, "Mom, this is a decision you have to make for yourself, but . . ."

"I know it is . . ."

". . . but I've testified in cases where the victim's spouse was present . . ."

"The victim's *spouse*," Louise said, almost spitting the word.

". . . and I can tell you it's not an easy thing to live through."

"He's right, Mom," Angela said.

"They'll be showing pictures, Mom . . ."

"I saw what he looked like, the pictures can't be any worse."

"Mom, that was a long time ago, you don't have to relive it all over again."

"It was yesterday," Louise said.

"It was last . . ."

"It'll always be yesterday," she said.

Teddy missed this. Carella signed it to her. She nodded.

"Until I can look that bastard straight in the eye," Louise said.

Carella had already looked that bastard straight in the eye. Had rammed the muzzle of his service revolver into the hollow of Sonny Cole's throat, had heard Detective Randy Wade whispering beside him, "Do it." He had not squeezed the trigger, although in the narrow corridor of a house surrounded by vacant lots this would have been the easiest thing in the world to do. He had not done it. Now, seeing the look in his mother's eyes, he wondered if he'd been right.

"I'm coming to the trial," she said, and nodded curtly.

"Mom . . ." Angela started.

"What time next Monday?" she asked.

"Nine o'clock," Carella said, and sighed heavily. "The Criminal Courts Building downtown."